STAR WARS

LABYRINTH OF EVIL

JAMES LUCENO

BALLANTINE BOOKS • NEW YORK

2005 Del Rey Books Mass Market Edition

Copyright © 2005 by Lucasfilm Ltd. & ® or ™ where indicated. All Rights Reserved. Used Under Authorization.

Excerpt from *Star Wars: Dark Lord: The Rise of Darth Vader* copyright © 2005 by Lucasfilm Ltd. & ® or ™ where indicated. All Rights Reserved. Used Under Authorization.

Published in the United States by Del Rey Books, an imprint of The Random House Publishing Group, a division of Random House, Inc., New York.

Del Rey is a registered trademark and the Del Rey colophon is a trademark of Random House, Inc.

Originally published in hardcover in the United States by Del Rey Books, an imprint of The Random House Publishing Group, a division of Random House, Inc., in 2005.

This book contains an excerpt from the forthcoming book *Star Wars: Dark Lord: The Rise of Darth Vader* by James Luceno. This excerpt has been set for this edition only and may not reflect the final content of the forthcoming edition.

ISBN 0-345-47573-9

Printed in the United States of America

www.starwars.com
www.delreybooks.com
www.readstarwars.com

OPM   9   8   7   6   5   4   3   2   1

For my loving aunt and uncle,
Rosemary and Joe Savoca
And for my earliest mentors,
Pat Mathison, who was forever urging me
to tell him stories,
and Richard Thomas, who introduced me
to science fiction,
Ian Fleming, and Thomas Pynchon

ACKNOWLEDGMENTS

Heartfelt thanks to Shelly Shapiro, Sue Rostoni, and Howard Roffman, for remaining in my corner throughout this project; to George Lucas, for responding to my many queries; to Matt Stover, for providing additional material and creative inspiration; to Dan Wallace, for sending me an early version of his Prequel Era chronology; to Haden Blackman, for graciously yielding some of the Big Moments; to the staff of the Hotel Casona, in Flores, Guatemala, for keeping the espressos coming; and to Karen-Ann and Jake, for granting me the time and space to daydream.

THE STAR WARS NOVELS TIMELINE

33 YEARS BEFORE STAR WARS: A New Hope

Darth Maul: Saboteur*

32.5 YEARS BEFORE STAR WARS: A New Hope

Cloak of Deception
Darth Maul: Shadow Hunter

32 YEARS BEFORE STAR WARS: A New Hope

**STAR WARS: EPISODE I
THE PHANTOM MENACE**

29 YEARS BEFORE STAR WARS: A New Hope

Rogue Planet

27 YEARS BEFORE STAR WARS: A New Hope

Outbound Flight

22.5 YEARS BEFORE STAR WARS: A New Hope

The Approaching Storm

22 YEARS BEFORE STAR WARS: A New Hope

**STAR WARS: EPISODE II
ATTACK OF THE CLONES**

Star Wars Republic Commando:
Hard Contact

21.5 YEARS BEFORE STAR WARS: A New Hope

Shatterpoint

21 YEARS BEFORE STAR WARS: A New Hope

The Cestus Deception
The Hive*

20 YEARS BEFORE STAR WARS: A New Hope

MedStar I: Battle Surgeons
MedStar II: Jedi Healer

19.5 YEARS BEFORE STAR WARS: A New Hope

Jedi Trial
Yoda: Dark Rendezvous

19 YEARS BEFORE STAR WARS: A New Hope

Labyrinth of Evil

**STAR WARS: EPISODE III
REVENGE OF THE SITH**

10-0 YEARS BEFORE STAR WARS: A New Hope

The Han Solo Trilogy:
The Paradise Snare
The Hutt Gambit
Rebel Dawn

5-2 YEARS BEFORE STAR WARS: A New Hope

The Adventures of Lando Calrissian:
Lando Calrissian and the
Mindharp of Sharu
Lando Calrissian and the
Flamewind of Oseon
Lando Calrissian and the
Starcave of ThonBoka

The Han Solo Adventures:
Han Solo at Stars' End
Han Solo's Revenge
Han Solo and the Lost Legacy

STAR WARS: A New Hope YEAR 0

**STAR WARS: EPISODE IV
A NEW HOPE**

0-3 YEARS AFTER STAR WARS: A New Hope

Tales from the Mos Eisley
Cantina
Star Wars: Galaxies: The Ruins
of Dantooine
Splinter of the Mind's Eye

3 YEARS AFTER STAR WARS: A New Hope

**STAR WARS: EPISODE V
THE EMPIRE STRIKES BACK**

Tales of the Bounty Hunters

3.5 YEARS AFTER STAR WARS: A New Hope

Shadows of the Empire

4 YEARS AFTER STAR WARS: A New Hope

**STAR WARS: EPISODE VI
RETURN OF THE JEDI**

Tales from Jabba's Palace
Tales from the Empire
Tales from the New Republic

LABYRINTH OF EVIL

Darkness was encroaching on Cato Neimoidia's western hemisphere, though exchanges of coherent light high above the beleaguered world ripped looming night to shreds. Well under the fractured sky, in an orchard of manax trees that studded the lower ramparts of Viceroy Gunray's majestic redoubt, companies of clone troopers and battle droids were slaughtering one another with bloodless precision.

A flashing fan of blue energy lit the undersides of a cluster of trees: the lightsaber of Obi-Wan Kenobi.

Attacked by two sentry droids, Obi-Wan stood his ground, twisting his upraised blade right and left to swat blaster bolts back at his enemies. Caught midsection by their own salvos, both droids came apart, with a scattering of alloy limbs.

Obi-Wan moved again.

Tumbling under the segmented thorax of a Neimoidian harvester beetle, he sprang to his feet and raced forward. Explosive light shunted from the citadel's deflector shield dappled the loamy ground between the trees, casting long shadows of their buttressed trunks. Oblivious to the chaos occurring in their midst, columns of the five-meter-long harvesters continued their stalwart march toward a mound that supported the fortress. In their cutting jaws or on their upsweeping backs they carried cargoes of pruned foliage. The crushing sounds of their ceaseless gnawing provided an eerie cadence to the rumbling detonations and the hiss and whine of blaster bolts.

From off to Obi-Wan's left came a sudden click of servos; to his right, a hushed cry of warning.

"Down, Master!"

He dropped into a crouch even before Anakin's lips formed the final word, lightsaber aimed to the ground to keep from impaling his onrushing former Padawan. A blur of thrumming blue energy sizzled through the humid air, followed by a sharp smell of cauterized circuitry, the tang of ozone. A blaster discharged into soft soil, then the stalked, elongated head of a battle droid struck the ground not a meter from Obi-Wan's feet, sparking as it bounced and rolled out of sight, repeating: *"Roger, roger . . . Roger, roger . . . "*

In a tuck, Obi-Wan pivoted on his right foot in time to see the droid's spindly body collapse. The fact that Anakin had saved his life was nothing new, but Anakin's blade had passed a little too close for comfort. Eyes somewhat wide with surprise, he came to his feet.

"You nearly took my head off."

Anakin held his blade to one side. In the strobing light of battle his blue eyes shone with wry amusement. "Sorry, Master, but your head was where my lightsaber needed to go."

Master.

Anakin used the honorific not as learner to teacher, but as Jedi Knight to Jedi Council member. The braid

that had defined his earlier status had been ritually severed after his audacious actions at Praesitlyn. His tunic,
knee-high boots, and tight-fitting trousers were as black
as the night. His face scarred from a contest with
Dooku-trained Asajj Ventress. His mechanical right
hand sheathed in an elbow-length glove. He had let his
hair grow long the past few months, falling almost to his
shoulders now. His face he kept clean-shaven, unlike
Obi-Wan, whose strong jaw was defined by a short
beard.

"I suppose I should be grateful your lightsaber *needed*
to go there, rather than desired to."

Anakin's grin blossomed into a full-fledged smile.
"Last time I checked we were on the same side, Master."

"Still, if I'd been a moment slower . . . "

Anakin booted the battle droid's blaster aside. "Your
fears are only in your mind."

Obi-Wan scowled. "Without a head I wouldn't have
much mind left, now, would I?" He swept his lightsaber
in a flourishing pass, nodding up the alley of manax
trees. "After you."

They resumed their charge, moving with the supernatural speed and grace afforded by the Force, Obi-Wan's
brown cloak swirling behind him. Victims of the initial
bombardment, scores of battle droids lay sprawled on
the ground. Others dangled like broken marionettes
from the branches of the trees into which they had been
hurled.

Areas of the leafy canopy were in flames.

Two scorched droids little more than arms and torsos
lifted their weapons as the Jedi approached, but Anakin
only raised his left hand in a Force push that shoved the
droids flat onto their backs.

They jinked right, somersaulting under the wide bodies of two harvester beetles, then hurdling a tangle of

barbed underbrush that had managed to anchor itself in the otherwise meticulously tended orchard. They emerged from the tree line at the shore of a broad irrigation canal, fed by a lake that delimited the Neimoidians' citadel on three sides. In the west a trio of wedge-shaped *Venator*-class assault cruisers hung in scudding clouds. North and east the sky was in turmoil, crosshatched with ion trails, turbolaser beams, hyphens of scarlet light streaming upward from weapons emplacements outside the citadel's energy shield. Rising from high ground at the end of the peninsula, the tiered fastness was reminiscent of the command towers of the Trade Federation core ships, and indeed had been the inspiration for them.

Somewhere inside, trapped by Republic forces, were the Trade Federation elite.

With his homeworld threatened and the purse worlds of Deko and Koru Neimoidia devastated, Viceroy Gunray would have been wiser to retreat to the Outer Rim, as other members of the Separatist Council were thought to be doing. But rational thinking had never been a Neimoidian strong suit, especially when possessions remained on Cato Neimoidia the viceroy apparently couldn't live without. Backed by a battle group of Federation warships, he had slipped onto Cato Neimoidia, intent on looting the citadel before it fell. But Republic forces had been lying in wait, eager to capture him alive and bring him to justice—thirteen years late, in the judgment of many.

Cato Neimoidia was as close to Coruscant as Obi-Wan and Anakin had been in almost four standard months, and with the last remaining Separatist strongholds now cleared from the Core and Colonies, they expected to be back in the Outer Rim by week's end.

Obi-Wan heard movement on the far side of the irrigation canal.

An instant later, four clone troopers crept from the tree line on the opposite bank to take up firing positions amid the water-smoothed rocks that lined the ditch. Far behind them a crashed gunship was burning. Protruding from the canopy, the LAAT's blunt tail was stenciled with the eight-rayed battle standard of the Galactic Republic.

A gunboat glided into view from downstream, maneuvering to where the Jedi were waiting. Standing in the bow, a clone commander named Cody waved hand signals to the troopers on shore and to others in the gunboat, who immediately fanned out to create a safe perimeter.

Troopers could communicate with one another through the comlinks built into their T-visored helmets, but the Advanced Recon Commando teams had created an elaborate system of gestures meant to thwart enemy attempts at eavesdropping.

A few nimble leaps brought Cody face-to-face with Obi-Wan and Anakin.

"Sirs, I have the latest from airborne command."

"Show us," Anakin said.

Cody dropped to one knee, his right hand activating a device built into his left wrist gauntlet. A cone of blue light emanated from the device, and a hologram of task force commander Dodonna resolved.

"Generals Kenobi and Skywalker, provincial recon unit reports that Viceroy Gunray and his entourage are making their way to the north side of the redoubt. Our forces have been hammering at the shield from above and from points along the shore, but the shield generator is in a hardened site, and difficult to get at. Gunships are taking heavy fire from turbolaser cannons in the lower ramparts. If your team is still committed to taking Gunray alive, you're going to have to skirt those defenses and find an alternative way into the palace. At this point we cannot reinforce, repeat, cannot reinforce."

Obi-Wan looked at Cody when the hologram had faded. "Suggestions, Commander?"

Cody made an adjustment to the wrist projector, and a 3-D schematic of the redoubt formed in midair. "Assuming that Gunray's fortress is similar to what we found on Deko and Koru, the underground levels will contain fungus farms and processing and shipment areas. There will be access from the shipping areas into the midlevel grub hatcheries, and from the hatcheries we'll be able to infiltrate the upper reaches."

Cody carried a short-stocked DC-15 blaster rifle and wore the white armor and imaging system helmet that had come to symbolize the Grand Army of the Republic—grown, nurtured, and trained on the remote world of Kamino, three years earlier. Just now, though, areas of white showed only where there were no smears of mud or dried blood, no gouges, abrasions, or charred patches. Cody's position was designated by orange markings on his helmet crest and shoulder guards. His upper right arm bore stripes signifying campaigns in which he had participated: Aagonar, Praesitlyn, Paracelus Minor, Antar 4, Tibrin, Skor II, and dozens of other worlds from Core to Outer Rim.

Over the years Obi-Wan had formed battlefield partnerships with several Advanced Recon Commandos—Alpha, with whom he had been imprisoned on Rattatak, and Jangotat, on Ord Cestus. Early-generation ARCs had received training by the Mandalorian clone template, Jango Fett. While the Kaminoans had managed to breed some of Fett out of the regulars, they had been more selective in the case of the ARCs. As a consequence, ARCs displayed more individual initiative and leadership abilities. In short, they were more like the late bounty hunter himself, which was to say, more *human*. While Cody wasn't genetically an Advanced Recon Commando, he had ARC training and shared many ARC attributes.

In the initial stages of the war, clone troopers were treated no differently from the war machines they piloted or the weapons they fired. To many they had more in common with battle droids poured by the tens of thousands from Baktoid Armor Workshops on a host of Separatist-held worlds. But attitudes began to shift as more and more troopers died. The clones' unfaltering dedication to the Republic, and to the Jedi, showed them to be true comrades in arms, and deserving of all the respect and compassion they were now afforded. It was the Jedi themselves, in addition to other progressive-thinking officials in the Republic, who had urged that second- and third-generation troopers be given names rather than numbers, to foster a growing fellowship.

"I agree that we can probably reach the upper levels, Commander," Obi-Wan said at last. "But how do you propose we reach the fungus farms to begin with?"

Cody stood to his full height and pointed toward the orchards. "We go in with the harvesters."

Obi-Wan glanced uncertainly at Anakin and motioned him off to one side.

"It's just the two of us. What do you think?"

"I think you worry too much, Master."

Obi-Wan folded his arms across his chest. "And who'll worry about you if I don't?"

Anakin canted his head and grinned. "There are others."

"You can only be referring to See-Threepio. And you had to *build* him."

"Think what you will."

Obi-Wan narrowed his eyes with purpose. "Oh, I see. But I would have thought Senator Amidala of greater interest to you than Supreme Chancellor Palpatine." Before Anakin could respond, he added: "Despite that she's a politician also."

"Don't think I haven't tried to attract her interest, Master."

Obi-Wan regarded Anakin for a moment. "What's more, if Chancellor Palpatine had genuine concern for your welfare, he would have kept you closer to Coruscant."

Anakin placed his artificial hand on Obi-Wan's left shoulder. "Perhaps, Master. But then, who would look after you?"

Despite their two pairs of powerful legs and the saw-toothed pincers that extended from their lower mandibles, the broad-bodied harvesters were single-minded creatures, complaisant except when threatened directly. From their flat heads sprouted looping antennae, which served not only as feelers, but also as organs of communication, by means of powerful pheromones. Each beetle was capable of carrying five times its considerable weight in foliage and branches. Similar to the Neimoidians who had domesticated them, their society was hierarchical, and included laborers, harvesters, soldiers, and breeders, all of whom served a distant queen that rewarded effort with food.

Obi-Wan, Anakin, and the commandos who made up Squad Seven had to run to keep up with the beetles as they hurried their fresh-picked loads from the orchard to the cave-like entrance to a natural mound at the base of the redoubt. The beetles' carapaces afforded them cover from surveillance sorties by battle droid STAP patrols. More important, the harvesters knew safe routes through mined stretches of cleared ground that separated the trees from the fortress itself.

The beetles' frequent habit of lowering their heads to exchange information with hivemates moving in the opposite direction demanded that the Jedi and troopers keep between the harvesters' rear legs. Hunched over, Obi-Wan ran with his lightsaber in hand but deactivated. As the shielded royal residence came into view, a certain uneasiness seemed to take hold of the creatures, disrupting the ordered nature of their columns. Obi-Wan suspected that outbound beetles were relaying accounts of potential perils to the nest posed by the Republic's unrelenting barrage. In response to the crisis, soldier beetles were joining the procession, quick to shepherd nervous strays back into line.

Anakin's greater height required him to remain farther back, almost directly under the beetle's pug tail. To Obi-Wan's right ran Cody, with his teammates trailing behind and flanking him.

Soldier beetles or no, discipline was breaking down fast.

A harvester providing cover for one of the commandos veered from the column before it could be guided back into line. Instead of hurrying under another beetle, the commando stuck with the stray, and quickly found himself out in open ground.

Obi-Wan felt a ripple in the Force an instant before the harvester's right foreleg tripped a land mine.

A potent explosion fountained from the rocky ground, blowing away half the creature's foreleg. The commando threw himself to one side, rolling out from under a trio now of pounding legs, only to have to bob and weave as the harvester began to run in frantic circles, seemingly determined to trample the commando underfoot. A glancing blow from the beetle's left rear leg tipped the commando off his feet. Confused, the harvester lowered its head and butted at the hard white object in its path, again and again, until there wasn't a smooth area left in the commando's armor.

The harvester's distress was having an impact on the rest of the beetles, as well.

While most were pressed tightly together, others were suddenly scurrying away from the main column, sending the soldier beetles to high alert. Tripping two mines in succession, a second harvester was lifted off the ground by the ensuing explosions. With that, the column dissolved into disorder, with harvesters and soldiers running every which way, and commandos and Jedi alike doing their best to protect themselves.

"Stay close to the ones who are still headed for the nest!" Anakin shouted.

Obi-Wan was doing just that when he noticed that the trampled commando was back on his feet and staggering toward him, tapping the side of his helmet with the palm of his gloved hand, and obviously indifferent to where he placed his booted feet. Barreling straight for the maw of the mound, a harvester bore down on the commando, clamping its pincers around his waist, then lifting him high into the air. Summoning the last of his reserves, the commando twisted his body back and forth, but was unable to break free.

All at once Anakin was out from under his protective harvester.

Lightsaber tight in his gloved hand, he bounded across the denuded landscape toward the captive commando, the Force guiding him to safe landings among the mines. The harvesters might have taken him for a demented turfjumper were they not so fixed on safeguarding their loads and reaching the security of the nest.

Anakin's final leap dropped him directly in front of the harvester that had seized the commando. With one upward stroke of his lightsaber he rid the beetle of its pincers, freeing the commando, but also sending the soldier beetles into a frenzy. Obi-Wan could almost smell the pheromone release, and decipher the information being exchanged: *The area is rife with predators!*

From the brood rose a shriek so high-pitched as to be barely audible, and a stampede was under way. Mines began to detonate to all sides, and out from billowing smoke above the orchard canopy swarmed more than a hundred STAPs.

A Neimoidian version of the agile repulsorlift airhook used as an observation vehicle throughout the galaxy, each Single Trooper Aerial Platform was equipped with twin blasters that delivered more firepower than the stubby-barreled models carried by infantry droids.

From maximum range the swarm rained energy bolts on everything in sight, dropping harvesters in their tracks and turning the rocky ground into a killing field. Explosions erupted in jagged lines as scores of mines were detonated. Supporting the commando trooper with his left arm, Anakin warded off blaster bolts on the run. The rest of Squad Seven supplied cover, blowing STAPs out of the sky with uninterrupted fire.

Cody motioned everyone into a shallow irrigation trench just short of the mound. By the time Obi-Wan arrived, the troopers were deployed in a circle, and continuing to pour fire into the sky. Anakin slid into the trench a moment later, lowering the commando gently to the muddy slope. Squad Seven's medical specialist crawled over, removing the commando's ravaged utility belt and deeply dented helmet.

Obi-Wan gazed at the face of the injured clone.

A face he would never forget; now a face he *couldn't* forget.

All these years later, he could still recall his brief conversation with Jango Fett, on Kamino. He glanced at Cody and the rest. *An army of one man . . . But the right man for the job.*

The clones' rallying cry.

The injured commando had already prompted his armor to inject him with painkillers, so he remained pliant while his chest plastron was removed and the black bodyglove undergarment knifed open. The harvester's pincers had crushed the armor into the commando's abdomen. His skin was intact, but the bruising was severe.

With only half the original army of 1.2 million in fighting shape, the life of every clone was vital. Blood and replacement organs—what the regular troopers referred to as "spare parts"—were readily available— "easily requisitioned"—but with the war reaching a crescendo, battlefield casualties were on the rise and treated as high priority.

"Not much I can do for him here," the medspec told Anakin. "Maybe if we can get an FX-Seven airdropped—"

"We don't need a droid," Anakin interrupted. Kneeling, he placed his hands on the injured commando's abdomen and used a Jedi healing technique to keep the clone from going into deep shock.

A sudden noise from above caught everyone's attention.

Scores of boulder-sized objects were spewing from openings in the lower ramparts of the fortress. Cody pressed a pair of macrobinoculars to his eyes and gazed upward.

"That's no ordinary avalanche," he said, passing the glasses to Obi-Wan.

Obi-Wan raised the glasses and waited for the lens to autofocus.

Rolling toward the trench at better than eighty kilometers per hour were some of the most feared of the Separatists' infantry arsenal.

Droidekas.

Known also by the fearsome title *destroyer droids,*
droidekas were rapid-deployment killing machines produced by an alien species that encouraged mayhem at
every opportunity. A combination of sheer momentum
and sequenced microrepulsors allowed the bronzium-
armored droids to roll like balls then unfurl in a blink as
tripoded gunfighters, shielded by individual deflectors
and armed with paired, twin-barreled, high-output
blasters.

Since the shields were powerful enough to resist
lightsabers, blasters, even light artillery bolts, the proven
strategy for dealing with droidekas was simply to run
from them.

More so, because surrender was never an option.

But Anakin had another idea.

"Comm fire support for an artillery strike," he ordered Cody, loud enough to be heard above STAP and
DC-15 fire. "Do it now."

Cody was more than willing to comply. After all, the
order had come directly from "the Hero with no Fear,"

as Anakin was sometimes known. "The Warrior of the Infinite." There was, though, a chain of command to maintain, so Cody looked to Obi-Wan for confirmation.

Obi-Wan nodded. "Do as he says."

The commando called for his comm specialist, who splashed through the shallow water and flattened himself alongside Cody. When the spec had provided needed coordinates, Cody opened a frequency to the fire support base and spoke in a rush.

"To FSB from Squad Seven. We're taking continuous fire from STAPs in sector Jenth-Bacta-Ion, and are about to be buried under destroyer droids deployed from the redoubt. Request immediate artillery support at coordinates accompanying transmission. Recommend tactical electromagnetic pulse airburst, followed by SPHA-T barrage."

"Pulse weapons don't discriminate, Commander," Obi-Wan thought to point out.

Cody shrugged. "It's the only way, sir."

"Tell them we've got a wounded trooper for the Rimsoo," Anakin said. The term stood for "Republic Mobile Surgical Unit."

Cody relayed the message. "Warn the evac pilot that he'll be setting down in a hot area. We'll mark a safe landing zone with smoke, and leave two behind to assist."

The assistant squad leader moved his right hand through a series of gestures. When the gestures had been repeated down the line, the commandos removed their helmets and began to deactivate the electronic systems built into their armor.

To a clone, they hunkered down in the fetid water.

A screaming came from the south.

Then: a nova-bright flare of white light, followed two seconds later by a roar that turned Obi-Wan's eardrums to mush. A shock wave spread from the ramparts, down onto the clear ground at the foot of the mound and out over the already blazing orchards. Above the trench, half the droidekas deployed prematurely from ball position and began to tumble down the slope in a tangle of limbs and weapons. Behind the trench, STAPs fell like stones, plunging from the sky into the burning trees.

What harvesters remained alive ran in dizzying circles, spilling their precious loads.

Now from the south came an infernal wail as SPHA-Ts—the Republic's walking artillery—loosed lasers on those droidekas that had survived the pulse weapon. Deprived of shields and unable to fire, they melted like wax in the gushes of radiant energy that struck the slopes.

Still without helmet, Cody stood up, signaling with both hands.

Obi-Wan interpreted the gestures: *Sixty count, then suit up and break for the entrance to the nest.*

He prepared by calming himself.

For all their reliance on droids, for all their infatuation with high technology, for all their inborn cowardice, greed, and guile, Neimoidians had a soft spot for their youth—their seven formative years as grubs, struggling for limited food in communal hives, discovering early on the benefits of duplicity and self-regard. The fungus foodstuff of those early years was as dear to them as adults as it was to them as hatchlings, and no wonder, since it was that same fungus that had found favor with species galaxywide, and from which the Neimoidians had evolved into a wealthy, spacefaring society, with ships enough to attract the eye of the notorious Trade Federation and, ultimately, droids enough to equal an army.

It would have been natural to assume that the fungus—prized for its medicinal as well as nutritional value—was somehow concocted from manax foliage gathered by the harvesters. But in fact the leaves and branches provided little more than a growth medium. Enzymes produced by the beetles, coupled with the dank conditions within the burrows and grottoes of the nest mounds, encouraged the rapid growth of a product that required only a modicum of refinement to become palatable.

Elsewhere during the sieges of Deko and Koru Neimoidia, Obi-Wan had never visited a fungus farm, but no sooner had he and Anakin dashed through the cave-like opening to the nest than the briefings he had received more than ten standard years earlier came back to him in a flash.

Here were the partly masticated leaves, carefully arranged in layers; the clumps of branches and other impurities; the laborer beetles; the droid overseers; the conveyors and similar contraptions devoted to sorting and transport . . . Not a Neimoidian in sight, but that was consistent with their doctrine that exertion of any sort was anathema. In the deep recesses of the mound, untouched by sunlight, the starter fungi—molds, mildews, and sickly white mushrooms—would be undergoing treatments with natural and synthetic growth-acceleration agents. And higher up, in what constituted the basement of the citadel, the matured end product was probably being consumed by grubs, or packed and readied for shipment.

Cody ordered the squad to secure the area. Those in the rear were still taking sporadic fire from STAPs, but the droid pilots couldn't get close to the entrance because of the bodies of dead beetles piled outside.

Squad Seven's medspec hurried over to Obi-Wan and Anakin.

"Sirs, I recommend you keep your rebreathers close at

hand. Odds are we won't have to penetrate any deeper into the nest, but there's always a chance of encountering free-floating spores in other areas."

Obi-Wan quirked his brows together. "Toxic, Sergeant?"

"No, sir. But the spores have been known to have an adverse effect on humans."

"Adverse how?" Anakin asked.

"The effect is most often described as 'dislocating,' sir."

Obi-Wan glanced at Anakin. "Then I suggest we do as he says."

The fingers of his left hand were prizing the small, twin-tanked rebreather from its pouch on his utility belt when a volley of blaster bolts streaked into the grotto. Caught in their upper chests, two troopers were knocked off their feet.

The source of the sudden fire was the mouth of a narrow side tunnel that could be sealed by an overhead door. Anakin was already racing for the tunnel, lightsaber gripped in both hands, deflecting most of the bolts back through the entrance.

Obi-Wan leapt to one side, raising his blade to deal with two bolts that got past Anakin. The first he returned toward its source; the second, he parried at a deliberately downward angle. Striking the grotto's hard-packed floor, the deflected bolt ricocheted to one wall, then to the ceiling, to the other wall, and back to the floor, from which it caromed squarely into the control panel that operated the tunnel door.

Showering sparks, the device shorted out, and a slab of thick alloy dropped from its pocket in the wall, sealing the tunnel with a loud *thud!*

Switching off his lightsaber, Anakin cast a complimentary glance over his shoulder.

"Nicely done, Master."

"The beauty of Form Three," Obi-Wan said with theatrical nonchalance. "You should try it sometime."

"You've always been better at evasion than I have," Anakin said. "I prefer more straightforward tactics."

Obi-Wan rolled his eyes. "Master of understatement."

"General Kenobi," the comm spec said from across the grotto. "Provincial recon reports that Viceroy Gunray and his entourage are heading for the launching bays. They're protected by super battle droids, a group of which are now closing on our position."

Anakin swung to Obi-Wan. "One of us has to divert the droids."

"One of us," Obi-Wan repeated. "Haven't we been through this before?"

"The beauty of our partnership, Master. You lure the bodyguards away, I capture Gunray. It hasn't failed us yet, has it?"

Obi-Wan compressed his lips. "From a certain point of view, Anakin."

Anakin scowled. "Fine. Then I'll be the bait this time."

"That makes no sense," Obi-Wan said quickly, shaking his head. "We play to our separate strengths."

Anakin couldn't restrain a smile. "I knew you'd listen to reason, Master." He singled out four commandos. "You'll come with me."

"Sir!" they said in unison.

Obi-Wan, Cody, and the rest of Squad Seven set out for the turbolift shafts. Obi-Wan hadn't gone five meters when he stopped and swung around.

"Anakin, I know we've got a score to settle with Gunray, but don't make it personal. We want to take him *alive*!"

Oh, *but it is personal*, Anakin told himself while he watched Obi-Wan, Cody, and four troopers disappear into the turbolift.

It was personal because of what Nute Gunray had done to Naboo thirteen years ago.

It was personal because of Gunray's hiring of Jango Fett to assassinate Padmé three years ago—first with a bomb planted on her ship, then with the pair of kouhuns a changling had inserted into Padmé's Senatorial quarters on Coruscant.

The woman Anakin loved above all else. *His wife*. The deepest though brightest of his secrets. Even Obi-Wan didn't know, for that would have created problems.

Finally, it was personal because of all that had occurred on Geonosis: the mock trial, the sentencing, the executions that were to have taken place in the arena . . .

Even if he could put all that aside, as Obi-Wan plainly wanted him to do, it was personal because Gunray had aligned himself with Dooku and the Separatists, and the

war they had planned from the start had brought ruin to
a thousand worlds.

The deaths of the Separatist leaders was the only solution now. It had always been the solution, despite objec-
tions by certain members of the Jedi Council, who still
believed in peaceful resolutions. Despite the Senate's attempts to bind the hands of Supreme Chancellor Palpatine, so that corrupt politicians could continue to turn a
profit. Line the pockets of their shimmersilk cloaks with
kickbacks from the immoral corporations that funded
the war machine. Supplying both sides with weapons,
ships, whatever was needed to extend the conflict.

It made Anakin's blood boil.

Yes, just as Yoda had sensed after Qui-Gon Jinn and
Obi-Wan had freed him from slavery on Tatooine and
brought him to the Jedi Temple, he had a lot of anger in
him. But what Yoda failed to realize was that anger
could be a kind of fuel. In peaceful times Anakin might
have been able to bridle his rage, but now he relied on it
to drive him forward, to transform him into the person
he needed to be.

Cut off the head.

Twice he might have been able to kill Dooku himself
had Obi-Wan not held him back. But he didn't hold that
against his former Master. For all his skills, Anakin still
looked to Obi-Wan for guidance.

On occasion.

As he and the four troopers were exiting the grotto,
the tip of his boot sent some object skittering across the
floor. On the fly he used the Force to call the thing to his
left hand and realized that it was Obi-Wan's rebreather,
which must have fallen from its utility pouch during the
brief exchange with the unseen battle droids. But no
matter; Obi-Wan was probably already in the lower lev-

els of the redoubt, where there would be little need for the device.

Opening one of the pouches on his belt, Anakin wedged the rebreather inside.

He urged the troopers on, and they stayed close on his heels.

Upward: following burrows, ramps, and shafts used only by droids. Through processing and shipment areas, through hatcheries filled with squealing grubs. Upward: into the citadel's gleaming middle levels. Through rooms large as starship docking bays filled floor to ceiling with ... *stuff*. A boundless collection of junk, ritual gifts, impulsive purchases. Thousands of faddish devices never to be used but too prized as possessions to be thrown out, donated, handed down, or destroyed. More technology than existed on entire worlds, hoarded, stacked, piled about, crammed into every available space.

Anakin could only shake his head in wonder. In Mos Espa, on Tatooine, he and his mother had lived simply, and never wanted for anything.

His grin was short-lived.

Anger and despair made him grit his teeth.

Upward: until they reached the citadel's semicircular projection of launching bays, which overlooked the surrounding lake and a ridge of forested mountains.

Anakin brought his team to a halt. One of the commandos held up his hand, palm outward, then tapped the side of his helmet to indicate an incoming transmission. The commando listened, then spoke to Anakin with hand signals.

Gunray's party is nearby.

"They're testing escape vectors for the shuttle by lowering the defensive shield and launching decoys," the commando said quietly. "Turbolaser fire has allowed several of the decoys to get past our blockade and reach orbiting core ships."

The muscles in Anakin's jaw bunched. "Then we have to act quickly."

No one contested when Anakin held point position. The commandos accepted without question that body armor and imaging systems were primitive compared to the power of the Force. They moved vigilantly through a maze of elegant corridors, abandoned in a rush, strewn with belongings dropped during flight.

Approaching an intersection, Anakin made a halting gesture with his left hand.

He listened for a moment; heard from around the corner the telltale heavy footfalls of super battle droids. The commando to Anakin's left nodded in confirmation, then extended a finger-thin holocam around the corner and activated his gauntlet holoprojector. Noisy images of Nute Gunray and his entourage of elite officers formed in midair. Hurrying down the corridor, tall headpieces bobbing, rich robes aswirl, safeguarded front and rear by burly battle droids.

Anakin motioned for silence, and was just about to step into the intersecting corridor when a banged-up silver protocol droid appeared from across the hall, raising its hands in delighted surprise.

"Welcome, sirs!" it said loudly. "I can't tell you how good it is to find guests in the palace! I am TeeCee-Sixteen and I am at your service. Nearly everyone has left—because of the invasion, of course—but I'm sure that we can make you comfortable, and that Viceroy Gunray will be most pleased—"

One hand clamped over TC-16's small rectangle of vocabulator, a commando yanked the droid to one side, but it was too late. Anakin leapt around the corner in time to see the Neimoidians set off at a run, red-eyed, flat-nosed Gunray casting a nervous glance over his shoulder.

As for the super battle droids, they had about-faced and were marching stiff-legged in Anakin's direction. Catching sight of him, their right arms elevated, twisted downward, locked into firing position.

And the corridor began to fill with blaster bolts.

Qui-Gon Jinn hadn't believed in baiting, Obi-Wan thought as he and the commandos rode the turbolift to the fortress's lowest level. Baiting implied a certain amount of advance planning, and Qui-Gon had no patience for that. He took situations as they came, throwing back his shoulders and striding boldly to the center of things, relying as much on his instincts as his lightsaber to deal with the consequences. It must have been difficult for him to have served under a methodical master such as Dooku, consummate planner, consummate duelist.

Now a *Sith*.

But that made sense, of a sort.

The desire to dominate and control.

For a time the same issues had stood at the center of Obi-Wan's conflicts with Anakin. Clearly Anakin was as strong in the Force as any Jedi who had ever sat on the Council. But as Obi-Wan had told him time and again, the essence of being a Jedi didn't hinge on attaining mastery of the Force, but on attaining mastery over oneself.

Someday Anakin would come to accept that, and then he would be truly unstoppable. Qui-Gon had had the insight to recognize it more than a decade earlier, and Obi-Wan felt duty-bound to his former Master to help Anakin fulfill his destiny.

His faith in Anakin had grown so strong that he had become Anakin's staunchest defender to those on the Council who had grown apprehensive about the young man's prowess, and uncomfortable with his confidential, almost familial relationship with Supreme Chancellor Palpatine. If Obi-Wan was, as Anakin sometimes said, the father he never had, then Palpatine was his wise uncle, adviser, mentor in the ways of life outside the Temple.

Obi-Wan understood that Anakin envied him for having been appointed to the Council. But how could he not, having been all but anointed "the Chosen One," continually bolstered by Palpatine's praise, driven to prove to *his* former Master that he could be the perfect Jedi Knight.

On countless occasions Anakin's bold actions had allowed them to prevail against seemingly impossible odds. But just as often it had been Obi-Wan's circumspection that had pulled them back from the brink. Whether foresight was something innate in Obi-Wan or the result of his continuing fascination with the unifying Force—the long view—Obi-Wan couldn't say. What he could say was that he had learned to trust Anakin's instincts.

On occasion.

He wouldn't have been able to go on playing the bait, otherwise.

"The next stop is ours, General," Cody said from behind him.

Obi-Wan turned, watched Cody slam a new blaster-pack into his DC-15, heard the familiar whine of the weapon's repower mechanism.

Reflexively, he placed his thumb on the lightsaber's activator button.

"How do you want to handle this, sir?"

"You're the master of warcraft, Commander. I'll follow your lead."

Cody nodded, perhaps grinning beneath his helmet. "Well, sir, our mandate is a simple one: Kill as many of the enemy as possible."

Obi-Wan recalled a conversation he had had on Ord Cestus with a clone trooper named Nate, regarding analogies between the Jedi and the clones: the former ushered by midi-chlorians to serve the Force; the latter, grown and programmed to serve the Republic.

But the analogies ended there, because the troopers never paused to consider possible repercussions of their actions. Tasked, they executed their orders to the best of their abilities, whereas lately, even the most forceful Jedi knew moments of doubt. Qui-Gon had always criticized the Council for being too authoritative, and for cultivating inflexible methods of teaching. He saw the Temple as a place where candidates were *programmed* to become Jedi, instead of a place where beings were allowed to grow into Jedihood. Qui-Gon was no stranger to what the Jedi referred to as "aggressive negotiations," which typically involved lightsabers more than diplomacy. But Obi-Wan wondered what he would have had to say about the war. He recalled, as if yesterday, Dooku's taunt on Geonosis that Qui-Gon would have joined Dooku in championing the Separatist cause.

As soon as the turbolift came to rest, two commandos tossed concussion grenades into the corridor beyond. Right and left, battle droids were blown against the walls and ceiling. Obi-Wan knew, because the corridor quickly became a torrent of blaster bolts. He, Cody, and the others threw themselves into the horizontal hail. Repeating blasters roared to life. Staccato bursts made short work of the droids, but reinforcements were already appearing.

Two commandos fell to fire while Obi-Wan's team was making its way down the corridor in the direction of the citadel's packing and shipping rooms. Halfway there, they encountered the contingent of super battle droids the Neimoidians had sent to root out the infiltrators.

Comparing the spindly infantry droid to the black-bodied super battle droid was like comparing a Muun to a champion shock-ball player. Quick decapitations weren't possible because the droid's head was all but buried in and fused to its broad torso. Heavy-gauge armor protected long arms and legs. Monogrip hands were suited only for gripping and firing high-energy dispersal blasters.

"Looks like they've taken the bait, General!" Cody said while he, Obi-Wan, and two commandos fought their way into a side room.

"Another successful action! Now we just have to survive it!"

Cody pointed to the entrance to a second room, opposite their present position.

"Through there," he said. "A second bank of turbolifts on the far side." He tapped Obi-Wan on the shoulder. "You first. We'll provide cover. Go!"

Obi-Wan shot for the room, deflecting bolts and mangling two super battle droids that stood in his way. The room beyond was stacked with coffin-sized repulsorlift shipping containers, constructed of some lightweight alloy. Treaded labor droids were moving additional containers into the room from an adjacent packaging area. Without warning, a battle droid appeared in the entrance. Obi-Wan glanced at the wall-mounted mechanism that operated the sliding doors. Adopting a defensive stance, he did just as he had done in the grotto, returning the first of the droid's blaster bolts, and sending the second caroming around the room in a path calculated to disable the door apparatus.

Things might have gone as planned had a labor droid not entered the room at an inopportune moment, guiding a levitated shipping container behind him. Ricocheting from the floor, the deflected bolt passed completely through the container before it struck the door mechanism. The pair of sliding doors attempted to close, but the crippled container was now in the way, so they began to cycle through attempts to repocket themselves, close, repocket themselves . . .

Each time they opened, a battle droid would squeeze into the room, firing away, forcing Obi-Wan back toward the entryway through which he had originally come, where a brutal firefight was still raging between commandos and super battle droids.

While all this was occurring, something else was afoot. Strands of some gauzy white substance were beginning to drift from the holed shipping container.

Obi-Wan realized instantly what the substance was.

Taking one hand from the hilt of his lightsaber, he began to fumble for the rebreather pouched on his belt, only to find it empty.

"Stars' end," he cursed, more in disappointment than anger.

Already beginning to feel woozy.

Sirs, this a terrible mistake!" TC-16 inserted into a brief pause in the firefight.

"Keep him quiet," Anakin snapped at the commando closest to the droid.

"But, sirs—"

A second commando glanced at Anakin and motioned down the corridor behind them. "Six infantry droids advancing. We're going to be caught in a crossfire."

Anakin gave his head a quick shake. "Wrong. Follow me—and bring the droid."

A muffled sound of dismay escaped TC-16's vocabulator.

Fury clouded Anakin's eyes. Lightsaber held high in his crooked right arm, he whirled into the intersecting corridor. No need to *use* the Force, as many Jedi said, for he was never anywhere but fully in the Force. He called instead on his anger, bringing images to mind to fuel his rage. It wasn't difficult, with so many to choose from: images of a Tusken Raider camp on Tatooine, Yavin 4, the defeat at Jabiim, Praesitlyn . . .

Blue blade flashing, he cut a swath through the super battle droids, opening their burnished carapaces with diagonal slashes, cutting off blaster arms, hobbling the droids by deflecting bolts into their hermetically sealed knees. Scarcely letting a shot get past him, so that the commandos following in his wake could concentrate their fire on the ones Anakin only wounded.

Their enemies fell aside, almost as if surrendering.

Focused on the route Gunray and his lackeys had taken, Anakin raced through corridors, rounding corners without slowing down, sprinting for the launching bay at the far end of the final corridor. Confronted with an iris-hatch blast door, he thrust his glowing blade into the metal as if it were living flesh. Lips drawn back over his teeth, he tried to force the lightsaber to burn a fast circle in the door. He brought his will to bear on the task, but the lightsaber could accomplish only so much, even in the hands of a powerful Jedi.

Withdrawing the blade, he stepped back from the door and moved his hands through a Force pass, willing the iris portal to open. The door shuddered but remained sealed. Screaming through gnashed teeth, he tried again.

When the commandos finally caught up with him, he spun to them.

"Blow the door!"

A commando hurried forward to place magnetic charges against the alloy. Anakin paced behind him, waiting. Another commando had to tug him to a safe distance.

The charges blew, and the portal yielded. Anakin charged through the irising seal even before it had opened fully.

The launching bay was littered with containers, articles of clothing, objects the Neimoidians hadn't had time or space to take with them.

The shuttle was gone.

Wisps of vapor swirled about, and the air smelled faintly of fuel. Anakin ran to the platform's forward-curving edge, eyes scanning Cato Neimoidia's light-riddled night sky for some sign of the fleeing ship. The palace's defensive shield had been deactivated. Thick packets of crimson light lanced from laser cannon batteries on the slopes below.

Anakin's teammates joined him at the brink, one with a hand vised on TC-16's upper left arm.

"What type of ship is it?" Anakin demanded of the droid.

TC-16 tipped his head to one side. "Ship, sir?"

"The shuttle—Gunray's shuttle. What model?"

"Why, I believe it was a *Sheathipede*-class, sir."

"Haor Chall Engineering *Sheathipede*-class transport shuttle," one of the commandos explained. "Design is based on the soldier beetles. Upraised stern, bow ramp, clawfoot landing gear. Gunray's is named the *Lapiz Cutter*."

A second commando spoke up, signaling that he was receiving commo.

"General. From Commander Dodonna's flagship: more than sixty shuttles and landing craft launched from the redoubt. Thirteen destroyed, eighteen seized. An unknown quantity have managed to dock aboard Trade Federation core ships and open-ring Lucrehulk carriers. Additional shuttles are still in the envelope."

Anakin turned through a circle, gloved hand gripped on the lightsaber pommel, the other balled into a fist. A conduit nearby took the brunt of his anger. Cleaved by the blade, it fell in pieces to the landing platform's seamless floor. Anakin began to pace again, then stopped, yanking a commando around by his shoulder.

"Comm forward command. I want my ship and

astromech droid flown here immediately. One of the ARC-one-seventy pilots can fly it."

The commando nodded, relayed the message, then said: "FCC will comply, sir. You'll have your starfighter soonest."

Anakin returned to the lip of the platform, blowing his breath into the night. The battle appeared to be winding down, except within him. Not until he had Gunray in his grip—

"General Skywalker," a commando said from behind him. "Urgent from Commander Cody. He and General Kenobi are pinned down on level one."

Anakin shot him a questioning look. "By *droids*?"

"A lot of them, apparently."

Anakin glanced into the glowing sky, then back at the commando who had delivered Cody's message.

"General, forward command reports that your starfighter is on the way," another commando updated.

Again, Anakin glanced at the sky, only to turn back to the commando. "Where did you say Obi-Wan and Cody are?"

"Level one, sir. In the shipping area."

Anakin compressed his lips. "All right. Let's go rescue them."

7

In the shipping room, the sliding doors were still cycling—striking the punctured shipping container, retracting, attempting to close once more. Battle droids were still entering with each parting of the doors, and spores were still wafting through the air.

Not much had changed, except within Obi-Wan, who felt as if he had downed three bottles of Whyren's Reserve. Bleary-eyed but lucid, tipsy but sure-footed, weary but attentive, Obi-Wan seemed to be the sum of all contrasts.

More or less rooted in place, he swayed, wobbled, tottered, and reeled, evading or parrying an almost unremitting current of blaster bolts. His singed and burned cloak bore evidence of all the near hits, but the floor—heaped with droids, whole and in parts, bodies sparking and limbs twitching—spoke to the accuracy of his deflections.

He felt at times as if he were merely holding the lightsaber and letting it do all the work. In one hand, in both, it made no difference. Other times he was able to anticipate the bolts, twist himself aside at the last instant, and allow the walls and floor to handle the ricochets.

Sometimes he actually took a moment to congratulate himself on the skill of his returns.

He was in the Force, to be sure, but deep in some other zone as well, giddy with astonishment, as the world unfolded in slow motion.

Alerted by the commandos that the air was saturated with spores, Anakin had his rebreather in his mouth as he approached the room in which Obi-Wan had held his own against better than fifty droids, all of which lay scattered about the room. A weaving, shuffling, staggering Obi-Wan was dealing with the last of them when Anakin entered.

When the final droid collapsed, Obi-Wan aimed the blade of his lightsaber casually toward the floor and stood swaying in place, breathing hard but almost grinning.

"Anakin," he said happily. "How are you?"

When Anakin went to him, Obi-Wan promptly collapsed in his arms.

Anakin deactivated Obi-Wan's blade and inserted a rebreather into his mouth—the same one that had ended up on the floor of the grotto. Then he carried him from the room to where Cody and several commandos were waiting, some with their helmets removed.

"Exactly what lightsaber form were you using back there, Master?" Anakin asked when Obi-Wan had come around and the rebreathers were no longer necessary.

"Form?"

"More the absence of it." Anakin laughed shortly. "If only Mace, Kit, or Shaak Ti could have seen you."

Obi-Wan blinked in confusion and glanced around at the carnage of droids in the shipping area. "We did this?" he said to Cody.

"You did most of it, General."

Obi-Wan regarded Anakin in confusion.

"I'll explain later," Anakin said.

Obi-Wan ran his hand through his hair, then, as if just remembering, said: "Gunray! Did you get him?"

Anakin's shoulders dropped. "The entire entourage escaped the palace."

Obi-Wan mulled it over for a moment. "You could have gone after them."

Anakin shrugged. "And leave you?" He paused, then added: "Of course, if I'd known you'd become master of a new lightsaber form . . . "

Obi-Wan's eyes brightened. "They'll be taken in orbit."

"Maybe."

"If not, there'll be other times, Anakin. We'll see to it."

Anakin nodded. "I know that, Master."

Obi-Wan was about to add something when a helmeted commando stepped from a nearby turbolift and hurried over to them.

"General Kenobi, General Skywalker, we've found something of interest among the equipment the Neimoidians left behind."

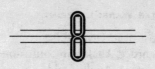

8

The fact that the Sheathipede shuttle had managed to thread its way through a storm of turbolaser bolts and dock in the core ship's port-side command tower was no guarantee of safety. Indeed, while everyone was filing down the shuttle's tongue-like boarding ramp, the core ship was still being pummeled by fire from Republic warships.

First to set foot on deck, Viceroy Nute Gunray, attired in blood-red robes and sporting a tall, helmet-like miter, asked for a situation report from one of the goggle-wearing technicians who was waiting in the docking bay.

"Even now coordinates for the jump to lightspeed are being calculated, Viceroy," the nearest one said. "A matter of moments and we will be well away from Cato Neimoidia. Your peers on the Council of Separatists await us in the Outer Rim."

"Let us hope so," Gunray said, as the vessel was rocked by a massive explosion.

Behind Gunray walked settlement officer Rune Haako, wearing a crested skullcap; and behind Haako, various financial, legal, and diplomatic officers, each wearing a distinctive headpiece. Droids were already beginning to unload the possessions—the treasures—for which Gunray had risked so much.

He called Haako aside while the others were exiting the sterile docking bay. "Do you think there will be a chance to return and reclaim what we had to leave behind?"

"Not a chance," puckered Haako said flatly. "Our purse worlds now belong to the Republic. Our only hope is to find sanctuary in the Outer Rim. Otherwise, this ship will have to serve as our home—and perhaps our final resting place!"

Sadness crept into Gunray's red orbs. "But my collections, my keepsakes . . . "

"Your most cherished items accompany you," Haako said, gesturing to the containers already piled at the foot of the boarding ramp. "More important, we escaped with our *lives*. Another instant and the Jedi would have had us."

Gunray allowed a nod of agreement. "You warned me."

"I did."

"Count Dooku will help us find new worlds to settle when the war is won."

"*If* the war is won, you mean. The Republic seems keen on driving us from the galaxy."

Gunray made a dismissive gesture with his fat fingers. "Temporary setbacks. The Republic has yet to see the face of its real enemy."

Haako hunched slightly at the reference. "But is even *he* enough, Viceroy?" he asked quietly.

Gunray said nothing, although he had been asking himself the same question for the past several weeks.

One thing was clear: the glory days of the Trade Federation had come to an untimely end. Ironically, the individual most responsible for that bright burning—for the rise of Nute Gunray himself—was the same individual who had repeatedly betrayed him, and to whom Gunray and the other Separatists were now forced to look for salvation.

The Sith Lord, Darth Sidious.

There at Dorvalla and Eriadu, manipulating events to shunt power and influence to the Neimoidians; there at Naboo, ordering a blockade of the planet, the murder of Jedi, assassination of the Queen . . . a debacle for the Trade Federation. Years of attempts by the Republic to try to convict Gunray and his chief officers, to break the hold the Trade Federation enjoyed on galactic shipping. But not once during that time of public disgrace did Gunray mention the role Sidious had played.

Out of fear?

Certainly.

But also because he had sensed that Sidious had not abandoned him completely. Rather, the Dark Lord was somehow seeing to it that the trials never came to fruition, that no lasting verdicts were rendered or punishments handed down. As the Separatist movement gained strength, threatening the security of ships and shipments in the far sectors, the Trade Federation had actually been able to increase the size of its standing army of battle droids by dealing directly with foundry worlds, such as Geonosis and Hypori. Making the most of the Republic's sudden instability, lucrative deals had been arranged between the Trade Federation and the Corporate Alliance, the InterGalactic Banking Clan, the Techno Union, the Commerce Guild, and other corporate entities.

It was during the final trial that Gunray had been approached by Count Dooku, who had promised that all would ultimately turn out well for the Trade Federation. In a moment of weakness, Gunray had revealed the truth about his dealings with Darth Sidious. Dooku has listened attentively; had promised to bring the matter to the attention of the Jedi Council, though he himself had left the Order some years earlier. Gunray had mixed feelings about Dooku's purpose in creating a Separatist movement, chiefly because corruption in the Republic Senate had so often worked to the Trade Federation's advantage. But if Dooku's Confederacy of Independent Systems could eliminate even some of the bribes and kickbacks commonplace in galactic trade, then so much the better.

By and by Dooku's real aims had been made clear: he was less interested in providing an alternative to the Republic than he was in bringing the Republic to its knees—through the use of force if necessary. In much the same way that the Trade Federation had amassed an army right under the nose of Supreme Chancellor Finis Valorum, Dooku—in plain sight—was seeing to it that Baktoid Armor Workshops was supplying weapons to any corporations that agreed to ally with him.

Regardless, Gunray had resisted offers to throw his full support to the Separatists—not when there were still profits to be made in countless Republic star systems. Playing a game of his own, teasing Dooku along, he had informed Dooku that a precondition to their entering into any exclusive arrangement was the death of former Naboo Queen Padmé Amidala, who had foiled Gunray on two occasions, and had been the loudest opposition voice at his trials.

Dooku had hired a bounty hunter to oversee the business, but two attempts at assassinating Senator Amidala had failed.

Then came Geonosis.

But just when Gunray finally had Amidala in his grasp—on trial, no less, for espionage—Dooku had equivocated, refusing to have Amidala killed outright, and not lifting a hand against the Jedi until some two hundred of them had showed up with a clone army the Republic had grown in secret!

That day had provided Gunray with the first in what would be a series of narrow escapes. Hurrying to the catacombs with Dooku at their side, Gunray and Haako had barely managed to flee the embattled surface and recall what core ships and droid carriers remained.

By then, though, it was too late for anyone to resign from Dooku's Confederacy.

The war was begun, and it was Dooku's turn for revelations: he, too, was Sith, and his Master was none other than Sidious! Whether a replacement for the fearsome Darth Maul, or a Sith even during his years in the Jedi Order, Gunray didn't care to know. What mattered was simply that Nute Gunray was right back where he had been so many years earlier: in service to forces over which he had no control whatsoever.

When the war had been going well, the issue of whom he served had been scarcely a problem. Trade had continued, and the Trade Federation had continued in the black. For a time it appeared that Sidious and Dooku's dreams of toppling the Republic might succeed after all. But they found themselves facing a worthy opponent in the person of Supreme Chancellor Palpatine—also from Naboo—who had never much impressed Gunray, but who had managed through a combination of charm and artfulness not only to remain in power long past his term of office, but also, in conjunction with the Jedi, to conduct the war. Slowly, the wheel began to turn, as one Separatist world after another was retaken by the Republic, and now Viceroy Nute Gunray himself had been driven from the Core.

A tragedy for the Trade Federation; a tragedy, he feared, for the entire Neimoidian species.

He gazed at the few possessions he had been able to gather: his costly robes and miters, resplendent jewelry, priceless works of art—

A sudden chill laddered up his spine. His bulging forehead and lower jaw tingled in dread. Eyes protruding from his mottled gray face, he swung to Rune Haako.

"The chair! Where is the chair?"

Haako stared at him.

"The mechno-chair!" Gunray said. "It's not here anywhere!"

Now Haako's eyes widened in apprehension. "Surely we couldn't have overlooked it."

Gunray paced worriedly, trying to recall when and where he had last seen the device. "I'm certain that I had it moved to the launching bay. Yes, yes, I remember seeing it there! But in the rush to launch—"

"But you armed it to self-destruct," Haako said. "Tell me you armed it!"

Gunray stared at him. "I thought you had armed it."

Haako gestured to himself. "I don't even know the sequence codes!"

Gunray fell silent for a moment. "Haako, what if they should decide to tamper with it?"

Haako's broad slash of mouth twitched with worry. "Without the codes, what could they possibly gain from it?"

"You're right. Of course, you're right."

Gunray tried to convince himself. It was just a mechno-chair, after all; finely wrought, but just a walking chair. A walking chair equipped with a hyperwave transceiver. A hyperwave transceiver given to him fourteen years ago by—

"What if he should learn that we left it behind?" Gunray rasped.

"Sidious," Haako said softly.

"Not Sidious!"

"Count Dooku, you mean."

"Are you brain-dead?" Gunray fairly screeched. "Grievous! What if *Grievous* should find out?"

Supreme Commander of the droid armies, General Grievous had been San Hill and Poggle the Lesser's gift to Dooku. Once merely a barbaric living being; now a cyborg monstrosity, devoted to death and destruction. Already the butcher of entire populations; the devastator of countless worlds—

"It's not too late," Haako said suddenly. "We can communicate with the chair from here."

"Can we arm it to self-destruct?"

Haako shook his head negatively. "But we might be able to instruct it to arm itself."

A technician intercepted them while they were hurrying toward a communications console.

"Viceroy, we are prepared to make the jump to lightspeed."

"You will do no such thing!" Gunray cried. "Not until I give the order!"

"But, Viceroy, our vessel can only withstand so much bombardment."

"Bombardment is the least of our concerns!"

"Hurry," Haako insisted, "we haven't much time!"

Gunray rushed to join him at the console. "Say nothing of this to *anyone,*" he warned.

9

Sickle-footed, humpbacked, incised with intricate designs, the mechno-chair sat in the launching bay of the now seized fortress, amid a heap of equally exquisite belongings left by the fleeing Neimoidians.

Obi-Wan was circling it, right hand caressing his bearded chin. "I think I've seen this chair before."

Squatting alongside it, Anakin looked up at him. "Where?"

Obi-Wan stopped. "On Naboo. Shortly after Viceroy Gunray and his entourage were taken into custody in Theed."

Anakin shook his head. "I don't remember seeing it."

Obi-Wan snorted. "I suspect you were too excited about having blown up the Droid Control Ship to take much notice of anything. What's more, I saw it only for a moment. But I do remember being struck by the design of the holoprojector plate. I'd never seen one quite like it—or since, for that matter."

On the far side of the spacious bay, up on its hard-stand, sat Anakin's sleek yellow starfighter. R2-D2 stood nearby, communing with TC-16. Commander Cody and the rest of Squad Seven were elsewhere in the palace, "mopping up," as the clones liked to say.

Anakin examined the chair's holoprojector without touching it. An oval of ribbed alloy, it was equipped with a pair of dorsal sockets sized to accept data cells of some sort. "It is unusual. You know, Master, these cells could contain valuable messages in storage."

"All the more reason to leave it be until someone from Intelligence can have a look at it."

Anakin frowned. "That could take forever."

Obi-Wan folded his arms and regarded him. "Are you in a rush, Anakin?"

"For all we know, the cells could be programmed to erase themselves."

"Do you see any evidence of that?"

"No, but—"

"Then we're better off waiting until we can run a proper diagnostic."

Anakin grimaced. "What do you know about running diagnostics? Master."

"I'm not exactly a stranger to the Temple's cyberlabs, Anakin."

"I know that. But Artoo can run the diagnostic." He beckoned for the droid to join him at the mechno-chair.

"Anakin," Obi-Wan started to say.

"Really, sirs, I must protest," TC-16 interrupted, hurrying behind R2-D2. "These items remain the property of Viceroy Gunray and other members of his party."

"You don't have a say in the matter," Anakin said.

R2-D2 trilled and hooted at the battered protocol droid. The two had been bickering since R2-D2's arrival a short time earlier.

"I'm fully aware that my circuits are corroded," TC-16 said. "As for my posture, there's little I can do about that until my pelvic joint is serviced. You astromechs think very highly of yourselves, just because you can pilot starfighters."

"Don't pay Artoo any mind, TeeCee," Anakin said. "He's been spoiled by another protocol droid. Haven't you, Artoo?"

Artoo toodled a response, extended his computer interface arm, and inserted the magnetic tip into an output socket in the chair.

"Anakin!" Obi-Wan said sharply.

Anakin stood up and joined Obi-Wan on the launch platform. Obi-Wan was pointing to a blinking light that was growing larger by the second in the night sky.

"Do you see that? That is very likely the ship we're waiting for. And the Intelligence officers aboard are not going to take kindly to our sticking our noses in their business."

"Sirs," TC-16 said from behind them.

"Not now," Obi-Wan said.

R2-D2 began to loose a long series of whistles, chirps, and chitters.

"If and when they give the okay," Obi-Wan went on, "then feel free to dissect the entire chair, if that's your objective."

"That's not my objective, Master."

"Maybe Qui-Gon should have left you at Watto's junk shop."

"You don't mean that, Master."

"Of course not. But I know how you love to tinker with things."

"Sirs—"

"Keep quiet, TeeCee," Anakin said.

R2-D2 honked and razzed, though as if from a distance.

"And you, too, Artoo."

Obi-Wan glanced over his shoulder, and his jaw dropped. "Where's the mechno-chair?"

Anakin swung around and scanned the bay. "Where's Artoo?"

"I've been trying to tell you, sirs," TC-16 said, gesturing toward the launching bay's ruined iris hatch. "The chair walked away—taking your high-thinking little droid with it!"

Obi-Wan stared at Anakin in bewilderment.

"Well, it couldn't have gotten far on foot, Master."

They rushed into the corridor, saw that it was deserted in both directions, and began searching the rooms that adjoined the bay. A prolonged electronic squeal brought both of them back into the main corridor.

"That's Artoo," Anakin said.

"Either that, or TeeCee has developed a talent for mimicry."

The protocol droid following behind, they hurried into a compact data room, where they saw R2-D2 with his interface arm still jacked into the chair, and the gripper of his grasping arm clamped to the bar handle of a storage cabinet. Stretched to its full extent, a computer interface cable now connected the mechno-chair to a control console of some sort. The chair's talon-like feet were in constant motion, attempting to gain purchase on the smooth floor in an effort to propel the chair closer to the console.

"What's it doing?" Obi-Wan asked.

Anakin made his face long and shook his head. "Recharging itself?"

"Never seen such tenacity in a mechno-chair."

R2-D2 chattered and wheezed.

"What's Artoo saying?" Obi-Wan asked TC-16.

"He's saying, sir, that the mechno-chair has *just armed itself to self-destruct*!"

Anakin made a mad dash for the console.

"Artoo, unplug yourself!" Obi-Wan shouted. "Anakin, get away from that thing!"

Anakin's fingers were already busy undoing leads that linked the holoprojector unit to the chair.

"Can't, Master. Now we know there's something stored in this chair no one wants us to see."

Obi-Wan glanced worriedly at R2-D2. "How much time, Artoo?"

TC-16 translated the astromech's response. "Seconds, sir!"

Obi-Wan rushed to Anakin's side. "There isn't time, Anakin. Besides, it could be rigged to detonate if tampered with."

"Almost there, Master . . . "

"You'll deactivate us in the process!"

Obi-Wan sensed a disturbance in the Force.

Without thinking, he pulled Anakin to the floor an instant before the chair shot a stream of white vapor into the space Anakin had occupied.

Coughing, Obi-Wan covered his mouth and nose with the wide sleeve of his robe. "Poison gas! Good bet it's the same one Gunray tried to use on Qui-Gon and me at Naboo."

"Thank you, Master," Anakin said. "What's that make it, twenty-five to thirty-seven?"

"Thirty-*six*—if you've any interest in accuracy."

Anakin studied the chair for a moment. "We have to take the chance."

Before Obi-Wan could even think about stopping him, Anakin had leaned forward and wrenched the interface cable from the control console.

R2-D2 yowled, and TC-16 moaned in distress.

A web of blue energy gamboled around the chair and the console, knocking Anakin onto his backside.

At the same time, a high-resolution blue hologram projected from the chair's holoplate.

R2-D2 mewled in alarm.

And to the meter-high figure in the hooded cloak, the unmistakable voice of Viceroy Nute Gunray was saying:

"Yes, yes, of course. Trust that I will see to it personally, my Lord Sidious."

These days, an appointment with Supreme Chancellor Palpatine was not something to be taken lightly—even for a member of the so-called Loyalist Committee.

Appointment?

More an *audience*.

Bail Organa had just arrived on Coruscant, and was still wearing the deep blue cloak, ruffle-collared shirt, and knee-high black boots his wife had laid out for him for the trip from Alderaan. He had been away from the galactic capital for only a standard month, and could scarcely believe the disturbing changes that had taken place during his short absence.

Alderaan never seemed more a paradise, a sanctuary. Just thinking about his beautiful blue-and-white home-world made Bail yearn to be there, yearn for the company of his loving wife.

"I'm going to need to see further identification," the clone trooper stationed at the landing platform's Home-world Security checkpoint told him.

Bail motioned to the identichip he had already slotted

in the scanner. "It's all there, Sergeant. I'm a member in good standing of the Republic Senate."

The helmeted noncom glanced at the display screen, then looked down at Bail. "So it says. But I'm still going to need to see further identification."

Bail sighed in exasperation and fished into the breast pocket of his brocaded tunic for his credit chip.

The new Coruscant, he thought.

Faceless, blaster-wielding soldiers on the shuttle landing platforms, in the plazas, arrayed in front of banks, hotels, theaters, wherever beings gathered or mingled. Scanning the crowds, stopping anyone who fit the current possible terrorist profile, conducting searches of individuals, belongings, residences. Not on a whim, because the cloned troopers didn't operate like that. They answered merely to their training, and the duties they performed were for the good of the Republic.

One heard rumors about antiwar demonstrations being put down by force; of disappearances and seizures of private property. Proof of such abuses of power rarely surfaced, and was quickly discredited.

The omnipresence of the soldiers seemed to bother Bail more than it did his few friends on Coruscant or his peers in the Senate. He had tried to attribute his agitation to the fact that he hailed from pacific Alderaan, but that explained only some of it. What bothered him most was the ease with which the majority of Coruscanti had acclimated to the changes. Their willingness—almost an eagerness—to surrender personal freedoms in the name of security. And a false security, at that. For while Coruscant seemed far from the war, it was also at the center of it.

Now, three years into a conflict that might have been ended as abruptly as it had begun, every new security measure was taken in stride. Except, of course, by members of those species most closely associated with the Separatist agenda—Geonosians, Muuns, Neimoidians, Gossams, and the rest—many of whom had been ostracized or forced to flee the capital. Having lived for so long in fear and ignorance, few Coruscanti stopped to question what was really going on. Least of all the Senate itself, which was so busy modifying the Constitution that it had completely abandoned its role as a balancing arm of the government.

Before the war, widespread corruption had stifled the legislative process. Bills languished, measures sat for years without being addressed, votes were protested and subjected to endless recounts . . . But one effect of the war had been to replace corruption and inertia with dereliction of duty. Reasoned discourse and debate had become so rare as to be archaic. In a political climate where representatives were afraid to speak their minds, it was easier—and thought to be safer—to cede power to those who at least appeared to have some grasp of the truth.

"You're free to go," the trooper said at last, apparently satisfied that Bail was in fact who his credentials claimed him to be.

Bail laughed to himself.

Free to go where? he wondered.

This high up on Coruscant, one couldn't be a pedestrian. Walking was an activity reserved for the bottom feeders who occupied Coruscant's reflectively lit sublevels. Bail hailed a free-travel air taxi and instructed the droid driver to take him to the Senate Building.

Even outside the normal skylanes, above the myriad and abysmal canyons that fissured the urbanscape, far from patrols of security soldiers or the prying eyes of Republic spies, Coruscant looked much as it had for as long as Bail had known it. Traffic was as dense as ever, with ships arriving perpetually from all points in the galaxy. New restaurants had opened; more art was being created. Paradoxically, there seemed to be more joviality in the air, and more opportunities than ever for vice. Even with trade disrupted to the Outer Rim, many Coruscanti were living the good life, and many Senators were continuing to avail themselves of the limitless privileges they had enjoyed in the prewar years.

From up here one had to look closely to observe the changes.

In the oval, twin-drive air taxi, for example.

Running in tiny print across the passenger's-seat display screen was a public service ad extolling the virtues of COMPOR—the Commission for the Protection of the Republic.

NONHUMANS NEED NOT APPLY.

And there, dazzling the sheer face of a towering office building, a piece of late-breaking HoloNet news detailing the Republic's victory at Cato Neimoidia. Lately it was triumph after triumph, praise for the Grand Army of the Republic, all glory to the clone troopers.

Rarely a mention of the Jedi, save for when one of them was commended by Palpatine in the Senate's Great Rotunda. Young Anakin Skywalker or some other. Otherwise one rarely saw an adult Jedi on Coruscant any longer. Spread thin throughout the galaxy, they led companies of troopers into battle. The holofeeds were fond of using the phrase *aggressive peacekeeping* to describe their actions. To the extent that friendships could be forged with them, Bail had come to know a few: Jedi Masters Obi-Wan Kenobi, Yoda, Mace Windu, Saesee Tiin—the privileged few who also were allowed to meet personally with Palpatine.

Bail stirred in his seat.

Even Palpatine's harshest critics in the Senate or in the

various media couldn't hold him fully accountable for
what Coruscant had become. Though hardly the innocent he sometimes pretended to be, Palpatine was not to
blame. His talent for being at once sincere and exacting
was what had gotten him elected in the first place. According to Bail Antilles, at any rate, Bail's predecessor in
the Senate.

*Thirteen years ago the Senate was interested only in
ridding itself of Finis Valorum,* Antilles had once told
Bail. Valorum, who had believed he could put honesty
on the Senate agenda. Even in those days Palpatine had
had his share of influential friends.

Still, Bail couldn't help but wonder who might have
succeeded Palpatine as Supreme Chancellor if the Separatist crises on Raxus Prime and Antar 4 had not occurred when they did, just as Palpatine's term of office
was ending. He remembered the arguments that had
raged over passage of the Emergency Powers Act; that it
was dangerous to "change dewbacks in the middle of a
sand dune." Back then, many Senators felt that the Republic should bide its time and simply allow Count
Dooku's movement to play itself out.

But not after the full extent of the Separatist threat became clear.

Not after some six thousand worlds, lured by the
promise of free and unrestricted trade, had seceded from
the Republic. Not after heavily armed corporations such
as the Commerce Guild and the Techno Union had part-
nered with Dooku. Not after the entire Rimward leg of
the Rimma Trade Route had become inaccessible to Republic shipping.

As a consequence—and by an overwhelming majority—the Senate had voted to amend the Constitution,
and to extend Palpatine's term indefinitely, with the understanding that he would voluntarily step down from

office when the crisis was resolved. In short order, however, the likelihood of a quick resolution evaporated. Formerly gracious and unassuming Palpatine was suddenly democracy's champion, vowing that he could not condone a Republic divided against itself.

Rumors of a Military Creation Act began to circulate. But Palpatine himself had refused to come out in favor of building an army for the Republic. He left that to others—the Senate's nominal Sand Panthers. Finally he attempted to arrange a peace summit, but Count Dooku had refused to attend.

Instead came war.

Bail could recall clearly the day he had stood with Palpatine, Mas Amedda, Malastarian Senators, and others on a balcony of the Senate Office Building, watching tens of thousands of clone troopers march into the enormous ships that would take the war to the Separatists. He could recall clearly his utter disconsolation. That after a thousand years of peace, war and evil had returned.

More accurately, been allowed to return.

Regardless, Bail had put his feelings aside and had played his part, endorsing bills he might have previously denounced, supporting Palpatine's "efficient streamlining of cumbersome bureaucracy." It wasn't until passage of the Reflex Amendment, some fourteen months back, that his fears had begun to resurface and intensify. The sudden disappearance of Senator Seti Ashgad after he had argued against installation of surveillance cams in the Senate Building; the suspicious explosion of a star freighter aboard which Finis Valorum was a passenger; the passage of a security bill that granted Palpatine wide-ranging powers over Coruscant . . .

The behavior of the Supreme Chancellor himself—frequently isolated by his covey of advisers and illegal cadre of red-robed personal bodyguards; his unbending resolve to continue fighting until the war was won. Gone was humble, self-deprecating Palpatine. And with him, tractable Bail Organa. Bail vowed to speak openly of his concerns, and he began to cultivate friendships with Senators who shared those concerns.

Some of them were waiting for him when the air taxi touched down in the broad plaza that fronted the mushroom-shaped Senate Building. Padmé Amidala, of Naboo; Mon Mothma of Chandrila; human Senators Terr Taneel, Bana Breemu, and Fang Zar; and alien Senator Chi Eekway.

Slender, short-haired Mon Mothma hurried to embrace Bail as he approached. "A momentous occasion, Bail," she said into his left ear. "An audience with Palpatine."

Bail laughed to himself. They did think alike.

Padmé hugged him, as well, though somewhat stiffly. She looked radiant. A bit more full-faced than Bail remembered, but the very picture of classic beauty in her elegant robes and elaborate coiffure. A golden protocol droid stood behind her. She told him she had just returned from a wonderful week on Naboo, visiting with her family.

"An extraordinary world, Naboo," Bail said. "I'll never understand how it spawned someone as stubborn as our Supreme Chancellor."

Padmé scolded him with a frown. "He's not stubborn, Bail. You just don't know him as I do. He'll take our concerns to heart."

"For all the good it will do," Chi Eekway said, displeasure wrinkling her blue face.

"You underestimate Palpatine's acuity," Padmé said. "Besides, he appreciates frank speech."

"We've been nothing if not frank, Senator," dark-complected, bib-bearded Fang Zar said. "With scant success."

Padmé glanced at everyone. "Surely, faced with all of us . . . "

"Had we a tenth of the Senate we would prove too few," Bana said, draped head-to-toe in shimmersilk. "But it is important that we hold to our intention."

Eekway nodded gravely.

"It can be hoped," Fang Zar said, "not counted on."

The conversation turned to personal matters as they entered the vast building. They were an animated group when they finally arrived at the holding office, directly beneath the Great Rotunda, where Palpatine's human appointments secretary asked them to wait in the receiving area.

After an hour of waiting, their spirits began to flag. But then the door to Palpatine's office slid open, and Sate Pestage, one of Palpatine's chief advisers, appeared.

"Senators, what a surprise," he said.

Bail came to his feet, speaking for everyone when he said: "It shouldn't be. The appointment was confirmed more than three weeks ago."

Pestage glanced at the appointments secretary. "Really? I wasn't informed."

"You most certainly were informed," Padmé said, "since the appointment was secured through your office."

"Several of us have risked much and traveled great distances," Eekway added.

Pestage spread his hands in a patronizing way. "Such times require sacrifices, Senator. Or perhaps you feel you've risked more than the Supreme Chancellor has."

Bail spoke up. "No one is implying that the Supreme Chancellor has been anything but tireless in his . . . devotion. But the fact remains that he agreed to see us, and we're not about to leave here until he honors his pledge."

"We're not asking for much of his time," Terr Taneel said, in a more placating tone.

"Maybe not, but you must realize how busy he is. What with new developments occurring daily." Pestage looked at Bail. "I understand you've become quite friendly with the Jedi Council. Why not visit with them while I attempt to reschedule you?"

Anger mottled Bail's bearded face. "We're not leaving until we see him, Sate."

Pestage forced a smile. "As is your prerogative, Senator."

The shuttle whose landing lights had caught Obi-Wan's attention on Cato Neimoidia carried more than Intelligence analysts and technicians. Yoda was aboard, eager to see for himself what Obi-Wan and Anakin had discovered.

The technicians had succeeded in inducing the mechno-chair's holoprojector to replay the image of Lord Sidious, and Republic cryptographers working with the Jedi were confident that the unique device would yield even greater secrets once it was relocated to Coruscant and examined thoroughly.

Refusing to let the mechno-chair out of his sight, Anakin had demanded to oversee its transfer to the waiting shuttle. Feeling unnecessary, Obi-Wan and Yoda decided to take a stroll down the corridor of Viceroy Gunray's now appropriated palace. The venerable Jedi Master was pensive as they walked, the silence broken only by the sounds of distant blasterfire and the *tick, tick* of Yoda's gimer stick as it struck the polished floor.

Yoda was unreadable.

Obi-Wan wasn't sure if Yoda was pondering the image of Sidious, or the fact that two Jedi had been killed during the fighting on Cato Neimoidia. Every day saw more Jedi die. Many were as shot up as the clone troopers. Wounded, blinded, scarred, deprived of arms or legs . . . patched up by bota and bacta. More than a thousand Padawans had lost their Masters; more than a thousand Masters, their Padawans. When Jedi gathered now they talked not about the Force, but about their military campaigns. New lightsabers were constructed not as a meditative exercise, but to handle the rigors of close combat.

Reaching the end of the long corridor, Obi-Wan and Yoda turned and started back. Without taking his eyes from the floor, Yoda said: "Found something important, you have, Obi-Wan. That Count Dooku is in league with someone, proof this is. That in this war a greater part the Sith play than we realize."

The name *Sidious* had come up only once since the war began—on Geonosis, when Dooku had told an imprisoned Obi-Wan that a Sith Lord by that name had hundreds of Republic Senators under his influence. At the time, Obi-Wan assumed that Dooku was lying, in order to persuade Obi-Wan that he was still aligned with the Jedi, although attempting to thwart the powers of the dark side by his own methods. And yet, even after Dooku had revealed himself to be Sith-trained, Yoda and others on the Council continued to believe that he had been lying about Sidious. Two Council members were convinced that Dooku *was* the Dark Lord, having somehow tutored himself—by Sith Holocron, perhaps—in the use of dark side powers.

Now that Sidious appeared to be real, Obi-Wan didn't know what to think.

A hunt for Dooku's Sith allies had been going on almost since the start of the war. Dooku was known to have trained Jedi in the dark arts—Jedi Knights who had lost faith in the ideals of the Republic, Padawans fascinated by the power of the dark side, misinformed novices such as Asajj Ventress, who had been mentored by a Jedi—but the question remained, who, if anyone, had been Dooku's teacher?

Thirteen years earlier, when Obi-Wan had fought and killed a Sith on Naboo, had he killed a Master or an apprentice? The question was rooted in the belief that the Sith, having essentially defeated themselves a millennium earlier, had learned that an army of Sith could never stand, and that there should be only two at any given time, lest a pair of apprentices conspire to combine their strengths to eliminate a Master.

More a doctrine than a rule; but a doctrine that had managed to keep the Sith order alive, if well concealed, for going on a thousand years.

But the horned and tattooed Sith whom Obi-Wan killed could not have trained Dooku, because Dooku had still been a member of the Jedi Order then. As clouded as the dark side made some things, there was simply no way Dooku could have been living a double life within the walls of the Temple itself.

"Master Yoda," Obi-Wan said, "is it possible that Dooku wasn't lying about the Senate being under the control of Sidious?"

Yoda gave his head a quick shake while they walked. "Looked hard at the Senate, we did. And risked much we did by doing so—questioning in secret those we serve. But no evidence we found." He glanced up at Obi-Wan. "If in control of the Senate Sidious was, would not defeated the Republic already be? Would not to the Confederacy the Core and Inner Rim belong?"

Yoda paused for a moment, then added: "Perhaps at Geonosis, an accident it was that Dooku revealed himself. Had he not, searched we would have for Sidious, leaving Dooku to escalate his war. What think you, Obi-Wan? Hmmm?"

Obi-Wan folded his arms. "I've thought long and hard about that day, Master, and I believe Dooku couldn't help revealing himself—even though he may have regretted it. When he was fleeing for his ship, it was almost as if he *allowed* himself to be seen; almost as if he was attempting to draw us into an engagement. My first thought was that he was trying to ensure the safe escape of Gunray and the other Separatist leaders. But my instincts tell me that he wanted desperately to demonstrate how powerful he had become. I think he was genuinely surprised to see you turn up. But instead of killing Anakin or me, he deliberately left us alive, to send a message to the Jedi."

"Right you are, Obi-Wan. *Pride* undid him. Forced him, it did, to show us his true face."

"Could he have been trained by this . . . Sidious?"

"Stands to reason, it does. *Accepted* by Sidious he was, following the death of the one you killed."

Obi-Wan considered it. "I've heard rumors about Dooku's early fascination with the dark side. Was there not an incident in the Temple involving a stolen Sith Holocron?"

Yoda squeezed his eyes shut and nodded. "True that rumor is. But understand, Obi-Wan, a *Jedi* Dooku was. For many, many years. Difficult the decision is to leave the Order. Influenced he was by many things. The death of your former Master, for one—even though avenged Qui-Gon was."

He glanced at Obi-Wan. "Complicated this is. Not merely by what we know, but by what we do not know; what we have to *assume.*"

Yoda stopped, then gestured to a carved bench.

"Sit for a while, we will. Enlighten you, I can."

Obi-Wan sat, his heart wanting to race.

"A stern Master Dooku was, to Qui-Gon and others," Yoda began. "Powerful he was; skilled, disdainful. More important, convinced that lowering the shroud of the dark side was. Signs there were, all about us, long before to the Temple you came; long before Qui-Gon came. Gross injustices, favoritism, corruption . . . More and more, called the Jedi were to enforce the peace. More and more deaths there were. Out of control events were becoming."

"Did the Council sense that the Sith had returned?"

"Never absent they were, Obi-Wan. But stronger suddenly. Closer to the surface. Spoke much of the prophecy, Dooku did."

"The prophecy of the Chosen One?"

"The larger prophecy: that *unfold* the dark times would. Born into their midst the Chosen One is, to return balance to the Force."

"Anakin," Obi-Wan said.

Yoda regarded him for a long moment. "Difficult to say," he said quickly. "Maybe, yes; maybe, no. More important the shroud of the dark side is. Many, many discussions Dooku had. With me, with other members of the Council. Most of all, with Master Sifo-Dyas."

Obi-Wan waited.

"Close friends they were. Bound together by the unifying Force. But worried about Master Dooku, Sifo-Dyas was. Worried about his disenchantment with the Republic; about self-absorption among the Jedi. Saw in Dooku the effect of Qui-Gon's death, Sifo-Dyas did. The effect that resurfaced the Sith had." Yoda shook his head mournfully. "Knew of Dooku's imminent departure, Master Sifo-Dyas did. Sensed, he may have, the birth of the Separatist movement."

"And yet the Council dismissed Dooku as an idealist," Obi-Wan said.

Yoda gazed at the floor. "Saw with my own eyes what he had become, and refused to believe it, I did."

"But how could Dooku have searched out Sidious? Or was it the other way around?"

"Impossible to know. But accept Sidious as a mentor Dooku did."

"Could Sifo-Dyas have foreseen that, as well?"

"Also impossible to know. Believed he might have, that Sidious Dooku would hunt down. To *destroy*."

"Could that have motivated Dooku to leave the Order?"

"Perhaps. But by the power of the dark side, even the most steadfast heart can be seduced."

Obi-Wan turned to face Yoda. "Master, did Sifo-Dyas order the clone army?"

Yoda nodded. "Contacted the Kaminoans, he did."

"Without your knowledge?"

"Without it, yes. But *exists,* a record of his initial contact."

Obi-Wan gave in to some of his frustration. "I should have questioned Lama Su more extensively."

"Questioned, the Kaminoans were. Furnished much they did."

"Did they?" Obi-Wan said in surprise. "When?"

"Reticent they were when first to Kamino I went. Only what already they had told you, I heard. That Sifo-Dyas the order placed; that Tyranus the donor clone furnished. That for the Republic the clones were. Seen by the Kaminoans, neither Sifo-Dyas nor Tyranus was. But later, after attacked Kamino was, *more* I learned from Taun We and Ko Sai. About the payments."

"From Sifo-Dyas?"

"From Tyranus."

"Could *Tyranus* have been an alias for Sifo-Dyas?

Could he have adopted the name to provide deniability for the Jedi in case the clone army was discovered?"

"Wished for that I did. But killed Sifo-Dyas was, *before* on Kamino Jango Fett arrived."

"Murdered?"

Yoda compressed his thin lips. "Unsolved the crime remains, but, yes: murdered."

"Someone knew," Obi-Wan said, more to himself. "Dooku?" he asked Yoda.

"A theory I have—nothing more. *Murder,* Dooku committed. Then, from the Jedi archives erased Kamino, he did. Of that tampering, proof Master Jocasta Nu found—proof of Dooku's action, though well concealed it was."

Obi-Wan recalled his visit to the archives to search out the location of Kamino, only to be told by Jocasta Nu that the planetary system didn't exist. What had caused him that day three years earlier to stare so intently at the library's bronzium bust of Count Dooku?

"Nevertheless, the clone army continued to be financed and built," he said at last. "Could Sifo-Dyas and Tyranus have been partners?"

"Of our ignorance, another example this is. But playing both sides Jango Fett clearly was. By someone on the side of the Republic, chosen he was on Bogg Four to be the clone template. But serving Dooku he was, as a hired killer. With the changeling who targeted Amidala, an intermediary he was."

Obi-Wan pictured Fett in the execution arena on Geonosis, standing behind Dooku in a box reserved for dignitaries. "He had knowledge of both armies. Could he have killed Sifo-Dyas?"

"Perhaps."

"Were you able to trace the source of the payments—beyond Tyranus, I mean?"

"From Bogg Four into a maze of deception, they led."

"Did the Kaminoans say whether anyone had tried to persuade them *not* to build the army?"

"Intercede, none did. Reveal themselves too soon, our enemies would have."

"So Dooku had no choice but to create an army before the clones were trained and ready."

"Appears that way, it does."

Obi-Wan fell silent for a moment.

"When I was being held captive on Geonosis, Dooku told me that the Trade Federation had been allied with Sidious during the blockade of Naboo, but that they had later been betrayed by him. Dooku said that Gunray had gone to him for help, and that Dooku had tried to appeal to the Council. He claimed that, even after several warnings, the Council refused to believe him. Is any of that true, Master?"

"More lies," Yoda said. "Building a case to enlist you in his cause, Dooku was."

You must join me, Obi-Wan, Dooku had said, *and together we will destroy the Sith!*

"If Gunray hadn't been so keen on assassinating Padmé Amidala," Obi-Wan mused. "If I'd failed to trace the saberdart that killed the changeling . . . "

"Ignorant about the clone army, we might have remained."

"But surely the Kaminoans would have contacted us, Master."

"Eventually. But grown greater in numbers the Separatist army would have. Invincible, perhaps."

Obi-Wan's eyes narrowed. "Mine wasn't a case of blind luck."

Yoda shook his head. "Meant to learn of the clone army, we were. Destined to fight this war, we were."

"In the nick of time. The Council couldn't conceive of

Dooku as anything but an idealist. Perhaps he never believed that the Jedi could become generals."

"Nonsense," Yoda said. "Warriors always have we been."

"But are we helping to return balance to the Force, or are our actions contributing to the growth of the dark side?"

Yoda grimaced. "Impatient with such talk I grow. Cryptic this conflict is—the way it began, the way it unfolds. But for the ideals of the Republic we fight. To prevail and restore peace our priorities must remain. *Then* to the dark heart of this matter will we burrow. Expose the truth, we will."

Yoda was correct, Obi-Wan told himself. If the Jedi hadn't learned of the clone army, Dooku's Separatists would have suddenly appeared on the scene with tens of millions of battle droids, fleets of warships, and seceded from the Republic without contest. But there would have been no coexisting with the Confederacy. Ultimately it would have bled the Republic dry. War would have been inevitable, and the Jedi would have been caught in the middle, as they were now.

But why hadn't Yoda told him sooner about Sifo-Dyas?

Or was this yet another lesson, as the search for Kamino had been? Yoda's way of telling him to search for the thing that didn't seem to be there by analyzing its effects on the world around it. *The difference between knowledge and wisdom,* Obi-Wan's friend Dex might have said, as he did on identifying the source of the saberdart that had killed Zam Wessel, when the Temple analysis droids couldn't.

Yoda was regarding him when he lifted his head.

"Reveal you, your thoughts do, Obi-Wan. Believe I should have told you sooner, you do."

"Yours is the wisdom of centuries, Master."

"Years matter not. Busy fighting a war, you have been. Mentoring your headstrong Padawan. In pursuit of Dooku and his minions . . . *Darker,* events became. Attempting to turn this war to their own uses, Dooku and Sidious are."

"We'll have Dooku soon enough."

"Lifted the veil of the dark side wasn't after your success on Naboo. Grown beyond Dooku this war has. Now to justice *both* must be brought. And to justice all those Sidious to the dark side has turned." Yoda looked hard at Obi-Wan. "Uncover Sidious's tracks, you must. A chance this war to conclude, you and Anakin have been given."

In the launching bay Anakin kept his eyes on the mechno-chair, while R2-D2 and TC-16 kept their photoreceptors on Anakin. Now that the analysts had run their diagnostic routines, the technicians were preparing to pack the device for safe shipment to Coruscant.

Just as Obi-Wan had said, they resented the fact that Anakin had tampered with the chair, despite the fact that, had he not, the chair would have blown itself to pieces, taking with it the holoimage of Sidious and whatever other communications memories it might contain.

Maybe Qui-Gon should have left you at Watto's junk shop.

Obi-Wan's little joke. But the words had stung, for some reason. Probably because of Anakin's own musings about what might have become of him had the Jedi not been forced to land on Tatooine to find a replacement part for Padmé's starship. It wasn't hard to imagine himself stuck in Mos Espa. With his mom; with C-3PO, without the bright shell he now wore—

No.

At nine years of age he had been an expert Podracer; by twenty-one he would have been a galactic champion. With or without Qui-Gon's or Watto's help, he would eventually have won the Boonta Eve race, and his reputation would have been made. He would have bought freedom for himself, his mother, all the slaves in Mos Espa, gone on to win the Grand Races on Malastare, been hailed in the gambling casinos on Ord Mantell and Coruscant. He wouldn't have become a Jedi—he would have been too old to train—would never have learned to wield a lightsaber. But he would have been able to fly rings around the finest of Jedi pilots, including Saesee Tiin.

And he still would have been stronger in the Force than any of them.

He might never have met Padmé . . .

He had thought her an Angel, arrived on Tatooine from the Moons of Iego. A playful remark on his part, but not as entirely innocent as it had sounded. Even so, to her he was just a funny little boy. Padmé didn't know then that his precocity wasn't limited to a skill for building and fixing things. He had an uncanny sense for knowing what was going to happen; a certainty that he would become celebrated. He was different—chosen long before the Jedi Order had bestowed the title. Mythical beings came to him—Angels and Jedi—and he excelled in contests in which humans weren't even meant to participate. And yet, even with an Angel and Jedi for guests in his home, he hadn't divined the sudden departure from Tatooine, the Jedi training, his marriage.

He was no longer the funny little boy. But Padmé remained his Angel—

A vision of her broke his reverie.

Something . . . something had changed. His heart filled with longing for her. Even through the Force he couldn't clarify what he was feeling. He simply knew that he should be with her. That he should be there to protect her . . .

He flexed his artificial hand.

Remain in the living Force, he told himself. A Jedi didn't dwell in the past. A Jedi surrendered attachment to persons and things that passed out of his or her life. A Jedi didn't fantasize, or think: *What if—*

He cut his eyes to the three human technicians who were fitting the mechno-chair into a crash-foam safety harness. One of them was working too fast, and almost knocked the chair over.

Anakin shot to his feet and stormed across the bay.

"Be careful with that!" he shouted.

The oldest of the three gave him a scornful glance. "Relax, kid, we know our job."

Kid.

He waved his hand, calling on the Force to keep the mechno-chair fixed in place. The three techs strained to move it, baffled until they realized what Anakin had done. Then the same one straightened and glared.

"All right, let go of it."

"When I'm convinced you actually know what you're doing."

"Look, kid—"

Anakin beetled his brows in anger and advanced a step. The three techs began to back away from the chair.

They're afraid of me. They've heard about me.

For an instant, their fear empowered him; then he felt shame, and averted his glance.

The eldest was holding up his hands. "Take it easy, Jedi. I didn't mean to offend you."

"Pack it yourself if you want to," another said.

Anakin swallowed hard. "It's important, that's all. I

don't want anything to happen to it." He let the mechno-chair settle to the floor.

"Carefully, this time," the eldest said, refusing to so much as glance at Anakin.

"General Skywalker!" a trooper called from behind him.

Anakin turned, saw the trooper motioning to the shuttle.

"Hyperwave commo for you—from the office of the Supreme Chancellor."

Now the three technicians looked at him again. *As well they should.*

Without a word, Anakin spun on his heel and ascended the shuttle's boarding ramp. Above a holoprojector plate in the ship's comm center, a flickering image of Supreme Chancellor Palpatine was resolving. When Anakin had positioned himself on the transmission grate, Palpatine smiled.

"Congratulations, Anakin, on your victory at Cato Neimoidia."

"Thank you, sir. But I'm sorry to report that Viceroy Gunray escaped, and that fighting continues in the rock-arch cities."

Palpatine's smile faltered. "Yes, I was informed as much."

It wasn't the first time Anakin had heard from Palpatine in the field. At Jabiim, Palpatine had ordered Anakin to retreat before the planet fell to the Separatists; at Praesitlyn he had praised Anakin for having saved the day. Still, the communications were often as awkward as they were flattering.

"What's wrong, my boy?" Palpatine asked. "I sense that you're troubled about something. If it involves Gunray, accept my word that he won't be able to hide from us forever. None of them will. One day you'll have your chance for complete victory."

Anakin wet his lips. "It's not about Gunray, sir. Just a small incident here that made me angry."

"What incident?"

Anakin was tempted to disclose the details of his and Obi-Wan's discovery, but Yoda had told him to remain silent about the mechno-chair. "Nothing important," he said. "But I always feel guilty when I become angry."

"That's a mistake," Palpatine said gently. "Anger is natural, Anakin. I thought we'd been through all this—regarding what took place on Tatooine?"

"Obi-Wan doesn't show anger—except, of course, at me. Even then, it's more like . . . aggravation."

"Anakin, you're a passionate young man. That's what separates you from your Jedi comrades. Unlike Obi-Wan and the others, you weren't raised in the Temple, where younglings are taught to conquer their anger by transcending it. You enjoyed a natural childhood. You can dream, you have imagination and vision. You're not some unthinking machine, some heartless piece of technology. Not that I'm suggesting that the Jedi are," Palpatine was quick to add. "But for someone like you, any threat to someone or something important to you is likely to evoke an emotional response. It happened with your mother; it will happen again. But you shouldn't fight those responses. Learn from them, but don't fight them."

Anakin suppressed an impulse to reveal his marriage to Padmé, as well.

"Do you think I'm immune to anger?" Palpatine said into the short silence.

"I've never seen you angry."

"Well, perhaps I've grown adept at reserving my anger for private moments. But it grows more difficult to do so, in the face of the frustrations I face with the Senate. With the way this war persists . . . Oh, I know that you and the other Jedi are doing everything you can . . . But the Jedi Council and I don't always see eye-to-eye on how this war should be waged. You know my love for the Republic knows no bounds. That's why I'm struggling so hard to keep it from falling to pieces."

Anakin forced a derisive breath. "The Senate should simply follow your lead. Instead, they block you. They tie your hands. It's as if they envy the power they gave you."

"Yes, my boy, many do. But many support me, as well. More important, we must abide by the rules and regulations of the Constitution, or else we are no better than those who stand in the way of freedom."

"Some individuals should be above the rules," Anakin grumbled.

"A case can be made for it. And, indeed, you are one of those people, Anakin. But you must know when to act, and when not to."

Anakin nodded. "I understand." He paused, then said, "How is Coruscant, sir? I miss it."

"Coruscant is as ever, a shining example of what life could be. But I'm far too busy to indulge in its manifold pleasures."

Anakin searched for some way to frame the question he needed to ask. "I guess you've been meeting frequently with the Loyalist Committee."

"As a matter of fact, I have. A treasured group of Senators, who value the high standards of the Republic as much as you and I do." Palpatine smiled. "Senator Amidala, for example. So filled with vigor and compassion— the same qualities she brought to her term as Queen of Naboo. She causes a stir wherever she goes." He looked directly at Anakin. "I'm so glad that you and she have become such dear friends."

Anakin swallowed nervously. "Will you tell her . . . will you tell her hello from me?"

"Of course I will."

An ensuing silence lingered an instant too long.

"Anakin, I will somehow see to it that you return from the Outer Rim soon," Palpatine said. "But we cannot rest until those responsible for this war have been held accountable for their crimes and eliminated as a threat to lasting peace. Do you understand?"

"I'll do my part, sir."

"Yes, my boy. I know you will."

In the reception area of the holding office, Bail Organa paced restlessly. He was preparing to vent his exasperation on Palpatine's appointments secretary when the door to the Supreme Chancellor's office opened once again, and his advisers began to file out between the imposing, red-cowled guards that flanked the opening.

Advisers Sim Aloo and Janus Greejatus; director of Intelligence Armand Isard; senior member of the Security and Intelligence Council, Jannie Ha'Nook of Glithnos; Chagrian Speaker of the Senate Mas Amedda; and staff aide Sly Moore, tall and ethereal-looking in her Umbaran shadowcloak. Last to exit was Pestage.

"Senators, you're still here, I see."

"We're nothing if not patient," Bail said.

"Good to know, since the Supreme Chancellor still has much to attend to."

Just then Palpatine himself appeared, glancing at Bail and the others, then at Pestage.

"Senator Organa, Senator Amidala—all of you. What a delight to find you here."

"Supreme Chancellor," Bail said, "we were under the impression we had an appointment with you."

Palpatine lifted an eyebrow. "Indeed? Why wasn't I informed of this?" he asked Pestage.

"Your schedule is so full, I didn't want to overburden you."

Palpatine frowned. "My day is never so full that I can't take time to confer with members of the Loyalist Committee. Leave us, Sate, and don't allow us to be disturbed. I'll call for you when you're needed."

Stepping aside, he gestured Bail and the others into the circular office. C-3PO was last to cross the threshold, twisting his head to regard both of the motionless guards.

Bail took a seat directly across from Palpatine's high-backed chair, which was said to house some sort of shield generator—necessary for his protection, as were the guards, though something that would have been unheard of three years earlier. Saturated in red, the windowless, carpeted office contained several singular pieces of statuary, as did Palpatine's chambers in the Senate Office Building, and his suite in the crown of 500 Republica. Rumored to work for days on end without sleeping, Palpatine seemed alert, curious, somewhat imperious.

"So, what matters have brought you here on such a glorious Coruscant afternoon?" he said from his chair. "I can't help but sense a certain urgency . . . "

"We'll come directly to the point, Supreme Chancellor," Bail said. "Now that the Confederacy has been chased from the Core and Inner Rim, we wish to discuss the abrogation of some of the measures that were enacted in the name of public safety."

Palpatine gazed at Bail over steepled fingers. "Our recent victories have made you feel so secure?"

"They have, Supreme Chancellor," Padmé said.

"The Enhanced Security and Enforcement Act in particular," Bail continued. "Specifically those measures that permit the unrestricted use of observation droids, and searches and seizures without the need for warrants or due process."

"I see," Palpatine said slowly. "Unfortunately, the fact of the matter is that the war is far from won, and I, for one, am not entirely satisfied that traitors and terrorists are not a continued threat to public safety. Oh, I realize that our victories give all appearances of a quick resolution to the war, but as of this morning I was informed that the Separatists still hold many key worlds in the Outer Rim, and that our sieges there could go on indefinitely."

"Indefinitely?" Eekway said.

"Why not consider ceding some of those worlds," Fang Zar suggested. "Trade in the Core and Inner Rim has resumed almost to prewar standards."

Palpatine shook his head. "Some of those Outer Rim worlds were Republic worlds, taken by force. And I fear we risk setting a dangerous precedent by allowing the Confederacy to retain them. I believe, furthermore, that now is the very time to press our attack, until the Separatists no longer present a threat to our way of life."

"Is there not some other way than continued warfare?" Bail asked. "Surely Dooku can be persuaded to listen to reason now."

"You misjudge his resolve, Senator. But even if I'm wrong, suppose we decide to cede some worlds, as a conciliatory gesture. Who will choose which worlds? Me? You? Shall we submit the matter to a Senate vote? And how might the denizens of those ceded worlds respond to our gesture? How would the good people of Alderaan feel about being a Confederacy world? Should loyalty to the Republic count for so little? Such decisions were what prompted many worlds to ally with Count Dooku in the first place."

"But can we even triumph in the Outer Rim," Eekway said, "with the army so reduced, the Jedi so dispersed? Might it not appear that the Jedi are deliberately perpetuating this war?"

Palpatine stood up and paced away from his huge chair, turning his back to everyone. "This has become a very regrettable situation—one we have attempted to correct, with limited success." He swung around. "We must consider how others view this war. A former Jedi at the helm of the Separatist movement; the clone army of the Republic led by Jedi . . . Many remote worlds see this war as an attempt by the Jedi to dominate the galaxy. To many, the Jedi were not to be trusted before the war—in part as a result of the aggressive negotiations they were constrained to undertake during the terms of my predecessors. Word reaches those same worlds that it was the Jedi who invaded Geonosis, all because two of the Order had been sentenced to death for espionage. We know better, of course, but how to amend the misinterpretation?"

Realizing that he had allowed the discussion to go off track, Bail said: "Returning to the matter of rescinding the Security Act—"

"I serve the Republic, Senator Organa," Palpatine said, cutting him off. "Introduce a measure to repeal in the Senate. I will accept whatever outcome ensues from a vote."

"Will you remain impartial during the debates?"

"You have my word."

"And these amendments to the Constitution," Mon Mothma started to say.

"I view the Constitution as a *living* document," Palpatine interrupted. "As such, it must be allowed to expand

and contract according to circumstances. Otherwise, what do we have but stasis."

"If we can be assured of a certain . . . exhalation of power," Bana Breemu said.

Palpatine grinned faintly. "Of course."

"Then we've made a beginning," Padmé said. "Just as I knew we would."

Palpatine beamed at her. "Senator Amidala, is that not the droid Jedi Skywalker constructed?"

Padmé looked at C-3PO. "Yes, it is."

For a moment it appeared that C-3PO was speechless—but only for a moment.

"I am honored that you remember me, Your Majesty," he said.

Palpatine returned an abrupt laugh. "A title more fit for a king or emperor." He glanced at Padmé. "In fact, I have just spoken with him, Your Highness."

"Anakin?" Padmé said in surprise.

Palpatine held her gaze. "Why Senator Amidala, I do believe you're blushing."

14

Returning to the launching bay with Yoda, Obi-Wan observed Anakin and Yoda trade the briefest of looks, the meaning of which escaped him. Neither Jedi appeared to be bothered by the silent exchange, and yet Yoda doddered off without a word to speak with the Intelligence analysts huddled near the shuttle's boarding ramp.

"Jedi Council business?" Anakin asked when Obi-Wan joined him.

"Nothing of the sort. Yoda believes that the mechno-chair may yield clues to the whereabouts of Darth Sidious. He wants us to take up the search."

Anakin didn't respond immediately. "Master, aren't we obligated to notify the Supreme Chancellor of our find?"

"We are, Anakin, and we will."

"When the Council sees fit, you mean."

"No. After the matter has been discussed."

"But suppose one or two of you should disagree with the majority?"

"Decisions are not always unanimous. When we are truly divided, we defer to Yoda's counsel."

"Then the Force can sometimes be felt more strongly by one than by eleven."

Obi-Wan tried to discern Anakin's intent. "Even Yoda is not infallible, if that's what you're getting at."

"The Jedi should be." Anakin glanced furtively at Obi-Wan. "We *could* be."

"I'm listening."

"By going farther with the Force than we allow ourselves. By riding its crest."

"Master Sora Bulq and many others would agree, Anakin. But few Jedi have the stomach for such a ride. We're not all as self-composed as Yoda or Master Windu."

"But maybe we're wrong to attach ourselves to the Force at the expense of life as most beings know it, which includes lust, love, and a lot of other emotions that are forbidden to us. Devotion to a higher cause is fine and good, Master, but we shouldn't ignore what's going on in front of our own eyes. You said yourself that we're not infallible. Dooku understood that. He looked things squarely in the eye, and decided to do something about it."

"Dooku is a Sith, Anakin. He may have had his good reasons for leaving the Order, but he is nothing now but a master of deceit. He and Sidious prey on the weak-willed. They deceive themselves into *believing* that they are infallible."

"But I've seen instances where the Jedi lie to one another. Master Kolar lied about Quinlan Vos going to the dark side. We're lying now, by not sharing our information about Sidious with Chancellor Palpatine. What would Sidious or Dooku have to say about our lies?"

"Don't compare us to them," Obi-Wan said, more harshly than he meant. "The Jedi are not a cult, Anakin. We don't worship a leadership of elites. We're encouraged to find our paths; to validate through personal experience the value of what we have been taught. We don't offer facile justifications for exterminating a perceived enemy. We're guided by compassion, and the belief that the Force is greater than the sum of those who open themselves to it."

Anakin grew quiet. "I'm only asking, Master."

Obi-Wan took a calming breath. *Too sure of themselves, the Jedi have become,* Yoda had once told him. *Even the older, more experienced ones . . .*

How might Anakin have fared under Qui-Gon's guidance? he wondered. He was merely Anakin's adoptive mentor, and a flawed mentor in many ways. So eager to live up to the memory of Qui-Gon that he was continually overlooking Anakin's attempts to live up to him.

"Carries on his shoulders the weight of the galaxy, Obi-Wan does," Yoda said, approaching with one of the Intelligence analysts. "Ease your concerns, this news might," he added before Obi-Wan could respond.

The dark-haired, robust-looking analyst Captain Dyne perched himself on the edge of a shipping container. "While we still don't know whether the mechnochair was left behind deliberately, as some kind of trap, the image of Sidious is authentic. The transmission appears to have been received two days ago, local, but we're going to have trouble tracking its source because it was routed through a system of hyperwave transceivers used by the Confederacy as a substitute for the HoloNet, and was encrypted using a code developed by the Inter-Galactic Banking Clan. We've been working on cracking that code for some time now, and when we do, we might be able to use the chair's hyperwave receiver to eavesdrop on enemy communications."

"Better you feel already, *ummm*?" Yoda said to Obi-Wan, motioning with his gimer stick.

"The chair bears the stamps of several of the manufacturers affiliated with Dooku," Dyne continued. "The hyperwave receiver is equipped with summoning chips and transponding antennae similar to ones we discovered in a mine-laying chameleon droid Master Yoda brought back from Ilum."

"An image of *Dooku,* the droid contained."

"For the time being we're proceeding on the assumption that Dooku—or Sidious, for that matter—might have developed the chips, and had them installed in transceivers awarded to Gunray and other key members of the Council of Separatists."

"Is the mechno-chair the same one I saw on Naboo?" Obi-Wan asked.

"We think so," Dyne said. "But it has undergone some modifications in the years since. The self-destruct mechanism, for one, along with the self-defense gas." He looked at Obi-Wan. "Your hunch was right about it being the same one the Neimoidians have been using for years, and appears to have originally been developed by a Separatist researcher named Zan Arbor."

"Zan Arbor," Anakin said angrily. "The gas used on the Gungans at Ohma-D'un." He looked at Obi-Wan. "No wonder you were able to sense it!"

Dyne glanced from Anakin to Obi-Wan. "The gas-emitter mechanism is identical to what you find in some of the Techno Union's E-Five-Twenty-Two assassin droids."

Obi-Wan stroked his chin in thought. "If Gunray has had the chair for fourteen years, then he could have been using it to contact Sidious during the Naboo crisis. If we could learn who manufactured the chair . . . "

Yoda laughed. "Ahead of Obi-Wan, the experts are," he said to Anakin.

"We know who's responsible for the chair's Neimoidian engravings," Dyne explained. "A Xi Charrian whose name I'm not even going to attempt to pronounce."

"How do you know?" Anakin asked.

The analyst grinned. "Because he signed his work."

Padmé parted company with Bail and the others in the Senate Plaza. She spied Captain Typho waving to her from the landing platform, and hastened toward their waiting speeder. The towering statues that graced the plaza seemed to stare down at her; the building had never seemed so enormous.

The brief meeting with Palpatine had left her flustered—but for all the wrong reasons. Though her every other thought was of Anakin, she had resolved to put him from her mind for the meeting; to focus on what was expected of her both as a public servant and concerned citizen of the Republic. And yet, despite her best intentions, Palpatine had brought Anakin to the fore.

Had Anakin confessed to him? she wondered. Had the Supreme Chancellor learned of their secret ceremony on Naboo, from Anakin or others?

A feeling of light-headedness forced her to slow her pace. The heat of the afternoon. The glare. The enormity of recent events . . .

She could feel Anakin at a great remove. He was thinking of her; she was certain of it. Images of him riffled through her mind. She paused at one that made her smile: their first dinner together on Tatooine. Qui-Gon reprimanding Jar Jar Binks for his uncouth behavior.

Anakin sitting beside her. Shmi . . . Was she sitting opposite her? Wasn't Shmi's gaze fixed on her when Shmi said, referring to Anakin: *He was meant to help you.*

The truth didn't matter.

That was the way she remembered it.

Protected by two squadrons of Trade Federation Vulture fighters, Nute Gunray's organic-looking shuttle cut a blazing trail through the void of deep space, plasma bolts from a dozen Republic V-wings nipping at its upraised tail. The droid fighters were matching the twists and slaloms of the faster enemy ships, and the blaster cannons buried deep in the clefts of their narrow wings were spewing continuous cover fire.

From the bridge of the Trade Federation cruiser the *Invisible Hand*—flagship of the Confederacy fleet—General Grievous observed the whole mad dance.

To any other spectator it might appear that the viceroy was risking his wattled neck, but Grievous knew better. Late to arrive at the rendezvous because of his decision to detour to Cato Neimoidia, Gunray was putting on a show for the general's benefit, attempting to make it seem that he had been *chased* to the Outer Rim when, in fact, he had undoubtedly allowed his hyperspace vectors to be plotted by Republic forces. Where common sense would have dictated using secret routes pioneered by and known only to members of the Trade Federation, the core ship the shuttle had launched from had adhered to standard hyperlanes in jumping from the inner systems.

More to the point, Gunray's vessel was in no real peril. Outnumbered by better than two to one and flying head-long into the vanguard vessels of the Confederacy fleet, it was the pilots of the Republic starfighters who were risking their necks. At another time Grievous might have applauded their bravery by allowing them to escape with their lives, but Gunray's transparent attempts at pretense had exposed the fleet to surveillance, and now the Republic pilots would have to die.

But not immediately.

First, Gunray would have to be punished for his blunder; given a foretaste of what awaited him the next time he disobeyed a directive.

Grievous turned from the cruiser's forward viewports to the weapons stations, where a pair of rangy droids were monitoring the pursuit.

"Gunners, the Republic starfighters are not to leave this sector. Target and destroy their hyperdrive rings. Then you are to target and destroy one squadron of the shuttle's escort Vulture fighters."

"Acquiring targets," one of the droids said.

"Firing," the other said.

Grievous swung back to the viewport in time to see the half-dozen hyperdrive rings come apart in short-lived explosions. An instant later, clouds of billowing fire began to erupt to both sides of Gunray's shuttle, and twelve droid fighters vanished from sight. The unexpected explosions wreaked havoc on the rest of the escort, leaving the shuttle vulnerable to strafing runs by the starfighters. With the formation in tatters, the Vultures followed protocol by attempting to regroup, but in so doing left themselves open to precisely placed bolts from the starfighters.

A consequence of the Neimoidians' reluctance to augment the droid brains of the fighters with interface capabilities, Grievous noted. Although they functioned better now than they had five years earlier.

Three more Vulture fighters blew to pieces, this time due to Republic fire.

Now the Neimoidian pilots of the shuttle weren't sure what to do. Attempts to go evasive were sabotaged by the droid ships' attempts to keep the shuttle centered in their shield array.

Enemy laser bolts kept finding their marks.

The destruction of the hyperdrive rings had alerted the Republic pilots to the fact that they were well inside the range of the cruiser's weapons, and that they had to make their kill quickly if they hoped to escape. Jinking and weaving among the remaining escort droids, they pressed the attack on the shuttle.

Grievous wondered for a moment if any of the pilots might be Jedi, in which case he would opt to capture rather than kill. The more closely he studied the maneuvers, however, the more certain he grew that the pilots were clones. Skilled fliers nevertheless—as indeed their Mandalorian template had been—but they evinced none of the supernatural perception afforded to the Jedi by the Force.

Still, Gunray's shuttle was taking a beating. One of its landing appendages had been amputated, and vapor streamed from its pug tail. The vessel's primitive particle and ray shields were still holding, but they weakened steadily with each direct hit. The convergence of a few more plasma bolts would overwhelm them. Then the ship the shields protected could be sliced and diced or taken out by a well-placed proton torpedo.

Grievous pictured Gunray, Haako, and the others strapped into luxurious acceleration couches, shivering with dread, perhaps sorry for the brief detour to Cato Neimoidia, wondering how a handful of Republic pilots had so easily decimated their squadrons, certainly comlinking the core ship to dispatch reinforcements.

The general was almost of a mind to award the Republic pilots their kill, for he and Gunray had been at odds frequently over the past three years. One of the first spacefaring species to build a droid army, the Neimoidians had grown accustomed to thinking of their soldiers and workers as thoroughly expendable. Their extraordinary wealth had allowed them to replace whatever they lost, so they had never developed a sense of respect for the machines fashioned for them by Baktoid Armor Workshops, the Xi Char, Colicoids, or others.

From their first acquaintance, Gunray had made the mistake of treating Grievous as just another droid—even though he had been told that this was not the case.

Perhaps Gunray had thought of him as some mindless entity, like the reawakened Gen'Dai, Durge; or Dooku's misguided apprentice, Asajj Ventress; or the humanoid bounty hunter called Aurra Sing—all three of whom had been so driven by personal hatred of the Jedi that they had proved worthless, mere distractions while Grievous went about the real business of war.

The attitude of the Neimoidians had changed quickly enough, though, in part because they had been witness to Grievous's capabilities, but more as a result of what had occurred on Geonosis. Had it not been for Grievous, Gunray and the rest might have suffered the same fate as Poggle the Lesser's lieutenant, Sun Fac. Grievous's actions in the catacombs that day—with the Geonosians retreating by the thousands from the arena and companies of clone commandos following them in—had allowed Gunray to escape the planet alive.

Sometimes he wondered just how many clones he had killed or wounded that day.

And Jedi, of course—though none had lived to speak of him.

The Jedi corpses that were retrieved bespoke something atrocious that resided in those dark underground passages. Perhaps the Jedi believed that a rancor or a reek had shredded the bodies of their Forceful comrades; or perhaps they thought the damage had been done by Geonosian sonic weapons set to maximum power.

Either way, they must have wondered what became of the victims' lightsabers.

Grievous regretted that he hadn't been able to see the reactions, but he, too, had been forced to flee as Geonosis fell.

The revelation of his existence had had to wait until a handful of hapless Jedi had arrived on the foundry world of Hypori. By then, Grievous had already amassed a sizable collection of lightsabers, but at Hypori he had been able to add several more, two of which he wore inside his command cloak even now.

As trophies they were superior to the pelts of hunted beings he knew some bounty hunters to affect. He admired the precision and care that had gone into the construction of the lightsabers; more, each seemed to retain a faint memory of its wielder. As a former swordmaster, he could appreciate that each had been handcrafted, rather than turned out in quantity like blasters or pike weapons.

He could respect the Jedi for that, though he had nothing but hatred for them as an Order.

Because of the remoteness of their homeworld, his species, the Kaleesh, had had few dealings with the Jedi. But then war had broken out between the Kaleesh and their planetary neighbors—a savage, insectile species known as the Huk. Grievous had become infamous during the long conflict: conquering worlds, defeating grand armies, exterminating entire colonies of Huk. But instead of surrendering, as would have been the honorable course, the Huk had appealed to the Republic to intercede, and the Jedi had arrived on Kalee. In what passed for negotiations—fifty Jedi Knights and Masters ready to loose their lightsabers on Grievous and his army—the Kaleesh were made to appear the aggressors. The reason was plain: where Kalee had little to offer in the way of trade, the Huk worlds were rich in ore and other resources lusted after by the Trade Federation and others. Chastised by the Republic, the Kaleesh foundered. Sanctions and reparations were imposed; traders avoided the planet; Grievous's people starved and perished by the hundreds of thousands.

Ultimately the InterGalactic Banking Clan had come to their rescue, helping with funds, reinstating trade, providing Grievous with a new direction.

Years later, the Muuns would come again . . .

Grievous's eyes tracked the course of the now imperiled shuttle.

Count Dooku and his Sith Master would never forgive him if he allowed anything untoward to happen to Gunray. Neimoidians were clever. Their knowledge of secret hyperlanes was unparalleled, and their immense army of infantry and super battle droids were rigged with devices that compelled them to respond principally to Gunray and his elite. Should the Neimoidian chiefs die, the Confederacy would lose a powerful ally.

It was time to spring Gunray from the trap he had fashioned for him.

"Launch tri-fighters to assist the shuttle," Grievous instructed the gunners. "Target and destroy the Republic starfighters outright."

Deployed from the cruiser, a wing of the new red-eyed droid fighters was soon visible from the bridge viewports.

Alerted to the approaching tri-droids, the Republic pilots had sense enough to realize that they were severely outnumbered. Disengaging from the last of the Vulture fighters, they began to make for free space, the nearest habitable planets, wherever their sublight ion drives could deliver them, since their means of jumping to lightspeed had already been destroyed.

Two of the starfighters were slower than the rest to disengage. Calling for magnification of the shuttle pursuit, Grievous saw that the stragglers were newly minted ARC-170s, copiloted crafts equipped with powerful laser cannons at the tips of their outstretched wings and multiple torpedo launchers. He was eager to see what they were capable of.

"Instruct three squadrons of the tri-fighter wing to shield the shuttle and escort it to our docking bay. Set the rest against the fleeing starfighters, except for the ARC-one-seventies. The ARC-one-seventies should be lured into engagement, without disintegration—even if some of the tri-droids are forced to succumb to enemy fire."

Grievous sharpened his gaze.

The tri-fighters had split into two groups, the larger forming up around Gunray's impaired shuttle and pouncing on the retreating V-wings, while the diverted squadron began to tease the pair of ARC-170s into duels and sallies.

What impressed Grievous was how quickly the pilots came to each other's assistance. Combat camaraderie hadn't been bred into them by the Kaminoan cloners, or been something they had learned from the Jedi. It had come from the Mandalorian bounty hunter. Fett would have denied it, of course, would have insisted that he was out only for himself. But that was not the way of his warrior brethren, and that was not the way of the clone pilots now. Exaggerating the value of each life, as if the clones were uncontrived humans.

Was the Republic so shorthanded it couldn't afford losses?

Something to bear in mind. Something that could be exploited at some point.

Without glancing at the bridge gunners, Grievous said: "Finish them off."

Then, turning to a droid at the communications suite, he added: "See to it that the Neimoidians are ushered directly to the briefing room. Inform the others that I am on my way."

Still shaken from the ordeal of transiting from the core ship to the *Invisible Hand,* Nute Gunray sat restively in the cabin space to which he and Haako had been shown immediately on disembarking. He had expected that a few Republic starfighters might pursue the core ship from Cato Neimoidia—as they no doubt had other Trade Federation vessels launched to equally distant star systems in the Outer Rim. And he had hoped that the appearance of those starfighters would convey the impression that he had been chased from the Neimoidian purse world. But the scenario hadn't unfolded as planned. What should have been a quick, effortless crossing had ended up a flight for life, with the shuttle left seriously damaged and more than a squadron of Vulture fighters destroyed.

It was almost beyond explanation until the shuttle pilot confirmed that most of the Vultures had been atomized by fire from the cruiser's turbolaser batteries.

Grievous!

Castigating him for arriving late.

Gunray would have liked nothing more than to inform Dooku of the general's actions, but he feared that the Sith would stand with Grievous.

Every bit as shaken, Rune Haako sat alongside Gunray at the cabin's gleaming table. Other members of the Separatist Council occupied the choice seats: the almost two-dimensionally thin San Hill, Muun chairman of the InterGalactic Banking Clan; the Skakoan foreman of the Techno Union, Wat Tambor, encased in the cumbersome pressure suit that supplied him with methane; the vestigial-winged Geonosian Poggle the Lesser, Archduke of the Stalgasin Hive; the stalk-necked Gossam president of the Commerce Guild, Shu Mai; the cranial-horned Corporate Alliance Magistrate, Passel Argente; and former Republic Senators Po Nudo and Tikkes—Aqualish and Quarren, respectively.

Separate conversations were in progress when the sound of clanging footfalls echoed from the long corridor that led to the briefing room. Abruptly everyone fell silent, and a moment later General Grievous appeared in the hatchway, the rounded crown of his elongated death mask of a helmet grazing the top of the opening, his high-backed collar of ceramic armorplast reminiscent of a neck brace. Sheathed in metal more suited to a starfighter, his skeletal upper limbs were spread wide, clawlike duranium hands just touching the hatchway frame. His two feet, which also resembled claws, were capable of increasing his height by several centimeters. Legs of sleek alloy bones looked as if they could propel him into orbit. His campaign cloak, slit down one side from left shoulder to floor, was thrown back so that twin pectorals of armor plating were exposed, along with the reverse ribs that began at Grievous's hip girdle and extended upward to his shielded sternum. Beneath it all, encased in a kind of fluid-filled, forest-green gutsac, were the organs that nurtured the living part of him.

Behind helmet holes that rendered his visage at once mournful and fearsome, sallow reptilian eyes fixed Gunray with a gimlet stare. In a synthesized voice, deep and grating, he said: "Welcome aboard, Viceroy. For a moment we feared that you weren't going to arrive."

Gunray felt the gazes of everyone in the cabin fall on him. His distrust of the cyborg was no secret; nor was Grievous's enmity for him.

"And I can only assume that you were very troubled by the prospect, General."

"You must know how important you are to our cause."

"I know it, General. Though I confess to wondering if you do."

"I am your keeper, Viceroy. Your protector."

Striding into the cabin, he began to circle the table, stopping directly behind Gunray, towering over him. Peripherally, Gunray saw Haako slouch deeper into his chair, refusing to look either at him or at Grievous, circling his hands in a nervous gesture.

"I have no favorite among you," the general said at last. "I champion all of you. That is why I summoned you here: to ensure your continued protection."

No one said a word.

"The Republic fools itself believing that they have you on the run, but, in fact, Lord Sidious and Darth Tyranus have engineered this, for reasons that will be made clear soon enough. All is proceeding according to plan. However, with your homeworlds fallen to the Republic, your purse and colony worlds throughout the galaxy threatened, you are ordered to remain a group for the foreseeable future. I have been instructed to find a safe harbor for you here, in the Outer Rim."

"What world will accept us now?" equine-faced San Hill asked in a disconsolate voice.

"If none offers, Chairman, then I will take one."

Grievous walked to the hatchway, his talons screeching along the deck. "For now, return to your separate vessels. When a world has been selected, I will contact each of you in the usual manner, and provide you with new rendezvous coordinates."

Careful not to betray his sudden misgiving, Gunray traded covert glances with Haako.

The "usual manner" meant the mechno-chair inadvertently left behind on Cato Neimoidia.

16

A patchwork of dull red and pale brown, Charros IV filled the forward viewports of the Republic cruiser. The twin-piloted ship had been an antique twenty years earlier, but its sublight and hyperdrive engines were reliable, and with vessels deployed on so many fronts Obi-Wan and Anakin couldn't be choosy. The cruiser's once emblematic crimson color was obscured under fresh coats of white paint; as a result of the war, laser cannons were carefully tucked astern under the radiator panel wings, and forward, beneath the cockpit, in the space that had once functioned as a salon for passengers.

Obi-Wan had plotted the three jumps it had taken them to reach the Xi Char world from the Inner Rim, but Anakin had done all the piloting.

"Landing coordinates coming in," Anakin said, eyes fixed on a display screen set into the instrument panel.

Obi-Wan was pleasantly surprised. "That will teach me not to be skeptical. In the past when we've been informed that Intelligence has done the advance work, I've found that to be anything but the case."

Anakin looked at him and laughed.

"Something funny?"

"I was just thinking, *Here you are again . . .* "

Obi-Wan sat back in his chair, waiting for the rest of it.

"I only mean that, for someone with a reputation for hating space travel, you've certainly taken part in more than your share of exotic missions. Kamino, Geonosis, Ord Cestus . . . "

Obi-Wan plucked at his beard. "Let's just say that the war has prompted me to take a long view of things."

"Master Qui-Gon would have been proud of you."

"Don't be too sure."

Obi-Wan had argued against going to Charros IV. Dexter Jettster, his Besalisk friend on Coruscant, could probably have furnished the Intelligence analysts with everything they needed to know about Viceroy Gunray's mechno-chair. But Yoda had insisted that Obi-Wan and Anakin attempt to speak personally with the Xi Charrian whose sigil had been discovered on the walking chair.

Now Obi-Wan wondered why he had been so averse to making the trip. Compared to the past few months, the mission already felt like a furlough. Anakin was correct about Obi-Wan's having had more than his share of such assignments. But several other Jedi had also doubled as Intelligence operatives during the course of the war. Aayla Secura and the Caamasi Jedi Ylenic It'kla had taken a Techno Union defector into custody on Corellia; Quinlan Vos had gone undercover to infiltrate Dooku's circle of dark side apprentices . . .

And Supreme Chancellor Palpatine hadn't been told— or learned since—about any of the covert operations.

It wasn't that the Jedi Council didn't trust him; it was more a matter of no longer trusting *anyone.*

"Do you think the Xi Char will talk to us?" Anakin said.

Obi-Wan swiveled to face him. "They've every reason to be accommodating. After the Battle of Naboo, the Republic refused to do any business with them, for their having supplied the Neimoidians with proscribed weapons. They've been eager to atone ever since, especially now that their signature designs are being mass-produced more cheaply by Baktoid Armor and other Confederacy suppliers."

The Xi Char's principal contribution to the Neimoidian arsenal had been the so-called Variable Geometry Self-Propelled Battle Droid starfighter, a meticulously engineered solid-fuel craft that was capable of configuring itself into three separate modes.

Anakin adopted a thin-lipped expression of wariness. "I hope they won't hold it against us that I destroyed so many of their fighters."

Obi-Wan laughed shortly. "Yes, let's hope your fame hasn't spread this far into the Outer Rim. But in fact, our success hinges almost entirely on whether TeeCee-Sixteen can speak Xi Char as fluently as he claims."

"Master Kenobi, I assure you that I can speak the tongue almost as well as an indigenous Xi Charrian," the protocol droid chimed in from one of the cockpit's rear seats. "My term of service to Viceroy Gunray demanded that I familiarize myself with the trader's tongues used by all the hive species, including the Xi Char, the Geonosians, the Colicoids, and many others. My fluency will ensure complete cooperation on the part of the Xi Char. Although I expect that they will be rather disgusted by my physical appearance."

"Why's that?" Anakin asked.

"Devotion to precision technology forms the basis of

Xi Char religious beliefs. They accept as a matter of faith that meticulous work is no different from prayer; indeed, their workshops have more in common with temples than factories. When a Xi Charrian is injured, he goes into self-exile, so that others won't have to look upon his imperfections or deformities. A Xi Char adage has it that 'The deity is in the details.' "

"Wear your flaws proudly, TeeCee," Anakin said, raising and clenching his right hand. "I do, mine."

The cruiser was descending into Charros IV's ice-clouded atmosphere. Leaning toward the viewport, Obi-Wan gazed down on an arid, almost treeless world. The Xi Char lived on high plateaus, hemmed in by ranges of snowcapped mountains. Expansive black-water lakes dotted the landscape.

"A bleak planet," Obi-Wan said.

Anakin made adjustments to the controls to compensate for strong winds that were buffeting the ship. "I'll take it over Tatooine any day."

Obi-Wan shrugged. "I can think of far worse places to live than Tatooine."

Into view came the landing platform to which they had been directed. Oval in shape and perfectly sized to the cruiser, it looked newly built.

"I'm certain that it was constructed specifically for us," TC-16 said. "That's why the Xi Char were unremitting in their requests to know the cruiser's exact dimensions."

Anakin glanced at Obi-Wan. "The Republic could use the Xi Char right about now."

He set the cruiser down on its broad disks of landing gear and extended the vessel's starboard boarding ramp. At the top of the ramp, Obi-Wan raised the hood of his cloak against a frigid wind that howled down the slopes. Ahead, a gleaming alloy runner ran from the edge of the landing platform to a cathedral-like structure half a kilometer distant. To both sides of the runner stood hundreds of excited Xi Charrians.

"Guess they don't get many guests," Anakin said as he, Obi-Wan, and TC-16 started down the ramp.

As was often the case, the Xi Char's technological creations mirrored their own anatomy and physiology. With their short, chitinous bodies, quartets of pointed legs, scissor-action feet, and teardrop-shaped heads, they might have been living versions of the shapeshifting droid fighters they had helped produce for the Trade Federation—in walk/patrol mode, at any rate. The wild chitterings of the hundreds-strong mob of welcomers was so loud that Anakin had to raise his voice to be heard.

"Celebrity treatment! I think I'm going to enjoy this!"

"Just be sure to follow my lead, Anakin."

"I'll try, Master."

The closer the Jedi and the protocol droid drew to the edge of the landing platform, the louder the chitterings became. Obi-Wan didn't know what to make of the sheer eagerness he felt from the aliens. It was as if some sort of footrace were about to begin. Frequently, an individual Xi Charrian, carried away by enthusiasm, would leap onto the sleek runner, only to be yanked back into the crowd by others.

"TeeCee, are they normally so zealous?" Obi-Wan asked.

"Yes, Master Kenobi. But their zest has nothing to do with us. It's the ship!"

The meaning of the remark became clear the instant the three of them stepped from the landing platform. At once the Xi Charrians surged forward and swarmed the cruiser, covering it from flat-faced bow to barrel-thrustered stern. Obi-Wan and Anakin watched in awe as patches of carbon scoring disappeared, dents were straightened, pieces of superstructure were realigned, and transparisteel viewports were polished.

"Let's remember to tip them when we leave," Anakin said.

Occasionally a Xi Charrian would leap on TC-16 or make a grab for one of his limbs, but the droid was able to shake his assailants off.

"In their eagerness to perfect me, I'm afraid they'll wipe my memory!" the droid said.

"Would that be such a bad thing," Anakin said, "after what you claim to have been through?"

"How can I be expected to learn from my mistakes if I can no longer *remember* them?"

They were halfway down the runner when a pair of larger Xi Charrians scurried out to meet them. TC-16 exchanged chitterings and stridulations with them, and explained.

"These two will take us to the Prelate."

"No weapons," Anakin said quietly. "That's a good sign."

"The Xi Char are a peaceful species," the droid explained. "They care only about the engineering of a piece of technology, not its intended use. That was why they felt unjustly accused and harshly judged by the Republic for the part their droid fighters played in the Battle of Naboo."

The enormous building TC-16 had called a workshop topped two hundred meters in height and was crowned with latticework spires and towers that evoked strains of eerie music from the steady wind. Arrays of tall skylights lit the vast interior space, in which thousands of Xi Charrians toiled. Arcades of exquisitely engraved columns supported a vaulted ceiling of exposed roof trusses, among which roosted several thousand more Xi

Charrians, suspended by their scissor feet and humming contentedly.

"The night shift?" Anakin wondered aloud.

Their pair of escorts led them into a kind of chancery, whose tall doors opened on a spotless room that could have passed for the captain's cabin of a luxury space yacht. Occupying a throne-like chair in the center of the room was the largest Xi Charrian the Jedi had yet seen, being attended to by a dozen smaller ones. Elsewhere, groups of tool-wielding Xi Charrians were going over every square millimeter of the chamber, scrubbing, cleaning, polishing.

Without ceremony, TC-16 approached the Prelate and tendered a greeting. The droid had tasked his vocoder to provide Obi-Wan and Anakin with simultaneous translations of his utterances.

"May I present Jedi Obi-Wan Kenobi, and Jedi Anakin Skywalker," he began.

Waving away his retinue, the Prelate pivoted his long head to regard Obi-Wan.

"TeeCee," Obi-Wan said, "tell him we're sorry to have disturbed him during his ablutions."

"You're not disturbing him, sir. The Prelate is attended to in similar fashion at all hours of the day."

The Prelate chittered.

"Excellency, I speak your language as a result of my former employment in the court of Viceroy Nute Gunray." The droid listened to the Prelate's response, then said: "Yes, I realize that does not endear me to you. But may I say in defense that my time among the Neimoidians was the most trying of my existence. To which my physical appearance surely attests, and is cause for my great shame."

Clearly mollified, the Prelate chittered again.

"These Jedi have come to seek permission from you to

pose questions to a devotee in Workshop Xcan—a certain t'laalak-s'lalak-t'th'ak."

TC-16 supplied the glottal stops and clicking sounds necessary to pronounce the name.

"A virtuoso engraver, to be sure, Excellency. As to the Jedi's interest in him, it is hoped that a work of art to which he devoted himself will provide a clue as to the current whereabouts of an important Separatist leader." The droid listened, then added: "And may I add that anything that brings joy to the Xi Char brings contentment to the Republic."

The Prelate's eye grooves found the Jedi again.

"The lightsabers are not weapons, Excellency," TC-16 said after a brief exchange. "But if permission to speak with t'laalak-s'lalak-t'th'ak rests on their surrendering the lightsabers, then I'm certain they will comply."

Obi-Wan was already reaching for his lightsaber, but Anakin looked dubious.

"You did say you would follow my lead."

Anakin opened his cloak. "I said I'd try, Master."

They handed the lightsabers to TC-16, who presented them to the Prelate for inspection.

"It hardly surprises me that you see room for improvement, Excellency," the droid said after a moment. "But then, what tool could fail to benefit from the touch of a Xi Charrian?" He listened, then added: "I'm certain that the Jedi know you will honor your pledge to leave the imperfections intact."

"That went better than expected," Obi-Wan said as he, Anakin, and TC-16 were being escorted into the heart of Workshop Xcan.

Anakin wasn't convinced. "You're too trusting, Master. I sense much suspicion."

"We can thank Raith Sienar for some of that."

Almost two decades earlier, the wealthy and influential owner-president of Sienar Design Systems—a chief supplier of starfighters to the Republic—had spent time among the Xi Char, mastering ultraprecision engineering techniques he would later incorporate into his own designs. Revealed to be a "nonbeliever," Sienar had been exiled from Charros IV, and been made the target of bounty hunters, four of whom Sienar had managed to strand at a black hole known only to him and a handful of other hotshot hyperspace explorers. Sienar had engaged in similar acts of corporate espionage among the Trade Federation, Baktoid Armor, Corellian Engineering, and Incom Corporations, but the Xi Char had a long memory for what they considered sacrilege. Six years before the Battle of Naboo, a second attempt on Raith's life had resulted in the death of his father, Narro, at Dantooine. But once again the heretic had escaped.

Ten years back, Obi-Wan and Anakin had had their own brush with Sienar at the living world known as Zonama Sekot. Because Sienar had been partly responsible for Zonama Sekot's *disappearance,* he was also the reason that the Xi Char no longer accepted human apprentices.

Workshop Xcan was a marvel to behold.

Xi Char artisans worked individually or in groups of three to three hundred, on devices ranging from high-end home appliances to starfighters, adding enhancements or adornments, tweaking, personalizing, customizing in a thousand different ways. Here were all the priceless devices Obi-Wan and Anakin had found crammed into storage rooms in Gunray's Cato Neimoidia citadel. The environment was the antithesis of the deafening freneticism that characterized a Baktoid Armor foundry, such as the one the Republic had commandeered on Geonosis. Xi Charrians rarely conversed with one another while working, preferring instead to amplify their concentration through the repetition of high-pitched stridulations, analogous to chants. The few who did take notice of the three visitors in their midst showed more interest in TC-16 than in the Jedi.

And yet, for all the fine work that was performed in Workshop Xcan, the cathedral-factory was little more than a stepping-stone for many Xi Charrians, who aspired to work for the Haor Chall Engineering conglomerate which had abandoned Charros IV for other worlds in the Outer Rim.

The same pair of outsized aliens who had escorted Obi-Wan and Anakin to the Prelate's chancery guided them to t'laalak-s'lalak-t'th'ak's altar, which was located in the workshop's western colonnade, the piers of which were decorated with mosaics of engraved tiles. High overhead, resting Xi Charrians hung inverted from the great curving rafters that supported the roof, like configurable droid fighters arrayed inside a Trade Federation carrier.

Obi-Wan could see how the sound of their ceaseless humming could be slightly unnerving.

t'laalak-s'lalak-t'th'ak was engrossed in engraving a corporate logo into a piece of starship console. Dozens of yet-to-be-completed pieces walled him in on one side; completed pieces were on the other. On hearing his name called, he glanced up from his work.

The escorts chittered to him briefly before TC-16 took over.

"t'laalak-s'lalak-t'th'ak, first allow me to say that your work is of such exceptional quality that the deities themselves must be covetous."

The Xi Charrian accepted the compliment in humility, and chittered a response.

"We appreciate the offer to watch you at work. But in

fact, we are not unacquainted with some of your finer pieces, and it is because of one piece in particular that we have journeyed so far to speak with you. An example that recently came to light on Cato Neimoidia."

The Xi Charrian took a long moment to respond.

"A mechno-chair you adorned for Trade Federation viceroy, Nute Gunray, some fourteen standard years ago." TC-16 listened, then added: "But surely it was yours, for the inner portion of the rear leg bears your devotional symbol." Again he listened. "A Baktoid forgery? Are you suggesting that your work could so easily be imitated?"

Anakin nudged Obi-Wan in the upper arm: Xi Charrians working nearby were beginning to take a keen interest in the conversation.

"We understand your reluctance to discuss such matters," TC-16 was saying quietly. "Why, the very fact that you *autographed* a piece could be interpreted by the Prelate as a statement of pride."

t'laalak-s'lalak-t'th'ak's anger was apparent.

"Well, of course, you should be proud. But should the Prelate learn that the piece has for all these years resided with a personage such as Viceroy Gunray—"

Without another chitter, the Xi Charrian let go his tools and launched himself from his work pallet—not at TC-16 or either of the Jedi, but straight up into the web of overhead girders. Ignoring indignant squeals from rudely awakened Xi Charrians, he began to leap from one girder to the next, clearly determined to reach one of the tall skylights that perforated the roof.

Obi-Wan watched him for a moment, then turned to Anakin. "I don't think he wants to speak with us."

Anakin kept his eyes on t'laalak-s'lalak-t'th'ak. "Well, he has to."

And with that, he leapt in pursuit.

"Anakin, wait!" Obi-Wan said, then added, more to himself, "Oh, what's the use," and sprang up toward the ceiling.

Hurling himself from truss to truss like some circus performer, Anakin arrived quickly at the intricate tracery surrounding the partially opened roof window through which t'laalak-s'lalak-t'th'ak was desperately trying to squirm. The Xi Charrian's insectile forelegs were already outside the window when Anakin leapt again, clutching on to him in an effort to return him to the floor. But the alien was stronger than he looked. Chittering madly, he leapt for a higher window, this time taking Anakin with him.

Ten meters away, Obi-Wan paralleled the Xi Charrian's flight into the upper reaches of the vaulted ceiling, where the chase had now roused scores of roosting Xi Charrians, inciting more than a few to join in.

Anakin was still trying to drag his quarry down, but his weight was insufficient to the task. Fearing what might result should Anakin call too strongly on the Force—Obi-Wan had visions of the entire workshop crumbing to pieces!—he fairly flew after them, barely managing at the apex of his ascent to grab hold of t'laalak-s'lalak-t'th'ak's rear legs.

And down they came.

All three, entwined, and bringing with them more than thirty inverted Xi Charrians. Cascading onto the floor, Obi-Wan and Anakin lost their hold on t'laalak-s'lalak-t'th'ak, and suddenly couldn't tell one Xi Charrian from the next. Losing t'laalak-s'lalak-t'th'ak had ceased to be an immediate concern, in any case, because Xi Charrians throughout the workshop were rushing to the aid of those the two Jedi had caused to plummet from the rafters. Some were already attempting to zap the Jedi into submission by brandishing assorted solder-

ing and engraving tools, while others were busy constructing a plasteel hemisphere under which the violence
might be contained.

"No mayhem!" Obi-Wan shouted.

Anakin showed him a wide-eyed glance from beneath
a three-meter-tall heap of irate Xi Charrians.

"Who exactly are you talking to?"

Obi-Wan glanced around the workshop. "Topple
something—quickly! Before they complete the mound!"

With a shoving motion of his free hand, Obi-Wan
overturned a small table twenty meters away, spilling
several stacks of freshly engraved comlinks and droid
summoners. Chittering in panic, half the Xi Charrians
who were holding him to the floor—and most of the
ones rushing toward him—scampered off to repair the
damaged devices.

"Quickly, Anakin!'

Even with his hands pinned under him, Anakin managed to upend a pallet of kitchen appliances, then knock
over a carefully arranged collection of toys, then tear
from the wall more than half a dozen sconces.

Chittering in dismay, more Xi Charrians raced off.

"Stop making it look like fun!" Obi-Wan cautioned.

Eyes riveted on a bin filled with musical instruments,
he was about to rid himself of his remaining tormenters
when blasterfire erupted in the workshop, and into the
midst of the throng of infuriated Xi Char appeared the
Prelate himself, seated on a litter carried by six bearers
and grasping a weapon in each foot.

Twenty Xi Charrians flattened themselves to the floor
as the Prelate brought the blasters to bear on Obi-Wan
and Anakin. But before a bolt could be fired TC-16
emerged from a side gallery, his body realigned and polished to a dazzling luster, shouting: "Look what they've
done to me!"

The droid's tone of voice combined anguish and wonder, but the change in him was so unexpected and remarkable that the Prelate and his bearers could only gape, as if a miracle had occurred in their midst. A babble of chitterings was exchanged, before the Prelate swung back to Obi-Wan and Anakin, raising the blasters once more.

"But they meant no harm, Excellency!" the droid intervened. "t'laalak-s'lalak-t'th'ak fled in response to their questions! Master Obi-Wan and Jedi Skywalker sought merely to ascertain the reason!"

The Prelate's gaze singled out t'laalak-s'lalak-t'th'ak.

TC-16 translated.

"Master Kenobi, the Prelate advises you to pose your questions, and to leave Charros Four before he has a change of heart."

Obi-Wan looked at t'laalak-s'lalak-t'th'ak, then at TC-16. "Ask him if he remembers the chair."

The droid relayed the question.

"He remembers it now."

"Was the engraving done here?"

"He answers, 'yes,' sir."

"Was the chair brought to Charros Four by the Neimoidians or by another?"

"He says, sir: 'By another.' "

Obi-Wan and Anakin traded eager looks.

"Was the hyperwave transceiver already affixed to it?" Anakin asked.

TC-16 listened. "Both the transceiver and the holoprojector itself were already affixed to the chair. He says that he did little but inscribe the legs of the chair and tweak some of its motion systems." Lowering his voice, the droid added: "May I say, sirs, that t'laalak-s'lalak-t'th'ak's voice is . . . quavering. I suspect that he is hiding something."

"He's afraid," Anakin said. "And not of Nute Gunray."

Obi-Wan looked at TC-16. "Ask him who made the transceiver. Ask him where it shipped from."

t'laalak-s'lalak-t'th'ak's chitterings sounded contrite.

TC-16 said: "The transceiver unit arrived from a facility known as Escarte. He believes that the device's maker is still there."

"Escarte?" Anakin said.

"An asteroid mining facility," TC-16 explained, "belonging to the Commerce Guild."

Ten years ago it would have had all the makings of a full-blown diplomatic incident," Intelligence officer Dyne was explaining to Yoda and Mace Windu in the data room of the Jedi Temple.

Filled with computers, holoprojector tables, and communications apparatus, the windowless chamber also housed an emergency beacon that transmitted on a frequency known only to the Jedi, allowing the Temple to send and receive encrypted messages without having to rely on the more public HoloNet.

"Since when are the Xi Char so forgiving?" Mace asked. Dressed in a brown belted tunic and beige trousers, he was poised on the edge of a desk, one booted foot planted on the shiny floor.

"Since they've been forced to make do with subcontracting work," Dyne said. "What they want is to get back in the game by landing a nice fat Republic contract for starfighters or combat droids. It has to be driving them mad, knowing that Sienar is getting even richer on techniques he basically stole from them."

Mace glanced at Yoda, who was standing off to one side, both hands resting on the knob of his gimer stick. "Then the Xi Char Prelate isn't likely to report the incident to the Senate."

Dyne shook his head. "Not a chance. No real harm was done, anyway."

"Reach the ears of the Supreme Chancellor, it won't," Yoda said. "But surprised I was by Obi-Wan's report. Losing some of his better judgment, Obi-Wan is."

"We both know why," Mace said. "He's become Anakin's partisan."

"If the Chosen One Skywalker is, then a hundred such diplomatic incidents we should suffer without concern." Yoda shut his eyes for a moment, then looked at the Intelligence analyst. "But come to tell us of these things, Captain Dyne hasn't."

Dyne grinned. "We've succeeded in deciphering the code Dooku—and, we have to assume, Sidious—has been using to communicate with the Council of Separatists. Using the code, we were able to intercept a message sent to Viceroy Gunray, through the mechno-chair."

Mace came to his feet. "Your people have been working on cracking that code for years."

"The chair's hyperwave transceiver provided us with our first solid lead. We saw right away that the code embedded in the transceiver's memory was a variant on codes used by the InterGalactic Banking Clan. So we decided to offer a deal to one of the Muuns arrested after the Battle of Muunilinst. It took some convincing, but the Muun finally confirmed that the Confederacy code comes closest to a code used on Aargau, for transferring bank funds and such." Dyne paused, then added: "Remember the missing credits that became the basis for accusations leveled against Chancellor Valorum back in the day?"

Yoda nodded. "Remember the incident well, we do."

"The credits that allegedly disappeared into the pockets of Valorum's family members on Eriadu were routed through Aargau."

"Interesting, this is."

Dyne opened an alloy briefcase and removed a ribbed data cell. Moving to one of the holoprojector tables, he inserted the cell into a socket. A meter-high holoimage appeared in the table's cone of blue light.

"General *Grievous*," Yoda said, narrowing his eyes.

"*You'll be pleased to learn that I've chosen a world for us, Viceroy,*" Grievous was saying. "*Belderone will be our temporary home.*" The cyborg fell silent for a moment. "*Viceroy? Viceroy!*" Whirling to someone off cam, he barked: "*End transmission.*"

Dyne paused the message before Grievous had faded from view.

"As high-resolution an image as I've ever seen," he said. "Technology of a different order than we're used to seeing—even from the Confederacy."

"About his image, Sidious cares, *ummm?*"

Mace's clean-shaven upper lip curled. "What was the source of the transmission?"

"Deep in the Outer Rim," Dyne said. "Six clone pilots pursued a core ship that jumped to the sector following the Battle of Cato Neimoidia. None returned."

"Rendezvous of the Confederacy fleet, it is," Yoda said.

Mace nodded. "And Belderone next." Again his gaze fell on Dyne. "Anything further on the source of the original Sidious transmission?"

Dyne shook his head. "Still working on it."

Mace paced away from the table. "Belderone is not a highly populated world, but it is friendly to the Republic. Grievous will kill millions just to make a point." He glanced at Yoda. "We can't let that happen."

Dyne looked from Mace to Yoda and back again. "If Republic forces are waiting when Grievous attacks, the Separatists will realize that we've managed to eavesdrop on their transmissions."

Yoda pressed his fingers to his lips in thought. "Act, we must. Lying in wait, Republic forces will be."

Dyne nodded. "You're right, of course. If no actions are taken, and word of this intelligence were to leak . . ." He regarded Yoda. "Do we inform the Supreme Chancellor?"

Yoda's ears twitched. "Difficult, this decision is."

"The information stays here," Mace said firmly.

Yoda sighed with purpose. "Agree I do. Use the beacon we will, to gather a force."

"Obi-Wan and Anakin aren't far from Belderone," Mace said. "But they're pursuing another lead to Sidious's whereabouts."

"Wait, the lead will. Needed Obi-Wan and Anakin will be." Yoda turned to the still image of General Grievous. "Prepare carefully for this battle, we must."

In dreams, Grievous remembered his life.

His mortal life.

On Kalee, and in the aftermath of the Huk War.

After all the close calls on battlefields on his home system worlds, on Huk worlds, sowing destruction, exterminating as many of them as he could . . . After all the times he had returned home wounded, bloodied to the bone, surrounded by his wives and offspring, basking in their support—relying on it to recall him to life.

After all the brushes with death . . . to be fatally injured in *a shuttle crash*.

The unfairness, the indignity had cost him more pain than the injuries themselves. To be denied a warrior's death—as was his due!

Floating suspended in bacta, keenly aware that no healing fluid or gamma blade wielded by living being or droid could repair his body. In moments of consciousness: seeing his wives and offspring gazing on his ravaged body from the far side of the permaglass. Offering words of encouragement; prayers for his return to health.

He had asked himself: could he be content to be a mind in a body without feeling? More, could he abandon a life of combat for a life in which the only battles he fought were with himself? The struggle to endure, to live another day . . .

No. It was beyond him.

By then, the Huk War had ended—more accurately had been ended by the Jedi, and the Kaleesh were still reaping the whirlwind. Their world in ruins, their appeals for justice and fair play ignored by the Republic.

Ever on the alert for investment opportunities, members of the InterGalactic Banking Clan had offered Kalee a dubious sort of rescue. They would support the planet financially, assume its staggering debt, if Grievous would agree to serve the clan as an enforcer. Their hailfire weapons were proficient at delivering "payment reminders" to delinquent clients, and their IG-series assassin droids took care of the wet work. But the hailfires had to be programmed, the IGs were dangerously unpredictable, and assassination was bad for business.

The clan wanted someone with a talent for intimidation.

Both to save his world and to provide himself with a touch of the life he had known as a warrior, a strategist, a leader of armies, Grievous had accepted the offer. IBC chairman San Hill himself had overseen the details of the arrangement. Still, Grievous wasn't entirely proud of his decision. Debt collection was a far cry from warcraft. An arena for beings without principles; for beings so attached to their possessions that they feared death. But Kalee had profited from his work for IBC. And Grievous's previous notoriety was such that it could not be eclipsed.

Then: the shuttle crash. The accident. The misfortune . . .

He told his would-be healers to fish him from the bacta tank. He could bear to die in atmosphere or the vacuum of deep space, but not in liquid. In the shadow of felled trees that would fuel his funeral pyre, he lapsed in and out of consciousness. That was when San Hill had paid him a second visit. Something consequential in mind. Obvious even to someone who could barely see straight.

"We can keep you alive," rail-thin Hill had whispered into Grievous's unimpaired ear.

Others had promised as much. He pictured breathing devices, a hover platform, a surround of life-sustaining machines.

But Hill had said: "None of that. You will walk, you will speak, you will retain your memories—your mind."

"I have my mind," Grievous had said. "What I *lack* is a body."

"Most of your internal organs are damaged beyond the repair of the finest surgeons," Hill had continued. "And you will have to surrender even more than you already have. You will no longer know the pleasures of the flesh."

"Flesh is weak. You need only gaze on me to see that."

Encouraged by the remark, Hill had talked in glowing terms of the Geonosians: how they had raised cyborg technology to an art form, and how the blending of living and machine technology was the future.

"Consider the battle droids of the Trade Federation," Hill had said. "They answer to a brain that is also nothing more than a droid. Protocol droids, astromechs, even assassin droids—all require programming and frequent maintenance."

Two words had caught Grievous's attention: *battle droids*.

"A war is brewing that will call many droids to the front," Hill had said just loudly enough to be heard. "I am not privy to when it will begin, but when that day comes, the entire galaxy will be involved."

His interest piqued, Grievous had said: "A war begun by whom? The Banking Clan? The Trade Federation?"

"Someone more powerful."

"Who?"

"In time, you will meet him. And you will be impressed."

"Then why does he need me?"

"In every war, there are leaders and there are commanders."

"A commander of *droids*."

"More precisely, a *living* commander of droids."

So he had allowed the Geonosians to go to work on him, constructing a duranium and ceramic shell for what little of him remained. His recuperation had been long and difficult. Coming to terms with his new and in many ways improved self, even longer and more difficult. Only then had he been presented to Count Dooku, and only then had his real training begun. From the Geonosians and members of the Techno Union he had already come to understand the inner workings of droids. But from Dooku—Lord Tyranus—he came to understand the inner workings of the Sith.

Tyranus himself had trained him in lightsaber technique. In mere weeks he had surpassed any of Tyranus's previous students. It helped, of course, to have an indestructible body reminiscent of a Krath wardroid. The ability to tower over most sentient beings. Crystal circuitry. Four grasping appendages . . .

In dreams he remembered his past life.

But in fact, he was not dreaming, for dreams were a product of sleep, and General Grievous did not sleep. He endured instead brief periods of stasis in a pod-like chamber that had been created for him by his body's builders. While inside that chamber he could sometimes recall what it had felt like to live. And while inside, he was not to be disturbed—unless in the event of inimical circumstances.

The chamber was equipped with displays linked to devices that monitored the status of the *Invisible Hand*. But Grievous was aware of a problem even before the displays told him as much.

As he exited the chamber and hurried for the cruiser's bridge, a droid joined him, supplying updates.

No sooner had the Separatist fleet emerged from hyperspace at Belderone than it had come under attack—not by Belderone's meager planetary defense force, but by a Republic battle group.

"Wings of starfighters are converging on the fleet," the droid reported. "Assault cruisers, destroyers, and other capital vessels are arrayed in a screen formation above night-side Belderone."

Klaxons were blaring in the corridors, and gunner droids and Neimoidians were hastening to battle stations.

"Order our ships to raise shields and form up behind us. Vanguard pickets are to fall back in shield formation to protect the core vessels."

"Affirmative, General."

"Roll the ship starboard to minimize our profile, and reorient the deflector shields. Deploy all wings of droid tri-fighters and ready all port-side batteries for enfilade fire."

Grievous braced himself against a bulkhead as the cruiser was shaken by an explosion.

"Ranged fire from the Republic destroyers," the droid said. "No damage. Shields functioning at better than ninety percent."

Grievous quickened his pace.

On the bridge, a real-time hologram of the battle was running above the tactical console. Grievous took a moment to study the deployment of the Republic ships and starfighter squadrons. Made up of sixty capital vessels, the battle group wasn't large enough to overwhelm the Separatist fleet, but it packed enough combined firepower to defend trivial Belderone.

On the far side of the dun-colored planet, a convoy of transports was angling toward the lesser of Belderone's two inhabited moons, starfighters and corvettes flying escort.

"Evacuees, General," one of the droids explained.

Grievous was stunned. An organized evacuation could mean only one thing: the Republic had somehow learned that Belderone had been targeted! But how could that be, when only the Separatist leaders had been apprised?

He moved to the forward viewports to observe the strobing spectacle of battle.

He would learn how he had been foiled. But survival was the first order of business.

With its stubby wings and bulbous aft cockpit, Anakin's starfighter was closer in design to the Delta-7 Aethersprite he had flown at the start of the war than it was to the newer-generation V-wings and ARC-170s flown by clone pilots. But where the Delta-7 was triangular in shape, the two-tone starfighter had a blunt bow composed of two separate fuselages, each equipped with a missile launcher. Laser cannons occupied notches forward of the wings. As with the Delta-7, the astromech socket was located to one side of the humpbacked cockpit.

Plus, Anakin had made a few significant modifications.

Already a veteran of battles at Xagobah and other worlds, the craft looked as if it had been around for ten years. But it handled better than the *Azure Angel* he had flown at Praesitlyn, and was faster, as well.

Launched from the *Integrity,* Anakin poured on speed in an effort to catch up with the ARCs and V-wings that had been first to deploy from the assault cruiser's massive ventral bay. An instrument panel monitor indicated that the starfighter's ion drive was functioning at just under optimal.

"Artoo," he said toward the comlink, "run a diagnostic on the starboard thruster."

The starfighter's console display translated the droid's toodled response into Basic characters.

"I thought so. Well, go ahead and make the adjustments. We don't want to be last to arrive."

R2-D2's plaintive mewl needed no translation.

The drive readout graph pulsed and climbed, and the starfighter surged forward.

"That's it, pal. Now we're moving!"

Settling back into the padded seat, he flexed his gloved hands and exhaled slowly through his mouth. Enough spying, he told himself. He wasn't any closer to Coruscant, but at least he was back where he belonged, wedded to a starfighter, and prepared to show the enemy a thing or two about space combat.

Ahead of him—spearhead to groups of needle-nosed pickets that were screening the capital ships—slued hundreds of enemy craft. Some were thirteen-year-old Vulture fighters with paired wings that resembled seedpods; others were compact tri-fighter droids; and still others were space-capable Geonosian twin-beaked Nantex starfighters. Just now the lead ARC-170s were weaving through permutations of close combat with the droid fighters, the glowing pulses of energy beams turning local space into a web of devastation.

Not since Praesitlyn had he soared into such an enemy-rich environment.

Target practice, he thought, allowing a grin.

He took his right hand from the control yoke to activate the long-range scanners. The threat-assessment screen displayed the signatures and deployment of the Separatist capital vessels: Trade Federation Lucrehulks and core ships; Techno Union Hardcells, with their columnar thruster packages and egg-shaped fuselages; Commerce Guild Diamond cruisers and Corporate Alliance Fantails; frigates, gunboats, and communications ships featuring huge circular transponders.

The whole Separatist parade.

Switching his comlink over to the battle net, Anakin hailed his wingmate.

"I say we leave the small stuff to Odd Ball and the other pilots, and go straight for the ones that matter."

Accustomed to Anakin's disregard for call signs, Obi-Wan answered in kind.

"Anakin, there are approximately five hundred droids positioned between Grievous and us. What's more, the capital ships are too heavily shielded."

"Just follow my lead, Master."

Obi-Wan sighed into the comlink microphone. "I'll try. *Master.*"

Anakin scanned the threat-assessment display, committing to memory vector lines of the closest enemy fighters. Then he reopened a channel to R2-D2.

"Battle speed, Artoo!"

Again, the starfighter shot forward. Indicators on the console redlined. Just short of the roiling fray, when he could sense the droid ships drawing a bead on him, he shoved the yoke into a corner for a pushover and streaked out of the maneuver with all weapons blazing.

Droids flared and flamed to all sides of him.

Wending through clouds of expanding fire, he locked down the trigger of the laser cannons and made a second pass through the enemy wave, destroying a dozen more fighters in a heartbeat. But the tri-fighters were onto him now, eager for payback. A sunburst of scarlet beams seared past the bubble canopy, and a fighter appeared to starboard. An instant later, a second volley sizzled down from overhead. R2-D2 loosed a series of urgent whistles and tweets as the starfighter was rocked to its shields.

Blue lightning coruscated across the console, and droid fighters appeared to port and starboard. More bolts found their mark, throwing Anakin hard against the safety harness.

"Just what I needed," he said, in appreciation.

Swerving hard to starboard, he caught the first ship with a sideslip shot. The second fighter sheared off as quickly as it could from the expanding fragmentation cloud. As it did, Anakin raced into its aft wash and triggered the lasers.

A ball of fire, the droid careened into a flak-dazzled tri-fighter and the two of them exploded.

Anakin checked the display to make certain that Obi-Wan was still with him.

"Are you all right?"

"A bit toasted, but okay."

"Stay with me."

"Do I have a choice?"

"Always, Master."

Deeper into the melee now, ARC-170s, V-wings, and droid fighters were joined in a great cloverleaf of combat, chasing one another, colliding into one another, twirling out of the fight with engines smoking or wings blown away. Weapons themselves, the droids were accurate with their bolts, but slower to recover, and easily confused by random maneuvers. While at times this made for effortless kills, there were just so many of them . . .

Anakin squared off with the enemy leader of the cloverleaf clash, and began to harass it with laser bolts. Adapting to his tactics, Obi-Wan fell back; then leapt his starfighter into kill position and opened up.

"Nice shot!" Anakin said when the wing leader vanished.

"Nice setup!"

Signaling Obi-Wan to follow, Anakin climbed out of the main battle, veering tangent to it, and rocketed toward the nearest of the Separatists' needle-nosed picket ships. Loosing two missiles to draw the picket's attention, he yawed to port, pushed over, then came back at the vessel with lasers.

"Run the hull! Target the shield generator!"

"Any closer and we'll be inside the thing!"

"That's the idea!"

Obi-Wan followed, unleashing with all cannons.

They were in the thick of the heaviest fighting now, where ranged fire from the Republic capital ships was breaking against the particle and ray shields of their targets. Blinding light pulsed behind the canopy blast tinting. The picket Anakin had piqued with missiles was under heavy bombardment. He grasped that a high-yield torpedo would be too much for it, and rushed to deliver it.

The torpedo tore from between the starfighter's cockpit-linked fuselages and burned its way toward the picket.

The picket's shield failed for an instant, and in that instant the huge incoming turbolaser bolts did their worst. Struck broadside, the picket burst like an overripe fruit, venting long plumes of incandescence and spilling light and guts into space.

Anakin jinked away, whooping into the comlink.

"We've got a clear shot at Grievous!" he told Obi-Wan.

With its tapered bow and large outrigger fins, the general's cruiser resembled a classic-era Coruscant skyscraper laid on its side.

"This hardly seems the time to bait him, Anakin. Have you had a look at those point-defense arrays?"

"When are you going to learn to trust me?"

"I do trust you! I just can't keep up with you!"

"Fine. Then I'll be right back."

Anakin pushed the starfighter to its limits, paying out laser bolts and missiles that exploded harmlessly against the great ship's deflector shield. He peeled away from the fiery wash, only to fall back at the ship in predatory banks, breaking ultimately for its 200-meter-tall conning tower.

The cruiser's in-close batteries came alive, chundering, gushing enormous gouts of spun plasma at the pest that was attempting to besiege it. Snap-rolling, Anakin slid the starfighter hard to port, belly-up, and continued to fire.

Again he tried to harry the invulnerable bridge with bursts of his lasers. And again the batteries of the colossal vessel tried but failed to get him in target lock.

Anakin pictured Grievous standing stalwart behind the transparisteel viewports.

"A taste of what's coming when we meet in the flesh," he growled.

Grievous's reptilian eyes tracked the audacious maneuvers of the yellow-and-gray starfighter that was attempting to strafe the bridge. Firing with precision, anticipating the responses of the forward batteries, taking chances even a clone wouldn't take . . . the pilot could only be a Jedi.

But a Jedi unafraid to call on his rage.

Grievous could see that in the pilot's dauntless determination, his abandon. He could sense it, even through the *Invisible Hand*'s shimmering shields and the viewport's transparisteel. Oh, to have the lightsaber of that one dangling from his belt, he thought.

Anakin Skywalker.

Certainly it was him. And in the starfighter that was guarding Anakin's stern: Obi-Wan Kenobi.

Thorns in the Separatists' side.

Elsewhere in the battle arena Republic forces were demonstrating similar enthusiasm, atomizing droid fighters and punishing the capital ships with long-range cannon fire. Grievous was confident that, if pressed, he could turn the tide of battle, but that was not his present mandate. His Sith Masters had ordered him to safeguard the lives of the Council members—though, in fact, the Confederacy needed none other than Lords Sidious and Tyranus.

He turned to watch the simulation playing above the tactical console, then swung back to the viewports, re-calling the ARC-170 pilots who had hounded Gunray's shuttle only days earlier. He waved for one of the droids.

"Alert our vessel commanders to stand by to receive revised battle orders."

"Yes, General," the droid acknowledged in monotone.

"Raise the ship. Prepare to fire all guns on my command."

There is no death; there is only the Force.

Obi-Wan wondered if he had ever witnessed a more lucid demonstration of the Jedi axiom than Anakin's Force-centered, death-defying harassment of Grievous's ship. His speck of a starfighter all but nose-to-nose with the mammoth cruiser, leaving Obi-Wan to deal with the vengeful droid fighters Anakin was either ignorant of or deliberately disregarding.

"He really is going to be the death of me," Obi-Wan mumbled.

But he was indifferent to his own fate, wondering in-stead: What if Anakin should be killed?

Could he even be killed?

As the Chosen One, was he destined to fulfill both the title and the prophecy? Was he immune to real harm,

or—as someone born to restore balance to the Force—
did he require defenders to guide him to that destiny?
Was it Obi-Wan's duty—more, the duty of all the Jedi—
to see to it that he survived at all costs?

Was that what Qui-Gon had intuited so many years
earlier on Tatooine, and had motivated him to attack
with such resolve the Sith who had revealed himself in
that parched landscape?

Though the cruiser's shield was removing the sting of
Anakin's laser bolts, he could not be deterred from per-
severing. Even Obi-Wan's repeated attempts to hail him
through the battle net had had no effect. But now the
huge ship was beginning to climb and reorient itself.

Obi-Wan thought for a moment that Grievous was actually going to bring all forward guns to bear on
Anakin. Instead, the cruiser continued to rise until it was
well above the plane of the ecliptic, with its bow angled
slightly Coreward.

Then it fired.

Not at the Republic battle group, nor at Belderone itself,
but at the convoy of evacuees and its escort starfighters.

Obi-Wan felt a great disturbance in the Force, as ship
after ship disintegrated or erupted in flames. Thousands
of voices cried out, and the battle and command nets
grew shrill with shouts of dismay and outrage.

The follow-up volley Obi-Wan waited for never arrived.

Tri-fighters and Vulture droids were suddenly slinking
back to the ships from which they had been disgorged.
At the same time, the entire Separatist fleet was turning
tail. Of course Grievous realized that his barbaric act
had caught the Republic forces by surprise, but he had
nothing more in mind than escape into hyperspace. The
general had obviously made up his mind that Belderone
simply wasn't worth the risk—not with so many de-
fenseless Outer Rim worlds still up for grabs.

"Anakin, the evacuees need our help!" Obi-Wan said.

"I'm coming, Master."

Obi-Wan watched Anakin's starfighter break off its futile pursuit of the cruiser. Farther out, Separatist ships were disappearing from sight as they made the jump to lightspeed.

"Vessels of the main fleet are safely away," a droid reported to Grievous as soon as the cruiser entered hyperspace. "Expected arrival at the alternate rally point: ten standard hours."

"Losses at Belderone?" Grievous said.

"Acceptable."

Beyond the forward viewports, the smoky vortices of outraced light.

Grievous ran the fingers of his clawlike hand down the bulkhead.

"Instruct my elite to meet me in the shuttle launching bay on emergence from hyperspace," he said to no droid in particular. "When all ships have arrived at the rally point, advise Viceroy Gunray that I will be paying him a visit."

Trained well by Dooku, General Grievous was," Yoda said. He and Mace Windu were in Yoda's chambers in the Jedi Temple, each atop a meditation dais. "Entrapped, they strike at the weakest. Force us, they do, to choose between saving lives and continuing the fight."

Yoda recalled his duel with Dooku in the solar sailer's docking bay on Geonosis. Dooku bested, left with no alternative but to distract and flee . . .

"Representatives from Belderone have expressed their gratitude to the Senate," Mace said. "Despite the losses."

Yoda shook his head sadly. "More than ten thousand killed. *Twenty-seven* Jedi."

The muscles in Mace's jaw bunched. "Billions have died in this war. Belderone was saved, and, more important, we were able to keep Grievous on the run."

"Know where he jumped to, we do."

"We'll chase him to the ends of known space, if we have to."

Yoda fell silent for a moment, then said: "Speak with the Supreme Chancellor, we must."

"Without apology," Mace said bluntly. "Our deference to him has to end."

"With the war's end, it will." Yoda turned slightly to regard Mace. "A terrible warning, Belderone is. *Increasing,* the power of the dark side is. Rooted out, Sidious must be."

Mace nodded gravely. "Rooted out and eliminated."

General Grievous has left the docking bay," a Trade Federation lieutenant relayed to Gunray in his lavish quarters in the core ship's port-side command tower.

"Which docking bay?" Gunray said toward the comlink's audio pickup. "Below, or in the tower?"

"The general's shuttle availed itself of the tower docking ring, Viceroy."

Gunray swung around to face Rune Haako. "That means he will be here any moment!"

He turned to a large circular screen that displayed a real-time view of the antechamber outside his suite. The Neimoidian guards stationed there had also been alerted to Grievous's arrival. Armed with blaster rifles taller than they were, the four wore bulky torso and lower-leg armor, and pot-shaped helmets that left their red eyes and green faces exposed.

"It has to be the mechno-chair," Gunray said, striding back and forth in front of the screen.

"What did you tell him?" Haako asked.

Gunray came to a halt. "Immediately on being apprised by Shu Mai of the Belderone rendezvous, I contacted Grievous, expressing anger that he hadn't informed me personally. I accused him of purposely leaving me out of the command loop."

Haako was horrified. "You said that to him?"

Gunray nodded. "He maintained that he had attempted to communicate through the mechno-chair hyperwave transceiver. I said that I had received no such transmission."

"They're coming!" Haako said, aiming a quivering finger at the display screen.

Gunray saw that Grievous was accompanied by four of his elite MagnaGuards. Fearsome bipedal battle droids built to exacting specifications, they stood as tall as the general and were armed with combat staffs tipped with electromagnetic pulse generators. Armorweave capes fell diagonally across their broad-shouldered bodies, swathing the crowns of their heads and lower faces. Benefiting from Grievous's own programming, as well as from the instruction Grievous had received from Dooku, the elite were trained in the Jedi arts, and more than a match for most.

The four Neimoidians stood their ground, bringing their rifles across their chests in a gesture of warning.

Grievous's elite didn't even slow down. Mirroring the Neimoidians, they raised their double-tipped electroshock batons, then swung them forward with such speed and precision that Gunray's sentinels were literally swept off their feet, as if they were children.

Grievous glared into the lens of the holocam mounted outside the hatch.

"Admit us, Viceroy. Or shall I instruct my elite to lay waste to everything that stands between me and you?"

Haako spun on his heel and hurried for the suite's rear hatch.

"Where are you going?" Gunray said. "Running will only make us appear guilty!"

"We are guilty!" Haako threw over his shoulder.

"He doesn't know that."

"*Viceroy!*" Grievous rasped.

Haako stood in the open hatch. "He will." And disappeared through it.

Gunray paced for a moment, wringing his hands, then, straightening robes and miter and pulling his shoulders back, he pressed a fat finger to the hatch release.

The general swept into the suite, the four Magna-Guards in his angry wake spreading out to both sides, ready for violence.

"What is the meaning of this intrusion?" Gunray said from the center of the main room. "Your Masters will not tolerate such ill treatment of me!"

Grievous glowered at him. "They will when they learn what you've done."

Gunray touched himself in the chest. "What are you talking about, you . . . *abomination.* When Lord Sidious hears that you promised us a world you could not deliver—"

Stepping forward, a MagnaGuard thrust his staff to within a millimeter of Gunray's face.

"Lord Sidious's alloy puppet," Gunray said, his voice quavering. "If not for the Trade Federation, you would have no army to command."

Grievous raised his right claw and pointed to Gunray. "The mechno-chair. I want to see it."

Gunray gulped. "In a fit of anger, I had it destroyed and purged from the ship."

"You're lying. There was no problem with my transmission to you. The chair relayed my message."

"What are you suggesting?"

"The chair is no longer in your possession. It has

somehow fallen into enemy hands, and, through it, the Republic was able to learn of my plan to attack Belderone."

"You're brain-dead."

Grabbing Gunray by the neck, Grievous lifted him a meter off the floor.

"Before I leave here, you will tell me everything I wish to know."

Poor Gunray, Dooku thought. *Pitiful creature . . .*

But for having left the mechno-chair behind on Cato Neimoidia, he deserved all the fear Grievous had put into him.

Secluded in his castle on Kaon, Dooku had just spoken with the general and was pondering how best to handle the situation. While the incident at Belderone wasn't conclusive proof that the Republic had managed to decrypt the Separatist code and intercept Grievous's transmission to Gunray, it was prudent to assume that this was the case. Dooku had already ordered the general to refrain from using the code for the time being. But the matter of the expropriated hyperwave transceiver was cause for added concern. The very fact that the Republic had tipped its hand at Belderone, declaring the success of its eavesdropping, implied that the mechno-chair had furnished more than intelligence. Clues to secrets that would astonish even Grievous.

The general was not accustomed to losing in battle. Even when a general among his own species, he had suf-

fered few defeats. That was orginally what had brought
him to the attention of Sidious. After the Sith Lord had
expressed interest in Grievous to Dooku, Dooku, in
turn, had expressed interest in Grievous to Chairman
San Hill, of the InterGalactic Banking Clan.

Poor Grievous, Dooku thought. *Pitiful creature . . .*

During the Huk War, and later, while in the employ of
the IBC, Grievous had survived numerous attempts on
his life, so an assassination attempt was ruled out almost
immediately. Hill himself had come up with the idea of a
shuttle crash, though that, too, presented risks.

What if Grievous should actually die in the crash?

Then the Separatists would simply have to look elsewhere for a commander, Dooku had told Hill. But
Grievous had survived—and only too well. In fact, most
of the life-threatening injuries he sustained had occurred
after he had been pulled from the flaming shuttle wreck,
and with great calculation.

When at last he had agreed to be rebuilt, promises
were made that no critical alterations would be made to
his mind. But the Geonosians had ways of modifying the
mind without a patient ever being aware that he had
been tampered with. Grievous certainly believed that he
had always been the cold-blooded conqueror he was
now, when in truth his cruelty and prowess owed much
to his rebuilding.

Sidious and Dooku couldn't have been more pleased
with the result. Dooku, especially, since he had no interest in commanding an army of droids, and already had
his hands full nursemaiding the likes of Nute Gunray,
Shu Mai, and the hive-minded others who eventually
would form the Council of Separatists.

Grievous had been a delight to train, as well. No need
to coax him to release his anger and rage, as Dooku had
been forced to do during the training of his so-called

Dark Jedi disciples. The Geonosians had arranged for Grievous to be nothing but anger and rage. And as to the general's combat skills, few, if any, Jedi would be capable of defeating him. There had been moments during the extensive combat sessions when even Dooku had been hard-pressed to outduel the cyborg.

But then, Dooku had kept some secrets to himself.

Just in case.

Manipulation of the sort that had gone into the transformation of Grievous went to the heart of what it meant to be a Sith—if, indeed, the words *heart* and *Sith* could be used together. The essence of the dark side lay in a willingness to use any means possible to arrive at a desired end—which, in the case of Lord Sidious, meant a galaxy brought under the dominion of a single, brilliant mind.

The current war had been the result of a thousand years of careful planning by the Sith—generations of bequeathing knowledge of the dark side from mentor to apprentice. Rarely more than two in each generation, from Darth Bane forward, Master and apprentice would devote themselves to harnessing the strength that flowed from the dark side, and to making the most of every opportunity to allow darkness to wax. Facilitating war, murder, corruption, injustice, and avarice when- and wherever possible.

Analogous to introducing a covert malignancy to the body politic of the Republic, then monitoring its spread from one organ to another until the mass reached such size that it began to disrupt vital systems . . .

The Sith had learned from their own internecine struggles that systems were often brought down from within when power became their reason for being. The greater the threat to that power, the tighter the threatened would cling.

That had been the case with the Jedi Order.

For two hundred years before the coming of Darth Sidious the power of the dark side had been gaining strength, and yet the Jedi had made only minimal efforts to thwart it. The Sith were pleased by the fact that the Jedi, too, had been allowed to grow so powerful, because, in the end, their sense of entitlement would blind them to what was occurring in their midst.

So, let them be placed on a pedestal. Let them grow soft and set in their ways. Let them forget that good and evil coexist. Let them look no farther than their vaunted Temple, so that they would fail to see the proverbial forest for the trees. And, by all means, let them grow possessive of the power they had gained, so that they might be that much easier to topple.

Not that *all* of them were blind, of course. Many Jedi were aware of the changes, the drift toward darkness. None, perhaps, more than aged Yoda. But the Masters who made up the Jedi Council were enslaved to the *inevitability* of that drift. Instead of attempting to get to the root of the coming darkness, they merely did their best to contain it. They waited for the Chosen One to be born, mistakenly believing that only he or she would be capable of restoring balance.

Such was the danger of prophecy.

It was into such times that Dooku had been born, placed because of a strong connection to the Force among an Order that had grown complacent, self-involved, arrogant about the power they wielded in the name of the Republic. Turning a blind eye to injustices the Republic had little interest in eradicating, because of profitable deals forged among those who held the reins of command.

While midi-chlorians determined to some degree a Jedi's ability to use the Force, other inherited character-

istics also played a part—notwithstanding the Temple's
best efforts to eradicate them. Having hailed from nobil-
ity and great wealth, Dooku yearned for prestige. Even
as a youngster, he had been obsessed with learning all he
could about the Sith and the dark side of the Force. He
had toed the Jedi line; become the Temple's most agile
swordmaster and instructor. And yet the makings of his
eventual transformation had been there from the start.
Without the Jedi ever realizing it, Dooku had been as dis-
ruptive to the Order as would be a young boy raised in
slavery on Tatooine.

His discontent had continued to grow and fester; his
frustration with the Republic Senate, with ineffectual
Supreme Chancellor Valorum, with the shortsightedness
of the Jedi Council members themselves. A Trade Federation blockade of Naboo, rumors of a Chosen One
found on a desert world, the death of Qui-Gon Jinn at
the hands of a Sith . . . How could the Council members
not see what was happening? How could they continue
to claim that the dark side obscured all?

Dooku had said as much to anyone who would listen.
He wore his discontent on the sleeve of his robes.
Though they hadn't enjoyed the smoothest of
student–teacher relationships, he and Yoda had spoken
openly of the portents. But Yoda was living proof of a
conservatism that came with extended life. Dooku's true
confidant had been Master Sifo-Dyas, who, while also
disturbed by what was occurring, was too weak to take
action.

The Battle of Naboo had revealed that the Sith were
back in the open, and that a Sith Lord was at work
somewhere.

The Sith Lord: the one born with the power needed to
take the final step.

Dooku had given thought to seeking him out, perhaps

killing him. But even what little faith he placed in the prophecy was enough to raise doubt that the death of a Sith could halt the advance of the dark side.

Another would come, and another.

As it happened, there had been no need to hunt for Sidious, for it was Sidious who had approached him. Sidious's boldness surprised him at first, but it hadn't taken long for Dooku to become fascinated by the Sith. Instead of a lightsaber duel to the death, there had been much discussion, and a gradual understanding that their separate visions for how the galaxy might be rescued from depravity were not so different after all.

But partnership with a Sith didn't make one a Sith.

As the Jedi arts had to be taught, so, too, did the power of the dark side. And so began his long apprenticeship. The Jedi warned that anger was the quickest path to the dark side, but anger was nothing more than raw emotion. To know the dark side one had to be willing to rise above all morality, to throw love and compassion aside, and to do whatever was necessary to bring about the vision of a world brought under control—even if that meant taking lives.

Dooku was an eager student, and yet Sidious had continued to hold him at arm's length. Perhaps he had been working with other potential replacements for his earlier apprentice, the savage Darth Maul, who, in fact, had been nothing more than a minion, like Asajj Ventress and General Grievous. Sidious had recognized in Dooku the makings of a true accomplice—an equal from the other camp, already trained in the Jedi arts, a master duelist, a political visionary. But he needed to gauge the depth of Dooku's commitment.

One of your former confidants at the Jedi Temple has perceived the coming change, Sidious had told him. *This one has contacted a group of cloners, regarding the cre-*

*ation of an army for the Republic. The order for the
army can stand, for we will be able to make use of that
army someday. But Master Sifo-Dyas cannot stand, for
the Jedi cannot learn about the army until we are prepared to have them learn of it.*

And so with the murder of Sifo-Dyas, Dooku had em-
braced the dark side fully, and Sidious had conferred on
him the title *Darth Tyranus*. His final act before leaving
the Jedi Order was to erase all mentions of Kamino from
the Jedi archives. Then, as Tyranus, he had found Fett on
Bogg 4; had instructed the Mandalorian to deliver himself to Kamino; and had arranged for payments to be
made to the cloners through circuitous routes . . .

Ten years passed.

Under its new Supreme Chancellor, the Republic re-
covered somewhat, then grew more corrupt and beset
with problems than before. As best they could, Sidious
and Tyranus helped things along.

Sidious had the ability to see deep into the future, but
there was always the unexpected. With the power of the
dark side, however, came flexibility.

Having traced Fett to Kamino, Obi-Wan Kenobi had
turned up on Geonosis. All at once, here was Qui-Gon
Jinn's former Padawan, right under Dooku's nose. But
when he had informed Sidious of Obi-Wan's presence,
Sidious had only said, *Allow events to play out, Darth
Tyranus. For our plans are unfolding exactly as I have
foreseen. The Force is very much with us.*

And now, a new wrinkle: as a result of Nute Gunray's
blunder at Cato Neimoidia, the Republic and the Jedi
had chanced on a possible way to trace the whereabouts
of Sidious and expose him.

The mechno-chair's exceptional transceiver—and others like it—had been created for Sidious by a host of beings, a few of whom were still alive. And if agents of the

Republic—or the Jedi, for that matter—were clever and persistent enough, they could succeed in learning more about Sidious than he would want anyone to learn . . .

He had to be informed, Dooku thought.

Or did he?

For a heartbeat he hesitated, imagining the power that could be his.

Then he went directly to the hyperwave transmitter Sidious had given him, and began his transmission.

M ace Windu couldn't recall a visit to the Supreme Chancellor's chambers in the Senate Office Building when his attention hadn't been drawn to Palpatine's curious and somehow unsettling collection of quasi-religious statuary. On one occasion, picking up on Mace's interest, Palpatine had offered lengthy and enthusiastic accounts of when and how he had come by some of the pieces. Acquired at an auction on Commenor; procured after many years and at great expense from a Corellian dealer in antiquities; salvaged from an ancient temple discovered on a moon of the gas giant Yavin; a gift from the Theed Council of Naboo; another gift from that world's Gungans . . .

Just now Mace's eyes were on a small bronzium statue Palpatine had once identified as Wapoe, the mythical Sistros demigod of disguise.

"I'm relieved that you contacted me, Master Jedi," the Supreme Chancellor was saying from the far side of his expansive desk. "As I was about to contact you on a matter of some gravity."

"Then speak of your matter first, we will," Yoda said.

He was seated for a change, atop a cushioned chair that made him appear even smaller than he was. Mace was at Yoda's left hand, sitting with legs widely spread, forearms resting on his knees.

Palpatine touched his steepled fingers to his lower lip, then inhaled and sat back in his throne of a chair. "This is rather awkward, Master Yoda, but I suspect that the matter I have in mind is the very one that brought you and Master Windu here. By that I mean Belderone."

Yoda compressed his lips. "Fail you, your intuition doesn't. About Belderone, much to say, we have."

Palpatine smiled without showing his teeth. "Well, then, suppose I begin by saying that I was most pleased to learn of our recent victory there. I only wish I had been informed of your plans before the fact."

"We had no time to corroborate the intelligence we received," Mace said without hesitation. "We thought it best to commit as few Republic ships as could be spared. It was essentially a Jedi operation."

"A Jedi operation," Palpatine said slowly. "And by all accounts you, that is, the Jedi, were successful in routing General Grievous's forces."

"A rout it was not," Yoda said. "To hyperspace Grievous fled. But protecting the Separatist leaders, he was."

"I see. And now?"

Mace leaned forward. "Wait for him to resurface, and strike again."

Palpatine regarded him. "Might I be informed of your intelligence next time? Didn't you and I have this discussion after Master Yoda was thought to have been killed at Ithor?" Before Mace could respond, he continued: "You see, the problem here is one of appearances. While I can appreciate the need to keep secret some intelligence, many in the Senate do not. In the instance of

Belderone—and largely because it constituted a Republic victory—I was able to allay the fear of certain Senators that the Jedi are taking the war into their own hands, and are no longer accountable for their actions."

Mace's nostrils flared. "We can't allow the Senate to go on dictating the course of the war."

Yoda nodded, sagely. "Miring the Jedi in uncertainty, some of the Senate's decisions are." He looked askance at Palpatine. "A matter of *appearances,* this is."

Mace made it emphatic. "We're not rogues."

Palpatine spread his hands in a gesture of appeasement. "Of course you're not. Nothing could be further from the truth. But, as I say . . . Well, if nothing else, the Senate at least needs to *believe* that it is being kept informed—particularly in light of the extraordinary powers it has granted this office." He sat straighter in the chair. "Not a day passes that I am not subjected to suspicion, accusations, suggestions of ulterior motive. And, I will tell you, the suspicions do not end here, in this office. They extend to the role of the Jedi in the war. Master Jedi, we cannot, under any circumstances, be perceived as being in collusion."

Yoda frowned. "In *collusion* we must be, if victory the goal remains."

Palpatine smiled tolerantly. "Master Yoda, far be it from me to lecture someone of your vast experience on the nature of politics. But the truth of the matter is that with the war now exiled to the Outer Rim, we must be judicious about the campaigns we undertake, and about the targets to which we assign our forces. If a lasting peace is ever to be achieved when this madness concludes, each and every act from this point forward must be handled with utmost delicacy." He shook his head. "Many worlds, loyal to the Republic, circumstance forced us to sacrifice. Others that joined the Separatists may wish to return to the Republic. These aren't matters with which I wish to burden the Jedi. But they are the province of this office, and I need to place them first and foremost."

"The lessons learned from a thousand years of serving the Republic aren't entirely lost on us," Mace said strongly. "The Jedi Council is fully aware of such concerns."

Palpatine took the rebuke in stride. "Excellent. Then we can move on to other matters."

Mace and Yoda waited.

"May I inquire as to how the Jedi learned of Grievous's plan to attack Belderone?"

"A hyperwave transceiver that belonged to Viceroy Gunray was seized at Cato Neimoidia," Mace explained. "The device allowed Intelligence to decipher the Separatist code. A message transmitted by General Grievous to Viceroy Gunray regarding Belderone was monitored, and we acted on it."

Palpatine was staring at him in disbelief. "We have the ability to listen in on Separatist transmissions?"

"Unlikely," Yoda said. "After Belderone."

Palpatine considered it, then frowned. "For Belderone you forfeited the ability to continue monitoring the Separatists." He took a breath, and the frown ebbed. "Had I been included in this matter, I would have made the same choice. But I must add, Master Jedi, that I am greatly displeased about having been circumvented. Why wasn't I told? Am I to infer from this that you no longer trust me?"

"No," Yoda almost barked. "But into this office, come and go many. Our own counsel we kept."

Palpatine's face took on sudden color. "And yet you continue to place full trust in those around you? Do you realize how some might respond to that, when many of your Order have deliberately absented themselves from the war, and some have even gone over to the Separatist side?"

"A decade old, such reproaches are, Supreme Chancellor."

"I fear you delude yourself in this instance, Master Yoda, if you believe that the passage of time makes those 'reproaches' any less valid to your critics."

This is getting out of control, Mace thought. He calmed himself before speaking.

"There's a more important reason for your not being informed about the transceiver."

Now Palpatine waited.

"It contained a stored message—a message transmitted to Viceroy Gunray from Darth Sidious."

Palpatine's broad forehead wrinkled in uncertainty. "Sidious. I know the name . . . "

"Dooku's Sith Master, Sidious is. Learned of him on Geonosis, Master Kenobi did. But eluded us, proof of him has."

"Now I recall," Palpatine said. "Obi-Wan was told that this Sidious had somehow infiltrated the Senate."

"Dismissed that, we have. But lying about Sidious, Dooku wasn't."

Palpatine swiveled his chair toward the room's immense curved window, the panorama of Coruscant. "Another Sith." Turning back to Yoda, he said: "Forgive me, but why is this of such great concern?"

"Carefully balanced this war has been. Republic victories, Separatist victories . . . In prolonging it, a part the Sith may play."

Again, Palpatine paused to consider Yoda's words. "I think I begin to understand the reasons for your secrecy. The Jedi are attempting to expose Sidious."

"In pursuit of clues, we are."

"Might the capture of Sidious end the war?"

"Hasten the end," Mace said.

Palpatine nodded in finality. "Then I trust that you will accept my apologies. Do whatever you must to hunt Sidious down."

When the Xi Charrian said it was an asteroid mining operation, I wasn't picturing an actual asteroid," Obi-Wan said from the copilot's seat of the Republic cruiser.

"It was TeeCee-Sixteen who told us that," Anakin said. "Maybe something was lost in translation."

The protocol droid had been sent to Coruscant for further debriefing by Republic Intelligence; R2-D2 was on Belderone, where technicians were seeing to damages he had sustained during the battle there. Obi-Wan and Anakin had the old white ship to themselves, and had exchanged their Jedi robes for outfits more suitable to itinerant spacers.

Named for the asteroid belt in which it was prominent, the Escarte Commerce Guild facility orbited between massive, multimooned gas giants in an otherwise uninhabited star system two hyperspace jumps from Belderone, on the Rimward side of the Perlemian Trade Route. Oblate when mining operations had commenced twenty years earlier, Escarte was now a concave hemisphere, heavily cratered by the forces of nature and the gargantuan labor droids of the Commerce Guild. Satisfied that every bit of ore had been extracted from Escarte, the guild had converted the asteroid's consequent quarries, tunnels, and shafts into processing centers and field offices. State-of-the-art tractor beam technology allowed the guild to capture small asteroids and draw them directly into the facility, rather than have to use tugs or engage in on-site mining. In many ways Escarte was the ore-mining equivalent of the Tibanna-gas-mining facilities that floated in the dense atmosphere of Bespin, far across the stars.

Unfriendly space, the belt was defended by Commerce Guild corvettes and fleet patrol craft modeled on the Geonosian starfighter. Regardless, Republic Intelligence had managed to insert one of its agents onto Escarte. Obi-Wan and Anakin hadn't been told when or even if they were going to make contact with the agent, but moments before leaving Belderone they had been informed that Thal K'sar—the Bith artisan who allegedly had designed the hyperwave transceiver and holoprojector for Gunray's mechno-chair—had been arrested, on charges yet to be learned.

An alert chime sounded from the cruiser's instrument console.

"Escarte," Anakin said. "Demanding that we identify ourselves and state our intent."

"We're freelance merchants in search of work," Obi-Wan reminded him.

Anakin activated the comm and said as much into the microphone.

"Corellian cruiser," a husky voice returned, "negative on your request to dock. Escarte has no job openings. Suggest you try Ansion or Ord Mantell."

Obi-Wan's gaze drifted to the viewport. Off to starboard, a corvette was coming about.

"Intercept vector," Anakin said. "Any last-minute instructions, Master?"

"Yes: stick to the plan. Our best hope for getting close to K'sar is to get ourselves arrested."

Anakin grinned. "Shouldn't be a problem. Hang on."

Obi-Wan already was, and so was able to remain more or less upright in the chair as Anakin firewalled the thrusters and threw the cruiser into a hard turn—not away from the corvette, but aimed directly toward it.

The console chimed another alert.

"They're warning us away, Anakin."

Anakin kept the cruiser on course. "Quick flyby. Our way of saying we're not happy about being turned away."

"No lasers."

"Promise. We're just going to buzz them."

Obi-Wan watched the corvette grow larger in the viewport. The console continued to chime, in escalating alerts. An instant later, two turbolaser beams streaked across the cruiser's bow.

Obi-Wan clenched his hands on the chair armrests. "They're not amused."

"We'll just have to try harder."

Dropping the cruiser's nose, Anakin increased speed. He seemed bent on maneuvering directly under the corvette, but at the last moment he pulled back on the control yoke, taking the cruiser through a spiraling, high-boost climb. A fusillade from the corvette's forward batteries narrowly missed clipping the ship's tail.

"Enough plausibility," Obi-Wan said. "Level out and signal that we're complying."

"Master, you are not taking our assignment seriously

enough. If we make it too easy for them, they'll suspect we're up to something."

Obi-Wan saw that two patrol craft were rushing in to join the pursuit. With flashes of scarlet light racing alongside, Anakin whipped the cruiser through a teeth-rattling bank and shot for the thick of the asteroid belt.

"The only thing worse than being your wingmate is being your passenger!"

Anakin had the ship tipped to one side, intent on weaving it through a cluster of rocks, when a laser bolt struck the closest asteroid. Rubble from the explosion peppered the cruiser's shields, but the console displays confirmed Obi-Wan's hunch that no damage had been done.

Anakin took a firm grip on the control yoke and yanked the cruiser into a turn. The patrol craft clung doggedly, angling to outflank the larger ship, but Anakin kept cheating the turn tighter and tighter, forcing the fighters to break off. The cruiser had no sooner re-aligned itself then it gave a sudden lurch, snapping Obi-Wan and Anakin back into their seats, then forward into the console. Anakin reached over his head to make adjustments, and the cruiser raced forward once more, only to freeze, then tremble.

Obi-Wan scanned the displays. "Are we hit?"

"No."

"Asteroid?"

"Not that, either."

"Don't tell me you've come to your senses and decided to surrender?"

Anakin showed him a long-suffering look. "Tractor beam."

"From Escarte? Impossible. We're much too far away."

"That's what I thought."

Anakin's hands flew across the instruments, shutting down some systems and activating others.

"Don't try to fight it, Anakin. This ship won't hold together."

A deep shudder from the bowels of the cruiser reinforced his words.

Anakin clenched his jaw, then let his hands fall to his sides.

"Look at it this way," Obi-Wan said, as the cruiser was being drawn toward the distant facility. "At least you made them work for it."

Gentle with the cruiser, the tractor beam had deposited it in a guild-made crater that was now a docking bay. Ordered out of the ship, Obi-Wan and Anakin stood at the foot of the boarding ramp with their hands clamped on top of their heads. Uniformed Neimoidians and Gossams surrounded the cruiser, and a security team comprising humans, Geonosians, and battle droids was marching toward them.

"Not exactly the warm welcome we received on Charros Four," Obi-Wan said.

Anakin nodded slightly. "Almost makes me nostalgic for the Xi Charrians."

"Keep your hands where we can see them!" the human chief of the security detail shouted as he stepped onto the landing platform. "Make no sudden moves!"

"Such drama," Anakin said.

"No mind tricks," Obi-Wan cautioned.

"Spoilsport."

The light-complected, blond security officer was as tall as Anakin and wider in the shoulders. A Commerce Guild badge affixed to the collar of his gray uniform showed him to be a captain in the Escarte Guard. He brought the security detail to a halt when everyone was still three meters from the boarding ramp. At his signal, the Geonosians spread out to both sides, brandishing wide-muzzled sonic blasters.

The captain looked Obi-Wan and Anakin up and down, then circled them once, hands clasped behind his back. Eyeing the ship, he said, "I haven't seen one of these in a while. But judging by the retrofitted cannons, I'd have to guess you're not ambassadors of goodwill."

"Let's just say we've been forced to adapt to the times," Obi-Wan said.

The captain scowled at him. "What's your business in this sector?"

"We were hoping to find freelance work," Anakin said.

"You were informed otherwise. Why create problems for yourselves by harassing one of our corvettes?"

"We felt that you'd been impolite—when all we wanted was to introduce ourselves."

The captain almost laughed. "Then this has all been a misunderstanding?"

"Exactly," Obi-Wan said.

The captain shook his head in amusement. "In that case we'd be glad to show you around—*starting with the detention level*!" He swung to two other humans in the detail. "Stun-cuff these comedians and search them for concealed weapons."

"Can't we simply pay a fine and be on our way?" Obi-Wan asked as the magnetic cuffs snapped into place around his wrists.

"Tell it to the judiciary."

Frisks completed, the two humans stepped away. "They're clean."

The captain nodded. "That's one thing in their favor. Search the ship and impound anything of value. And alert detention that I have two for containment." Drawing a blaster from his hip holster, he motioned Obi-Wan and Anakin toward the turbolifts.

The crater docking bay was accessed by several corridors, some unchanged since the days they had served as mining tunnels, others reinforced by plasteel girders and dressed up with ferrocrete panels. It was apparent also that some of the turbolifts were housed in former mine shafts.

The captain indicated an unoccupied lift and followed Obi-Wan and Anakin inside. When two Gossams hurried for the same lift, he waved them away. As soon as the door closed, he lowered his weapon and spoke with a sudden urgency.

"We have to make this quick."

"You're Travale," Obi-Wan said, using the code name he had been furnished.

"Things have gotten more complicated with the Bith. He's slated for execution."

Anakin's eyebrows met in a V. "What did he do, murder someone?"

"Some sort of accounting error."

"Execution seems a rather harsh penalty," Obi-Wan said.

"Escarte Judiciary claims it wants to make an example of him. But it's clear the charges were trumped up." Travale paused. "Could have something to do with your being here to see him."

Travale hadn't been given the reason, but Obi-Wan nodded in acknowledgment. "If he's expecting to die, he may not feel inclined to talk to us."

"My thought, too," Travale said. "But maybe if you could break him out . . . "

"You could arrange that?" Anakin said.

"I can try."

The turbolift car came to a rest and the door slid open.

"Welcome to the detention level," Travale said, back in character, and shoving Obi-Wan out into the anteroom beyond. Behind a semicircle of consoles stood five surly nonhumans—tusked and bald-domed Quara Aqualish—wearing Commerce Guild uniforms and sporting heavy sidearms.

"Show our two guests to cell four-eight-one-six," Travale told the sergeant among them.

"Already occupied by the Bith—K'sar."

"Misery loves company," Travale said.

Executing a crisp about-face, he returned to the turbolift. Emerged from the enclosure of display screens, a four-eyed Aqualish led Obi-Wan and Anakin into a narrow corridor lined with detention cells. Thirty meters along he stopped to enter a code into a wall-mounted touch pad, and the bloodstained door to 4816 slid open.

Square and squalid, it contained neither cots nor refresher.

The smell of waste was almost overpowering.

"Word of warning," the Aqualish said in Basic, "the quality of the cuisine is surpassed only by the cleanliness of the accommodations."

"Then we'll hope to be released before lunch," Obi-Wan said.

Thal K'sar was slumped in a corner, his long-fingered hands cuffed in front of him. Slender even for a Bith, he was well dressed and seemingly unharmed. Obi-Wan recalled that he had been arrested only the previous day.

K'sar glanced up, but didn't return Obi-Wan's nod of greeting.

"Some fix," Anakin said loudly when the cell sealed. "Good job back there."

Obi-Wan played along. "You didn't help matters any by flooring that security guard."

"Ah, she had it coming."

Anakin ambled over to where K'sar was huddled.

"What landed you in here?" he asked.

Though surprised to hear his own language spoken by a human, K'sar kept silent. When Anakin made a second attempt, the Bith said in Basic, "It's none of your concern. Please leave me alone."

Anakin shrugged and joined Obi-Wan on the far side of the room.

"Patience," Obi-Wan said quietly.

Backs pressed to the filthy wall, the two of them sank down onto their haunches.

Less than a standard hour had passed when they heard voices in the corridor. The door grated open, revealing Travale and two Aqualish security officers. Without a word, the aliens standing to either side of Travale grabbed him by the arms and hurled him headlong into the cell.

Obi-Wan caught him before he hit the floor.

"Another unexpected development?"

Travale was cuffed, and rattled. "My cover's blown," he said quietly. "Don't know how, or by whom."

Anakin glanced at Obi-Wan. "No coincidence."

"Someone is onto us." Obi-Wan left it at that.

"Now what?"

"Were you able to arrange anything?" Obi-Wan asked Travale.

He nodded. "Power failure. Brief, but more than enough time for you to get out of here."

"*Us,*" Anakin amended. "You're coming along."

"I appreciate that." He frowned in uncertainty. "Hope I wasn't wrong in figuring that you two will be able to open the door . . . manually, I mean."

"We can open the door," Obi-Wan assured him.

"How long before the power fails?" Anakin asked.

"An hour from now." Travale glanced at K'sar. "What about him?"

Anakin stood up and crossed the room. "I know you're not interested in small talk, but we think we may have a way out of here. Does that interest you?"

The Bith's lidless black eyes grew considerably larger. "Yes. Yes! Thank you."

"Just be ready."

"Take the tunnel to the left of the guard station," Travale was telling Obi-Wan when Anakin returned. "Keep taking lefts until you reach a stairway, then follow that to the docking level."

"You're going a different way?" Anakin said.

"Someone has to deactivate the tractor beam, or your ship's not leaving. Two levels below this one there's a power coupling station. I know just enough to disable it temporarily."

"You're not going alone," Obi-Wan said.

Anakin grinned at him. "I believe it's your turn . . . "

Obi-Wan didn't argue. "That means K'sar goes with you. Don't allow him out of your sight, Anakin."

Travale nodded toward the cell block corridor. "We'll still have the guards to deal with."

"Don't worry about them," Anakin said.

Spreading his hands, he snapped the cuffs from his wrists. Obi-Wan did the same, then snapped Travale's open.

Travale smiled broadly. "I love a good plan."

Anakin and Obi-Wan were standing by the door when the cell's grime-encrusted illuminator faltered and died. Obi-Wan shoved his hands sideways through the air, and the door retracted.

Travale shook his head in wonderment. "It never ceases to amaze me."

Anakin swung to K'sar. "Now! Hurry!"

The four of them moved into the unlit hall.

"Emergency power should come on shortly," Travale said.

Ahead of them they could hear the five guards toggling switches on the console and speaking in excited voices. Anakin wasn't halfway to the anteroom when one of the guards appeared at the end of the narrow corridor. The Aqualish's huge eyes allowed him to see in the dark, but not as well as the Bith, nor as well as the Jedi. Before the guard could realize what was happening, his raised blaster was soaring down the corridor into Anakin's hand. A Force push from Obi-Wan sent the Aqualish flailing back into the anteroom and slamming into the turbolift wall.

The rest of the guards hurried out from behind the darkened console to counterattack. By then Obi-Wan and Anakin were on them, dropping them with punches, side kicks, Force pushes. Bodies sailed across the anteroom, tumbled over one another, smashed into display screens. One Aqualish managed to get off a shot, but the blaster bolt missed anyone during its mad carom around the room.

The fracas was over almost before it began.

In the red glow of emergency lights, K'sar cast a dumbfounded look around.

"You're Jedi!"

"Two out of three," Travale said.

"But . . . what are you doing here—on Escarte?"

Anakin pressed his forefinger to his lips with elaborate seriousness. "Republic business." Then into K'sar's hands he pressed the blaster he had summoned from the guard.

K'sar stared at the weapon. "But—"

"I won't need it."

"Here's where we part company," Travale said to Anakin. "Remember: stay left until you reach the stairway."

"Where are you sending him?" K'sar asked.

"Docking Bay Thirty-Six."

The Bith nodded. "I know the way."

Travale chuckled. "This just keeps getting better and better." He swung back to Anakin. "K'sar will also know the way to Docking Bay Forty. That's where we'll be waiting for you. Escarte Control won't be able to bring the tractor beam back online immediately, and judging by the way you fly, you shouldn't have much trouble dodging the patrol craft. But good luck, anyway."

"Thanks, but there's no such thing."

As Travale and Obi-Wan were running off, Anakin noticed that one of the turbolift cars was descending.

"Security detail coming to check on the guards," K'sar said.

Anakin nodded toward the dark corridor they were supposed to take. "Go!"

K'sar's long legs propelled him at a fast clip. But instead of going left as Travale had advised, he turned right at the first intersection.

Anakin grabbed him by the shoulder and spun him around. "This isn't the way we were told to go."

"The captain's a newcomer to Escarte," the Bith said, short of breath. "I've been here for fifteen years. I know every route through this rock."

Anakin regarded him in silence.

"Trust me, Jedi, I have nothing to gain by lying to you and remaining here."

Anakin tapped him into motion. Several minutes of running brought them to a rickety stairway, which K'sar didn't hesitate to climb.

"I'd still like to know what you did to end up in detention," Anakin asked from behind K'sar.

"And I wish I could tell you," he said. "My superior—a Gossam—said I had made an accounting error that would cost the Commerce Guild a small fortune."

"You were always an exec?"

"I started out as a technician—design, installation, the whole gamut. Gradually, I worked my way up."

"Up, maybe. But you're on the wrong side in this war. Your entire species."

K'sar stopped to catch his breath. "Clak'dor Seven had little choice," he said. "The Separatists were offering unrestricted access to hyperspace routes, better deals on trade goods, no interference . . . As for me, I was already working for the guild. One day it was business as usual, the next—on the heels of what happened on Geonosis, at any rate—the guild was suddenly at war with the Republic." He raised his gaze. "We go left at the top of the stairs."

Anakin heard a note of indecision in his voice. "You don't sound as sure as you did."

"I haven't been in this area for a long while, but I'm certain we can reach the docking level."

The rock walls of the corridor into which they raced bore the scars of the giant drills that had hollowed Escarte. Light and oxygen were scant, and the uneven floor was slippery. Anakin clamped his right arm around the Bith's narrow waist to help him along.

"Wait, wait!" K'sar said suddenly.

"What's wrong?'

K'sar eyes filled with dread. "I made a mistake! We shouldn't have come this way!"

Anakin prevented him from moving. "Too late to turn back."

"We have to! You don't understand—"

K'sar words were swallowed by the sound of servomotors and hydraulics. Around a bend in the gloomy tunnel raced a dwarf spider droid, its long-barreled blaster cannon already sweeping side to side, in search of targets.

S omeone's coming," Obi-Wan warned Travale.

They were standing on a narrow gantry that accessed the control panel for Escarte's number three tractor beam coupling station. Six meters high, the tower rose from a circular platform that projected from the wall of a deep air shaft. They'd had to wait for full power to return to the area before seeing to the task of disabling the tractor beam. Initially, Travale had made a few mistakes, but he had sorted through his confusion and was almost done.

Obi-Wan peered around the corner of the tower in the direction of the voices he had heard. Three Geonosian security guards were approaching the coupling station from a corridor on the far side of the shaft.

"Never a lightsaber when you need one," Travale whispered. "Can you divert them somehow?"

Obi-Wan considered his options, then made a flicking motion with the fingers of his right hand. An unidentifiable sound issued from deeper in the corridor the guards had taken. Whirling, the three Geonosians hurried off to investigate.

Travale shook his head back and forth in appreciation of Obi-Wan's skill. "It's a wonder the war isn't over yet."

"Too few of us."

Travale studied Obi-Wan for a moment. "Is that the reason?"

Obi-Wan touched Travale on the arm, and motioned with his bearded chin to the tower. "No time to waste."

The Jedi watched over Travale's shoulder as he dialed the coupling power feed to zero.

"These things are the future," Travale said. "Fill a ship with enough tractor beam arrays and you could prevent an enemy from jumping to hyperspace."

"There aren't ships large enough."

"There will be," Travale said. "To ensure that another war doesn't happen."

Mainstay of the Commerce Guild's mining operations, the dwarf spider droid was a hunter-killer. The spider didn't stand much taller than a Trade Federation battle droid, but it was agile and equipped with two powerful blaster cannons. Perched at the juncture of four splayed legs, the hemispherical body was dominated by two huge circular photoreceptors, which appeared to be fixed on Anakin and K'sar as the droid rushed in to make the kill.

Anakin threw K'sar to one side and rolled as the dwarf spider fired. Two glaring bolts gouged a trench in the hewn floor of the tunnel, and the report of the cannon resounded deafeningly from the walls. The head pivoted, photoreceptors finding Anakin, and the weapon discharged again.

Anakin flipped himself away. Calling on the Force, he swirled his hands in front of him to prevent the intense heat from engulfing him. Rolling once more, he tried to get underneath the droid's striding legs, but the spider anticipated him, skittered backward, and loosed another burst.

Anakin leapt.

Propelled by the Force, as well as the force of the explosion, he struck the arched ceiling and fell hard to the floor. Blacking out for a moment, he awoke to find the droid charging toward him, reorienting the smaller of its cannons to place him in the crosshairs. Catapulting to his feet, he flew forward, intent on ripping the power cells from beneath the droid's dome. No less determined, the droid countered by retreating and rearing up. Falling short of the mark, Anakin curled his body, counting on momentum to carry him forward.

The spider continued to retreat, then dropped back on all fours, traversing its cannon.

Feigning a sidestep, Anakin hurled himself completely under the droid, but still couldn't find cover. He heard the sound of the spider's dome rotating, then the sound of the muzzle of the long cannon hitting the scabrous wall. Realizing that it had entered a section of the tunnel too narrow to allow for a half turn, the droid stamped its legs in frustration, then began to back itself into the wider stretch.

Without a clear plan in mind, Anakin chased it, heard the dome begin to pivot once more, then the sound of a hand blaster set on full automatic.

Ten meters down the corridor, K'sar was on his feet, the heavy weapon held in front of him in a two-handed grip, firing directly into the spider's bulging red photoreceptors and power cells. Confused, the droid tried desperately to spin around, but there wasn't room. Loose rock calved from the walls as the barrel of the cannon struck again and again. All the while, the Bith continued to advance, emptying the blaster's power cell. An elec-

tronic shriek tore from somewhere inside the spider, and
sparks began to geyser from its perforated dome. The
four legs danced in anger for a moment longer, then
stopped, and the tunnel began to fill with smoke. Finally
the droid collapsed, the tip of its cannon slamming into
the floor at K'sar's feet.

Anakin eased around the smoking machine and gently
removed the blaster from the Bith's shaking grip. The
droid's dome pinged as it cooled; a steady susurration escaped the blaster's gas chamber.

"How much farther?" Anakin asked after a moment.

"We're close," K'sar said in a daze. "Half a kilometer
or so past the bend."

"Can you make it?"

K'sar nodded, and they hurried through the final
stretch, emerging from a tunnel opening at the rear of
the docking bay. A hundred meters away the cruiser was
sitting just where the tractor beam had left it. Few
guards were about, and most of them were battle droids.

Anakin took a moment to study the disposition of the
droids, then turned to K'sar, who seemed to have recov-
ered from the ordeal in the tunnel.

"No matter what I do, I want you to head straight for
the boarding ramp. Don't stop running until you're inside the ship, understand?"

K'sar nodded.

Anakin leapt out of the corridor, deliberately calling
attention to himself to distract the droids from firing at
K'sar. Evading blaster bolts with perfectly timed jumps
and rolls, he got close enough to the droids to wave some
of them into others, toppling them as if they had been
picked up by a strong wind. From one, he called a
blaster rifle into his own hands, and mowed down those
that were still on their feet.

Following K'sar up the boarding ramp, he rushed into

the cockpit and began to power up the cruiser's defensive systems. Bolts from the droids' blasters ricocheted from the fuselage and transparisteel panels. Traversing the cruiser's fore and aft cannons, Anakin fired, burying the droids under huge chunks of ferrocrete blown from the walls and ceiling.

When the flight systems were online he left the cockpit to search for K'sar, who was sitting on the floor of the main hold, panting.

"Why aren't you raising the ship?" the Bith said. "Guild corvettes are probably already on the way."

Anakin stepped closer to him, his expression darkening visibly. "You and I need to talk first. And either you answer my questions, or I jettison you here, and let the Gossams do what they will with you."

The Bith's eyes expanded. "Talk? About what?"

"A hyperwave transceiver you designed fourteen years ago."

"Fourteen years ago? I can barely remember last *week*."

Anakin glared at him from beneath an angrily furrowed brow. "Think harder."

"Why are you doing this to me? I just saved your life!"

"Remind me to thank you later. Right now you're going to tell me about the transceiver. It would have been a special order. More than the usual secrecy. You would have been well paid. You installed it in a mechno-chair."

K'sar started. His wrinkled mouth puckered and he stared at Anakin in terror. "Now it all comes together— my arrest and imprisonment, the death sentence! The transceiver . . . that's what brought you here."

"Who placed the order?"

"I suspect you already know the answer."

"How did he contact you?"

"Through my personal comlink. He needed someone

of great skill. Someone willing to follow his every instruction without question. The designs he sent were like nothing I had ever seen. The end result was almost . . . artistic."

"Why did he allow you to live—afterward?"

"I was never sure. I knew I'd been useful. I thought he might require additional devices, but I never heard from him again."

"If you're right about your arrest, that means he *has* been keeping an eye on you. Tell me the rest and we might be able to keep you from his long reach."

"That's everything!"

"You're holding something back," Anakin said in a flat, menacing tone. "I can feel it."

K'sar gulped, and clutched at his neck. "I built two of them!"

"Who received the second one? One of the Separatist leaders?"

Swallowing with difficulty, K'sar said: "It went to Sienar!"

Anakin blinked in surprise. "Raith Sienar?"

"To Sienar Advanced Projects. It was designed for some sort of experimental spacecraft they were building."

"Who was the craft meant for?"

"I don't know—I swear, Jedi, I don't." K'sar paused, then added: "But I knew the pilot Sienar hired to deliver the ship."

"Knew?"

"I don't know if she's still alive. But I know where you could begin to look."

Obi-Wan and Travale negotiated the cofferdam that linked Escarte's air lock to a docking ring just forward of the cruiser's tri-barreled thruster fantail.

Stepping into the main hold, Travale gave a shout of joy.

"Good to be alive!"

Obi-Wan glanced at Thal K'sar, thinking the Bith might feel the same. Instead, K'sar was curled up on the hold's worn acceleration couch. Obi-Wan hurried on to the cockpit and strapped into the copilot's seat.

"Any problems reaching the ship?"

"The usual close calls," Anakin said evasively. "Obviously you were successful at disabling the tractor beam."

"Not a skill I expect to draw on again, but, yes, thanks to Travale."

Anakin glanced at the console, waiting for the cofferdam telltale to go off, then called on the thrusters to move the cruiser away from Escarte. Off to port, Obi-Wan saw two Guild corvettes dead in space.

"And here I was certain we weren't out of this yet."

Anakin shrugged. "Anticlimactic."

Obi-Wan regarded him for a moment. "K'sar seemed rather . . . subdued. Were you able to question him?"

Anakin busied himself with the controls. "Briefly."

"And?"

"We have a new lead." Before Obi-Wan could reply, Anakin said: "Hyperspace coordinates coming in."

Banking widely, the cruiser left Escarte and sluggish light behind.

Coruscant had places one couldn't persuade a droid air taxi driver to take one, even with the promise of a free year of lubrication baths at Industrial Automaton.

The labyrinth of dark back streets south of Corusca Circus.

Daring Way, where it crossed Vos Gesal in upper Uscru.

Hazad's Skytunnel in the Manarai Uplift.

And just about anywhere in the sector known colloquially as "The Works."

Foot mat to the Senate District, with its New Architecture spires and domes, its blade-thin obelisks that resembled oft-used candles dipped in gleaming alloy, The Works had been a booming manufacturing area until escalating costs had driven the production of spacecraft parts, labor droids, and construction materials offworld.

Kilometer after cheerless kilometer of flat-roofed factories and assembly plants; towering cranes and enormous gantries; endless stretches of pitted mag-lev tracks that might have been overgrown with weeds if weeds grew on Coruscant; skyscraping clusters of vacant corporate buildings with rocket-fin buttresses . . . For standard centuries, the sector had been the destination for billions of hardworking immigrants from the Inner Rim and the Colonies, seeking employment and new lives in the Core. Now The Works was a destination for fugitives from Nar Shaddaa who needed a hole to crawl into. A Coruscanti might risk a visit to The Works if he had just been laid off by the Bank of Aargau and was looking for someone to disintegrate his former boss. Or perhaps when death sticks no longer satisfied and a capsule of Crude was in order . . .

It was the gritty, toxic smoke that still belched from the stacks of factories closed for generations that made for the crimson-and-gold splendor of Coruscant's sunsets, gawked at by the affluent habitués of the Senate District's Skysitter Restaurant.

The entire sector might have been demolished if it could be determined with any certainty just who owned what. Rumors persisted that hired assassins and crime syndicates had buried so many bodies in The Works that it should be considered a cemetery.

And yet Dooku loved the place.

The antithesis of his native Serenno, The Works was very much a home away from home for the human who had earned the title *Darth Tyranus*.

One structure in particular—columnar in shape, round-topped, propped by angular ramparts—rising from the defiled core of The Works like a stake driven into its heart. Strong in the dark side—made so by Darth Sidious—the building had been the place of Dooku's apprenticeship, just as it had served as a training ground for Darth Maul before Dooku, and who knew who or how many other Sith disciples before Maul.

During the ten years preceding the outbreak of the

war—when Count Dooku of Serenno was believed to
have been peddling his Separatist agenda to disenfranchised worlds in the Mid and Outer Rims—he had, in
fact, spent long periods of time in The Works, coming
and going at will, or as required of him by Darth Sidious. Even in the three years since, he had been able to
visit Coruscant without fear of detection, thanks in part
to unique countermeasures the Geonosians had engineered into his interstellar sloop.

The modified Punworcca 116 rested on its slight landing gear in the building's vast docking space. With its
needle-tipped bow carapaces and the spherical cockpit
module they gripped, the sloop was typically Geonosian
in design. Its signature sail, however, had been obtained
with Sidious's help from a dealer in pre-Republic antiquities in the Gree Enclave. Furled into the ventral cara-
pace now—seldom used any longer—it had been created
by an ancient spacefaring race that had taken to the
grave the secrets of supralight emission propulsion.

Having ordered the sloop's FA-4 pilot droid to remain
in the ball cockpit, Dooku was walking some of the
stiffness of the long voyage out of his legs. His black
trousers were tucked into black dress boots, and his
black tunic was cinched by a wide belt of costly leather.
Thrown back over his shoulders, the Serenno armor-
weave-lined cape shimmered behind him. He made no
efforts to disguise himself for such trips to Coruscant.
The silver hair, mustache, beard, and flaring eyebrows
that gave him the look of a stage magician were as
meticulously groomed as ever.

Normally measured, Dooku's pace was rushed and
somewhat haphazard—evidence to anyone who knew
him that the Count was troubled. If asked, he might have
admitted as much. Even so, in moments when he could
put aside the reasons for his visit, he surveyed the dock-

ing bay with a certain fondness, recalling the years he had spent under Sidious's tutelage, learning the ways of the Sith, practicing the dark arts, perfecting himself.

Mastering evil, Yoda would have said.

The problem was partly semantic, in that the Jedi Order had seen to it that the dark side of the Force had become equated with evil. But was shade more evil than stark sunlight? Recognizing that the dark side was on the ascendant, the Jedi—in service to the Force—should have known enough to embrace it, to ally themselves with it. After all, it was all a matter of balance, and if the preservation of balance required the dark side to be on top, then so be it.

With Dooku, Sidious hadn't had to waste precious hours on lightsaber technique, nor on ridding Dooku of ill habits born of a lifetime spent in the Jedi Temple, for Dooku had long before rid himself of those. Instead, Sidious had focused on giving Dooku what had amounted to a crash course in tapping into the power of the dark side—a mere taste of which had proved intoxicating. Enough to convince Dooku that no course was left open to him but to abandon the Order; more, that his entire life had been preparation for his apprenticeship to Sidious.

That at long last he had found a true mentor.

The Sith saw no need to take on only young disciples, though they often did. Sometimes the training went smoother with disciples who had lived long enough to grow disillusioned or angry or vengeful. The Jedi, by contrast, were shackled by compassion. Their penchant for showing mercy, for granting forgiveness, for heeding the dictates of conscience, prevented them from giving themselves over to the dark side. From becoming as a force of nature itself, paranormally strong and quick, capable of conjuring Sith lightning, of exteriorizing rage, all without the need for the magic hand passes the Jedi were so fond of employing.

The Sith understood that the elitism and mobsterism of the Republic could be ended only by bringing the diverse beings of the galaxy under the control of a single hand. The galaxy could only be saved from itself by the imposition of order.

What fools the Jedi were not to see it. Blind to their own downfall, the coming of their endtime.

What fools—

The sound of soft footfalls made Dooku turn.

From off to one side of the docking bay a figure approached. Dressed in a hooded cloak of burgundy material, closed at the neck by a distinctive clasp, and so soft and voluminous that it covered everything but the lower portion of the figure's face and his hands. Rarely was that hood lowered, allowing the wearer to walk unnoticed through the byways and plazas of Coruscant's blurred underground, just another recluse or religious initiate arrived in the Core from some world beyond imagining.

Of his youth, Sidious had offered little these past thirteen years; of his Master, Darth Plagueis, even less.

More than once it had occurred to Dooku that Sidious and Yoda had certain qualities in common. Principally, that neither was entirely what he appeared to be—that is, made frail by age, or by the intensity required to master the Sith or Jedi arts.

On Geonosis, Yoda's easy parrying and, indeed, *handling* of the Sith lightning Dooku hurled at him had come as a surprise. Had made him wonder if, on some level during the course of Yoda's eight-hundred-odd years, the Jedi Master hadn't delved into the dark arts, if only as a means of familiarizing himself with his perceived enemy. And on Vjun, only months ago, Yoda himself had admitted as much. *Carry a darkness within me, I do,* he had said. Yoda probably believed that he had defeated Dooku on Geonosis. But in fact, Dooku had only fled the fight to safeguard the plans he had been carrying—the technical readouts to what would one day become the Ultimate Weapon . . .

"Welcome, Darth Tyranus," Sidious said as he drew nearer.

"Lord Sidious," Dooku said, bowing slightly at the waist. "I spared no haste in leaving Kaon."

"And took a great risk you did, my apprentice."

Whether by nature or design, Sidious's words came slowly, sibilantly.

"A calculated risk, my lord."

"Do you fear that the Republic has become so adept at eavesdropping that they can now listen in on our private transmissions?"

"No, my lord. As I told you, the Republic has probably deciphered the code we have been using to communicate with our . . . partners, shall we say. But I am confident that the Intelligence division knew nothing of our plans for dealing with the Bith at Escarte."

"Then my instructions were carried out?"

"They were."

"And still you have come here," Sidious said.

"Some matters are best discussed in real time."

Sidious nodded. "Then let us speak of these things in real time."

They walked in silence to a balcony that overlooked the desolate sprawl of The Works. In the far distance the glassy towers of the Senate District disappeared into clouds. One of Dooku's previous visits had followed the assassination of a faithless Senator by Jedi Knight Quinlan Vos. Duped by Dooku on several occasions, Vos had managed to track Dooku to The Works, though he apparently hadn't perceived just how deeply the dark side had taken root there.

"I suspect that the planned disappearance of Thal K'sar did not go according to plan," Sidious said finally.

"Regretfully, my lord. He *was* taken into custody, but our guild confederates at Escarte failed to act quickly enough. Hours from execution, K'sar was rescued and spirited from the facility by a Republic Intelligence agent, who had the help of two Jedi."

Dooku had been able to count on one hand the number of times he had seen Sidious angry.

Suddenly he needed two hands.

"I would hear more of this, Lord Tyranus," Sidious said with purposeful slowness.

"I have since learned that these same two Jedi recently visited the Xi Char world of Charros Four."

Well ahead of Dooku, Sidious said: "The engraver of the mechno-chair . . . "

"The same."

Sidious pondered it for a moment. "From Viceroy Gunray to the Xi Char engraver to the Bith who implemented my designs for the hyperwave transceiver and holoprojector . . . "

"The Jedi mean to expose you, my lord."

"And what if they should?" Sidious snapped. "Do you think that would bring an end to what I have set in motion?"

"No, my lord. But this is unexpected."

Sidious eyed Dooku from beneath the hood of his cloak. "Yes. Yes, it is, as you say, unexpected." He returned his gaze to the far-off towers. "Someday I may choose to reveal myself to the galaxy, but not now. This war must be made to continue a while longer. There are worlds and persons we still need to convert to our side."

"I understand."

"Tell me, who is conducting this . . . search?"

Dooku exhaled with purpose. "Skywalker and Kenobi."

Sidious took a long moment to respond. "The so-called Chosen One, and a Jedi with enough good fortune to almost make one believe in luck." Without turning from the view, he added: "I am displeased by this turn of events, Lord Tyranus. Greatly displeased."

Once Master and Padawan, Kenobi and Skywalker had become the scourge of Dooku's existence. On Geonosis he had deliberately allowed them to pursue him—just as Sidious had instructed him to do. Also as instructed, Dooku had made Kenobi aware of the existence of Darth Sidious, as a means of confusing the Jedi Order by telling them the truth. In the sloop's docking bay he had demonstrated his mastery to Kenobi and Skywalker—although Skywalker hadn't been as easily defeated the second time they had dueled. Enraged, the young Jedi had proved a powerful opponent, and Dooku suspected that he had grown only more powerful since Geonosis.

Long have I watched young Skywalker, Sidious had once admitted.

And all the more so of late.

"My lord, the Jedi may search for others who contributed to fashioning the communications devices you distributed to Gunray, myself, and others. Also, there is the matter of Grievous's defeat at Belderone."

Sidious made a gesture accepting that defeat. "Do not trouble yourself about Belderone. It may suit our ultimate purpose to have the Republic believe that they have chased us from their precious Core. As regards your concern for keeping secret my whereabouts, I am moved. But here, too, I begin to see a way to engineer events in our favor." He paused to consider something, then said: "Yes, I begin to see the blazes along the trail Skywalker and Kenobi will follow."

Sidious turned to Dooku, grinning malevolently. "Their single-mindedness will deliver them into our hands, Lord Tyranus. We will set our trap for them on Naos Three."

Dooku allowed his skepticism to show. "As remote a world as can be found in known space, my lord."

"Nevertheless, Kenobi and young Skywalker will find their way to it."

Dooku decided to take it on faith. "What would you have me do?"

"Nothing more than make arrangements—for you are needed elsewhere. Employ outsiders."

Dooku nodded. "It is done."

"One small addendum. See to it that Obi-Wan Kenobi ceases to be an irritant." Sidious sneered the name.

"He represents so forceful a threat to our plans?"

Sidious shook his head. "But Skywalker does. And Kenobi . . . Kenobi has been as a father to him. Orphan Skywalker once and for all, and he will shift."

"Shift?"

"To the dark side."

"An apprentice?"

Sidious gazed at him. "In good time, Lord Tyranus. All in good time."

Having suffered through all four hours of Palpatine's State of the Republic address to the Senate, interrupted dozens of times by standing ovations—an archaic tradition not practiced since the era of Supreme Chancellor Valorum Eixes—Bail Organa watched from the backseat of the air taxi as a trio of assault cruisers lifted off into Coruscant's flame-orange sky, casting their wedge-shaped shadows on the spired roof of the Jedi Temple.

Bail's destination.

He instructed the droid pilot to set the taxi down on the Temple's northeast landing platform, where two Jedi younglings were waiting for him. The opulence of the Temple's wide corridors was lost on him as he followed his escort to the room the Order used for public meetings, rather than the circular chamber reserved for private conclaves in the summit of the High Council spire.

A holorecording of Palpatine's speech was running in the center of the room when Bail was admitted. Around the holoprojector table sat Council members Yoda, Mace

Windu, Saesee Tiin, Ki-Adi-Mundi, Shaak Ti, Stass Allie, Plo Koon, and Kit Fisto.

"And so it is with a heavy heart that I commit two
hundred thousand additional troopers to the Outer Rim
sieges," the holoimage of the Supreme Chancellor was
saying, "though in full confidence that the end of this
brutal conflict is now in sight. Cast from the Core, ex-
pelled from the Inner Rim and Colonies, driven from the
Mid Rim, and soon to be exiled in the spiral arms, the
Confederacy will pay a dear price for what they have
brought down on our fair house."

He paused for applause, which went on for far too long.

Droid cams buzzed around the Great Rotunda to high-
light the more well-known of the Palpatine-friendly fac-
tions then, coming full circle, closed on Palpatine's
thirty-meter-tall podium to linger on the two dozen human naval officers who were standing just below the
summit, clapping enthusiastically.

"A show of force, this is," Yoda remarked.

Dressed in robes of magenta and forest green, Palpatine continued.

"Some of you may question why my heart is heavy
when my tidings bring news of such long-awaited re-
dress. The decision weighs on me because I would
sooner say: *Enough is enough, let the Confederacy—the
Separatists—wither and die on their own in the Outer
Rim. Let us keep our best and brightest home; let us refrain from bringing bloodshed to any more worlds,
harm to our noble soldiers, our trusted Jedi Knights.*"

Yoda harrumphed.

"Sadly, though, I cannot decide with my heart alone.
Because we cannot allow the enemies of democracy to
rest and recuperate. Like a life-threatening growth
taken hold in the body, they must be excised. As a con-
tagious disease, they must be eradicated. If not, our chil-

dren's generation and generations to come will live under the threat that those who brought chaos to the
galaxy will find the strength to regroup and attack
anew."

"Applause break," Bail said—because he had been
there.

The Jedi Masters stirred in their high-backed chairs
but said nothing.

"Lest my statements convey an impression that the
hardest decisions are behind us, let me hasten to add that
much work remains to be done. So much rebuilding; so
much reordering . . . To you, all of you, will I look for
guidance in determining which worlds we should welcome back into the Republic's embrace, and which, if
any, should be kept at arm's length, or shunned for the
injuries they have heaped upon us. Similarly will I look
to you for guidance in reshaping our Constitution to
conform to the needs of the new epoch."

"What does he mean by that?" Mace Windu inter-
jected.

"Finally will I look to you, all of you, to author a new
spirit in Coruscant, in the Core, throughout the star systems where the light of democracy continues to shine, so
that we can look forward to another thousand years of
peace, and another thousand beyond that, and so on, until war itself is stamped from our just domain."

"Had enough?" Stass Allie asked while the Senate
broke into extended applause. Tall, slender, and dark-
complected, she wore a Tholoth headdress similar in design to that worn by her immediate predecessor on the
Council, Adi Gallia. When no one objected, she deactivated the holoprojector.

Turning to Bail, Yoda said, "Appreciate your visit, we
do, Senator Organa."

"I just wanted all of you to know that, despite what

the HoloNet news might lead you to believe, not all of us were on our feet."

"Aware of this, we are."

Bail gestured broadly to the room's triangular windows and shook his head in dismay. "Coruscant is already in a celebratory mood. You can practically taste it in the air."

"Premature, any celebration is," Yoda said ruefully.

Mace leaned forward in his chair. "What can Palpatine be thinking—committing half of Coruscant's home force to the Outer Rim sieges?"

"Emboldened Palpatine is, by what we achieved at Belderone."

"The Supreme Chancellor singles out Mygeeto, Saleucami, and Felucia," Plo Koon said from beneath the mask that supplied him with life gases.

Ki-Adi-Mundi's elongated head made a subtle nod. "A 'triad of evil,' he labeled them."

"Separatist bastions, they are," Yoda said. "But so remote, so insignificant."

"A danger to the body of the Republic," Bail said.

Mace ridiculed the idea. "When the body is damaged, it prioritizes. It doesn't rally its defenses to deal with a pinprick when the chest has been holed by a blaster bolt."

Bail glanced around the room. "Some of us are concerned that the Supreme Chancellor has been persuaded to press these sieges as a means of acquiring worlds by force. There are bills before the Senate now that could grant him the authority to overrule local system governments."

Yoda compressed his lips in indignation. "A labyrinth of evil, this war has become. But protect ourselves, we must. Safeguard the traditions the Jedi have upheld for one thousand generations."

Mace ran a hand over his shaven head. "We can only hope that Obi-Wan and Anakin find their way to the source of this war before it's too late."

With a slurping sound, Anakin's right leg sank almost to the knee in the muck that passed for Naos III's main street. An equally onomatopoeic sound accompanied Anakin's reclaiming of the leg, and expletives flew from his lips as he hopped off on his left foot toward solid ground. Crossing his right leg over his left while standing, he tried to shake some of the filth from his boot, then pointed to a pinkish strand that refused to let go.

"What is that?" he asked in alarmed disgust, with breath clouds punctuating his every word.

Reluctantly, Obi-Wan leaned in to peer at the slick boot, not wanting to get too close.

"It could be something alive, or something that was once alive, or something that came from something alive."

"Well, whatever it is, it's going to have to catch a ride on someone else."

Obi-Wan straightened and shoved his hands deeper into the sleeves of his robe. "I warned you there are worse places than Tatooine."

Lining both sides of the puddled street were low-slung prefab buildings, their alloy roofs capped with crystalline snow and bearded with thick icicles. Pieces of a collapsed skyway had been moved to one side of the street, left to marinate in a puddle much like the one Anakin had inadvertently waded into, and fashioned by areas of radiant heating that still functioned beneath the mostly ruined ceramacrete paving.

Anakin began stomping his boot on the solid ice. Ultimately the clingy, unidentifiable pink thing decided that it had had enough and flew off into a snowdrift.

"Worse places than Tatooine," he mumbled. "And, what, you feel we need to visit every last one of them? When are we going to be allowed to return to Coruscant?"

"Blame Thal K'sar. He was the one who suggested we should start here."

Anakin gazed around. "I just can't help thinking the next place will be worse."

They both fell silent for a moment, then said in unison: "Almost makes me nostalgic for Escarte."

Anakin winced. "You know it's time to end the partnership when that happens. In fact, I could see you and Yoda teaming up. You share the same fondness for caution and lectures."

"Yes, we're two of a kind, old Yoda and me."

They continued their slog toward what seemed to be the heart of the place.

For most of its short year the moon known as Naos III was a frigid little orb with days that never seemed to end. Indigenous herbivores and carnivores had been hunted to extinction early on by colonists from Rodia and Ryloth, lured by the hope of discovering rich veins of ryll spice in Naos III's volcanically heated cave systems. The creatures one saw most often now were bovine rycrits and woollier-than-normal banthas.

The moon's continued habitation owed to a pink-fleshed delicacy fished from the ice-covered rivers that plunged turbulent and roaring from a surround of nearly sheer mountains. Known as the Naos sharptooth, the fish spawned only in the coldest months, was shipped offworld, flash-frozen, and sold at exorbitant prices in eateries from Mon Calamari to Corellia. Still, few locals banked enough credits to buy passage off Naos III, preferring instead to return their meager earnings to Naos III Mercantile, which oversaw the sharptooth industry and owned nearly every store, hotel, gambling parlor, and cantina.

The dispirited humanoids who had colonized the moon had never bothered to award a name to their principal population center, so it, too, was known as Naos III. Visitors expecting to find a typical spaceport found instead a cluster of fortified hilltops, interconnected by bridges that spanned a delta of waterways. As befitted a place with such a dearth of creativity, the moon had attracted nomads and spacers of dubious character, eager either to lose or reinvent themselves. While Rodians and Lethan Twi'leks comprised the majority, humans and other humanoids were well represented. A few wealthy sportfishers arrived each year, but Naos III was simply too remote and too lacking in infrastructure to support a tourist trade.

Despite the fact that the moon seemed a perfect place for a red-complected Twi'lek to hide, Obi-Wan doubted that Fa'ale Leh would be found here. To begin with, she would have certainly changed her name by now, possibly even the color of her complexion. More important, Naos III didn't offer much in the way of job opportunities for a former spicerunner—unless Leh was one of the death-defying few who piloted loads of flash-frozen sharptooths to the Tion or Coreward on the Perlemian.

According to K'sar, Leh had been in the business of transporting shipments of spice from Ryloth to worlds in Hutt space when Sienar had hired her to deliver the experimental spacecraft for which K'sar had constructed a transceiver identical to the one he had affixed to Gunray's mechno-chair.

To Obi-Wan's mind the ship in question could only be the modified star courier that had belonged to the Sith he had killed on Naboo, and had been confiscated by the Republic after the battle there. Flight, weapons, and communications systems had self-destructed when Republic Intelligence agents had bungled an attempt to enter the courier, but, unknown to many, its burned-out carcass still sat in a clandestine docking bay in Theed. It had long been assumed that the tattooed Zabrak Sith had performed the modifications, but information supplied by K'sar suggested that Raith Sienar's Advanced Projects Laboratory had been responsible not only for building the ship, but also for implementing Darth Sidious's designs.

Obi-Wan and Anakin might have gone directly to the source—to Raith Sienar—had Supreme Chancellor Palpatine not vetoed the idea.

The Republic's other major supplier of weapons, Kuat Drive Yards, was known to have contributed to both sides during the war. Under its subsidiary, Rothana Heavy Engineering—the builders of the *Acclamator*-class assault ships, as well as the AT-TE walkers—KDY had also supplied the Confederacy with the Storm Fleet, which had been "the Terror of the Perlemian" until retired from service with the help of Obi-Wan and Anakin.

With snow falling harder in Naos III, the two

STAR WARS: LABYRINTH OF EVIL   191

stopped to get their bearings. Obi-Wan gestured to a nearby cantina. "This has to be the fifteenth we've passed."

"On this street," Anakin said. "If we stop for a drink in each one, we'll be drunk before we reach the bridge."

"With any luck. Still, they're likely to be our best source of information."

"As opposed to just looking up her name in the local comm directory."

"And a lot more fun."

Anakin grinned. "Fine with me. Where do you want to start?"

Completing a circle, Obi-Wan pointed to a cantina diagonally across from them. The Desperate Pilot.

Four hours later, half drunk and near frozen, they entered the final cantina before the bridge. Brushing snow from the shoulders of their cloaks and lowering the hoods, they scanned the patrons crowding the bar and occupying nearly every table.

"Not a lot to do in Naos Three when you're not fishing," Anakin said.

"I've the distinct impression that some drinking goes on even during work hours."

Replacing two Rodians who stumbled away from the curved bar, they ordered drinks.

Anakin sipped from his glass. "Ten cantinas, as many Lethan females, and every one of them claims to have been born onworld. I'd say we're in for a long stay."

"K'sar didn't supply you with anything else to go on—scars, tattooed lekku, anything?"

Anakin shook his head. "Nothing." When Obi-Wan signaled for the human bartender, he added: "You order one more Twi'lek appetizer, I promise I'm going to cut your arm off."

Obi-Wan laughed. "I found the izzy-mold at the last place to be very flavorful."

Anakin took another sip. "And speaking of arms."

"Were we?"

"We were. At least I think we were. Anyway, remember in the Outlander Club when you went off to get a drink? Did you have an inkling that Zam Wessel would follow you?"

"On the contrary. I knew she would follow you."

"Implying that shapeshifters have a special fondness for me?"

"The way you were strutting around, what female could help herself?" Mimicking Anakin's voice, Obi-Wan said: " 'Jedi business.' "

"Then you admit it—you were using me as bait."

"A privilege that comes with being a Master. You have more than repaid me in kind, in any case."

Anakin raised his glass. "A toast to that."

Seeing the bartender approach, Obi-Wan placed a sizable credit chip under his empty glass and slid it forward. "Another drink. And the rest is for you."

An athletic man with red hair that fell almost to his waist, the bartender eyed the credit chip. "Rather large remuneration for such a rudimentary libation. Perhaps you'd permit me to concoct something a trifle more flavorsome."

"What I'd actually prefer is a bit of information."

"Now, how did I guess."

"We're looking for a Lethan female," Anakin said.

"Who isn't."

Obi-Wan shook his head. "Strictly business."

"That's what it often is with them. I suggest you try the Palace Hotel."

"You don't understand."

"Oh, I think I do."

"Look," Anakin said, "this one probably isn't a . . . masseuse."

"Or a dancer," Obi-Wan thought to add.

"Then what would she be doing on Naos Three?"

"She used to be a pilot—with a taste for spice."

Obi-Wan watched the bartender closely. "She would have arrived on Naos Three within the past ten or so years."

The bartender's eyes narrowed. "Why didn't you say so to begin with? You mean Genne."

"The name we know her by is Fa'ale Leh."

"My friends, on Naos Three a name is nothing more than a convenient handle."

"But you do know her," Obi-Wan said.

"I do."

"Then you know where she can be found."

The bartender jerked a thumb. "Upstairs. Room seven. She said you should go right up."

Anakin and Obi-Wan traded confused glances.

"She's expecting us?" Obi-Wan said.

The bartender heaved his massive shoulders in a shrug. "She didn't say who she was expecting. Just that if anyone came looking for her, I should send them up."

They canceled the drink order and walked to the foot of a long flight of stairs.

"Jedi mind trick?" Anakin asked.

"If it was, I wasn't aware of performing it."

"Ten drinks will do that to you."

"Yes, and maybe it was the Twi'lek izzy-mold. What seems infinitely more likely is that we're about to walk into a trap."

"So we should be on guard."

"Yes, Anakin, we should be on guard."

Obi-Wan led the way up the stairs and rapped his hand on room seven's green plastoid door.

"Door's unlocked," a voice said in Basic from within.

They made certain that their lightsabers were in easy reach, but left them affixed to their belts and concealed. Obi-Wan hit the door-release stud, then followed Anakin into the chill room.

Wearing trousers, boots, and an insulated jacket, Genne—perhaps Fa'ale Leh—was lounging on a narrow bed, her back and lekku against the headboard, long legs extended and crossed at the ankle. Beside her on a small table stood a half-full bottle of what Obi-Wan guessed was the local rocket-fuel homebrew.

Reaching for two clearly unwashed glasses, she said: "Fix you a drink?"

"We're already at the legal limit," Anakin said, vigilant.

The remark made her smile. "Naos Three doesn't have a legal limit, kid." She took a healthy swallow from her own glass, eyeing them over the rim. "I have to say, you're not what I expected."

"Was that surprise or disappointment?" Anakin asked Obi-Wan.

"Who were you expecting?" Obi-Wan said.

"Your classic rough-and-tumble types. Black Sun lackeys, bounty hunters. You two . . . You look more like lost Jedi." She paused, then said: "Maybe that's exactly what you are. Jedi have been known to outpunish even the punishers."

"Only when necessary," Anakin said.

She shrugged absently. "You want to do it here, or are you going to buy me a last meal?"

"Do what here?" Obi-Wan said.

"Kill me, of course."

Anakin took a forward step. "There's always that possibility."

She glanced from him to Obi-Wan. "Bad Jedi. Good Jedi."

"We want to talk to you about a star courier you piloted for Sienar Advanced Projects."

She nodded at Obi-Wan. "Of course you do. A round of questions and answers, then a blaster—no, a lightsaber to the side of the head."

"Then you are Fa'ale Leh."

"Who told you where to find me? Had to be Thal K'sar, am I right? He's the only one still alive. That betraying little Bith—"

"Tell us about the courier," Anakin said, cutting her off.

She smiled in apparent recollection. "An extraordinary ship—a work of genius. But I knew going in, it was a job that would come back to haunt me. And so it has."

Obi-Wan looked around the room. "You've been in hiding here for more than ten years."

"No, I came for the beaches." She motioned in dismissal. "You know, they killed the engineers, the mechanics, just about everyone who worked on that craft. But I knew. I made the delivery, grabbed what was due me, and I was away. Not far enough, though. They tracked me to Ryloth, Nar Shaddaa, half the starforsaken worlds in the Tingel Arm. I had my share of close calls. I could show you the scars."

"No need," Obi-Wan said as Fa'ale was bringing her left head-tail over her shoulder.

She threw back another drink. "So who sent you—Sienar? Or was it the one the courier was built for?"

"Who *was* it built for?" Anakin said.

She regarded him for a moment. "That's the funny thing. Sienar—Raith Sienar himself—told me it was for a Jedi. But the guy I handed the yoke over to—he was no Jedi. Oh, he had a lightsaber and all, but . . . I don't know, there was something off about him."

Obi-Wan nodded. "We've had dealings with him."

"Where did you deliver it?" Anakin pressed.

"Well, to Coruscant, of course."

Obi-Wan glanced at the ceiling.

An instant before it blew inward—raining plastoid rafters, ice-covered roof panels, ceiling tiles, and two heavily armed Trandoshans—he had rushed to the bed and overturned it, dumping Fa'ale Leh, foam mattresses, and bedcovers onto the cold floor.

In hand and activated, Anakin's lightsaber was already a streak of blue light, deflecting blaster bolts and parrying swings of a vibro-ax in the meaty hands of a red-skinned Falleen who had burst through the door. Behind the Falleen came two humans who, in their eagerness to race into the room, had wedged themselves in the door frame.

Whirling, Obi-Wan called his lightsaber from his belt and leapt to the doorway, his blade slicing both hands off one of the humans. An agonized howl pierced the frigid air as the man sank to his knees. Unstuck, the second one fell forward, directly onto Obi-Wan's blade. The smell of burned flesh filled the room, swirling about with smoke from the explosive that had taken out three square meters of roof, and big wet snowflakes that were drifting though the opening.

Off to Obi-Wan's left Anakin stood unmoving in the center of the room, holding his own against the two reptilian aliens and the wielder of the vibro-ax. Parried bolts flew directly through the thin walls, rousing shrieks from Fa'ale's neighbors to both sides. Doors opened and slammed, and footfalls pounded on the hallway floor.

Pivoting on his left foot, the Falleen swung the vibro-ax at Obi-Wan's head. Ducking the swing, Obi-Wan got underneath the blade and just managed to nick the Falleen in the left thigh.

The strike only fueled the humanoid's rage. Raising the ax over his head, he rushed forward, intent on splitting Obi-Wan down the middle. A backflip carried Obi-Wan out of the blade's path, but Fa'ale's bedside table wasn't as fortunate. Cleaved, each half table fell to the floor, launching the Twi'lek's bottle of firewater clear across the room and square into the face of the larger of the two Trandoshans. Screaming in anger, the alien raised a clawed hand to his bleeding brow ridge, even while his other hand continued to trigger bolts at Anakin. As the bolts began to go wide, Anakin raised his left hand, pushing it through the air in the Trandoshan's direction and blowing him backward through the room's only window.

Determined to make the most of Anakin's split attention, the reptiloid's partner risked a lunge forward.

Obi-Wan tracked the flight of the alien's head across the room, out the door, and into the hallway, where someone loosed a bloodcurdling screech. The Falleen, finding himself on his own with the two Jedi, extended the ax in front of him and began to whirl.

Anakin backed away from the circling blade, then dived forward, sliding across the wet floor on his belly with his lightsaber held out in front of him and amputating the Falleen's legs at the knees. Shorter by half a meter but no less enraged, the humanoid sent the vibro-ax flying straight for Obi-Wan, then drew from his hip holster a large blaster and began firing.

In midflight from the vibrating blade, Obi-Wan watched Anakin rid the Falleen of blaster and hand, and thrust his lightsaber directly into the Falleen's chest.

Whatever torso armor the humanoid was wearing beneath his jacket gave the energy blade pause, but heat from the lightsaber set fire to the Falleen's bandolier of explosive rounds.

Backing away from the lightsaber on the cauterized stumps of his legs, the Falleen began swatting at the growing flames in mounting panic, then turned and executed a perfect front dive out the window—only to explode short of the snowdrift that might have been his destination.

The room fell suddenly silent, except for the sizzle of huge snowflakes hitting the lightsabers.

Obi-Wan shouted: "Get her out of here!"

Deactivating his blade, Anakin pulled Fa'ale out from under the mattresses and bedding, and yanked her to her feet.

Wobbling drunkenly, she took in the ruined room.

"You two seem like decent folk—even for Jedi. Sorry you have to get mixed up in this."

Catching sight of a bottle that had somehow survived the violence, she started for it. When Anakin tightened his hold on her, she balled her hands and hammered at his chest and upper arms.

"Stop trying to be a hero, kid! I'm tired of running. It's over—for all of us."

"Not till we say it is," Anakin said.

She sagged in his grip. "That's the problem. That's why we're in a war to begin with."

Anakin began to drag her toward the door.

"Right on time," Obi-Wan said from the window. "Six more that I can see." A blaster bolt destroyed what was left of the window frame.

Anakin hauled Fa'ale to her feet once more and planted himself face-to-face with her. "You've outwitted assassins for ten years. You have a way out of here." He shook her forcefully. "Where?"

She remained still for a moment, then shut her eyes and nodded.

Obi-Wan and Anakin followed her out the door to a utility closet at the end of the hall. Concealed behind a false rear wall, two shiny poles dropped into darkness. Fa'ale took hold of one of the poles and vanished from sight. Anakin went next. Through the closed door, Obi-Wan could hear a crowd of beings race past the closet, heading for the Twi'lek's room. Gripping the pole with hands and feet, he let gravity take over.

The descent was longer than expected. Instead of ending up in the basement of the cantina, the poles ran completely through the hill on which that portion of Naos III had been built, all the way to the river itself. The bottom of the poles disappeared into thick ice. In dim natural light Obi-Wan saw that he was in a cavern that had become an inlet for the river. Close to the base of the poles sat three surface-effect sleds of the sort the locals used for ice fishing, outfitted with powerful-looking engines and pairs of long skis.

"I'm too drunk to drive," Fa'ale was saying.

Anakin had already straddled the machine's narrow seat, and was studying the controls. "You leave that to me," he told her. With the flip of a switch, the speeder's engine coughed to life, then began to purr loudly in the hollow of the cave.

Obi-Wan mounted a second sled, while Fa'ale was positioning herself behind Anakin.

"That one, then that one," Anakin said, pointing out the ignition switch and the warmer. Demonstrating, he added: "Thrusters, pitch control, steer like this."

Obi-Wan was instantly confused.

"Like this?"

"Like this, like this!" Anakin emphasized, demon-strating again, then indicating another set of switches on the control panel of Obi-Wan's machine. "Repulsorlift. But strictly for handling small ice mounds, frozen debris, that sort of thing. This isn't a conventional speeder—or even a swoop."

"Do you remember where we parked the cruiser?"

"I don't even remember landing. But the field can't be far off."

"Downriver," Fa'ale said. "Swing south around the hillock, go under the bridge, then west around the next hillock. Under two more bridges, slalom south again, and we're there."

Obi-Wan stared at her. "I'll follow you two."

They roared from the mouth of the cavern and out onto the glacial river.

Blaster bolts began to sear into the ice around them before they made the first bridge. Glancing over his shoulder, Obi-Wan saw three sleds gaining on them from upriver.

On the bridge, two beings bundled up in cold-weather gear were drawing a bead on him with a pintle-mounted repeating blaster.

The star that warmed Naos III was a white blur, low on the horizon. Ominous clouds obscured the mountains to Obi-Wan's right.

Snow was falling harder.

Tearing into it as fast as the sled would carry him, he felt as if he had run smack into a blizzard. The lovely, crystalline flakes would have been like pellets against his face and hands if not for the Force. Even so, he could barely see, and the ice—gray, white, and sometimes blue—was nowhere near as smooth as he had thought it would be. Pebbly where surface water had thawed and refrozen countless times; mounded up over debris trapped during the freeze; pocked by fishing holes; heaped high with ice that had filled the holes . . .

Matters weren't helped any by the fact that he was being shot at.

Bolts from the repeating blaster on the bridge had him weaving all over the river, slaloming around ice dams and leaping small mounds. The repulsorlift would have allowed him to fly over the obstacles—as Anakin was doing, farther downriver—but Obi-Wan just couldn't get the hang of it. More to the point, engaging the repulsorlift required using two hands, and just now he had none to spare. His left was gripped on the control bar/throttle; his right, tight on the hilt of his ignited lightsaber, as he fended off bolts from above and behind.

For a moment he was back on Muunilinst, jousting with Durge's speeder-freak lancer droids.

Except for the snow.

A vacillating roar in his right ear told him that one of the pursuit sleds had caught up with him. Out of the corner of his streaming eye, Obi-Wan saw the sled's human pilot bend low over the control bars to provide his Rodian rider with the clearance he needed to send a blaster bolt through Obi-Wan's head. Braking, Obi-Wan allowed the sled to come alongside more quickly than the Rodian had planned. The rider's first shot raced past Obi-Wan's eyes; the second, he deflected slightly downward, straight into the sled's engine.

The machine exploded instantly, flinging pilot and rider head over heels in opposite directions.

Quickly, however, a second sled was catching up.

This one carried a pilot only, but a more skillful one. Twisting the throttle, the pilot drove his sled into Obi-Wan's, trying to send it spinning out of control or, better still, into the trunk of a massive tree that was protruding acutely from the thick ice. Narrowly missing the latter, Obi-Wan went into a sideways skid. Overcorrecting, he added spin to his slide and couldn't resume his course until the sled had whipped through half a dozen counter rotations. By then his crash-helmeted pursuer was well positioned to ram him a second time, but Obi-Wan was ready for him. Turning sharply, he steered into the pursuit sled, hanging on through the jarring collision, then directing a Force push at the rebounding pilot.

The sled shot forward as if supercharged, with the pilot all but dangling from the control bars. Speeding up the face of a hummock, the craft went airborne, then ballistic, plummeting into a thinly iced-over fishing hole at an angle that took machine and rider both deep under solid ice.

Water geysered into the air, drenching Obi-Wan as he raced past. The third sled was still clinging to his tail, and blaster bolts were whizzing past his ears. Up ahead, he saw Anakin and Fa'ale lean their sled through a sweeping turn to the south, between two of Naos III's many hills. Lethal hyphens of light streaked down from the bridge that linked the hills, but not one found Anakin or Fa'ale.

Unable to replicate Anakin's deft turns, Obi-Wan was falling farther behind with each quarter kilometer, and was now making himself an easy target for the assassins on the bridge. With no hope of negotiating the hail of fire, he maneuvered the sled through a long turn away from the span. But no sooner did he emerge from his half circle than he found himself on a collision course with the last of the pursuit sleds.

The inevitability of a head-on crash left him no choice but to abandon his machine for what was going to be a very long slide on the ice. But just short of his leap, a bolt in the jagged line the bridge gunners were stitching along the river caught the pilot of the onrushing machine in the chest, hurling him into the air. Twisting the throttle, Obi-Wan swerved around the pilotless sled and continued to race upriver, out of range of the blasters.

To his right a clamor built over the hill, and the shadow of something large and swift fell over him. A repeating blaster clacked repeatedly, fracturing the ice directly in his path and opening a wide, surging breach of agitated water.

Uncertain he could leap the gap even if he wanted to try, Obi-Wan applied the brakes—hard!

The sled was ten meters from the ice-chunked fissure when a metal claw dropped over him, snapping shut and plucking him from the seat. Wrenched from his hand, his lightsaber flew onto the ice, and the sled sailed off into the frothing water.

"Stars' end," Obi-Wan muttered.

Suspended on a swaying cable, the claw began to ascend toward the open belly of a graceless snow skiff.

Red hands clamped around Anakin's waist, Fa'ale whooped and shouted, clearly enjoying herself. Even through the daze of too many drinks—or more likely because of them.

"You missed your calling, Jedi," she shouted into his right ear. "You could have been a champion Podracer!"

"Been there, done that," Anakin said over his shoulder.

It was then that he caught sight of Obi-Wan being lifted from his sled. Bringing brakes and thrusters to bear, Anakin powered the sled through a fast 180 and shot back upriver, under the bridge they had just left behind, dodging the unrelenting fire of hand blasters.

"Sharptooth collector," Fa'ale explained when she saw the snow skiff. "Gathers catch, so the fishers won't have to ferry their loads into the city. That's what I do here— my job, such as it is."

The claw that had Obi-Wan in its grip was halfway to the skiff.

"I don't see any way of reaching him in time," Fa'ale said.

"Get ready to take the control bars!" Anakin said.

Fa'ale's hands clutched his robe. "Where are you planning to go?"

"Up."

Pouring on all speed, Anakin steered the sled up the side of the hill that supported one half of the bridge. At the zenith of the climb, he engaged the repulsorlift. Then, leaping from the now rocketing sled, he called on the Force to propel himself toward the swaying cage.

The pilots of the skiff saw him coming, and banked hard to starboard, but not soon enough to prevent Anakin from latching onto the claw. A Rodian in the copilot's chair cracked open the door and began firing down at his moving target.

"I had a feeling you'd show up," Obi-Wan said from inside the claw.

A lucky shot from above hit the cage and ricocheted.

"Hang on, Master! This isn't going to be pretty."

Obi-Wan heard the *snap-hiss* of Anakin's lightsaber. Peering through the metal fingers of the claw, he saw what was coming.

"Anakin, wait—"

But there was no stopping him.

As the claw came within reach of the cargo hold, Anakin swung his lightsaber and sliced open the floor of the skiff's cockpit. Sparks and smoke poured from the rend, and almost immediately the craft slued to starboard. Passing within a meter of one of the bridge towers, it began to twirl toward the hillside.

An instant before the crash, Anakin severed the claw cable, and the cage plummeted, striking the slippery ground and racing down to the frozen river, out onto the ice, spinning crazily, with Obi-Wan bouncing around inside and Anakin Force-fastened to the outside through all the unpredictable pitches and tumbles. The skiff crashed into the hillside. By the time the claw came to a rest on the far side of the river, the two Jedi were so covered in snow they looked like wampas.

Anakin's lightsaber made short work of the fingers of

the claw. Obi-Wan scrambled out, spitting snow, and shaking like a hound.

"Where's Fa'ale?"

Anakin scanned the hillsides. The assassins on the bridge had packed up and fled. Ultimately, he pointed toward the opposite bank of the river, where a sled was wedged between two mounds of ice.

When they reached her, Fa'ale was laying facedown a few meters from the machine, which had been holed by blasterfire. Gently turning her over, Anakin saw that one bolt had amputated the Twi'lek's right lekku. Her eyes blinked open, focusing on him as he cradled her in his arms.

"Don't tell me," she said weakly. "I'm going to live, right?"

"Sorry to be the bearer of bad news."

"A week in bacta and you'll be good as new," Obi-Wan said.

Fa'ale sighed. "I won't hold it against you. You did your best to get me killed." She gazed around. "Shouldn't we be looking for cover?"

"They're gone," Anakin said.

Fa'ale shook her head. "After all these years, they finally—"

"I don't think so," Obi-Wan interrupted. "Someone more important than Raith Sienar doesn't want us to learn too much about the star courier."

"Then I had better tell you the rest—about Coruscant, I mean."

Anakin raised her up. "Where did you deliver the ship?"

"To an old building in the industrial quarter, west of the Senate. An area called The Works."

Macrobinoculars pressed to his eyes, Mace studied the distant building top to bottom, his gaze lingering on broken windows, fissured ledges, canted balconies.

Central to a complex of half a dozen structures, the building was more than three centuries old and going to ruin. For two-thirds of its towering height it was an unadorned pillar with a rounded summit. Support for the superstructure was afforded by a circular base, reinforced by massive fins. Where the superstructure and the sloped tops of the buttresses met, the building was fenestrated by windows and antiquated gear-toothed docking gates. Many of the permaglass panels and skylights were intact, but time and corrosion had done their worst to the vertical hatches of the docking gates.

An investigation was under way to determine who had raised the building, and who owned it—although, judging by its location and prominence in The Works, it appeared to have served as corporate headquarters for the factories and assembly plants that surrounded it.

Mace and his team of Jedi, clone commandos, and Intelligence analysts were a kilometer east of the structure, in an area of squat, peak-roofed foundries, lorded over by smoke-belching permacrete stacks. A more dispiriting place this side of Eriadu or Korriban would have been hard to find, Mace told himself. Five hours spent here could take five years off someone's life. He could feel the damage with every breath he took, every grimy surface he touched, every vagrant-poisoned whiff that wafted his way. The acids in the air were fast digesting everything, but not quickly enough for some. Ambitious developers and urban renewalists had deliberately introduced stone mites, duracrete slugs, and conduit worms to aid and abet the caustic rain, without heed for the risk such vermin posed to the nearby skyscrapers of the Senate District.

All in all, the perfect environment for a Sith Lord.

"Probe remotes are away, General Windu," the ARC reported.

Mace trained the macrobinoculars on the flock of meter-wide spherical droids that were maneuvering with purposeful unevenness toward the building.

The Senate Intelligence Oversight Committee had attempted to interdict the use of commandos and probe droids. In the minds of the committee members, the idea that a Separatist stronghold could exist on Coruscant was absurd. Fortunately—and admittedly unexpectedly—Supreme Chancellor Palpatine had overruled the committee, and Mace had been allowed to compile a dream team that included not only ARC commander Valiant and Captain Dyne of Republic Intelligence, but also Jedi Master Shaak Ti and several capable Padawans.

"No indications that the probes are being targeted," the ARC updated.

Mace watched the black spheres begin to drift through shattered windows and into areas of the superstructure where the building's façade had disintegrated and the bones of its plasteel skeleton were exposed.

Moment of truth, he thought.

The Lethan pilot Obi-Wan and Anakin had searched out on Naos III hadn't been able to furnish anything more than a portrait of the building to which she had delivered the star courier. A product of Sienar Advanced Projects Laboratory, the craft had been modified—perhaps unwittingly by Sienar itself—for the Sith who had killed Qui-Gon Jinn. The pilot had been provided with landing coordinates on Coruscant, but, in fact, the courier itself had homed in on those. Paid in full for her services, she had been taxied to Westport, and had left for Ryloth soon after. The physical description of the courier's destination hadn't given the Jedi much to go on. Though more horizontal than most areas of equatorial Coruscant, The Works sprawled for hundreds of square kilometers and contained thousands of buildings that could have fit the description.

A break hadn't come until Jedi Master Tholme had recalled a detail from the debriefing of his former Padawan, Quinlan Vos. As part of Vos's covert mission to penetrate Count Dooku's inner circle of dark side apprentices, Vos had been tasked with assassinating a duplicitous Senator, named Viento. Immediately following the assassination—and a brutal duel with Master K'Kruhk—Vos had met briefly with Dooku in The Works. There, Dooku had informed his would-be protégé that Vos had been incorrect in assuming that Viento was a Sith, and had again denied that he himself answered to any Master.

At the time, no one had paid much attention to Vos's remarks, because Vos seemed to have been seduced by the dark side and lost to the Order. The rendezvous was considered to have been only that: an out-of-the-way meeting place. Of greater interest to the Jedi and Republic Intelligence was the fact that Dooku had managed to arrive at and depart Coruscant without detection.

"Holoimages of the interior coming in," Valiant said.

Mace lowered the macrobinoculars and shifted his gaze to the field holoprojector. Dazzled by diagonal lines of static, the 3-D images were of forlorn rooms, stretches of dark corridor, vast empty spaces.

"The building appears to be completely abandoned, General. No signs of droids or living beings—other than varieties common to similar manufacturing slums."

"Abandoned, perhaps, but not forgotten," Captain Dyne said from behind Valiant. "The building's *live*. It has power and illumination."

"Doesn't mean much," Mace said. "Many structures in this district were self-powered, often by dangerous, highly unstable fuels." He gestured broadly. "They're still belching smoke."

Dyne nodded. "But this one shows periodic and recent use of power."

Mace turned to Valiant. "All right, Commander. Give the go-ahead."

From behind and to both sides of the observation post, LAATs lifted off into the smoke-filled sky, doorway gunners traversing their repeating blasters and commandos standing ready to deploy from the gunship's troop bay. Elsewhere, AT-TEs and other mobile artillery vehicles began to lumber across the debris-filled urbanscape toward the target.

Valiant turned to the troopers who made up Aurek Team.

"The building is a free-strike zone. You are to consider anyone we find inside to be hostile." He slammed a fresh power pack into his short-stocked blaster. "Troopers: find, fix, finish!"

No matter how often he heard it, the grunting, communal response to the ARC's rallying cry continued to disturb Mace on some level. Although it was probably no different from what the clone troopers heard when the Jedi said to one another, *May the Force be with you*.

He swung and waved a signal to Shaak Ti.

"I'll ride with Aurek Team. You have Bacta."

As beautiful as a flower, as deadly as a viper, Shaak Ti was the Jedi Master one wanted by one's side in chaotic circumstances. Graced with the ability to move quickly through crowds or tight spots, she was often the first to wade into close-quarter engagements, her striped montrals and lengthy head-tail alert to distances, her blue lightsaber quick to find its mark. She had proved instrumental in the defense of Kamino and Brentaal IV, and Mace was glad to have her with him now.

Aurek Team's gunship was already packed with commandos and Padawans by the time he clambered inside. Lifting off, the LAAT/i aimed straight for the summit of the building. The strategy was to work from the top down, in the hope of flushing hostiles out through the lowest levels, where infantry and artillery units were already taking up firing positions around the buttressed base. The entire area was undermined with tunnels that had been used for transporting workers, droids, and materials. While it wasn't possible to monitor every entrance and egress, many of the principal tunnels that opened on the building's sub-basements had been outfitted with sensors capable of detecting droids or flesh-and-bloods.

No functioning docking bay large enough to accommodate a gunship had been discovered. The commandos had advocated blowing a gaping hole in the side of the superstructure, but engineers feared that an explosion of the strength required could very well collapse the entire structure. Instead the LAAT/i carried the team to the largest of the blown-out windows below the summit, and hovered there while everyone was inserted.

Leaping the gap, Mace activated his lightsaber and instructed the Padawans to follow suit.

Weapons raised to their chests, the commandos spread out in fire-and-maneuver squads and began to move deeper into the building, checking out each room and alcove before declaring any level secure. Mace's blade glowed amethyst in the gloom. Stretching out with the Force, he could feel the presence of the dark side. The only explanation for Quinlan Vos not having felt it was that he, too, had gone dark.

Yoda had warned Mace that the dark side might cloud his mind to certain rooms and passageways—places that the Sith Lords didn't want Mace to discover—but he felt alert in all ways. Besides, that was what the commandos were for.

They worked their way down and down, without encountering resistance or finding anything of interest.

"Quiet as a tomb, General," Valiant said when the top ten levels had been secured.

Mace studied the 3-D map displayed by the ARC's wrist gauntlet projector.

"Inform Bacta Team that we will rally with them in designated sector three."

Valiant was about to speak when his comlink toned.

"Commander, this is Bacta Team leader," a voice said. "We have a functioning docking gate on level six that shows evidence of recent use. And, sir, wait until you get a look at the landing zone."

*   *   *

The floor that served as a landing area was scarcely large enough for a gunship, but it gleamed as if scrubbed and polished daily by custodial droids. Parallel to the long sides of the rectangle were banks of slender blue illuminators.

"Everyone stay exactly where you are," Captain Dyne said when Mace and the rest of Aurek Team appeared at the mouth of a corridor that intersected the docking bay at its lengthwise centerpoint.

Deployed in a circle formation, Shaak Ti and the Padawans who had entered with Bacta were clustered in the middle of the floor.

Thirty meters to Mace's right, Dyne and two other Intelligence officers were interpreting the data being sent to them by several probe droids meandering with design throughout the room, some of them misting the floor with a highly volatile substance. The well-lubricated vertical docking gate was open, revealing an oval of blackened sky.

"A Huppla Pasa Tisc sloop occupied this docking bay less than two standard weeks ago," Dyne said, loud enough for everyone to hear. "The arrangement of its landing gear and aft boarding ramp match the footprint of the *Punworcca 116*–class that launched from Geonosis during the battle there."

"Dooku's ship," Mace said.

"A reasonable supposition, Master Windu," Dyne said loudly. After several moments of gazing at the monitor screens of his equipment and conferring with his associates, he added: "The floor reveals traces of two beings who were here contemporaneous with the sloop."

Green light from one of the drifting droids played across the alloy floor panels. Dyne directed the droid to concentrate on certain areas, and studied the data again.

"The first being exited the sloop and walked to this

point." He indicated an area close to the open gate. "Taking into consideration trace impressions and the length of the being's stride, I would hazard that being one stands one hundred and ninety-five centimeters in height, and was wearing boots."

It was *Dooku!* Mace thought.

The droid focused its lights on another area, and Dyne continued.

"Here, being one met with being two, lighter in weight, perhaps shorter in stature, and wearing—" Dyne consulted what Mace assumed to be some sort of database. "—what can best be described as soft-soled footwear or slippers. This unknown being came from the direction of the building's east turbolifts, and accompanied . . . Dooku—for all intents and purposes—to a balconied niche above the docking gate. Following the same route, the pair returned to the docking bay and separated: Dooku to his ship; our unknown quarry, presumably to the turbolifts."

Tasking the probe droids to track the prints of the second being, Dyne began to trail them, waving for Mace, Shaak Ti, and the commandos to follow.

"Single file behind me," Dyne cautioned. "No straying out of line."

Mace and Shaak Ti took the point, with the Padawans and commandos strung out behind. By the time the two Jedi Masters caught up with Dyne and his droids, the Intelligence analyst was standing at the door to a dated turbolift.

"Verified," Dyne said, grinning in self-satisfaction. "Being two used the turbolift."

Turning to the wall, he pressed his gloved right hand to the call stud. When the summoned car appeared, he affixed a scanner to the control pad inside.

"The car's memory tells us that it arrived from sub-basement two. If we fail to discover evidence of our unknown quarry there, we'll have to work our way back up, one level at a time, until we do."

The turbolift was just roomy enough for Dyne, his associates, Mace, Shaak Ti, the two team commanders, and two probe droids. Comlinking troopers outside the building, Valiant ordered them to make their way to sub-basement two, but forewarned them to stay clear of the east turbolift and any nearby corridors or tunnels.

The probe droids were first to exit the car when it stopped, misting the corridor in both directions. One of the droids hadn't gone five meters before it stopped in midflight and began playing its detection lights across the floor.

"Footprints," Dyne said with enthusiasm. "We're still on track."

Stepping carefully from the car, he followed the probe droids to the entrance of a wide tunnel. After the droids had disappeared inside and returned, Dyne swung to Mace, who was waiting with everyone else at the base of the turbolift.

"The prints end here. From this point on the unknown used a vehicle—certainly a repulsorlift of some sort, although the droids aren't detecting any phantom emissions."

Mace and Shaak Ti joined Dyne and his teammates at the tunnel entrance.

Shaak Ti peered into the darkness. "Where does it lead?"

Dyne consulted a holomap. "If we can trust a map that's older than any of us, it connects to tunnels all over The Works—to adjacent buildings, to the foundries, to a one-time landing field . . . There must be a hundred branches."

"Forget the branches," Mace said. "What's at the far end of this one?"

Dyne called up a series of displays and studied them in silence. At last, he said: "The principal tunnel leads all the way to the western limit of the Senate District."

Mace walked two meters into the darkness, and ran his hand down the tunnel's tiled wall.

Hundreds of Senators are now under the influence of a Sith Lord called Darth Sidious, Dooku had told Obi-Wan on Geonosis.

Turning to face Shaak Ti and the clone commanders, Mace said: "We're going to need more troops."

In the Supreme Chancellor's Senate Office Building chambers, Yoda sat staring across the desk at Palpatine, silhouetted against the long window that overlooked western Coruscant. How many Supreme Chancellors had he sat with in this office and others like it? he asked himself. Half a hundred now. But why with this one did discussion so often skirt the edge of confrontation—especially when the topic turned to the Force. As ineffectual a leader as he was, Finis Valorum had tried to comport himself as if he placed the Force above all. With Palpatine, the Force was not placed last. It wasn't even on the agenda.

"I understand your concerns entirely, Master Yoda," he was saying. "More important, I am *sympathetic* to them. But the Outer Rim sieges must continue. Despite what you may think—and notwithstanding the extraordinary powers the Senate has deemed fit to bestow on me these past five years—I am one voice in a welter. At long last the Senate is galvanized to end this destructive conflict, and it will not permit me to stand in the way."

"Exhort me, you need not, Supreme Chancellor," Yoda said.

Palpatine smiled dryly. "I apologize if I sounded sermonizing."

"Galvanized by your State of the Republic address, the Senate was."

"My address was a reflection of the spirit of the times, Master Yoda. What's more, I spoke from my heart."

"Doubt you, I do not. But too soon, your encouragements came. Celebrates imminent victory, Coruscant does, when far from ended the war is."

Palpatine's frown contained a hint of warning, of malice. "After three years of fear, Coruscant craves relief."

"Agree with you, I do. But how from the seizure of Outer Rim worlds is relief sustained? Too many new fronts, the Senate urges us to open. Too dispersed the Jedi are, to serve effectively. A reasonable strategy, we lack."

"My military advisers would not be pleased to hear you categorize their strategy as irrational."

"Need to hear it, they do. *Say* it to them, I will."

Palpatine paused to consider the remark, then leveled a hard gaze. "Master Yoda, forgive my frankness, but if the Jedi are indeed too widely scattered to coordinate the sieges, then the burden will have to fall to my naval commanders."

Yoda compressed his lips and shook his head. "Answer foremost to the Jedi, our troopers do. Forged an alliance with them, we have. Forged in fire, this fidelity has been."

Palpatine sat upright, as if struck. "I'm certain I misconstrue your meaning, but you almost make it sound as if our army was created for the Jedi."

"Not true," Yoda snapped. "For the Republic, and none other."

Appeased, Palpatine said: "Then perhaps the clones can be trained to respond to others, as well as they respond to the Jedi."

Yoda made a glum face. "Trained the troopers can be. But wrong this strategy remains."

"May I ask that you think back to Geonosis? Do you not agree that we erred then by not pursuing the Separatists?"

"Unprepared, we were. New, the army was."

"Granted. But we are prepared now. We have the Confederacy on the run from the inner systems, and I will not allow us to repeat the mistake we made at Geonosis."

"No, a *different* mistake we make now."

Palpatine interlocked his fingers. "This is the wisdom of the Council?"

"It is."

"Then you will challenge the Senate's decision?"

Yoda shook his head. "Sworn by oath to uphold you, we are."

Palpatine spread his hands. "That does not instill confidence, Master Yoda. If it's nothing more than an oath, then you are duty-bound to reconsider."

"Reconsidered we *have*, Supreme Chancellor."

"You imply no threat, I trust."

"No threat."

Palpatine forced a fatigued exhale. "As I've told you on many occasions, I do not have the luxury of seeing this world through the Force. I see only the real world."

"No problem there would be, if the 'real world,' all there was."

"Unfortunately, we who are not attuned to the Force have that on Jedi authority only."

Yoda wagged his forefinger at Palpatine. "To end this war, *more* we will have to do than defeat Grievous and his army of war machines. More we will have to do than seize remote worlds."

"These Sith to whom you keep referring." Palpatine fell silent in thought, then said: "When you were believed killed at Ithor, Master Windu said as much to me."

"More attentive to his concerns, were you?"

Palpatine regarded him. "A skilled duelist you are."

"When need be, Supreme Chancellor."

"You never fully described what went on between you and Count Dooku on Vjun. Was he at all inclined to return to the Order—to the side of the Republic?"

Yoda allowed his sadness to show. "From the dark path, no returning there is. Forever, the direction of your life it dominates."

"That may make Dooku difficult to rehabilitate."

Yoda raised his gaze. "Captured, he will never be. Die fighting, he will."

"This Darth Sidious, as well—should Dooku be found and killed?"

Yoda's eyes fidgeted. "Difficult to say. Deprived of an apprentice, Sidious may withdraw—to preserve the Sith."

"One person is all that's required to preserve the Sith traditions?"

"Traditions they are not. The *dark* side, it is."

"Then what if you should find Sidious first, and kill him? Would Dooku's power increase?"

"Only Dooku's determination. Different it will be, because a Sith late he has become." Yoda shook his head. "Hard to know if Dooku a true Sith is, or simply with the power of the dark side infatuated."

"And General Grievous?"

Yoda made a gesture of dismissal. "More machine than alive, Grievous is—though more dangerous for it. But without Dooku's or Sidious's leadership, collapse the

Separatists will. Bound together by the Sith they are. Mortared by the dark side of the Force."

Palpatine leaned forward with interest. "Then the Council is of the opinion that we must kill the leadership—that this war is more a battle within the Force?"

"United we are in that matter."

"You are persuasive, Master Yoda. You have my word that I will bear this conversation in mind when I meet with the Senate to discuss our campaigns."

"Relieved, I am, Supreme Chancellor."

Palpatine reclined in his chair. "Tell me, how goes the hunt for Darth Sidious?"

Yoda leaned forward for emphasis. "Coming *closer* to him, are we."

32

In a forward hold of Grievous's flagship, Dooku watched the cyborg general duel with his elite Magna-Guards, three of his trophy lightsabers in constant motion, parrying thrusts of the guards' pulse-weaponed staffs, slicing the recycled air a hairbreadth from the expressionless faces of his opponents, incapacitating arm and leg servos when he could. Grievous was a force to be reckoned with, to be sure, but Dooku deplored his habit of collecting lightsabers. It had merely bothered him that Ventress and lesser combatants such as the bounty hunter Aurra Sing had adopted the foul practice. Grievous's habit struck Dooku as the worst kind of profanation. Even so, he was not about to discourage the practice. The more Jedi that could be dispatched, the better.

The only aspect of Grievous's technique that vexed him more was the general's penchant for using four blades. Two was bad enough—in the form they had been used by Darth Maul, or in Anakin Skywalker's sad attempt to employ the technique on Geonosis.

But *three*?

What was to become of elegance and gallantry if a duelist couldn't make do with one blade?

Well, what had become of elegance and gallantry, in any case?

Grievous was fast, and so were his IG 100-series sparring partners. They had the advantage of size and brute strength. They executed moves almost faster than the human eye could follow. Their thrusts and lunges demonstrated a singular lack of hesitancy. Once committed to a maneuver, they never faltered. They never stopped to recalculate their actions. Their weapons went exactly where they meant them to go. And they always aimed for points beyond their opponents in order to slice clear through.

Dooku had taught Grievous well, and Grievous had taught his elite well. Coupled with Dooku's coaching, their programming in the seven classic forms of lightsaber dueling—in the Jedi arts—made them lethal opponents. But they were not invincible, not even Grievous, because they could be confused by unpredictability, and they had no understanding of finesse. A player of dejarik could memorize all the classic openings and countermoves, and still not be a master of the game. Defeat often came at the hands of less experienced players who knew nothing about the traditional strategies. A professional fighter, a combat artist, could be defeated by a cantina brawler who knew nothing about form but everything about ending a conflict quickly, without a thought to winning gracefully or elegantly.

Enslavement to form opened one to defeat by the unforeseen.

This was often the failing of trained duelists, and it would be the failing of the Jedi Order.

Given that elegance, gallantry, and enchantment were

gone from the galaxy, it was only fitting that the Order's days were numbered; that the fire that had been the Jedi was guttering and dying out. As with the corrupt Republic itself, the Order's time had come. The noble Jedi, bound to the Force, sworn to uphold peace and justice, were seldom seen as heroes or saviors any longer, but more often as bullies or mobsters.

Still, it was sad that it had fallen to Dooku to help usher them out.

The conversation he had had with Yoda on dreary Vjun was never far from his thoughts these days. For all his flair with words, all his Force-given personal power, Yoda was nothing more than an old one, unwilling to embrace anything new, indisposed to see any way but his own. Yet how terrible not simply to fade away but to expire in full knowledge that the galaxy had tipped inexorably and at long last to the dark side, to the Sith, and might remain so for as long as the Jedi themselves had ruled.

The unforeseen . . .

Grievous and his guards were dancing. Going through their programmed motions.

An Ataro attack answered by Shii-Cho; Soresu answered by Lus-ma . . .

Dooku couldn't suffer another moment of it.

"No, no, stop, stop," he yelled, coming to his feet and striding to the middle of the training circle, his arms extended to both sides. When he was certain that he had their attention, he swung to Grievous. "Power moves served you well on Hypori against Jedi such as Daakman Barrek and Tarr Seir. But I pity you should you have to face off against any of the Council Masters." He called into hand his courtly, curve-handled lightsaber and drew a rapid X in the air—a Makashi flourish. "Do I need to demonstrate what responses you can expect from Cin

STAR WARS: LABYRINTH OF EVIL   225

Drallig or Obi-Wan Kenobi? From Mace Windu or, stars help you, *Yoda*?"

He flicked his blade quickly, ridding two of the guards of their staffs, then placing the glowing tip a millimeter from Grievous's death-helmeted visage. "Finesse. Artfulness. Economy. Otherwise, my friend, I fear that you will end up beyond the repair of even the Geonosians. Do you take my meaning?"

His vertically slit eyes unfathomable, Grievous nodded. "I take your meaning, my lord."

Dooku withdrew his blade. "Again, then. With some measure of polish, if I'm not asking for too much."

Dooku seated himself and watched them go at it.

Hopeless, he thought.

But he knew that he was partly to blame. He had made the same mistake with Grievous that he had made with Ventress, by allowing her to fill herself with hate, as if hate could substitute for dispassion. Even the most hateful could be defeated. Even the most angry. There should be no emotion in killing, no self, only the act. When he should have been helping Ventress rid herself of *self,* he had instead permitted her to grow impassioned. Sidious had once confessed that he had erred similarly in his training of Darth Maul. Ventress and Maul had been driven by a desire to excel—to be the best—instead of merely allowing themselves to be pure instruments of the dark side.

The Jedi knew this about the Force: that the best of them were nothing more than instruments.

Dooku grew troubled.

Was Sidious thinking the same of him now? Thinking: *This is where I failed poor Dooku. Pitiful creature . . .*

It was entirely possible, considering how wrong things had gone on Naos III. Standard days earlier, Dooku had sent Sidious a coded transmission that was as much apology as explanation, and had yet to hear from him.

He watched Grievous disarm two of the MagnaGuards. In fact, Grievous was *all* instrument.

And Dooku. What was Count Dooku of Serenno?

He glanced at the hold's holoprojector table a moment before a blue holoimage of Sidious appeared above it.

My time is at hand, he told himself as he centered himself proudly on the transmission grid, Grievous behind him, down on one knee, with head lowered.

"My lord," he said, bowing slightly at the waist. "I've been waiting."

"There have been matters that warranted my close attention, Lord Tyranus."

"Born, no doubt, of my failure at Naos Three. The ones I sent had every opportunity to kill Kenobi, Skywalker, and the Twi'lek pilot. Instead, they decided to attempt their capture, to extract additional funds from me, as well as to bolster their reputations."

Sidious was dismissive. "Such is the way of bounty hunters. I should have foreseen this."

Dooku blinked. Was this an admission of failure on Sidious's part? Was Sidious's upper lip twitching, or was it nothing more than noise in the transmission?

"The Force is strong in Skywalker," Sidious went on.

"Yes, my lord. Very strong. Next time I will deal with the Jedi personally."

"Yes, that time is drawing near, Lord Tyranus. But first we need to provide the Jedi with something that distracts them from hunting me."

Sidious's upper lip was definitely twitching. Was this worry? Worry from someone fond of saying that things were going precisely as planned?

"What has happened, my lord?"

"The Twi'lek's information led them to our rendezvous on Coruscant," Sidious said in a scurrilous voice.

Dooku was stunned. "Is there a greater danger?"

"They think they have my scent, Lord Tyranus, and perhaps they do."

"Can you leave Coruscant, my lord?"

From parsecs distant, Sidious stared at him. "Leave Coruscant?"

"For a time, my lord. Surely we can find some way."

Sidious fell silent for a long moment, then said: "Perhaps, Lord Tyranus. Perhaps."

"If not, then I will come to you."

Sidious shook his head. "That won't be necessary. I told you that their search for me would benefit us before too long, and thanks to you I begin to see a way."

"What is thy bidding, Master?" Grievous asked from behind Dooku.

Sidious turned slightly toward Grievous, but continued to speak to Dooku. "The Jedi have divided their forces. We must do the same. I will deal with the ones on Coruscant. I need you to deal with the rest."

"My fleet stands ready, Master," Grievous said, still without raising his gaze from the grid.

"The Republic is monitoring you?" Sidious asked the general.

"Yes, Master."

"Can you divide the fleet—judiciously?"

"It can be done, Master."

"Good, good. Then move however many ships are needed to crush and occupy Tythe."

Again Dooku was stunned. So, too, was Grievous.

"Is that wise, Master," the general asked carefully, "after what happened at Belderone?"

Sidious adopted a faint grin. "More than wise, General. *Inspired.*"

"But Tythe, my lord," Dooku said with equal care. "Less a world than a corpse."

"It has some strategic value, does it not, General?"

"As a jump point, Master. But a dubious prize, regardless, when far better targets exist."

"It may prove costly to us, my lord. The Republic will almost certainly flatten it," Dooku said.

"Not if the Jedi are convinced that it must be retaken rather than destroyed."

Confusion wrinkled Dooku's forehead. "How will we convince them?"

"We won't have to, Lord Tyranus. Their own investigations will lead them to that conclusion. Moreover, Kenobi and Skywalker will oversee the counterattack."

"Indeed, my lord?"

"They will not pass up an opportunity to capture Count Dooku."

Dooku saw Grievous's armorplast head elevate in surprise. "What leads you to believe that the Republic will not simply flatten me at this point?"

"The Jedi are predictable, Lord Tyranus. I needn't tell you this. Look what they risked on Cato Neimoidia in an effort to capture Viceroy Gunray. They are obsessed with bringing their enemies to justice, instead of merely administering justice themselves."

"It is their way."

"Then you don't mind serving as bait to lure them there?"

Dooku inclined his head. "As ever, I am at your disposal, my lord."

Sidious grinned once more. "Hold Kenobi and Skywalker, Lord Tyranus. Entertain them. Play to their weakness. Demonstrate your mastery, as you have on previous occasions."

Grievous made a meaningful sound. "I will do the same with their warships, Master."

"No, General," Sidious cut in. "I have something else in

mind for you and the rest of the fleet. But tell me, can you tuck your charges somewhere safe for the time being?"

"The planet Utapau comes to mind, Lord Sidious."

"I will leave that to you."

"And when I have seen to that, Master?"

"General, I'm certain you recall the plans we discussed some time ago, regarding the final stage of the war."

"Regarding Coruscant."

"Regarding Coruscant, yes." Sidious paused, then said: "We must accelerate those plans. Prepare, General, for what will be your finest hour."

33

Fa'ale is doing fine," Anakin said as he approached Obi-Wan jauntily. "Two more days of bacta and she'll be on her feet. She says she's through with Naos Three, though. She might even remain here on Belderone."

Obi-Wan looked at him askance. "Your relationship with females is an interesting one. The more jeopardy they're in, the more you worry about them. And the more you worry about them, the more they worry about *you*."

Anakin frowned. "You're basing this on, what, exactly?"

Obi-Wan looked away. "HoloNet gossip."

Anakin stepped deliberately into Obi-Wan's gaze. "Something's wrong. What is it?"

Obi-Wan sighed. "We won't be returning to Coruscant."

They were in a visitors' lounge in the largest of the MedStars orbiting Belderone. For four standard days they had been awaiting instructions from the Jedi Council and visiting the medical ward to check on Fa'ale's progress, and the strain of so much inactivity was beginning to show.

Anakin was staring dumbfounded at Obi-Wan.

"Hear me out before you go critical. Mace and Shaak Ti were able to locate the building in The Works. Not surprisingly, it turns out to have been the same one where Quinlan Vos met with Dooku last year. Once inside, Mace's team discovered more than we could have even hoped for—evidence of a more recent visit by Dooku, and of the person he apparently went to Coruscant to see."

"Sidious?"

"Possibly. Even if it wasn't, it's likely that Dooku has other confederates on Coruscant, and tracking them down could eventually lead us to Sidious. Other evidence has come to light, as well. Intelligence discovered that the building belonged to a corporation called LiMerge Power, which was believed to have been involved in the manufacture and distribution of prohibited weapons during Finis Valorum's term as Supreme Chancellor. It was rumored at the time that LiMerge was responsible for funding acts of piracy directed against Trade Federation vessels in the Outer Rim. And it was those acts of piracy that led ultimately to the Trade Federation being granted the right to defend their vessels with battle droids."

"Are you telling me that LiMerge might have been in league with the Sith?"

"Why not? At Naboo, the Trade Federation was in league with Sidious. The entire Confederacy is in league with him now."

Anakin shrugged impatiently. "I still don't understand how this keeps us from returning to Coruscant."

"I've just been informed that the Separatists have attacked a Republic garrison base on Tythe, and occupied the planet."

"Who cares? I mean, I'm sorry for any troopers we lost, but Tythe is a wasteland."

"Exactly," Obi-Wan said. "But before it became a wasteland, it was headquarters for LiMerge Power."

Anakin mulled it over for a moment. "Another attempt by Sidious to erase the trail we've been following?"

Obi-Wan ran his hand over his mouth. "The Council was able to convince Palpatine of the need to retake Tythe, and he has authorized a full battle group to divert there. It seems he is finally willing to follow Master Yoda's advice about concentrating on dismantling the Confederacy leadership."

"Grievous is on Tythe?"

Obi-Wan grinned. "Better: Dooku is there."

Anakin turned his back to Obi-Wan. His face was flushed when he finally swung around. "Not good enough."

Obi-Wan blinked. "Not good enough?"

"The search for Sidious began with us. We discovered the first clues. If he's thought to be on Coruscant, then we're the ones who should be there to capture him."

"Anakin, Mace and Shaak Ti are more than capable of seeing to that—*if* Sidious is even there."

Anakin was shaking his head. "Not as easily as . . . we could. Sidious is a Sith Lord!"

Obi-Wan took a moment to respond. "The way I remember it, we didn't fare all that well against Dooku."

"All that's changed!" Anakin said, becoming angrier as he spoke. "I'm stronger than I was. You're stronger. Together, we can defeat any Sith."

"Anakin, is this really about capturing Sidious?"

"Of course it is. We deserve the honor."

"Honor? Since when did this war become a contest for first place? If you're thinking that the capture of Sidious will earn you a place on the Council—"

"I don't care about the Council! I'm telling you we need to return to Coruscant. People are counting us."

"What people?"

"The . . . people of Coruscant."

Obi-Wan inhaled slowly. "Why don't I believe you?"

"I don't know, Master? Suppose you tell me?"

Obi-Wan narrowed his eyes. "Don't turn this into a game. There's something else at work here. Have you had a vision I should know about?"

Anakin started to reply, bit back whatever it was he had in mind to say, and began again. "The truth is . . . I want to be home. We've been out here longer than anyone—trooper or Jedi."

"That's what you get for being so good at what you do," Obi-Wan said, hoping to lighten the mood.

"I'm tired of it, Master. I want to be home."

Obi-Wan studied him. "You miss the Temple so much? The food? The lights of Coruscant?"

"Yes."

"Yes, to what?"

"All of it."

"Then your protests have nothing to do with capturing Sidious."

"No. They do."

"Well, which is it—home or Sidious?"

"Why can't it be both?"

Obi-Wan fell silent, as if struck by a sudden suspicion. "Anakin, is it Padmé?"

Anakin rolled his eyes. "Here you go again."

"Well, is it?"

Anakin compressed his lips, then said, "I won't lie to you and say that I don't miss her."

Obi-Wan frowned sympathetically. "You can't afford to miss her in that way."

"And exactly why is that, Master?"

"Because you cannot be married to both."

"Who said anything about *marriage*? She's a friend. I miss her as a friend!"

"You would forgo your destiny for Padmé?"

Anakin's brows beetled in anger. "I never claimed to be the Chosen One. That was Qui-Gon. Even the Council doesn't believe it anymore, so why should you?"

"Because I think you believe it," Obi-Wan said calmly. "I think you know in your heart that you're meant for something extraordinary."

"And you, Master. What does your heart tell you you're meant for?"

"Infinite sadness," Obi-Wan said, even while smiling.

Anakin regarded him. "If you believe in destiny, then everything we do becomes part of that destiny—whether we go to Tythe or we return to Coruscant."

"You may be right. I don't have the answer. I wish I did."

"Then where does that leave us?"

Obi-Wan rested his hands on Anakin's shoulders. "Speak with Palpatine. Maybe he'll see something in this that I've missed."

Fifty meters ahead of Mace in the tunnel, Shaak Ti held up her hand, motioning for him to stop. Angling his purple blade to the floor, Mace turned to relay the signal to the commandos behind him.

Shaak Ti's whisper reached him through the Force: *Movement ahead.*

She gestured to the mouth of an intersecting tunnel just beyond where she stood, her profile limned blue by the glow of her raised lightsaber. Faint light spilled from the opening, as if someone with a handheld luma was approaching on foot.

Mace waved a signal to Commander Valiant, whose team moved forward stealthily, hugging the walls, their T-visor helmets allowing them to see in the dark.

Normally the probe droids would have the point, playing their lights and sensors across the dusty floor and tiled walls, sending data to Dyne and his team of analysts. Mace and Shaak Ti would ride in separate speeders behind the agents, intermingled with those of the commandos. Occasionally, however, the Jedi would assume the lead on foot for a couple of kilometers, usually in response to some anomaly discovered by the droids. Ventilation, such as it was, came courtesy of ancient blowers that did little more than drag in the sooty air from above, and illumination was provided by what the team brought with them.

They were deep below an area of The Works called the Grungeon Block. Encompassing twenty square kilometers, the block had originally been a production center for Serv-O-Droid, Huvicko, and Nebula Manufacturing, but it had fallen on hard times when its three principal clients had declared bankruptcy. Unable to attract new businesses, the developers who owned the Grungeon had allowed stratts and other vermin to overrun the stamping plants, and cashed out.

In the days since the raid, Mace's team had searched nearly every nook and cranny of the confusion of tunnels and shafts that undermined the Grungeon and similar assembly areas. Ten kilometers into the tunnel that led to the LiMerge building's sub-basement, a shaft had been found, leading to a deeper, older tunnel that also ran east toward the Senate District. In appearance the parallel tunnels were similar, save for the fact that the floor of the older one hosted an ancient mag-lev rail. The probe droids had discovered places along the rail where the accumulated decades of dust and debris had been blown away by the rapid passage of a repulsorlift vehicle of some sort. With no other clues to go on, the team had made the mag-lev tunnel the focus of the investigation.

Still, Mace felt that the team was on the right track.

An extensive search of the LiMerge building had revealed the remains of several Trang Robotics Duelist Elite droids that had been reduced to durasteel pieces by a lightsaber. Only Sidious, Dooku, or Sidious's previous apprentice could have performed the amputations.

And there was more.

Shortly before Dooku had left the Jedi Order to return to his native Serenno—during the period when he had taken the title *Count* and had first gone public with his discontents about the Republic—he had been known to frequent a tavern called the Golden Cuff, which had been a watering hole for Senators, lobbyists, and aides. Analysts at the Temple were going through files of security cam holoimages thirteen years old, hoping to find images of Dooku and anyone he may have met with repeatedly.

Thus far, no images of Dooku had surfaced in the recordings that had survived. Even if images of Dooku's tavern mates did surface, the Jedi had no means of identifying any of them as Darth Sidious, but the images could provide an additional starting point for further investigation.

By now Mace could hear movement and soft voices ahead.

Hardly a good tactic for hostiles intent on springing an ambush, but one never knew. He stretched out with his feelings, alert for diversions or clues he might have overlooked—obscured by the dark side, or owing to his own neglect.

Standing nearby, Valiant looked to Mace for the go signal.

When Mace nodded, Valiant said: "Light it up!"

Weapons raised, gas and fragmentation grenades enabled, the commandos sprinted into the intersecting tunnel, firing tracer bolts into the gloom.

Tight on their heels, Mace heard Valiant yell: "Down on the floor! Don't move! I said, don't move!"

More fire erupted, then several commando voices were shouting: "Stay still! Down on your faces! Hands up— all four of them!"

All four of them? Mace thought.

Edging through the commandos, he reached Valiant, whose BlasTech was aimed at a cowering crowd of thirty or so four-armed insectoid aliens, who were babbling in some language other than Basic, or speaking it with an accent so thick as to make their words unintelligible.

"Lower your weapons," Mace told the commandos. "And someone bring that interpreter droid forward!"

Mace's command was relayed down the line, and a moment later a highly polished silver protocol droid tottered into the tunnel, muttering to itself.

"I don't understand how I've gone from serving the Separatists to serving the Republic. Did I undergo a partial memory wipe?"

"Consider yourself lucky," one of the commandos said. "Now you're on the side of the good guys."

"Good guys, bad guys . . . who can tell anymore? What's more, you won't be so quick to say that should someone compel you to shift loyalties at a moment's notice."

"Droid!" Mace shouted.

"I do have a name, sir."

Mace glanced at Valiant.

"TeeCee something or other," the ARC said.

"Fine," Mace said, grabbing hold of TC-16 and pointing him in the direction of the terrified aliens. "See if you can make sense of what these folk are saying."

The droid listened to the babbling, responded in kind, and turned to face Mace. "They are Unets, General. Speaking their native language, which is called Une."

Mace regarded the huddled, shivering group. "What are they doing down here?"

TC-16 listened, then said: "They say that they haven't the slightest idea where they are, General. They arrived on Coruscant in a shipping container that was air-dropped at a decrepit landing platform some twenty kilometers from here. The personage who was to have guided them into the depths of the Uscru Sector stole all their credits and abandoned them in The Works."

"Undocumented refugees," Valiant said.

Mace frowned. The tunnels beneath the Grungeon Block held countless surprises.

"They almost got themselves killed."

"Apparently that's nothing new for them," TC-16 said. "Their planet fell to the Separatists, the freighter they originally took passage on was attacked by pirates, several of them—"

"That's enough," Mace said. "Assure them that they're not going to be harmed, and that we'll see to it they reach a refugee camp." He nodded to Valiant, who in turn told two of his troopers to carry out Mace's command.

"Talk about your corridor ghouls," Dyne said, eyeing the aliens as he approached Mace.

"Squatters, death stick runners, lost droids, now un-documented refugees . . ."

"Next it'll be Cthons," Dyne said, referring to the flesh-eating humanoids believed by many Coruscanti to inhabit the world's underground.

Shaak Ti joined them. "These corridors are highways for people who want to enter central Coruscant illegally."

Dyne sighed in disappointment. "Our chances for picking up Sidious's trail decrease with each person who passes."

"How far are we from the Senate District?" Shaak Ti asked.

"Within a couple of kilometers," Dyne said. "We might think about going directly to the buildings

LiMerge Power once owned in the city core, and see if we can't work our way *toward* The Works from those."

Mace considered the idea, then shook his head.

"Not yet."

Mace waved everyone back into motion, then fell into step with Shaak Ti.

"Wild gundark chase?"

She nodded. "Only because our quarry is aware that we're closing in on him. He failed to silence the ones Obi-Wan and Anakin searched out, and by now he knows that we've discovered his and Dooku's den. It's unlikely he will wait around for us to surprise him."

"That's true. But there's much to gain from simply identifying him. If not here, then by means of something Obi-Wan and Anakin discover on Tythe."

"Assuming there's anything left after Dooku sterilizes the place. From everything we've seen, Sidious and Dooku don't make many mistakes."

They walked in silence for a long while. They were a kilometer closer to the outlying areas of the Senate District when Dyne called to them from behind.

Mace saw that the Intelligence analysts and commandos were gathered some twenty meters away. He and Shaak Ti had been so engrossed in their private thoughts that neither of them had noticed the probe droids stopping to investigate something. Joining the others, the Jedi watched the droids hover with clear purpose in front of a large niche in the tunnel wall.

Dyne's handheld sensor needed only a moment to discover a small control panel that operated the niche's sliding door.

The door concealed the entrance to a narrow, dimly lit corridor.

And all but hiding in plain sight: a repulsorlift speeder

bike, semicircular in design, with an arc of a concentric seat and a single steering handle.

Mace and Shaak Ti traded astonished looks.

"How did we miss seeing this?" she asked.

Mace's brow furrowed. "The answer is in the question."

35

As big as life, Palpatine's holoimage spoke from atop a projector table in a private comlink lounge aboard the medical frigate. With R2-D2 standing off to one side of the transmission grid, Anakin hung on the Supreme Chancellor's every word.

"Of course, the Council doesn't understand," Palpatine said. "Surely you don't find that surprising."

"They reject every suggestion I make—on principle, I'm beginning to think."

"It's obvious that you're upset, Anakin, but you must be patient. Your time will come."

"When, sir?"

Palpatine smiled lightly. "I can't see into the future, my boy."

Anakin's face contorted. "What if I told you that *I* could?"

"I would believe you," Palpatine said without pause. "Tell me what you see."

"Coruscant."

"Are we in danger?"

"I'm not certain. I just feel that I need to be there."

Palpatine gazed away from the holocam. "I suppose I could invent some pretext . . . " His gaze returned to Anakin. "But is that wise?"

"I'm not the wise one. Ask anybody."

"What does Master Kenobi say?"

"He's the one who suggested I contact *you*," Anakin said sharply.

"Really? But what does he think you should do?"

Anakin blew out his breath. "Obi-Wan is under the illusion that I can't deny my destiny—no matter what I do."

"Your former Master is wiser than you think, Anakin."

"Yes, yes, and he is the only Jedi in a thousand years to have killed a Sith."

Palpatine spread his hands. "That alone has to count for something. Though I'm at a loss to know precisely what."

"Obi-Wan is wise. But he has no heart, sir. He sees everything in terms of the Force."

"If you want advice about the Force, you must look to him, because I'm of no help."

"That's exactly what I *don't* want. I live in the Force, but I also live in the real world. I came from . . . the real world. Just as you said, I had the advantage of a normal childhood. Well, sort of."

Palpatine waited until he was certain Anakin was finished. "My boy, I don't know that it's healthy to have a foot in each world. Soon you may have to make a choice."

Anakin nodded. "I'm ready."

Palpatine smiled again. "But back to the matter at hand. It sounds to me as if the recapture of Tythe could prove very important toward ending the war. I don't understand all of it. The Jedi Council is being very secretive with me."

Anakin fought the temptation to reveal everything about the search for Darth Sidious. He glanced at R2-D2, as if expecting commiseration, but the astromech only swiveled his dome, his processor status indicator flashing from blue to red.

Finally Anakin said: "I don't know what to do, sir." ·

Palpatine adopted a sympathetic expression. "It's decided. I shall prevail upon the Council to order you back to the Core. No one needs further proof of how intrepid you are, or how committed you are to defeating our enemies."

In time you will learn to trust your feelings; then you will be invincible.

Palpatine's advice to him, three years earlier.

"No," Anakin said in a rush. "No. Thank you, sir, but . . . I'm needed on Tythe. Dooku is there."

I'm sorry, Padmé. I'm so, so sorry. I miss you so much—

"Yes," Palpatine was saying. "Dooku is the key to everything just now. Despite all our victories in the inner systems . . . Do you suspect he and General Grievous may have some secret strategy?"

"If they do, Obi-Wan and I will defeat them before they can implement it."

"The Republic counts on it."

"Safeguard Coruscant, sir. Safeguard everyone there."

"I will, my boy. And rest assured that I will call on you if I need you."

Obi-Wan was in the MedStar's docking bay, waiting for the shuttle that would take him to the light cruiser *Integrity*. His arms were folded across his chest, and his small rucksack was sitting on the deck.

"Did you get through to him?" he asked as Anakin and R2-D2 approached.

"Well, I spoke to him."

"That's what I meant. And?"

Anakin averted his gaze. "We both decided that my place is here, Master." He sounded on the verge of tears.

Obi-Wan merely nodded. "For a moment I thought you were going to leave it to me to retake Tythe."

Anakin looked at him. "I know better than that."

"You don't think I'm capable?" Obi-Wan asked around a forming grin.

"I know you'd be willing to die trying."

"There is no trying—"

"Yes, there is," Anakin cut him off. "And you're living proof of it."

Obi-Wan smiled, then glanced out the hold's magcon transparency. "The shuttle's coming."

Anakin's eyes tracked the approaching light. "I'm as ready as I'll ever be." He still wasn't smiling.

Obi-Wan closed his hand around Anakin's upper right arm. "Anakin, let's get Dooku and end this."

Anakin swallowed and nodded. "If it's meant to be, Master."

36

With assistance from the probe droids, the discolored panels at the end of the corridor unlocked and parted. Brown robe swirling behind him and lightsaber in hand, Mace barreled through the doorway, with Shaak Ti and the commandos close behind.

By rote the troopers spread out, quickly and efficiently, but also unnecessarily.

"Surprise," Shaak Ti said flatly. "Another corridor."

"Another corridor closer," Mace said, determined to put a good spin on it.

The tunnel the team had followed from the hidden niche had led them through a maze of twists, turns, forks, steep climbs, and sudden drops. For stretches the dark corridor had been wide enough to contain a speeder; then it grew so narrow that everyone had had to edge through. For two kilometers, walls, ceiling, and floor were damp from water that had trickled down through Coruscant's layered surface. There, the prints of their prey had disappeared, but the probe droids had managed to pick up the trail farther along. Some of the prints were so recent and well preserved that Dyne had been able to calculate the human's slipper size.

Human.

That much the droids had determined from smudged fingerprints found on the speeder bike's steering grip and cushioned seat. The repulsorlift machine had also provided the droids with fibers, hairs, and other detritus. Slowly, a portrait of Dooku's unknown confederate was being compiled.

His eyes fixed on the display screen of his data processor, Captain Dyne ambled toward Mace and Shaak Ti.

"Master Jedi, our search is about to take us to a whole new level."

Mace looked around the tunnel for signs of a concealed turbolift or staircase.

"Up or down?" Shaak Ti asked, equally bewildered.

Dyne glanced up, blinking at her. "I didn't mean 'new level' in the literal sense." He indicated the hovering probe droids, which were eager to have the team follow them east. "If the prints lead us far enough, we're going to end up in the sub-basements of 500 Republica."

Mace tracked the droids as they moved deeper into the corridor.

Five Hundred Republica: home to thousands of Coruscant's wealthiest Senators, celebrities, shipping magnates, and media tycoons.

And one of them, very possibly a Sith Lord.

37

There was little the Confederacy or the Republic could add to the damage LiMerge Power had inflicted on Tythe generations earlier. From deep space, the surface—glimpsed through a pall of ash-gray clouds—looked as if it had been licked by a flare from its primary, or had had a brush with an enormous meteor. But Tythe's scars owed to none of that. The planet had been spared everything but LiMerge itself, whose attempts to exploit Tythe's abundant deposits of natural plasma had invoked a cataclysm of global proportions.

The three drifting hulks that had been Republic cruisers might have been caught up in the cataclysm but were, in fact, casualties of the Separatist attack, which had come swiftly and without quarter. Nimbused by what vacuum had drawn from their interiors, the scorched and lanced trio lazed midway between opposing battle groups of Separatist and Republic vessels.

"Just once I wish we could repay Dooku and Grievous in kind," Anakin said over the tactical net, as Red

Squadron dropped from the belly of the *Integrity* and rocketed toward Tythe.

"The fact that we don't is what keeps us centered in the Force," Obi-Wan said.

Anakin grunted. "There'll come a time when they'll have to answer to us personally, and it will be the Force that guides our blades."

The two starfighters were flying abreast, almost wingtip-to-wingtip, astromech droids R2-D2 and R4-P17 in their respective sockets. Tythe's rubicund star was at their backs, and the ships that made up the Separatist flotilla were strung menacingly above the planet's northern hemisphere.

With Tythe's brood of moons clustered in a two-hundred-degree arc, the Separatists had worked quickly to strew mines at several hyperspace jump points, leaving the Republic ships with only a narrow window in which to revert to realspace. Trade Federation, Techno Union, and Commerce Guild capital ships occupied the apex of that window, deployed from north pole to equator above Tythe's bright side, with wings of droid fighters boiling into space to the fore of the arrayed vessels.

To minimize their profiles, the Republic ships—widely dispositioned, like a group of predatory fish—had their triangular bows pointed toward the planet. Red and other squadrons were streaking forward, but well short of engaging the vanguard Vultures and tri-fighters.

"Prepare to break hard to starboard," Anakin said over the net to the entire squadron. "Watch your countdown displays. On my mark, ten seconds to break . . . "

Obi-Wan kept his eyes on the counter at the bottom of the instrument panel's tactical display screen. At the zero mark, he yanked the yoke to one side and peeled away for clear space.

Behind the squadrons of V-wings and Jedi and ARC-170 starfighters, the Republic battle group broke to port, drenching the distant Separatist ships with furious broadsides. Blinding payloads of spun plasma hurtled through space, detonating against the shields of the enemy vessels, atomizing any droid fighters unlucky enough to have been caught in the way.

The Separatist ships absorbed the first hits without flinching. Vessels that sustained damage began to drift to the rear. Then the battle group responded with an equally ferocious barrage. Turbolasers silenced, the Republic ships had already broken formation. Small suns flared in their midst and blue energy capered over their shielded hulls. No sooner did the barrage end than the starfighter squadrons regrouped, accelerating in an effort to reach the big enemy ships before their cannons or shields could repower.

The droid fighters swooped in to meet them halfway, and the tight formations observed by both sides dissolved into dozens of separate skirmishes. Those Republic starfighters that managed to steal through the chaos drew into tight clusters and continued their fiery advance. The rest became embroiled in swift attacks and evasive maneuvers. Local space became a scrawl of scarlet lines and white spirals, punctuated by expanding explosions. Craft of both camps came apart, tumbling and spinning from the arena, wingless or in flames.

"They're being shot to pieces," Red Seven said over the net.

"They know their job," Anakin responded.

That job was to buy Red Squadron enough time to skirt the main action and race down Tythe's gravity well.

A burst-transmission from survivors of the assault on the Republic's small base had confirmed Dooku's presence on the surface. But on the possibility that Tythe was a calculated diversion, Palpatine's naval command staff had agreed to committing only a single battle group from the Outer Rim fleet. In the view of those same naval commanders, invasion was senseless; a Base Delta Zero attack, justified. In the end it was decided that saturation bombardment, augmented by limited starfighter engagement, would send Dooku fleeing, in keeping with the Republic's strategy to force the Separatists deeper into the galaxy's spiral arms.

The Jedi had insisted nevertheless that an attempt be made to take Dooku alive.

Obi-Wan and Anakin didn't need to be reminded of what had happened only weeks earlier on Cato Neimoidia when they had gone after Viceroy Gunray, but they were not about to forgo a chance to capture the Sith Lord.

Red Squadron's intended insertion point was twenty degrees south of Tythe's north pole, where the Separatist line was most dispersed. With droid fighters still pouring from the curving arms of Trade Federation Lucrehulks, and the recoiling barrels of Commerce Guild cannons filling local space with storms of unleashed energy, Anakin led the starfighters on a weaving course through the heart of the enemy fleet.

"No signature for Grievous's cruiser," he said to Obi-Wan. "None of the ships of the Separatist leadership are here."

Obi-Wan glanced at the wire-frame display of his threat-assessment screen. "All the more reason to believe that Dooku was ordered here by Sidious."

"Then where's everyone else?"

Obi-Wan was troubled by the thought, but didn't admit to it. "Dooku will know," he started to say, when the starfighter's proximity scanners stammered a warning. "Techno Union starship is veering to intercept us."

"Droid fighters are away and locking on," Red Three added.

Obi-Wan acknowledged. "Angle shields. We can out-fly them."

"We'll end up too far off course," Anakin said.

"We're almost at the insertion point," Obi-Wan said. "That starship isn't just going to move aside. Form up on me. We'll show them how well we improvise."

There was no time to argue the point. Rolling to port, Obi-Wan fell in behind Anakin and fired his thrusters. Trailing behind, Red Squadron accelerated and banked for the narrow-waisted vessel.

"Ready proton torpedoes," Anakin said. "Sow them just above the fuel cells."

Point-defense turbolasers sought the starfighters as they fell on the ship, needling space with outpourings of gaudy energy. Corkscrewing missiles claimed Red Ten and Red Twelve, both of which disappeared in angry blossoms of fire. Sensing its sudden vulnerability, the huge vessel launched additional droid fighters. In the instant it lowered its shields to route power to the sublight drives, Red Squadron attacked.

Tight on Anakin, the ten remaining starfighters yawed for the waist of the ship, just forward of its cluster of cylindrical fuel cells. Dropping his craft to within one hundred meters of the pinched hull, Anakin began to hug the surface, surging onto a course that would whip Red Squadron through a tight circle around the forward ends of the fuel cells.

"Torpedoes away!" he said at the halfway mark.

Obi-Wan triggered the launchers and watched two torpedoes burn toward the target. Behind him, the rest of Red Squadron did the same. Hits began to score, fire and gas fountaining from breaches in the ship's dark hull.

The disabling run completed, Anakin boosted for Tythe.

"She's finished!"

In single file, Red Squadron followed.

Almost instantly the punctured vessel exploded, stunning the fleeing starfighters with a wave of force. Red Nine disappeared at the edge of the roiling detonation zone, and Red Seven wheeled off into the void with both wings sheared away.

Obi-Wan regained control of his craft and once more attached himself to Anakin's six.

"Insertion point in fifteen seconds," Anakin updated. "Dial inertial compensators to maximum. All power to the ablative shields. Deceleration burn on my mark . . . "

Obi-Wan clamped his hands on the violently shaking yoke as Red Squadron ripped into Tythe's plundered atmosphere. He thought his teeth might rattle out of his jaws and drop into his lap; eyes and ears might implode from the pressure; chest might cave in and crush his heart.

Light flashed behind him; streaked past the cockpit.

Half a dozen droid fighters were chasing them down the well.

Not having to concern themselves with endangering living systems, the Vultures should have been able to descend even more rapidly and more acutely than the starfighters. But as the heat of entry built in the ships, survival protocols began to kick in, tasking the fighters to adjust the angle of their descents. For some of the droids it was already too late. Single contrails became particle showers as gravity summoned the broken fighters to their doom.

Punching through the blankets of clouds at suicidal velocity, Obi-Wan's starfighter went into a roll. Pinwheeling before his eyes, Tythe was a kaleidoscopic furor of white and brown, smeared occasionally with striations of blue-green.

Anakin's voice grew loud in his ears. "Nose up! Nose up!"

With effort, Obi-Wan leveled out of his plummet, his stomach lurching up into his throat. Reaching forward, he engaged the starfighter's topographic sensors. The ship was dropping toward ice floes and bergs. Then, far below, peninsulas of rocky islands came into view. The surging waves of a dead gray ocean. The denuded shelf of a continent. Barren land fissured by dry, sinuous riverbeds, and mounded by brown hills strewn with toppled trees.

A ruined world.

"Head count," he said into his helmet microphone.

Five voices responded. Reds Eight and Eleven were lost.

"Locking in target coordinates," Anakin said.

Red Squadron flew just above the contours of land that had once been as lush as the area surrounding Theed, on Naboo. Now a desert, save for areas where exotic species of vegetation thrived in lakes of red-brown water, their jagged shorelines crusted yellow and black.

Also like Naboo, Tythe had once mined plasma in sufficient quantities to ship offworld. But greed had driven LiMerge Power to experiment with dangerous methods for keeping the ionized gas under adequate heat. A chain reaction set in motion by nuclear fuels had destroyed facilities throughout Tythe's northern hemisphere and had left the planet uninhabitable for a generation.

"Target facility is ten kilometers west," Anakin said. "We should be hearing from artillery soon enough."

Soaring from the edge of a high plateau, the six starfighters dropped into a broad valley, disturbingly

reminiscent of Geonosis, right down to the berthed starships and war machines spread across the floor.

Hailfire droids wheeled out to greet them with volleys
of surface-to-air missiles. Turbolaser cannons affixed to
Trade Federation landing ships cut the gray-yellow sky
to ribbons. STAPs lifted into the air, and squads of infantry droids hurried for armed skimmers.

Unequipped to defend itself against the onslaught, tat-
tered Red Squadron banked broadly to the north, evading plasma beams and flak from exploding heat seekers.
Anakin and Obi-Wan paid out the last of their proton
torpedoes in futile attempts to save Reds Three, Four,
and Five. Bursts from their laser cannons crippled two
enemy speeders and countless droid fighters, sending
them crashing into the contaminated terrain. R4-P17
howled as Obi-Wan twisted the starfighter through violent airbursts and superheated clouds of billowing
smoke.

Red Six vanished.

When they had juked their way through the worst of
it, Anakin came alongside Obi-Wan.

It was just the two of them now.

"Point three-oh," Anakin said. "On the landing platform."

Obi-Wan gazed out the right side of the cockpit at
what had been an enormous plasma-generating facility.
Fractured containment domes and adjacent roofless
structures revealed toppled extraction shafts, exploded
activators, and tumbled walkways. In the center of the
complex stood an elevated square of corroded ferrocrete,
crowded with enemy fighter craft and bearing a single
Geonosian fantail of distinctive design.

"Dooku's sloop."

The words had scarcely left Obi-Wan's mouth when
battle droids began to gush from the facility and out

onto the landing platform. Bolts from the droids' blasters clawed at the pair of prowling starfighters.

"I guess we're not going in through the front door," Obi-Wan said.

"There's another way," Anakin said, as they were emerging from their flyby. "We go in through the north dome."

Obi-Wan looked over his left shoulder at the partially collapsed hemisphere. The lid that had once topped the plasma containment structure was long gone, and the resultant circular opening was large enough for a starfighter to thread.

Obi-Wan had misgivings, nevertheless.

"What about residual radiation inside the dome?"

"Radiation?" Anakin laughed. "The maneuver alone will probably kill us!"

38

With its fifty-three skydocks, hundreds of private turbolifts, arrays of hidden security armaments, and towering atria, 500 Republica was a world unto itself. Containing more technology than many Outer Rim worlds and more residents than some, the sky-piercing structure was the unrivaled gem of the Senate District, and the elegant cynosure of the district's prestigious Ambassadorial Sector.

What had begun as a stately building in the classic style had, over the course of centuries, become a veritable mountain of steps and setbacks—some with flat roofs, others as gently rounded as shoulders, and still others as massive as any structure in the district. Up and up they climbed, profuse, organic, in seeming competition for Coruscant's sunlight, culminating in a graceful crown, banded with penthouses and topped by a lithe spire. Gilded by the rising sun, its head in the clouds, buttressed by the towers that had allowed it to outgrow all its neighbors, 500 Republica was the lofty vantage from which a privileged few could actually gaze *down* on Coruscant.

Which was precisely why the building had become the landmark the galaxy's disenfranchised pointed to when they spoke of Coruscant's disproportionate wealth and elitism. Why 500 Republica was viewed by many as more emblematic of the bloated, indulgent Senate than the Senate's own squat mushroom of a home.

Mace could feel the oppressive weight of the structure bearing down on him as the team entered 500 Republica's level-one sub-basement—square kilometers of supportive ferrocrete and durasteel, crammed with whining, whirring machines that kept the tower stable, aloft, secure, climate-controlled, and supplied with water and power. As deep as it was, the sub-basement was still a hundred meters above Coruscant's true underground, and twice that above the original surface of the planet.

The team had had to wait hours for Republica security to grant them permission to enter and carry on with the investigation. For a time, Mace had considered appealing to Palpatine for permission, since the Supreme Chancellor had an upper-level suite in the building. For company, the probe droids had scores of custodial and maintenance droids, but the trail to Sidious had gone cold.

Lost among countless footprints that covered the floor.

"Unless we can find prints that say otherwise, there's no guarantee our quarry gained entrance to the sub-basement from Five Hundred Republica itself," Dyne pronounced, switching his handheld processor to standby mode. "He may have entered from the tunnels that connect to the east or west skydocks."

"In other words, he could have arrived here from just about anywhere on Coruscant," Shaak Ti said.

Dyne nodded. "Presumably."

Mace gazed down the tunnel the team had taken.

"Could we have missed something along the way?"

"The droids wouldn't."

Mace gestured to the smudged and stained ferrocrete floor. "Why would the prints suddenly end right here?"

Dyne compressed his lips and shook his head. "Maybe someone carried him here by repulsorlift. Unless you're suggesting he levitated across the floor." He thought about it for a long moment, then said: "All right, for the sake of argument, let's say that he *did* levitate here."

"There'll be prints at his starting point," Mace said.

Dyne scanned the sub-basement, pursed his lips, and blew out his breath. "We're going to need a lot more probe droids."

"How many more?" Mace said.

"A *lot*."

"How long to bring them here and search this entire level?"

"With all this machinery, the skydock access tunnels, the waste and supply turbolifts . . . I couldn't begin to guess. What's more, we're going to need additional security clearance to search the tunnels."

"You'll have whatever clearance you need," Shaak Ti promised.

Mace glanced around. "You'll have to run imaging scans of the partitions and the exterior walls."

"That could require several weeks," Dyne said cautiously.

"Then the sooner we begin, the better."

Dyne took a comlink from his belt and was about to activate it when the floor began to tremble.

"A quake?" Mace asked Shaak Ti.

She shook her head. "I'm not sure—"

A second jolt shook the sub-basement, strong enough to dust the team with loose ferrocrete from the high ceiling.

"Feels like something rammed the building," Dyne said.

It wouldn't be the first time an intoxicated or exhausted driver had veered from one of the free-travel skylanes and plowed into the side of a building, Mace told himself. And yet—

The next shudder was accompanied by the distant sound of a powerful explosion. Lights in the subbasement faded momentarily, then returned to full illumination, sending the custodial and maintenance droids into frantic activity.

Also at a far remove, klaxons and sirens blared.

"My comlink isn't working," Dyne said, jabbing at the device's frequency search control with his forefinger.

"We're tiers below midlevel," Shaak Ti said.

Dyne shook his head. "That shouldn't matter. Not in here."

Stretching out with the Force, Mace sensed danger, frenzy, pain, and death. "Where's the nearest exit?"

Dyne pointed to his left. "The tunnel to the east skydock."

Mace's thoughts swirled. He turned to Valiant. "Commander, Shaak Ti and I will need half your squad. You and the rest of your team will assist Captain Dyne with the search. Keep me informed of your progress."

"What about me, sir?"

Mace looked at TC-16, then at Dyne. "The droid stays with you."

Flanked by commandos, Mace and Shaak Ti raced off. The tunnel to the east skydock shook as they hurried through mixed-species crowds of frightened pedestrians heading toward and away from 500 Republica. Ahead of them loomed a square of dim sunlight, almost aquatic in quality, typical of the lower reaches of Coruscant's urban canyons.

On the huge quadrangular skydock, humans, humanoids, and aliens were crouched behind parked limos, taxis, and private yachts, or hurrying for the entrance to the upper-level mag-lev platform. Shouts and screams punctuated the drone of overhead traffic. Panic gripped the free-travel skylanes. Taxis and transports were swerving in all directions, careening into one another and the sides of buildings, making desperate rooftop and plaza landings.

Higher, a plunging vehicle—a boxy cargo ship, engulfed in flames—came streaking through a horizontal autonavigation lane, surrendering some of its velocity to a violent collision with a public transport pod before continuing its fiery plunge toward the bottom of the canyon.

Mace tracked the ill-fated ship for a moment, then tilted his head back and put the edge of his hand to his brow. Distant buildings shimmered, as if miraged by heat.

The district's defensive shield had been raised!

Higher still, something was wrong with the flickering sky. Light flared behind stratified clouds, and thunder of a kind reverberated from the summits of the taller buildings. Far to the south, Coruscant's pale blue mantle was hashed into triangles and slivers by white contrails.

In their oblate pools of white skin, Shaak Ti's eyes were wide when she looked at Mace.

"An attack," she said in stunned disbelief.

Comlink already in hand, Mace activated the Jedi Temple frequency and held the device to his ear.

"Nothing but noise."

"The deflector shield," Shaak Ti said.

She craned her neck, striped montrals and head-tail quivering. "Or could they be jamming transmissions?"

Mace's nostrils flared. "Crowd control!" he told the commandos. To Shaak Ti, he said: "Find Palpatine. See to it he's conveyed to safety. I'll send backup."

39

In the ruined archive hall of LiMerge Power's plasma facility, Count Dooku waited for Kenobi and Skywalker to arrive. The room was enormous by any standard, thirty meters high and three times that in circumference. Dooku could imagine it when it had hummed with life and activity, before the catastrophe. Still, that it had remained intact was a testament to its builders. And with its curved walls of holobooks and data storage disks—irradiated beyond salvage—he accepted that some might believe that secrets of the most sinister sort were concealed here.

Jedi like Kenobi and Skywalker, who *wanted* to believe as much.

Despite their gullibility, they were nothing if not tenacious and—dare he admit it?—exceptional.

In the risks they undertook.

In how deluded they were—about so many things.

In their unabashed zeal to capture him they had actually piloted their starfighters straight through the roof of the largest of the facility's containment domes, and had managed to survive. Such superhuman feats were almost enough to convince Dooku that they still had the Force with them.

If only they weren't so naïve and easily manipulated.

Once again, Darth Sidious had divined the actions they would take well in advance of their own deciding. The talent had less to do with being able to peer into the future than with having access to streams of possibilities. Sidious wasn't unerring. He could be surprised or taken off his guard—as at Geonosis, as in the case of Gunray's mechno-chair—but not for long. His mastery of the dark side of the Force endowed him with the power to decipher the currents that comprised the future, and to comprehend that while those currents were manifold, they were not boundless.

Such mastery was one of the skills that distinguished Sidious from Yoda, who believed the future was so much in motion it could not be read with any clarity—especially during times when the dark side was on the ascendant. But how could Yoda be expected to see the whole picture with one eye closed?

Deliberately closed.

The Jedi accepted as a matter of faith that embracing the dark side meant cutting themselves off from the light, when in fact the dark side opened one to the full range of the Force.

There was, after all, only the Force.

It was unfortunate for the Jedi that they believed the Force was theirs alone to use and honor. That sense of entitlement was evident in the way Kenobi and Skywalker called on the Force in their fervor to confront him: opening doors with waves of their hands, clearing obstacles from their path with similar gestures, moving with what appeared to be numinous speed and agility, flourishing their blue blades as if they were powered by the will of the Force itself . . .

While at the same time oblivious.

Dooku took a moment to set in place his compact welcoming device, then hurried through a series of decontamination chambers into the facility's control room, which overlooked the rear of the archive hall and the vast space enclosed by the containment dome itself. There he activated a second small holoprojector and positioned himself for the holocam. Owing to interference, images of the archive hall were nowhere near as clear as he might have wished, and the audio feed was worse. It was more important, though, that Kenobi and Skywalker be able to see him than he them.

At long last the two Jedi rushed headlong into the hall, only to *stop* upon spying his life-sized holoimage emanating from the compact holoprojector he had left behind.

"Dooku!" young Skywalker said, as if his tone of voice should suffice to send shivers down the backbones of his opponents. "Show yourself!"

Rooms distant, Dooku merely spread his hands in a gesture of greeting, and aimed his words at the holoprojector's microphone. "Stand not amazed, young Jedi. Is this not the way you had your first glimpse of Lord Sidious?"

Instead of replying, Kenobi touched Skywalker on the arm, and the two of them began to scan the hall, no doubt in an attempt to locate him through the Force.

"You won't find me, Jedi—"

"We know you're here, Dooku," Kenobi said suddenly—and with irksome audio distortion. "We can sense you."

Dooku sighed in disappointment. They weren't hearing him. Worse, the video feed was also becoming hopelessly corrupted. More through the Force than the holocam feed he saw them moving toward the very doorway he had taken to reach the control room.

Exceptional, he thought.

Despite his mastery of the Quey'tek technique for hiding oneself in the Force, they had located him! Ah, well then, time to *entertain* them, in observance of Sidious's wishes.

Plucking his comlink from his belt, Dooku's right thumb leapt across the small touch pad.

Heralded by the sound of metallic footfalls, fifty infantry droids crowded into the archive hall through two opposing doorways, perpendicular to the one through which the Jedi had entered.

"—beginning to . . . things almost as much . . . I hate sand," Skywalker was saying to his former mentor as he raised his lightsaber over one shoulder.

Kenobi spread his legs and brought his blade directly in front of him. "Then . . . sweep up."

Touched by their camaraderie, Dooku smiled to himself. Darth Sidious had his work cut out for him if he ever expected to turn Skywalker to the dark side.

He thumbed a final comlink key.

And with that, the droids leveled their blaster rifles at the Jedi and opened fire.

Yoda surrendered himself to the current of the Force. Sometimes, when the current was swift and steadfast, he could see through the eyes of his fellow Jedi, almost as if they were the Temple's remote sensors. And sometimes when the current was especially forceful, when it surged as if descending from great heights, he could hear the voice of Qui-Gon Jinn, as clearly as if he were still alive.

Master Yoda, he might say, *we still have much to learn. The Force remains a code only partially deciphered. But another key has been found. We will become stronger than we have ever been . . .*

Today was not one of those days. Today the current was interrupted by eddies and whirlpools, hydraulic traps whose roar overpowered the voices Yoda sought to hear. Today the current was not pellucid, but muddied by red soil eroded from distant shores, treacherous with obstacles, tainted.

Though he was scarcely aware of it, his eyelids were squeezed tight, his eyeballs dancing beneath as if incapable of focusing on any one thing. He had an image of himself drawing aside a veil only to find another, and another beyond that.

The dark side frustrated his every effort to see clearly.

The experience was still something new to him.

Even though he'd had centuries to grow accustomed to foreboding, he had lived far longer without it. The dark side never completely disappeared—it scratched at the surface like an insect crawling across a transparisteel panel—and he had been able to sense its incremental increases in strength when the Jedi erred, or when the Republic erred, and soon the two were hand in hand.

Drawn into the mistakes of the Republic, the Jedi had been. But knowingly, and sometimes with full complicity. Allowed the dark side to take root, the Jedi had. Allowed arrogance to infect the Order, the Jedi had. A priority, holding on to power had become. Inflated by their own conquests, the Jedi became.

Some Jedi believed that Yoda wasn't aware of these things, or that he hadn't done enough to stem the tide of the dark side. Some believed that the Council had acted improperly or, worse, ineptly. What they failed to understand was that, once rooted, the growth of the dark side was inexorable, and could only be reversed by the one born to restore balance.

Yoda was not that one.

Aged, experienced, diplomatic, informative, brilliant with a lightsaber . . . Yes, all of these things. And not unacquainted with the power of the dark side. For that reason he understood just how dangerous this new Sith Lord was. He hadn't had a sense of that danger until he had fought Dooku on Geonosis.

Then he understood.

In self-exile for a thousand years, the Sith had not merely been waiting for an appropriate time to reemerge and exact revenge, but for the birth of one strong enough to embrace the dark side fully and become its dedicated instrument. This was Sidious: powerful enough to hide in plain sight. Powerful enough to instruct his apprentice, Dooku, to expose him, and still remain hidden from the Jedi.

And as arrogant as the Jedi. Convinced that his way was the one and only way.

Did he know about Skywalker?

Surely he did. What better way to ensure total victory than by killing or corrupting the Chosen One? Even if not that One, someone so strong in midi-chlorians . . . *Someone birthed by the Force itself,* Qui-Gon would have said—never a doubt that Anakin's mother might have been lying.

The boy had no father.

None I choose to remember. None I would honor with that title.

The Sith were aware of Skywalker. How would he react when they tried finally to ensnare him?

Yoda's eyes snapped open. A disturbance in the Force—of such magnitude that he had been hurled from the current.

At his thought command, the window shutters in his quarters opened, and he gazed out on Coruscant, over the plain of The Works and beyond. Something was wrong with the sky. Behind gathered clouds turned red and gold by noxious smoke: a lightstorm. Pulsing light, brighter than the waning rays of Coruscant's sun. Movement, as well; outside Coruscant's busy envelope, not seen but sensed.

An attack.

The Sith Lord's response to his being chased? Was it possible?

He perceived Mace running down corridors in the Temple; then turned as Mace rushed through the doorway. At the same instant, a flaming Republic ship streaked past the Temple's crowning spires and crashed violently in the heart of The Works.

"Tiin, Koon, Ki-Adi-Mundi, and some of the others are on their way up the well," Mace said. "I sent Stass Allie to assist Shaak Ti in guarding Chancellor Palpatine."

Yoda nodded sagely. "Well trained the Supreme Chancellor's Red Guards are. But display due concern for his safety, the Jedi must."

"Reports from naval command are garbled," Mace continued. "It's clear that the attack caught the home fleet by surprise. Groups of Separatist ships managed to penetrate the envelope before the fleet had time to engage. Now, by all accounts, our vessels are holding the line."

Yoda adopted an expression that mixed anger and bafflement. "Monitoring hyperspace reversion points, our commanders weren't?"

Mace's eyes narrowed. "The Separatist fleet jumped from the Deep Core."

"*Secret,* those routes were. Known to us and few others." Yoda looked at Mace. "Unrestricted access to the archives, Dooku had. Access enough to erase all mentions of Kamino. Access enough to learn of explorations in the Deep Core."

Mace went to the window wall and stared at the sky. "Dooku isn't leading this attack. Obi-Wan confirmed that he is on Tythe."

"Revealed, the importance of Tythe is. To draw into the Outer Rim additional Jedi."

"Maybe Palpatine will heed the Council's warnings next time."

"Improbable. But as you say: perhaps."

Mace swung back to Yoda. "It's Grievous. But he can't be planning to occupy Coruscant. There aren't enough battle droids in the entire galaxy for that."

"Desperate he is," Yoda said, more to himself.

"It's not in his programming."

Yoda looked up. "Not Grievous—*Sidious.*"

Mace took a moment to answer. "If that's true, then we're closer to finding him than we thought. Still, he can't believe we'd call off the search now."

"Demoralize Coruscant, Grievous will. Harry those who live in the heights and who wield power. Send them fleeing for safer havens, the attack will. Disrupt the Senate."

Mace paced in front of the windows. "This will only encourage Palpatine to triple the size of the clone army, construct more and more starships and fighters, strike at more worlds. With the Senate crippled, no one will oppose him."

"*Modulate,* this war does. Recall every available Jedi, we must."

"The HoloNet is down," Mace said. "Surface communications are distorted by the defensive shields."

Yoda nodded. "Use the beacon, we will."

In the wake of the erratic and mostly unintelligible messages that had reached 500 Republica regarding the Separatists' surprise attack, Dyne had considered the sub-basement to be the safest place on Coruscant. But now that the team had discovered a possible finish to the long trail they had followed from The Works, the building's vast underground seemed the most dangerous place to be.

With a battle raging in space, and notwithstanding Mace Windu's command to the contrary, Dyne had been tempted to suspend the search for Sidious's lair and report back to the Intelligence division, as he had ordered the other analysts to do. But as ARC commander Valiant had pointed out, the search team's objective was as important to the war as the actions of the ships that were protecting Coruscant.

So, while the team waited for Intelligence to deliver additional probe droids, a search of the sub-basement had begun—admittedly superficial and somewhat desultory, but only in response to the seeming impossibility of the task. Electronically tethered to the probe droids, Dyne and the commandos had performed imagings of some of the partitions and walls, and investigated numerous unlit hollows and recesses. The basement became a kind of microcosm for the entire war, with everyone on the team contributing separate skills.

Only the interpreter droid, TC-16, was at a loss for something to do.

Five Hundred Republica hadn't sustained any follow-up jolts. Dyne had learned that the initial jolts had owed not to bombardment, but to the fall of ships destroyed at the edge of space. With thousands of cargo and passenger vessels arriving at Coruscant at any given moment, he could scarcely imagine the chaos upside. Secondary shocks that had rocked the huge building had been traced to the firing of plasma weapons concealed in 500 Republica's cake of a crown.

Several hours into the cursory search, Dyne had been struck by the possibility that certain Coruscanti—perhaps the Sith Lord himself—could be helping to coordinate the attack. With HoloNet transmissions jammed and surface communications sabotaged by the defensive shields, he had theorized that the probe droids might be able to home in on exchanges occurring on eccentric frequencies.

He was as astonished as anyone when the hovering probe droids had led the team right back to where they had begun the search: where the footprints of their as-yet-unidentified quarry ended.

The source of the unusual frequency was determined to be directly beneath them. The droids had discovered further that the ferrocrete floor panel thought to have been the end of the trail was actually a movable platform, not unlike a turbolift, but powered hydraulically rather than by antigrav repulsor. The search for a hidden control panel, such as had been detected at the niche, hadn't come to anything. But by broadcasting sounds—both within and outside the range of human hearing—the probe droids had ultimately conjured a response from the platform.

Following what had sounded like a debate, the probe droids had chirped and bleated at the panel a second time. Issuing a resolved *click,* the panel had descended a couple of centimeters, then come to a halt.

Dyne recalled wondering where the platform's shaft could lead.

Unlike many of Coruscant's tallest buildings, 500 Republica did not rely on the support of earlier structures for its foundation, but was solid almost all the way down to bedrock. Or at least was thought to be. This far below Coruscant's civilized crust, there remained areas as unfamiliar as the surfaces of some distant worlds.

Dyne had decided to contact Mace Windu at the Jedi Temple for advice on how to proceed. But when his repeated attempts failed, he and Valiant had made a command decision to carry on without the Jedi.

Ground imaging scans had already shown the shaft to be fifty meters deep. Four meters in diameter, the panel was large enough to accommodate the entire team, including the interpreter droid.

Definitely the most dangerous place to be, Dyne thought as he wedged himself among the commandos.

The probe droids chirped instructions to the panel, and it began to drop.

Slower than would have been the case had it answered to a repulsorlift.

The wall of the circular shaft was ancient ceramacrete, cracked and stained in places.

"If anyone's down here," Dyne said to Valiant, "they're probably aware we're on the way."

The commandos didn't need to be told. Weapons enabled, they hurried to firing positions the moment the platform came to a rest.

Ribboned with conduits and crowded with ancient machinery, the dismal space bore some resemblance to the tunnels and rooms they had passed through and explored since leaving The Works. But this one, Dyne told himself, was an archaeologist's dream. Probably a maintenance node for buildings that had stood here in Coruscant's dim past.

Twenty meters ahead of them, flickering light lanced from around the edges of a large metal door.

Dyne sent the droids to investigate, then studied the processor's data screen.

"One flesh-and-blood behind the door," he whispered to Valiant. "Readings also indicate the presence of droids." He looked at the ARC. "It's your call, Commander."

Valiant regarded the door. "We've come this far. I say we go in like we own the place."

Dyne's heart began to race. "Find, fix, finish."

In what had served as the archive room for LiMerge Power's plasma facility, droid parts were piling up so fast and so high that Obi-Wan and Anakin could scarcely see Dooku's wavering holoimage any longer.

The business of destroying infantry droids—for that's precisely what the confrontation had come down to— was beginning to take a toll on Obi-Wan. The decapitations and amputations were no longer as surgical as they had been when Dooku had first unleashed the droids. The slices that halved his spindly opponents and the thrusts that pierced chest plastrons had lost some of their initial accuracy.

Neither he nor Anakin was relying on lightsabers only. Calling on the Force, they hurled whatever could be lifted from the floor or yanked from the walls. Force-pushing four droids to the floor, hewing half a dozen more with his flashing blade, Anakin leapt from Obi-Wan's side, landed on the head of a perplexed droid, and began to race toward the far side of the hall, using other heads as stepping-stones.

But for every droid either of them destroyed, five more would appear, creating an impenetrable barrier between them and the doorway through which Dooku had certainly disappeared moments before they had arrived.

"Dooku!" Anakin snarled through clenched teeth. "I will kill you!"

"Control your rage, Anakin," Obi-Wan managed to say between breaths. "Don't give him the satisfaction."

Anakin shot him a worrisome scowl. "Can't have me becoming *too* powerful, now, can we, Master?"

Before Obi-Wan could reply, twenty battle droids hurried into the room through the door behind him. Whirling, he deflected their first barrage, then fought his way to cover behind a heap of dismembered droids, where Anakin joined him.

In the hope that Dooku was listening from afar, he shouted: "Whatever happens here, Dooku, your Confederacy is finished! The Republic has all of you on the run—even your master, *Sidious*."

More droids appeared.

To Dooku, this was nothing more than a *game*, Obi-Wan told himself. But if it was a demonstration of Force ability Dooku wanted, then Anakin was still more than willing to provide it.

"Dooku!" he howled.

With such force and wrath that the ceiling of the vast hall began to collapse.

Hurry, Threepio," Padmé said over her shoulder. "Unless you want the Senate to be your final resting place."

The protocol droid hastened his pace. "I assure you, Mistress, I'm moving as quickly as my limbs permit. Oh, curse my metal body! I'll become entombed here!"

The broad, ornate hallways leading from the Great Rotunda were packed with Senators, their aides, staff members, and droids, many laden with armloads of documents and data disks, and in some cases expensive gifts received from appreciative lobbyists. Blue-robed Senate Guards and helmeted clone troopers were doing their best to oversee the evacuation, but, what with the warbling sirens and flying rumors, alarm was beginning to yield to panic.

"How could this happen?" a Sullustan was posing to the Gotal next to him. "How?"

To all sides of her—among Bith, Gran, Wookiees, Rodians—Padmé heard the same question being asked.

How could Coruscant be invaded?

She wondered, as well. But she had more to worry about than Coruscant.

Where is Anakin?

She reached for him in her thoughts, with her heart.

I need you. Come back to me—quickly!

Grievous's strike was impeccably timed. Many delegates who might not have been on Coruscant had come to hear Palpatine's State of the Republic address, and had remained onworld to attend the endless parties that followed. In light of the surprise attack, Palpatine's reassurances seemed even more woefully premature now than when he had uttered them. And despite the fact that the Supreme Chancellor's optimistic remarks had been echoed throughout the Great Rotunda, Padmé couldn't help notice that many of her peers were surrounded by cadres of bodyguards, or sporting body armor, jet packs, or other emergency escape devices.

Clearly Palpatine had failed to lull everyone into complacency.

Thirteen years earlier Padmé could have claimed to be one of the few dignitaries whose homeworld had succumbed to an invasion and occupation. Targeted by the Trade Federation, Naboo had fallen to the Neimoidians; her parents and advisers were arrested and jailed. Now she was just one of thousands of Senators whose worlds had been similarly invaded and ransacked. Regardless, she refused to accept that Coruscant could fall to the Confederacy—even with the home fleet reduced to half its former strength. Word of mouth had it that buildings in the Ambassadorial Sector had been toppled, that battle droids were surging through Loijin Plaza, that midlevel skylanes overflowed with Geonosian Fanblades and droid fighters . . . Even if the rumors proved true, Padmé was convinced that Palpatine would find some way to drive Grievous from the Core—*again.*

Perhaps he would recall battle groups participating in the Outer Rim sieges.

That meant that Anakin would be recalled.

She chided herself for being selfish. But didn't she have the right? Hadn't she *earned* the right?

Just this once?

Thus far, the Senate Building was unscathed. Nevertheless, Homeworld Security felt it prudent to move everyone to the shelters deep beneath the hemisphere and the enormous plaza that fronted it. With most of the autonavigation lanes congested, it wasn't as if anyone could flee Coruscant. And there was always the likelihood that Grievous would single out civilian targets, as he had done on countless occasions.

Jostled by the surging crowd, Padmé collided with a Gran delegate who fixed his trio of eyestalks on her.

"And you originally *opposed* the Military Creation Act," he barked. "What do you say now?"

There was really no answer. Besides, she had been on the receiving end of similar reproofs since the start of the war. Typically voiced by those who failed to grasp that her concern was for the Constitution, not for the ultimate fate of the free-trade zones.

She heard her name called, and turned to see Bail Organa and Mon Mothma angling toward where she and C-3PO were momentarily hampered. With them were two female Jedi—Masters Shaak Ti and Stass Allie.

"Have you seen the Chancellor?" Bail asked when he could.

She shook her head. "He's probably in the holding office."

"We were just there," Shaak Ti said. "The office is empty. Even his guards are gone."

"They must have escorted him to the shelters," Padmé said.

Bail glanced at something over her shoulder and raised his hand over his head to call attention to himself. "Mas Amedda," he explained for Padmé's benefit. "He'll know where to find the Chancellor."

The tall, horned, gray-complected Chagrian fairly shouldered his way through the crowd.

"The Supreme Chancellor had no meetings scheduled until later today," he said in answer to Bail's question. "I assume he is in his residence."

"Five Hundred Republica," Shaak Ti muttered to herself in seeming frustration. "I was just there."

Amedda gazed down at her in sudden concern. "And the Chancellor wasn't?"

"I wasn't looking for him then," the Jedi started to say, then allowed her words to trail off. "Master Allie and I will check the Senate Office Building and Republica." She glanced at Padmé, Bail, and the others. "Where are you going?"

"Wherever we're directed to go," Bail said.

"The turbolifts to the shelters are overwhelmed," Stass Allie said. "It'll be hours before the Senate is evacuated. My skimmer is at the plaza's northwest landing platform. You can pilot that directly to the shelters."

"Won't you and Shaak Ti need it?" Padmé asked.

"We'll use the speeder bike I arrived on," Shaak Ti said.

"We appreciate the gesture," Bail said. "But I heard that the front plaza is cordoned off."

Stass Allie took his arm. "We'll escort you."

Troopers stationed in the corridor opened a path for the group, and before long they reached the doorways to the main plaza. There, however, a commando blocked their path.

"You can't exit this way," the commando told Bail.

"They're with us," Shaak Ti said.

Waving signals to several of his white-armored comrades, the commando stood aside and allowed Padmé's group to pass. The sky above the statue-studded plaza was crowded with gunships and personnel carriers. AT-TEs and other mobile artillery pieces had already been deployed.

The Jedi led Padmé, C-3PO, Bail, and Mon Mothma to the open-roofed skimmer. The speeder bike was parked alongside. Shaak Ti swung one leg over the seat and started the engine. Stass Allie settled in behind her.

"Good luck," she said.

The Senators and the droid watched the two Jedi race off in the direction of the Senate Office Building; then, with Bail piloting, they boarded the oval-shaped Flash skimmer and dropped down into the wide canyon below the plaza.

Free-travel traffic was thick even there, but Bail's skill got them through the worst of it and on course for the shelter entrances, which were just below the main sky-docks of the Senate Medcenter.

Without warning, two beams of scarlet light stabbed at them from somewhere above the dome of the Senate.

"Vulture droids!" Bail said.

Padmé clutched on to C-3PO as Bail veered away from the plasma bolts. The pod-winged droid fighter that had fired was one of several that were strafing vehicles, landing platforms, and buildings in the canyon. Republic gunships were in close pursuit, unleashing with powerful wingtip cannons.

Padmé's mouth fell open in astonishment. This was something she had never expected to witness on Coruscant.

Bail was doing everything he could to keep clear of blaster bolts, plasma, and flak, but so was every other driver, and collisions quickly became part of the obstacle course. Dropping the skimmer lower still, Bail began to

head for the nearest shelter entrance, as friendly and unfriendly fire ranged closer.

A flash of intense light blinded Padmé momentarily.
The skimmer tipped harshly, almost spilling its occu-
pants into midair. Smoke poured from the starboard tur-
bine nacelle, and the small craft went into a shallow dive.

"Hold tight!" Bail yelled.

"We're doomed!" C-3PO said.

Padmé understood that Bail was swerving for a landing platform that abutted a wide skybridge. Tears
streaming from her eyes, stricken with a sudden nausea,
she placed her right hand on her abdomen.

Anakin! she said to herself. *Anakin!*

43

Flagship of the Separatist flotilla, General Grievous's kilometers-long cruiser the *Invisible Hand* held to a stationary orbit above Coruscant's Senate District, just now in full sunlight, the most majestic of its forest of aeries standing tall above the clouds. Magnified holoimages of the buildings rose from the tactical table on the cruiser's bridge. Grievous studied the images for a moment before returning to his customary place at the forward viewscreens.

Glinting in daylight, the gargantuan wedge-shaped assault ships that were, for good reason, the pride of the Republic fleet were positioned to provide cover for the planet's most important centers. In the first moments of the sneak attack, Grievous had caught a few of the ships with their shields contracted, and those hapless few glided now like flaming torches above Coruscant's pearl-strung night side, fire-suppression tenders and rescue ships following in their wake, gobbling up escape pods and lifeboats. The surviving cruisers were managing to keep their Separatist counterparts at bay. Although that scarcely mattered, since neither aerial bombardment nor invasion was important to the plan.

From the point of view of Republic naval commanders, it must have appeared that Grievous lacked a plan; that desperation resulting from his previous defeats in the Mid and Outer Rims had driven him to gather what remained of his fleet and hurl it into a battle he couldn't possibly hope to win. And indeed, Grievous was doing everything he could to encourage that misconception. The warships under his command were haphazardly dispersed, vulnerable to counterattack, concentrating fire on communications satellites and orbital mirrors, lobbing occasional and largely ineffectual volleys of plasma at the world they had come so far and risked so much to assail.

All this was crucial to the plan.

The tactics of terror had their place.

From hundreds of areas on Coruscant's bright and dark sides streamed columns of passenger and cargo ships, determined to reach the safety of deep space. Indeed, there were almost as many vessels attempting to depart as there were arriving, constrained to autonavigation lanes and easy prey because of that. Elsewhere in local space, inward-bound ships that had reverted to realspace outside the battle zone had diverted from their approach vectors and were either hanging well to the rear, close to Coruscant's small moons, or deviating for the star system's inner worlds at sublight speeds.

In the middle distance, droid fighters and clone-piloted starfighters were destroying one another with a vengeance. Perhaps a wing of Vulture fighters had penetrated Republic lines at the start of the battle, but many had since been destroyed by orbital platform cannons, flights of high-altitude patrol craft, or ground-based artillery. Others had dashed themselves against the defensive shields that provided additional safeguards for Coruscant's political districts. But that, too, was part of the plan to inspire panic, since the sight of laser bolts or plummeting ships detonating against those transparent domes of energy could be terrifying. Smoke billowing from some of the capital world's deepest canyons told Grievous that a few of the spearhead droids had succeeded in evading both shields and antiaircraft fire.

Similarly, tentative maneuvers on the part of Coruscant's home fleet vessels told him how eager their commanders were to break formation and engage Grievous head-on. But they had a world to protect and, more important, were too meager in number to proceed with certainty. No doubt they were waiting for reinforcements to arrive from distant systems. Anticipating as much, Grievous had planted surprises for those Republic battle groups closest to the Core, surprises in the form of mass-shadow mines, and had station warships at reversion points along the hyperlanes. If he couldn't prevent reinforcements from arriving, he could at least delay them.

If everything went according to plan, the Separatist flotilla would be ready to jump to lightspeed long before reinforcements reverted in sufficient numbers to pose a serious threat.

Grievous took a long moment to absorb the silent battle that flared beyond the thick transparisteel of the bridge viewports. He loathed being so far from the action and bloodshed. But he knew that he had to be patient a while longer. Then all the waiting and frustration would be justified.

A Neimoidian addressed him from one of the duty stations.

"General: comlink transmissions are returning to normal in sectors of the planet. The enemy appears to have comprehended that we are using the jamming suite we employed to our advantage at Praesitlyn."

"This is not unexpected," Grievous said, without turning from the view. "Instruct Group One commanders that they should continue targeting orbital mirrors and communication satellites. Relocate the jamming platform to zero-one-zero ecliptic, and intensify the shields."

"Yes, General." The Neimoidian paused, then added: "I am compelled to report that we are sustaining heavy losses in all groups."

Grievous glanced at the tactical table. Group One alone had lost two Trade Federation carriers. The Neimoidians had managed to jettison the spherical core of one of the carriers, but the other had been blown completely in half. In the holofield, the tiny dots spilling from the carrier's curved and now separated arms were droid fighters.

"Override the survival and engagement programs of those droid fighters," Grievous ordered. "Issue a command that they speed directly for Coruscant. They are to convert to explosive devices."

"Are any specific targets assigned?"

"The outskirts of the Senate District."

"General, some of our fighters have already infiltrated that sector."

"Excellent. Command those to target landing platforms, skyways, pedestrian plazas, and shelters. Wherever possible, they are to dedicate themselves to overwhelming Coruscant's civil defense forces."

"Affirmative."

"Have any Republic auxiliaries arrived?"

"A task force comprising four light cruisers is decanting from hyperspace and advancing from Coruscant's night side."

"Order our commanders there to engage them."

Sooner than expected, Grievous thought. Ordinarily he would have given thought to contingency plans, but he trusted that Lords Sidious and Tyranus would apprise him of any changes. Had it not been for the Deep Core hyperspace routes the flotilla had taken, the attack could not have been launched successfully. Those little-known routes had been furnished by Sidious, who was less concerned with battlefield tactics than with long-range strategies. It was warcraft of a sort Grievous had never practiced. Warcraft in which seeming defeats had resulted in victories; seeming foes proved to be allies. Warcraft of a sort that left the losers with nothing, and the winners with everything.

The galaxy itself.

The Neimoidian communications officer had fallen silent, apparently in reception of an update from one of the duty stations. Now he said: "General, a group of Jedi starfighters has emerged from Coruscant's gravity well."

"How large a group?"

"Twenty-two craft."

"Deploy as many tri-fighters against them as are needed."

"Yes, sir."

Grievous turned from the viewports. "Is the strike force assembled?"

The gunnery officer took a moment to reply. "Your gunboat is ready, and your elites are standing by in the launching bay."

"Battle droids, as well?"

"Fifty, General."

Grievous nodded. "That should suffice." He glanced at the viewport a final time, then turned his gaze on the Neimoidian bridge crew. "Carry on. Consider every Republic vessel a target of opportunity."

* * *

"I'm sorry, Master, but the beacon still isn't transmitting."

Yoda continued to pace the floor of the Temple's computer room, then stopped and pointed the business end of his gimer stick at the Jedi seated at the beacon's control console.

"Nothing for which to be sorry," he said in reprimand. "The *Separatists'* fault this is. Jamming transmissions from this sector of Coruscant, Grievous is."

The Jedi—a brown-haired human female named Lari Oll—lifted her hands from the console and shook her head in confusion. "How could Grievous—"

"Dooku," Yoda cut her off. "Shares our secrets with his confederates, he does."

"If one of our starfighters could get past the Separatist blockade, there might be a way of relaying a message through the HoloNet."

Yoda nodded. "Already considered that, Master Tiin has. Attempt to recall Jedi from Belderone, Tythe, and other worlds, he will."

"Can they get back here in time?"

"*Hmph.* On Grievous's objective, that depends. Leave Coruscant soon and only slightly bruised, he might. Wait, we must, until he reveals his plan." Yoda paused to consider his own words, then leaned his weight on the gimer stick and looked hard at Lari Oll. "Enabled the comm is?"

"Intermittently, Master Yoda."

He nodded his chin to the communications console. "Call Master Windu."

Moments later, Windu's voice issued indistinctly from the console's annunciators.

" . . . Fisto and I . . . Senate building. Shaak . . . Allie . . . to the Chancellor's quarters in Five Hundred Republica. We . . . with them—"

"Raised, the defense shields are. Among one another, districts are unable to communicate." Yoda grimaced, then nodded once more. "Master Ti, try."

Lari Oll tried several frequencies before giving up. "I'm sor—" She caught herself. "No response."

Yoda paced away from the console, deliberately turning his back to the glut of devices, screens, data displays, in a kind of countermeasure.

Shutting his eyes to distance himself further, he stretched out with his feelings, placing in his mind's eye Mace and Kit Fisto skimming through the deranged sky; Shaak Ti and Allie Stass hurrying toward Palpatine's quarters in 500 Republica; Saesee Tiin, Agen Kolar, Bultar Swan, and other Jedi Masters and Jedi Knights streaking from Coruscant's envelope in their starfighters, local space flashing with energy bolts and globular explosions, ships too numerous to count embroiled in a monumental battle . . .

Grievous was loosing his war machines against both military and civilian targets, firing at anything and everything that wandered into his sights, commanding his droid fighters to dash themselves against Coruscant's defensive umbrellas or race down through traffic lanes, initiating chain reactions of collisions.

And yet, for all the diversion, disruption, and terror those stratagems incited, they had little to do with the real battle.

As was true of the war itself, the real battle was being fought in the Force.

Yoda stretched out further, immersing himself fully in the Force—only to feel his breath catch in his throat.

Frigid, the current became.

Arctic.

And for the first time he could feel Sidious. *Feel him on Coruscant!*

* * *

Captain Dyne stepped cautiously from the platform that had dropped the team into the unexplored depths of 500 Republica. Here, at an intersection of spooky corridors made of permacrete and surfaced with panels of plasteel, no water dripped, no insects constructed hives, no conduit worms nursed on electrical current. Strangely, however, the air was stirred by a faint and fresh breeze.

Dyne took a breath to steady his nerves. He was trained for combat, but had spent so many of the past few years doing routine Intelligence work that his once sharp reflexes were shot. Commanding the hovering probe droids to go to stasis mode, he deactivated the handheld processor and hooked it on his belt.

Drawing his Merr-Sonn blaster from its holster, he hefted it, then thumbed off the stun setting switch.

Ahead of him, ghost-like in the dismal light, the commandos were moving toward the thick door at the end of the hall, keeping close to the walls, with weapons raised. Valiant had the point, with the squad's explosives expert close behind, a thermal detonator in hand.

Dyne stepped between the powered-down pair of probe droids, TC-16 following in his footsteps.

They hadn't advanced three meters down the corridor when Dyne's ears pricked up at the sound of gurgled voices.

He could sense TC-16 come to a sudden halt behind him.

"Why, someone is speaking Geonosian," the protocol droid started to say.

Whirling, Dyne found himself staring down the wide muzzles of two organic-looking sonic weapons, grasped in the thick-fingered hands of two Geonosian soldier drones, barely visible in the shadows, their wings angled down toward the corridor's grimy floor.

The next few moments unfurled in silent slow motion.

Dyne understood that it wasn't his life flashing before his eyes, but his death.

He saw the commandos drop in their tracks, as if blown over by a gale-force wind. He watched Valiant and the explosives expert leave the floor and hurtle headlong into the door. He observed a storm of probe droid parts whirl past him. He felt himself go airborne and crash into the wall, and his insides turn spongy.

It was possible, in that eternal moment of silence, that the troopers had reacted quickly enough to get off a few bolts, because when Dyne looked to his right, along the way he had come, there were no signs of the Geonosians or, for that matter, TC-16.

Then again, for all he knew he had lapsed into unconsciousness for an undetermined amount of time. He was vaguely aware of being slumped against the wall in a position that didn't come naturally to a human being. It was as if every bone in his body had been made pliant.

Soundlessly, the distant door opened inward, and light flooded into the corridor. The light was either red or tinted so by the blood that was filling his ruptured eyeballs.

Still set on slow motion, the immediate world came in and out of focus. What remained of his vision registered a room filled with blinking equipment, screens filled with scrolling data, a holoprojector table, above which drifted a Trade Federation battleship, halved and in flames. Two machine intelligences emerged from the room, their slender, tubular bodies identifying them as assassin droids. Behind them walked a human of medium height and build, who stepped nonchalantly over Valiant's grotesquely twisted body.

His liquefying brain notwithstanding, Dyne found a

moment to be astonished, because he recognized the man instantly.

Incredible, he thought.

As the Jedi suspected, the Sith had managed to infiltrate the highest levels of the Republic government.

The fact that the man had made no attempt to mask himself assured and comforted Dyne that he was about to die, and shortly after the realization, he did.

Where is the Chancellor?" Shaak Ti demanded of the three Red Guards stationed outside the entrance to Palpatine's suite in 500 Republica.

Alongside her hurried Stass Allie, one hand on the hilt of her lightsaber. In their adamant wake followed four members of the building's small army of security personnel, who had escorted the Jedi women from a midlevel skydock to the penthouse level.

Despite having been notified of their arrival, the imposing Red Guards kept their force pikes raised in defensive postures.

"Where?" Stass Allie said, making it clear that she was going to get past them, one way or another.

Shaak Ti had her hand raised to part the doors with a Force wave when the guards lowered their pikes and stepped aside.

One punched a code into a wall panel, and the pair of burnished doors opened.

"This way," the same guard said, gesturing the Jedi inside.

A broad hallway lined with sculptures and holo-art images led into the suite itself, which, like Palpatine's chambers in the Senate Office Building, was predominantly red. There was no telling how large the suite was, but the exterior wall of the vast main room followed the curve of the building's crown and looked down on patchy clouds, typical of those that gathered around the building in late afternoon. Distant autonavigation lanes—transverse, and to and from orbit—were motionless with stalled traffic. Between them and 500 Republica hovered two LAAT gunships and a small flock of patrol skimmers.

A distinct disturbance at the crest of the Senate District's defensive umbrella meant that continued bombardment by Separatist forces had rendered the shield permeable. Beyond the superhot edge of the shield, light flashed within banks of gray clouds.

Lightning or plasma, Shaak Ti told herself.

Scarcely acknowledging her presence, Palpatine paced into the room like a caged animal, hands clasped behind his back, Senatorial robes trailing along the richly carpeted floor.

Additional Red Guards and several of Palpatine's advisers stood watching him, some with comlinks plugged into their ears, others with devices Shaak Ti understood to be vital to the continued operation of the Republic military. Should anything befall the Chancellor, authority to initiate battle campaigns and issue war codes would pass temporarily to Speaker of the Senate, Mas Amedda, who, Shaak Ti had learned, was already safely ensconced in a hardened bunker deep beneath the Great Rotunda.

She couldn't help noticing that Pestage and Isard—two of Palpatine's closest advisers—looked nervous.

"Why is he still here?" Stass Allie directed at Isard.

Isard made his lips a thin line. "Ask him yourself."

Shaak Ti practically had to plant herself in Palpatine's path to get his attention.

"Supreme Chancellor, we need to escort you to shelter."

They were not strangers. Palpatine had personally commended her for her actions at Geonosis, Kamino, Dagu, Brentaal IV, and Centares.

He stopped briefly to regard her, then swung around and paced away from her. "Master Ti, while I appreciate your concern, I've no need of rescue. As I've made abundantly plain to my advisers and protectors, I feel that my place is here, where I can best communicate with our commanders. If I were to go anywhere, it would be to the holding office."

"Chancellor, communications will be clearer from the bunker," Pestage said.

Isard added: "All those familiarization drills you so despised were conducted for just this scenario, sir."

Palpatine sent him a skewered grin. "Practice and reality are different matters. The Supreme Chancellor of the Galactic Senate does not hide from enemies of the Republic. Can I be any clearer?"

The fact that Palpatine was flustered, confused, possibly frightened was obvious. But when Shaak Ti attempted to read him through the Force, she found it difficult to get a sense of what he was truly feeling.

"Chancellor, I'm sorry," Stass Allie chimed in, "but the Jedi are obliged to make this decision for you."

He swung to her. "I thought you answered to me!"

She remained unfazed. "We answer first to the Republic, and safeguarding you is tantamount to safeguarding the Republic."

Palpatine deployed his signature penetrating gaze. "And what will you do should I refuse? Use the Force to drag me from my quarters? Pit your lightsabers against the weapons of my guards, who are also sworn to safe-guard me?"

Shaak Ti traded looks with one of the guards, wishing she could see through the face shield of his red cowl. The situation was becoming dangerous. A shiver born in the Force moved her to glance out the window.

"Supreme Chancellor," Pestage was saying. "You must listen to reason—"

"Reason?" Palpatine snapped. He aimed a finger toward the window. "Have you gazed into our once tranquil skies? Is there anything *reasonable* about what's occurring there?"

"All the more reason to move you to safety as quickly as possible," Isard said. "So that you conduct Corus-cant's defense from a hardened site."

Palpatine stared at him. "In other words, you agree with the Jedi."

"We do, sir," Isard said.

"And you?" Palpatine asked the captain of his guards. The guard nodded.

"Then all of you are in error." Palpatine stormed to the window. "Perhaps you need to take a closer look—"

Before a further word could fly from his mouth, Shaak Ti and Stass Allie were in motion; Shaak Ti tackling Pal-patine to the floor, while Allie ignited her blade and brought it vertically in front of her.

Without warning, the gunships closest to 500 Repub-lica were lanced by plasma bolts. Their door gunners blown into midair, the two ships veered and began to fall through the clouds, trailing plumes of fire and thick black smoke.

"Unhand me!" Palpatine said. "How dare you?"

Shaak Ti kept him pinned to the floor and called her lightsaber into her hand.

A shrill sound overrode the window's noise cancellation feature, and a Separatist assault craft rose into view from somewhere below the suite. Crowded at the side hatches and ready to deploy stood a band of battle droids and others. As the craft hovered closer to the window Shaak Ti gaped in disbelief.

Grievous!

"Down!" Stass Allie shouted a moment before the entire window wall blew inward, filling the air with permaglass pebbles. Through the shattered window, droids leapt into the room, opening up with blaster rifles.

Stass Allie stood immobile in the rush of wind, noise, and blaster bolts. Six Red Guards raced to her side, their activated force pikes humming in concert with Allie's lightsaber. Droids fell armless, legless, headless before they made it two meters into the room. Blaster bolts deflected by Allie's flashing blue blade blazed out of the window opening, ripping into the other droids waiting to hurdle the gap between craft and building.

For a moment Shaak Ti was certain that Allie was going to throw herself aboard the hovering gunboat, but there were simply too many droids standing in the way. Keeping Palpatine in a crouch, she grabbed a handful of his robes and began to guide him deeper into the room, her upraised lightsaber parrying bolts that ricocheted from the walls and ceiling.

Beaten back, the battle droids broke off their attack. Outside the window, the gunboat was taking heavy fire from a surround of patrol skimmers. As Allie and the Red Guards were felling the final few droids, the Separatist craft dropped back into the clouds, with bolts from the skimmers chasing it.

Releasing Palpatine to the custody of two guards, Shaak Ti raced to the window and gazed down into the clouds. By then, there was little to see but angry exchanges of cyan and crimson light.

She turned to face Isard. "Alert Homeworld Security that General Grievous has broken through the perimeter."

Elsewhere in the room, Pestage was helping Palpatine to his feet.

"Ready now, sir?"

Palpatine returned a wide-eyed nod.

"These familiarization drills you've been conducting," Stass Allie started to say.

Isard gestured to one of the side rooms. "The suite is equipped with a secret turbolift that serves a secure, midlevel skydock. An armored gunship is standing by to transport the Chancellor to a bunker complex in the Sah'c District."

"Negative," Shaak Ti said, shaking her head. "Grievous knew enough to come here. We have to assume that the escape route has been compromised, as well."

"We can't just take him to a public shelter," Isard said.

"No," Shaak Ti agreed. "But there are other ways to reach the bunker complex."

"Why not use Republica's private turbolifts," one of the security guards suggested. "Ride them to the basement levels and you'll have access to any number of landing platforms."

Stass Allie nodded, then glanced at Palpatine. "Supreme Chancellor, your guards are going to encircle you. You are not to attempt to leave that circle under any circumstances. Do you understand?"

Palpatine nodded. "I'll do whatever you say."

Allie waited until the Red Guards had gathered around him. "Now—quickly!"

When everyone had moved into the hallway, Shaak Ti used her comlink to find Mace Windu.

"Mace, Grievous is onworld," she said the moment she heard his voice.

The response was noisy but intelligible. "I just heard."

"The Chancellor's escape route may be in jeopardy," she continued. "We're heading for Republica's sub-basements. Can you meet us there?"

"Kit and I are nearby."

Pressed into the turbolift with Stass Allie, Palpatine's guards and advisers, and Republica's security personnel, Shaak Ti watched the display tick off the floors.

No one spoke until the car had reached the first sub-level.

"Don't stop," Shaak Ti told the security man closest to the controls. "The deeper we go, the better."

"All the way to the bottom?" the man asked.

She nodded. "All the way to the bottom."

Again.

The turbolift deposited them not far from where she had been earlier, though on the opposite side of the tunnel leading to the east skydock. As they hurried for the tunnel, Shaak Ti took a moment to survey the huge space for some sign of Captain Dyne's team. Considering all that had happened since she left, it was likely that Dyne and Commander Valiant had curtailed the search for Sidious's hideaway. Or perhaps they were still at it, somewhere in the sub-basement. Just short of entering the tunnel, she caught a glance of a bright silver protocol droid that might have been TC-16 hastening toward the exit to the west skydock.

The tunnel was darker than it should have been at that time of day, and the lower reaches of the canyon were darker still.

"Wait here," Shaak Ti instructed the Red Guards and Palpatine when they had reached the mouth of the tunnel.

Stass Allie strode to the center of the platform and gazed up at the buildings that loomed on all sides. "Grievous's forces must have destroyed the orbital mirror that feeds this sector."

Shaak Ti looked straight up at the sliver of sky.

"The shield is down. They must have taken out the generator."

Allie blew out her breath. "I'll find an appropriate vehicle to confiscate."

Shaak Ti laid a hand on her upper arm. "Too risky. We should remain as close to ground as possible."

Allie indicated the stairway that led to the mag-lev platform. "The train won't take us to the bunker complex, but close enough."

Shaak Ti smiled at her and reactivated the comlink.

"Mace," she said when he answered. "Another change in plans . . . "

Dragging himself out from under plasteel girders and chunks of ferrocrete, Count Dooku came shakily to his feet and gazed in astonished disbelief at the shambles of the control room. Had the containment dome been so weak that it had succumbed to flurries of ricocheting blaster bolts, or had Skywalker's voiced rage actually called the ceiling down?

Had Dooku not leapt forcefully at the last moment, he might have been buried, as the two Jedi were, somewhere below, in the expanse of rubble that covered the archive room. He was certain that they had survived. But if nothing else they were trapped, which had been the intent from the start.

But Skywalker . . . Assuming that he had grown powerful enough to have collapsed the dome, the end result was simply further evidence that he would someday undo himself. Wasn't it? Because admitting to any alternative explanation meant accepting that Skywalker was potentially a greater threat to the Sith than anyone realized.

Initially, it had cheered him to observe that Skywalker

and Kenobi had finally learned to fight together; to see
how powerful they had become in partnership. Comple-
menting each other's strengths, compensating for each
other's weaknesses. Kenobi making full use of his inher-
ent discretion to balance young Skywalker's inattentive
rowdiness. He could have watched them until the light
faded on fair Tythe. And he wished that General Grievous could have been there to witness the display for
himself.

Now he wasn't so sure.

What if it should all *come crashing down?* he found
himself thinking, as he dusted himself off and raced to
exit the ruined facility.

What if Grievous was outwitted and destroyed at Coruscant? Sidious, apprehended and defeated? What if the
Jedi should triumph, after all?

What would become of his dream of a galaxy brought
under eminent stewardship?

On Vjun, Yoda had implied that the Jedi Temple
would always be open to Dooku's return . . . But, no.
There was no turning back from the dark side, especially
from the depths in which he had swum. Was there, then,
a life of retirement somewhere in the galaxy for the former Count Dooku of Serenno?

So much rested on what would take place over the
next few standard days.

So much rested on whether Lord Sidious's plan could
succeed on all fronts—even though forced to unfold
hastily, because of a foolish oversight by Nute Gunray.

Outside, under Tythe's yellow-gray sky, his sloop was
waiting, and standing alongside it the ship's pilot droid.

"A recorded message," the droid announced. "From
General Grievous."

"Play it!" Dooku said as he hurried up the sloop's aft
boarding ramp and into the instrument-filled main hold.

A paused holoimage of the cyborg floated in blue light.

Throwing off his dusty cape, Dooku paced while the FA-4 triggered the recording to replay.

"*Lord Tyranus,*" Grievous said, in motion suddenly and genuflecting. "*Supreme Chancellor Palpatine will soon be ours.*"

Dooku exhaled in satisfaction. "And just in time," he muttered.

As if recalled to life, he positioned himself on the transmission grid and sent a simple return message: "General, I will join you shortly."

Padmé's eyes fluttered open.

Into focus swam the faintly smiling face of Mon Mothma.

"No sleeping on the job, Senator," Mon Mothma said, as if from underwater. "We have to get you out of here."

Padmé took stock of herself; realized that she was reclined in the rear seat of Stass Allie's skimmer. Her head was pillowed on Mon Mothma's left arm, and her ears felt as if they were plugged with cotton.

"How long—"

"Just for a moment," Mon Mothma said in the same watery tone. "I don't think you struck your head. You were fine after the crash. Then you fainted. Can you move?"

Padmé sat up and saw that the skimmer's safety mechanisms had deployed. Light-headed but unhurt, she brushed her hair from her face. "I can barely hear you."

Mon Mothma regarded her in knowing silence, then

extended a hand to help her climb from the craft. "Padmé, you have to be careful. Quickly, now."

She nodded. "Crashing wasn't exactly on my agenda."

Mon Mothma hurried her away from the skimmer, to where Bail and C-3PO were hiding behind the blockish pedestal of a modernistic sculpture.

"Master Allie doesn't strike me as someone who will sue for damages," the droid was saying.

Still in a daze, Padmé grasped that they had skidded into the plaza that fronted the Embassy Mall, taking out a large holosign and three news kiosks along the way. Bail's skill had somehow kept them from mowing down pedestrians, who had apparently scattered on first sight of the nose-diving ship. Or perhaps at sight of the craft that had fallen to Separatist fire *ahead* of the skimmer— a military police vehicle, similar to a Naboo Gian speeder, tipped on its side against the façade of the mall and belching smoke. Sprawled on the plaza close to the vehicle were the charred corpses of three clone troopers.

Reality reasserted itself in a rush of deafening noise, flashing light, and acrid smells. From nearby came anguished moans and terrified screams; from the tiered heights above the plaza, distant discharges of artillery. Higher still, plasma bolts raked the sky; fire bloomed, detonations thundered.

Padmé saw a smear of blood on Bail's cheek. "You're hurt—"

"It's nothing," he said. "Besides, we have more to worry about."

She followed his grim gaze, and understood immediately why Coruscanti were fleeing the pedestrian skybridge that linked the mall to the midlevel entrances of the Senate Hospital. Five Vulture droids had alit on the far side of the span and reconfigured to patrol mode.

Four-legged gargoyles, with heads deployed forward and sensor slits red as arterial blood, they were striding through Hospital Plaza, sowing destruction. Their four laser cannons were aimed downward, but from paired launchers in their semicircular fuselage flew torpedoes aimed at air taxis, craft attempting to dock at the hospital's emergency platforms, the tunnel entrances to the Senate shelters . . .

Republic LAATs had dropped from the Senate Plaza to engage the three-and-a-half-meter-tall droids but were maintaining a wary distance just now, pilots and gunners clearly worried about adding energy weapons or EMP missiles to the chaos.

"Xi Char monstrosities," Mon Mothma said.

Padmé remembered standing helplessly at the tall windows of Theed Palace, watching squadrons of Vulture fighters fill the sky, like cave creatures loosed on Naboo by darkness . . .

Caught in the crossfire, pedestrians had raced across the skybridge, hoping to find sanctuary in the Embassy Mall—midlevel in the dome-topped Nicandra Counterrevolutionary Signalmen's Memorial Building—but thick security grates had been lowered over the entrances, leaving crowds of Coruscanti to scramble for whatever cover could be found.

Padmé felt faint once more.

Huddled, frightened, panicked masses of Coruscanti were suddenly getting a taste of what the inhabitants of Jabiim, Brentaal, and countless other worlds had faced during the past three years. Caught up in a war of ideologies, often by dint of circumstance or location. Caught between the forces of a droid army led by a self-styled revolutionary and a cyborg butcher, and an army of vat-grown soldiers led by a monastic order of Jedi Knights who had once been the galaxy's peacekeepers.

Caught in the middle, with no allegiance to either side.

It was tragic and senseless, and she might have broken down and cried if her current circumstances had been different. She felt sick at heart, and in despair for the future of sentient life.

"Palpatine will never live this down," Mon Mothma was saying. "Committing so many of our ships and troopers to the Outer Rim sieges. As if this war he is so intent on winning could never come to Coruscant."

Bail frowned in sympathy. "Not only will he live it down, he'll profit from it. The Senate will be blamed for voting to escalate the sieges, and while we're mired in accusations and counteraccusations of accountability, Palpatine will quietly accrue more and more power. Without realizing it, the Separatists have played right into his hands by launching this attack."

Padmé wanted to argue with him but didn't have the strength.

"They're all mad," Bail continued. "Dooku, Grievous, Gunray, Palpatine."

Mon Mothma nodded sadly. "The Jedi could have stopped this war. Now they're Palpatine's pawns."

Padmé squeezed her eyes shut. Even if she managed to summon the strength, how could she respond, when her own husband was one of them—a *general*? What had the Jedi gotten Anakin into—taking him from Tatooine, from his youth, his mother? And yet hadn't she done as much as anyone to encourage him to remain a Jedi; to heed the tutelage of Obi-Wan, Mace, and the others; to perpetuate the lie that was their secret life as husband and wife?

She hugged herself.

What had *she* gotten Anakin into? What had she gotten both of them into?

Bail's voice snapped her from self-pity.

"They're coming." He aimed a finger across the plaza. "They're coming across the bridge."

From somewhere in the Vultures' droid brains had come a revelation that the pedestrian skyway offered a better vantage for targeting buildings and craft to both sides of the kilometer-deep canyon. More important, the gunships were even less likely to fire on them there, lest they destroy the span and send it plummeting to the busy thoroughfares and mag-lev lines two hundred stories below.

"Perhaps if we throw ourselves on the mercy of the owners of the mall, they will raise the security grate," C-3PO started to say.

Bail looked at Padmé and Mon Mothma. "We have to keep those droids on the far side of the bridge, so the gunships can take them out."

Mon Mothma glanced at the overturned military craft. "I see a way to try."

The craft sat scarcely fifty meters from the base of the sculpture. Without further word, the three of them hurried for it.

"What could I have been thinking?" C-3PO shouted as he watched them search the craft for weapons. "It can never be the easy answer!"

The three humans returned momentarily, carrying three blaster rifles.

"Not much power left," Bail said, checking one of them. "Yours?"

"Low on blaster gas," Padmé said.

Mon Mothma ejected the powerpack from hers. "Empty."

Bail nodded glumly. "We'll have to make do."

Hunkering down behind the pedestal, he and Padmé took careful aim on the closest of the walking droids.

By then three had started onto the skyway, firing at random. Exploding against the façades of buildings above and below, torpedoes sent slabs of durasteel-reinforced ferrocrete avalanching onto plazas, landing platforms, and balconies, burying scores of hapless Coruscanti.

"Be prepared to move as soon as we fire," Bail said. He indicated one of the kiosks that had survived the crashes of both speeders. "There's our first cover."

Padmé centered the lead droid in the blaster's targeting reticle and squeezed the trigger. Her initial bursts did little more than catch the droid's attention, but subsequent bolts from both blasters started to score hits on vital components. The droid actually retreated a couple of steps toward Hospital Plaza, only to launch a trio of torpedoes straight across the skyway.

Padmé and company were already in motion. One torpedo hit the pedestal, blowing it and the sculpture to fragments. A second slagged what was left of Stass Allie's skimmer. The third detonated against the lowered security grate, blowing a gaping hole into the mall. Pedestrians to both sides hastened for it, fighting with one another to be first through the smoking maw. Padmé thought that one of the Vultures would target them, but in their moment of inattention, the droids had left themselves open to strafing runs by the gunships. Converging beams of brilliant light streaked from the fire dishes of the LAATs' wing- and armature-mounted ball turrets, and staccato bursts erupted from the forward guns.

Two droids exploded.

One turned to answer the volleys, but not in time. Missiles from the gunships' mass-drive launchers took off the droid's left legs, then the head, then blew the rest

clear across the plaza. The remaining two Vultures skittered onto the skyway to increase their odds of survival.

Bail and Padmé laid down steady lines of fire, but the
droids were undeterred.

"And I thought the Senate was a battlefield!" Mon
Mothma said.

The sight of smoke curling from holes in the lead
droid's fuselage seemed to invigorate the one behind.
Driving Padmé and the others in search of new cover
with a single torpedo, the droid scurried forward, edging
around its stricken comrade and stepping brazenly into
the mall plaza, red sensors gleaming.

A gunship made a quick pass, but couldn't find a clear
field of fire.

"I'm out," Bail said, dropping his rifle.

Padmé checked her weapon's display screen. "Same."

C-3PO shook his head. "How will I ever explain this
to Artoo-Detoo?"

They broke for cover a final time, hoping to throw
themselves through the ragged hole in the still-smoking
security grate, but the droid hurried to intercept them;
then, in seeming sadistic delight, began to back the four
of them against the wall of the Nicandra Building.

A rage began to build in Padmé, born of instincts as
old as life itself. She was on the verge of hurling herself
against the towering machine, ripping the sensors from
its teardrop-shaped head, when the droid came to a sudden halt, obviously in reception of some remote communication. Retracting its head and stiffening its
scissor-like legs into wings, it turned and launched itself
over the edge of the plaza into the canyon below.

The droid on the skyway did the same, even with two
gunships in close pursuit.

Padmé was first to reach the skyway railing. Far below, the Senate District mag-lev was racing south toward the skytunnel that would take it through the kilometer-wide Heorem Complex and on into the wealthy Sah'c District. The two Vulture droids were swooping down to join ranks with a Separatist gunboat that was already chasing the train.

How had Grievous known to attack 500 Republica? Mace asked himself as the mag-lev rushed at three hundred kilometers per hour toward the skytunnel that would spirit the train from the Senate District.

Having boarded the mag-lev at its 500 Republica platform, he, Kit Fisto, Shaak Ti, and Stass Allie were in the car the Supreme Chancellor's Red Guards had commandeered—second in a train of some twenty cars. Through a gap in the protective circle the guards had forged, Mace caught a glimpse of Palpatine, his head of wavy gray hair lowered in what might have been anguish or deep concentration.

How had Grievous known? Mace asked himself.

Many Coruscanti knew that Palpatine resided in 500 Republica, but the location of his suite was a well-kept secret. More important, how had Grievous known that Palpatine wasn't to be found in either of his offices?

Not everything could be traced to Dooku.

It was conceivable that Dooku had furnished Grievous with data on hyperlanes that skimmed the outer limits of the Deep Core. That much, Dooku could have pilfered from the Jedi archives before he left the Order, presumably when he was erasing mentions of Kamino from the data banks. Similarly, Dooku could have supplied Grievous with the orbital coordinates of specific communications satellites and mirrors, or with tactical information regarding the location of dedicated shield generators on the surface. But Palpatine had only just been elected Supreme Chancellor when Dooku left Coruscant to return to Serenno, and back then, some thirteen years ago, Palpatine had relocated to a high-rise tower close to the Senate Building.

So how had Grievous known to go to 500 Republica? Sidious?

If it was true that hundreds of Senators had, for a time, been under the Sith Lord's influence, then he may have had access to the highest levels of confidential information. As many on the Jedi Council feared, Sidious's network of agents and assets might have infiltrated the Republic military command itself. Which suggested that the sneak attack on Coruscant may have been years in the planning!

Mace caught another glimpse of Palpatine, insulated by the flowing red robes of his handpicked bodyguards.

This was hardly the time to question him about his closest confidants.

But Mace would make it his business to find the time later.

Briefly, he wondered what had become of Captain Dyne's team. Surmising that Dyne had called off the search for Sidious shortly after the attack had commenced, Intelligence hadn't dispatched a second search team—aimed at locating Dyne and Valiant—until neither of them had been heard from, even after communications had been restored to the Senate District.

Shaak Ti hadn't seen them when she and Palpatine's protectors had whisked the Supreme Chancellor through 500 Republica's sub-basement.

So had Dyne and the commandos fallen victim to Grievous's attack? Were they trapped somewhere under a crashed cargo ship or tons of ferrocrete rubble?

Yet another ill-timed concern, Mace thought.

The mag-lev's other cars were packed cheek-to-jowl with Coruscanti attempting to flee the Senate and Financial Districts. Palpatine's guards would have commandeered the entire train if Palpatine hadn't intervened, refusing to allow it. Shaak Ti had told Mace and Kit about the Supreme Chancellor's earlier reluctance to leave his suite. Mace didn't know what to make of it. But now at least they were on the way to the bunker. The mag-lev line didn't run past the complex, but the first stop in Sah'c was close to a system of skyways and turbolifts that did.

Light filtering into the car through the tinted windows dimmed.

The mag-lev was entering the Heorem Skytunnel, a broad burrow that accommodated not only the speeding train, but also opposing lanes of autonavigation and free-travel traffic, passing through several of the Senate District's largest buildings. Lanes leading south—away from the district, and off to the right side of the mag-lev—were crawling with public transports and air taxis. By contrast, the northbound lanes were almost empty, the result of traffic having been rerouted well before it reached the Senate District.

A blur of light off to the left-hand side of the car caught Mace's eye, and he hurried to the closest window. Streaking southbound in the northbound free-travel lane, two droid fighters were trying to overtake the train. Before Mace could utter a word of warning, cannon fire from one of the twin-winged ships stitched a broken line of holes across the blunt nose of a transport in the autonavigation lane. Instantly the transport exploded, savaging nearby vehicles with shrapnel and nearly rocking the mag-lev from its elevated guide rails.

Screams issued from Coruscanti wedged into the cars to the front and rear of Palpatine's.

"Vulture fighters!" Mace told the Jedi and Red Guards.

Leaning low at the window, he saw one of the droids climb over the mag-lev, only to descend on the opposite side of the train in the midst of the free-travel lane, initiating a succession of collisions that flung speeders, taxis, and buses all over the skytunnel. Two vehicles careened into the train, only to rebound back into the travel lane, starting a second series of fatal crashes. Racing alongside Palpatine's car, the same droid responsible for the collisions surged into a steep climb and disappeared from view.

Not a moment later an earsplitting sound reached Mace from somewhere in the rear of the train and overhead. Behind the tinted glass, sparks showered down the rounded sides of the car, and the smell of molten metal wafted from the ventilation grilles. A tumult of terrified cries rose from the car directly behind Palpatine's, and hands and feet began to pound against the passageway door.

Part of a group of mag-lev security personnel stationed there, a Weequay looked to Mace.

"We won't be able to hold them back!"

In turn, Mace whirled to Shaak Ti and Allie. "Move the Chancellor into the forward car!"

Shaak Ti regarded him as if he had lost his mind. "It's packed, Mace!"

"I know that. Find a way!"

He gestured for Kit Fisto, and the two of them shouldered through the cluster of security personnel at the rear of the car and activated their lightsabers. Faced with the purple and blue blades, passengers on the far side of the door's window began to retreat into the vestibule, battling with those behind them who were attempting to press into the forward car.

When there was space enough in the vestibule, Mace instructed the Weequay to unlock the door. Without hesitation he and Kit dashed through the vestibule and on into the rear car, where most of the mixed-species passengers were heaped atop seats on both sides of the wide aisle. Wind howled through the car from a jagged rend that had been opened in the roof, and through which had dropped half a dozen infantry droids.

Mace allowed himself a moment of bewilderment. Since the battle droids couldn't have been delivered by the droid fighters, there had to be a *third* Separatist craft racing alongside the train.

The battle droids opened fire.

To many of the passengers all but fused to the tinted windows, the situation must have seemed hopeless. Not because the two Jedi couldn't deflect the hail of blaster bolts aimed at them, but because they couldn't deflect them without sending some into or through people in the car. But those passengers failed to recognize that one of the Jedi was Mace Windu—rumored to have single-handedly destroyed a seismic tank on Dantooine—and that the other was Kit Fisto, Nautolan hero of the Battle of Mon Calamari.

Together they returned some of the sizzling bolts into the advancing droids. Others they sent whizzing through the opening in the roof, managing in the process to catch one of the Vultures in the belly and send it spiraling to its death somewhere below the mag-lev line. Sparks and

smoke whirled through the car, and parts of spindly
arms and legs flew about unavoidably, but Mace and Kit
called on the Force to control even those. A few Coruscanti were struck, but, against all odds, the Jedi saw to it
that none was critically injured.

No sooner had the final droid dropped than Mace
leapt straight up through the rend, landing in a crouch
on the roof of the next car down the line, holding himself in place by the Force with the wind whipping at the
back of his shaved skull and coarse tunic. Senses on
alert, he saw a Separatist craft drop down behind the
final car in the line. Farther away, but quickly making up
the distance, flew two Republic gunships.

Instinctively he glanced to the right just as the second
Vulture droid was rocketing into view. Seeing him, the
droid sprayed the roof of the car with cannon fire. Mace
turned into the powerful wind and focused all his intention on a front flip that carried him back through the
rend. The Vulture veered, positioning itself directly over
the laceration its partner had opened, and reorienting its
wing cannons.

In what would surely have been a futile act, Mace
raised his lightsaber.

But the expected cannon blast never arrived. Wings
clipped and repulsors damaged by missiles fired from the
gunships, the Vulture slammed down onto the roof of
the speeding train, then rolled out of sight.

Deactivating their blades, Mace and Kit rushed into
the forward car, which was now filled with Palpatine's
advisers and those passengers the Jedi women and Red
Guards had relocated from the train's lead car. Mace and
Kit continued to squirm forward, arriving in the
Supreme Chancellor's car just as the mag-lev was emerging from the skytunnel. The sun was going down, and
the tall buildings that rose to the west cast enormous

shadows across the city canyon and the busy thoroughfares far below the cantilevered mag-lev line.

In the middle of the car, Palpatine stood at the center
of the cordon the Red Guards had formed around him.
And at a fixed-pane window they had deliberately shattered, Shaak Ti and Stass Allie were gazing toward the
rear of the train.

"Those fighters could easily have derailed us with a
torpedo," Shaak Ti said as Mace and Kit approached.

Mace leaned partway out the window, eyes searching
the canyon. "And battle droids don't just drop from the
sky. There's a third craft."

Kit's bulging black eyes indicated Palpatine. "They
want to take him alive."

The words had scarcely left his mouth when something hit the train with sufficient force to whip everyone
from one side of the car to the other, then back again.
The Red Guards were just regaining their balance when
the roof began to resound with the cadence of heavy,
clanging footfalls, advancing from the rear of the train.

"Grievous," Mace grumbled.

Kit glanced at him. "Here we go again."

Hurrying into the vestibule between the two lead cars,
they launched themselves to the roof. Three cars distant
marched General Grievous and two of his elite droids,
their capes snapping behind them in the wind, pulse-
tipped batons angled across their barrel chests.

Farther back, clamped by animal-like claws to the roof
of the train, was the gunboat from which the frightful
trio had been released.

Without pausing, Grievous drew two lightsabers from
inside his billowing cloak. By the time they were ignited,
Mace was already on and all over the cyborg, batting
away at the two blades, swinging low at Grievous's artificial legs, thrusting at his skeletal face.

The lightsabers thrummed and hissed, meeting one another in bursts of dazzling light. In a corner of Mace's mind he wondered to which Jedi Grievous's blades had belonged. Just as the Force was keeping Mace from being blown from the mag-lev's roof, magnetism of some sort was keeping the general fastened in place. For the cyborg, though, the coherence hindered as much as it helped, whereas Mace never remained in one place for very long. Again and again the three blades joined, in snarling attacks and parries.

Grievous was well trained in the Jedi arts. Mace could recognize the hand of Dooku in the general's training and technique. His strikes were as forceful as any Mace had ever had to counter, and his speed was astonishing.

But he didn't know Vaapad—the technique of dark flirtation in which Mace excelled.

To the rear of the car, where Grievous's pair of MagnaGuards had made the mistake of pitting themselves against Kit Fisto, the Nautolan's blade was a cyclone of blazing blue light. Resistant to the energy outpourings of a lightsaber, the phrik alloy staffs were potent weapons, but like any weapon they needed to find their target, and Kit simply wasn't allowing that. In moves a Twi'lek dancer might envy, he spun around the guards, claiming a limb from both with each rotation: left legs, right arms, right legs . . .

The speed of the train saw to the rest, ultimately whisking the droids into the canyon like insects blown from the windscreen of a speeder bike.

The loss of his confederates was noted by whatever computers were slaved to Grievous's organic brain, but the loss neither distracted nor slowed him. His sole setting was *attack*. Successful at analyzing Mace's lightsaber style, those same computers suggested that

Grievous alter his stance and posture, along with the angle of his parries, ripostes, and thrusts.

The result wasn't Vaapad, but it was close enough, and Mace wasn't interested in prolonging the contest any longer than necessary.

Crouching low, he angled the blade downward and slashed, guiding it through the roof of the car, perpendicular to Grievous's stalwart advance. Mace saw by the surprised look in the cyborg's reptilian eyes that, for all his strength, dexterity, and resolve, the living part of him wasn't always in perfect sync with his alloy servos. Clearly, Grievous—onetime courageous commander of sentient troops—realized what Mace had done and wanted to sidestep, where General Grievous—current commander of droids and other war machines—wanted nothing more than to impale Mace with lunging thrusts of the paired blades.

Slipping into the gap made by Mace's saber, Grievous's left talon lost magnetic purchase on the roof, and the general faltered. Mace came out of his crouch prepared to drive his sword into Grievous's guts, but some last-instant firing of the general's cybersynapses compelled the cyborg's torso through a swift half twist that would have sent Mace's head hurtling into the canyon had the maneuver prevailed. Instead Mace leapt backward, out of the range of the slicing blades, and Force-pushed outward, just at the instant of Grievous's single misstep.

Off the side of the car the general went, twisting and turning as he fell, Mace trying to track the general's contorted plunge, but unsuccessfully.

Had he fallen into the canyon? Had he managed to dig his duranium claws into the side of the car or grab hold of the mag-lev rail itself?

Mace couldn't take the time to puzzle it out. One hundred meters away, the gunboat retracted its landing gear and rose from the roof on repulsorlift power. Reckless shots from one of the pursuing gunships obliged the Separatist craft to skew, then dive, with the gunship following close behind.

Mace and Kit watched in awe as the two ships began to helix forward around the speeding mag-lev, exchanging constant fire. Climbing away from the train's sharp nose, within which the magnetic controls were housed, the gunboat made as if to bank west, only to bank east at the last instant.

By then, however, the gunship—leading its target west—had already fired.

Drilled by a swarm of deadly hyphens, the mag-lev's control system blew apart, and the entire train began to drop.

In the darkness, buried alive, Anakin stretched out with his feelings.

In his mind's eye he saw Padmé stalked by a dark, towering creature with a mechanical head, poised at the edge of a deep abyss, her world turned upside down. A surprise attack. Opponents locked in combat. Ground and sky filled with fire, smoke billowing in the air, clouding everything.

Death, destruction, deceit . . . A labyrinth of lies. *His* world turned upside down.

He shuddered, as if plunged into liquid gas. One touch would break him into a million shards.

His fear for Padmé expanded until he couldn't see past it. Yoda's voice in his ear: *Fear leads to anger; anger to hated; hatred to the dark side . . .*

He was as afraid to lose her as he was to hold on to her, and the pain of that contradiction made him wish he had never been born. There was no solace, even in the Force. As Qui-Gon had told him, he needed to make his focus his reality. But how?

How?

Qui-Gon, who had died—even though, to his young mind, Jedi weren't supposed to . . .

Beside him, Obi-Wan stirred and coughed.

"You're getting awfully good at destroying things," he said. "On Vjun, you needed a grenade to do this much damage."

Anakin shook the vision from his mind. "I told you I was becoming more powerful."

"Then do us both a favor by getting us out from under all this."

They used the Force, their hands and backs to extricate themselves. Getting to their feet, they stood staring at each other, dusted white head-to-toe from the debris.

"Go ahead," Anakin said. "If you don't say it, I will."

"If you insist." Obi-Wan snorted dust from his nose. "Almost makes me nostalgic for Naos Three."

"Once more, with feeling."

"Some other time. Dooku, first."

Scampering over the remains of the dome, droid parts, buried pieces of furniture, overturned shelves of holodocuments, they raced for the landing platform, arriving in time to see Dooku's sloop, one among dozens of Separatist vessels, streaking for space.

"Coward," Obi-Wan said. "He flees."

Anakin watched the sloop for a moment longer, then looked at Obi-Wan. "That's not the reason, Master. We've been tricked. Tythe was never the target. *We* were."

49

Bleeding speed and loft, the mag-lev settled hard onto the guide rail that projected from the skyscraper-lined rim of Sah'c Canyon. Counterpoint to the sobs and moans of the passengers, the two dozen cars—two now with slashed-open roofs—pinged and creaked.

Balanced on the balls of their feet, Mace and Kit hooked their lightsabers to their belts and drifted back down into the vestibule, as gently as the Force allowed. As if buffeted by thermals, the train swayed lazily from side to side. But with traffic halted in both directions, the air at midlevel should have been unruffled.

A quick glance out the right side of the vestibule supplied Mace with the explanation.

The aged, cantilevered supports anchored to the sides of the buildings were beginning to bend under the weight of the train.

In the distance, sirens wailed and dopplered as emergency craft hurried to render aid. Left of the stricken mag-lev, two enormous repulsorlift platforms were making a careful approach. Waiting for the train to quiet,

Mace and Kit stood like statues in the vestibule. When the rocking motion had subsided somewhat, they pressed the release stud for the passageway door and eased themselves into the lead car.

The train continued to protest its peculiar circumstance with an assortment of stressful sounds, but the sagging supports held.

Held for a few seconds more.

Then, with explosive reports, the rail supports beneath the center of the train tore away from the canyon rim, taking a lengthy portion of the rail with them. The train V'ed into the sudden gap, and would have plunged completely but for the fact that enough forward and rear cars remained clasped to the rail to support the few that now formed an inverted triangle. Even so, Coruscanti in the rear were propelled forward by the collapse, while those in the lead cars were jerked violently backward.

Steps into Palpatine's car, Mace and Kit called on the Force to prevent everyone from flailing toward the vestibule door. Farther forward in the car, Shaak Ti and Stass Allie were keeping the Supreme Chancellor on his feet.

Strident sounds issued from the guide rail. The maglev lurched, and another two cars slipped into the V-notch, their motion adding a sudden twist to the train that turned some of the cars onto their sides, and sent passengers sliding and tumbling toward the tinted windows. Coruscanti screamed in terror, bracing themselves as best they could, or clawing at one another for support.

Centered in the Force, Mace directed all his energy toward keeping the Red Guards and others rooted in place. He wondered if he, Kit, Shaak Ti, and Allie—acting in concert—could support the entire train, but dismissed the idea immediately.

They would need Yoda.

Perhaps five Yodas.

Unexpectedly, a feeling of relief flowed through him.

"The emergency repulsorlifts," Kit said.

Once more the train lurched, but this time the cars began to level out as antigrav repulsors levitated those that had dropped into the notch.

By then, too, the pair of repulsorlift platforms had cozied up to the train's left side, and scores of emergency craft were rushing in from all sides. Mace could feel an increasing sense of desperation sweep through the cars as passengers grew frantic to exit. He knew that it was only going to get worse, since none of them would be allowed to leave until Palpatine had been moved to safety.

He and Kit did their best to make that happen as quickly as possible. Within moments, they had ushered everyone who had been in the lead car onto one of the platforms. Pressed in among his Red Guards, Palpatine couldn't even be seen. Disengaging from the mag-lev, the platform was moving away from the train before a single passenger—even any of Palpatine's advisers—could scramble out onto its twin.

The air was filled with escort craft and gunships, two of which put down on the platform as it was closing on the canyon's eastern rim. Leaping out of the craft, two platoons of commandos assumed firing positions along the platform's perimeter. Behind them came four Jedi Knights, who rushed to join Shaak Ti and Stass Allie in guarding Palpatine.

Mace recognized the more scorched of the pair of gunships as one of two that had been in pursuit of Grievous's gunboat. Hurrying over to it, he signaled the pilot to raise the bubble canopy.

Cupping his hands to his mouth, he said: "What became of the gunboat?"

"My wingmate is in pursuit, General," the pilot said. "We're awaiting word."

"Did Grievous fall from the mag-lev?"

"I was too far back to see much of anything, sir. But I didn't see him fall, and I didn't see anyone on the train."

Mace replayed the events in his mind. Saw himself Force-pushing Grievous from the roof of the car; saw Grievous plunging over the edge, down out of sight, toward the rail or the canyon floor. The cyborg's gunboat disengaging from the train, descending into the canyon before it and the second gunship had commenced their corkscrewing race around the mag-lev . . .

Mace clenched his hands, and swung to Kit. "The gunboat could have caught him—somehow." He gazed up at the pilot again. "Any word yet?"

"Coming in now, sir . . . Sector H-Fifty-Two. My wingmate is in close pursuit. I'd better get a move on."

"General Fisto and I are going with you." Mace turned to Shaak Ti, Allie, and the four newly arrived Jedi Knights.

Shaak Ti nodded at him. "We'll see the Chancellor the rest of the way to the bunker."

Shaak Ti was the last to board the gunship that would deliver Palpatine to shelter, somewhere deep in the narrow service chasms that fractured the exclusive Sah'c neighborhood. Encircled by the contingent of Red Guards, Palpatine stood silently in the rear of the troop bay. His hair and robes were mussed, and he looked pale and feeble among his striking protectors. Stass Allie and the four Jedi Knights Yoda had dispatched from the Temple stood just inside the door, shoulder-to-shoulder with commandos and government agents. Shaak Ti knew the human male Jedi and the female Twi'lek by sight, but she couldn't recall ever running into the other

two—a male Talz and a male Ithorian. All four of them
looked able enough, though she hoped there would be
no call for them to demonstrate their skills.

Moments earlier, the gunship carrying Mace and Kit
had banked north, back toward the Senate District, in
apparent pursuit of Grievous's gunboat. Palpatine's gunship had taken off to the south, and had immediately begun to descend. Dusk had already fallen on the rim of
the canyon. Bruised by the day's events, Coruscant's
skies were a swirl of blood red, orange, and deep laven-
der. Down below, the buildings and thoroughfares were
illuminated.

Halfway to the floor of the canyon, a gunship that had
seen recent action fell in alongside the Supreme Chancellor's, and remained just off to starboard and slightly
astern through the numerous twists and turns that led ultimately to the mountainous structure that served as the
bunker complex.

A final turn to the north brought the two gunships to
the mouth of a narrow urban ravine, where they hovered
for the moment it took to lower the particle shield that
safeguarded the shelters, tactical and communications
centers, landing platforms, and the network of tunnels
that linked them. The complex could be reached by alternative means—under normal circumstances, Palpatine
would have been conveyed by repulsorlift speeder
through deep tunnels that arrived from 500 Republica,
the Great Rotunda, and the Senate Office Building—but
the ravine was the best way of entering from anywhere
west of the Senate or Financial Districts.

Shaak Ti didn't allow herself to relax until the gunships had been cleared through the shimmering screen
and had been issued approach vectors for landing.

Her relieved exhale seemed to go on and on.

The escort gunship shot ahead and was already on the

pad when Shaak Ti and the rest arrived moments later. The craft bearing the Supreme Chancellor had scarcely touched down when the side doors flew out and back, and the Red Guards hurried Palpatine off to a waiting speeder. The commandos leapt out to reinforce the bunker's contingent of troopers.

Shaak Ti instructed the four Jedi Knights to accompany the Red Guards, promising to join them after she and Stass Allie had apprised the Temple of their safe arrival.

The two Jedi women watched the speeder race off into the broad tunnel that accessed the bunker, then swung themselves down to the landing pad. Allie grabbed her comlink and depressed the SEND button. After several failed attempts to reach the Temple, she glanced at Shaak Ti.

"Too much interference. Let's move away from the ship."

It was the interference that saved them from the explosion that mangled and consumed the gunship. As it was, the blast set their robes on fire and hurled them ten meters through the air. Retaining consciousness, Shaak Ti used the momentum to propel herself through a tucked roll that carried her almost to the edge of the landing platform. Stass Allie lay facedown nearby. The missile that had destroyed the gunship had been launched by the craft that had preceded them into the ravine. That same craft's several cannons were firing now, laying waste to other vessels and making short work of the troopers.

Shaak Ti saw several soldiers jump from the gunship's doors and move with astounding speed into the mouth of the access tunnel. She raised herself to one knee, then sprinted to Stass Allie's side to put out the flames that had engulfed her cloak.

Allie stirred and raised herself on the palms of her hands.

"Stay down," Shaak Ti warned.

As the gunship was lifting off—no doubt to gain a better vantage on the landing platform—additional troopers appeared from somewhere below the landing pad. Rocket-propelled grenades swarmed after the rising craft, several of them infiltrating the vented nacelles of the repulsorlift engines. The ensuing detonation resounded in the ravine and cast fiery hunks of metal in all directions.

Shaak Ti curled her body and tucked her head to her chest. A wave of intense heat washed over her and Allie, and a hail of fragments clanged and clattered down around her.

One of the last pieces to land—not two meters from her face—was the charred head of a battle droid.

Mace and Kit stood in the open doorway of the Republic gunship as it threaded its way among the monads and skyscrapers of the Senate District. Grievous's gunboat raced ahead, darting left and right as it fired continuously at its pursuer.

Mace backed into the gunship as bolts sizzled past the doorway, nearly catching the underside of the starboard wing. The fact that it had taken so little effort to track and catch up with the Separatist craft gnawed at Mace. Neither he nor Kit could shake the feeling that the gunboat had practically been waiting for them above the squat Senate Building, and had only then attempted to go evasive. And yet it had obviously eluded the original gunship that had chased it through the Sah'c skytunnel.

Mace leaned into the hatch to the gunner's compartment and called up to him. "Where's your wingmate?"

"Lost him, sir," the gunner shouted. "He's not anywhere on the tactical screen."

"The ship could have gone down," Kit suggested.

Mace's brow furrowed. "I don't think so. Something's wrong about this."

Overhead, missiles roared from the launchers and an explosion boomed and echoed from the surround of buildings. Black smoke and debris swept past the doorway, and the gunner whooped.

"We got him, sir! He's trailing fire, and surface-bound!"

Mace and Kit leaned out the doorway in time to see the gunboat tip to one side, then begin a rapid downward spiral.

"Stay with him, pilot!" Mace yelled.

Coiling into a city chasm east of the Senate, the craft clipped the edge of a skydock and started to come apart. The pilot of the gunship jinked to avoid airborne wreckage, but managed to remain in the wake of the doomed ship. The collision with the skydock had added an end-over-end flip to the gunboat's spiral, and now the craft was simply falling like a stone, straight down toward brightly illuminated Uscru Boulevard, which was blessedly free of traffic. Fires sputtering out, it hit the surface nose-first, cratering the street and shattering windows in buildings to all sides.

Maintaining a safe distance from the crash site, the gunship pilot engaged the repulsorlift engines and hovered to a landing at the frayed edge of the impact crater. Mace, Kit, and a dozen commandos jumped to the hot ground to secure the area. Crowds of startled onlookers formed almost immediately, and the sirens of emergency vehicles began to wail in the distance.

Lightsabers ignited, Mace and Kit strode along the perimeter of the shallow well, alert to the slightest movements. The crumpled ship had been torn open from bow to stern along one side, and they had clear views into every cabin space. Neither Grievous nor any of his elite guards were anywhere to be found.

Only battle droids: slagged, mangled, twisted into peculiar shapes.

"I can accept that Grievous might have fallen from the mag-lev," Mace said, "but not that he would have included only *two* of his elite on a mission like this."

Kit gazed at the wedge of night sky. "There could be a second assault craft."

"Pilot!" Mace called toward the gunship. "Comlink the Supreme Chancellor's bunker, and arrange for us to be cleared through the shield."

Grievous and six MagnaGuards cut a bloody swath through the broad corridors that led ultimately to Palpatine's sanctuary. Republic soldiers—cloned and otherwise—fell to Grievous's lightsabers and the deadly staffs of his elite. Behind them, the firefight at the landing platform was raging. If nothing else, Grievous told himself, the clash would tie up two of the Jedi and dozens of troopers.

Thus far, things were still on target—if not proceeding according to plan.

At Palpatine's apartment, Grievous had managed to fool everyone by placing the gunboat on display, then clandestinely transferring himself and his combat droids into the Republic gunship Lord Tyranus had promised would be waiting for them. He had been forced to improvise when Palpatine's protectors had opted to follow an alternate route to the bunker, and he had enjoyed chasing the mag-lev—if not the brief duel on the roof of the train car.

Tyranus had warned him about Mace Windu's prowess with a blade, and now he understood. His literal "misstep" had shamed him, and he was grateful that the two MagnaGuards that had fought at his side had not survived to bear witness to it. Had he not managed at

the last instant to grab hold of the mag-lev rail and be retrieved by the borrowed gunship, all the efforts the
Banking Clan had undertaken to have him rebuilt would
have been for nothing.

But as it happened he was now about to give the Separatists more than their credits' worth. Perhaps a means
to proclaim themselves victors of the war.

Grievous and five remaining droids completed their
march to the bunker, deflecting the fire of three troopers
guarding the entrance, then decapitating them. Hexagonal, the sturdy portal was impervious to blaster bolts, radiation, or electromagnetic pulse. Grievous was well
aware that his lightsabers were capable of burning
through the door. While doing so would have heightened
the drama of his entry, he did the next best thing.

He used the code Tyranus had provided.

"Under no circumstances are you to harm the Chancellor," he exhorted his elite, while layers of the thick
hatch were retracting.

The astonishment registered by Palpatine and his quar-
tet of Jedi Knights assured Grievous that he could not
have made a more dramatic entry. A large desk dominated the circular room, and banks of communications
consoles formed the circumference. Centered in the
curved wall opposite the entrance was a second door.
Posing for effect in the polygonal opening, Grievous
granted his opponents a moment to activate their lightsabers, force pikes, and other weapons. Also for effect,
he deflected the initial flurry of blaster bolts with his
clawed hands, before drawing two of his lightsabers.

His brazenness summoned the Jedi to him in a flash,
but he knew in the first moments of contest that he had
nothing to worry about. Compared to Mace Windu, the
four were mere novices, whose lightsaber techniques
were some of the earliest Grievous had mastered.

Behind him rushed his elite droids, with a single purpose in mind: to tear into the guards and soldiers arrayed in a defensive semicircle in front of Palpatine. Tall, elegant-looking, dramatic in their red robes and face-masked cowls, the Supreme Chancellor's protectors were well trained and fought with passion. Their fists and feet were fast and powerful, and their force pikes sliced and jabbed through the near-impervious armor of the droids. But they were no real match for fearless war machines, programmed to kill by any means possible. Perhaps if Palpatine had been intelligent enough to have surrounded himself with *real* Jedi—Jedi of the caliber of Windu and the tentacle-headed Kit Fisto—the engagement might have gone differently.

Fencing with his four adversaries—for that's all the fight amounted to—Grievous saw six of the soldiers and three of the Red Guards jolted to spasming deaths by the MagnaGuards' double-tipped scepters. One of his elite had gone down, as well, but even though blinded and savagely slashed by the guards' staffs, the droid was continuing to fight. And those elite still on their feet had altered their combat stances and offensive moves to adapt to the guards' defensive strategies.

Grievous enjoyed going against so many Jedi simultaneously. If time wasn't of the essence, he might have protracted the fight. Feinting with the blade in his right hand, he removed the head of one Jedi with the blade in his left. Distracted when his right foot inadvertently booted the rolling head of his comrade, the Ithorian dropped his guard momentarily, and received as penalty a thrust to the heart that dropped him to his knees before he pitched forward.

Stepping back to absorb what had happened, the two remaining Jedi came at Grievous in concert, twirling and leaping about as if putting on some sort of crowd-pleasing martial arts demonstration. For practice, Grievous called two more blades from his belt, grasping them in his feet even as the antigrav repulsors built into his legs were lifting him from the floor, making him every bit as agile as the Force did the Jedi.

With his four blades to the Jedi's two, the duel had come full circle.

Whirling, he severed the blade hand of the Talz, then his opposing foot, then took his life, as well. Mists of blood formed in the air, swirled about by the ventilators.

The fourth he intimidated into retreat by wheeling all four blades, transforming himself into a veritable chopping machine. Fear blossomed in the Twi'lek Jedi's dark eyes as she backed away. He had her on the run, poor thing. But he awarded her some measure of dignity by allowing her to land glancing blows on his forearms and shoulders. The burns did little more than add a new odor to the room. Emboldened, she pressed her attack, but was fast exhausting herself from the effort of trying to amputate one of his limbs—to *hurt* him in some fashion.

And all for what? Grievous asked himself. The timid old man backed to the bunker's rear wall? The would-be champion of democracy, who had loosed his clone army against the merchants and builders and traders who opposed his rule—his *Republic*?

Best to put the Jedi out of her misery, Grievous thought. Which he did with a single blade to the heart—for it would have been cruel to do otherwise.

Elsewhere his three surviving elites were doing well against five Red Guards. With time counting down, he waded into the thick of the action. Sensing him, one guard feinted a rotation to the left, then pivoted to the right with his force pike raised at face level. A move Grievous could appreciate, although he was no longer in the space through which the weapon sliced. Using two blades, he nipped the guard's cowled head from his torso. The next he speared from behind in both kidneys. Opening the backs of another's thighs, he moved on, disemboweling the fourth.

The last guard was already dead by the time he reached him.

With a gesture, Grievous instructed his elite to secure the bunker's hexagonal door. Then, deactivating his lightsabers, he turned to Palpatine.

"Now, Chancellor," he announced, "you're coming with us."

Palpatine neither cowered nor protested. He merely said: "You will be a true loss to the forces you represent."

The remark took Grievous by surprise. Was this praise?

"Four Jedi Knights, all these soldiers and guards," Palpatine went on, gesturing broadly. "Why not wait until Shaak Ti and Stass Allie arrive." He cocked his head to one side. "I think I hear them coming. They are *Masters,* after all."

Grievous didn't respond immediately. Was Palpatine trying to trick him? "I might at any other time," he said finally. "But a ship awaits us that will take you from Coruscant—and from your cherished Republic, as well."

Palpatine mocked him with a sneer. "Do you actually believe that this plan will succeed?"

Grievous returned the look. "You're more defiant than I was led to believe, Chancellor. But, yes, the plan will succeed—and to your deficit. I would gladly kill you now but for my orders."

"So you take orders," Palpatine said, moving with deliberate lethargy. "Which of us, then, is the lesser?" Before Grievous could reply, he added: "My death won't end this war, General."

Grievous had wondered about that. Understandably,

Lord Sidious had his plan, but did he actually believe that Palpatine's death would prompt the Jedi to lay down their lightsabers? Thrown into turmoil by the Chancellor's death, could the Senate *order* the Jedi to stand down? After years of warfare, would the Republic suddenly capitulate?

The sound of rapid footfalls roused him, and he gestured to the bunker's rear door. "Move," he told Palpatine.

The MagnaGuards stepped forward to make certain that Palpatine obeyed.

Grievous hurried to the bunker's communication console. The stud switch and control pad for the emergency beacon were precisely where Tyranus said they would be. After entering the code Tyranus had provided, Grievous pressed his alloy hand to the switch.

Palpatine watched him from the doorway. "That will call many Jedi down on you, General—some of whom you may regret having summoned."

Grievous glared at him. "Only if they fail to challenge me."

Word of the firefight on the landing platform reached Mace and Kit in the gunship while they were returning to Sah'c. It hadn't taken long to piece together what had happened: the Separatists had managed to hijack a Republic gunship and infiltrate the bunker complex shield by timing their arrival to coincide with that of the ship carrying Palpatine, Shaak Ti, and the others. An ARC commander verified that the hijacked gunship had been piloted by droids, but the same ARC would neither confirm nor deny that Grievous had been aboard the destroyed ship.

That, alone, was cause for concern.

Mace and Kit thought they knew what had occurred, and hoped they were wrong.

In the white glare of spotlights, the gunship that had been brought down by RPGs was a flaming hulk, dangling from the edge of the landing pad. Even less remained of the gunship that had delivered Palpatine to the complex. Fatalities of the surprise attack—one in a series of terrible surprises now—had been removed from the scene, but the pad boasted a company of reinforcements, as well as two AT-STs that had been air-dropped by wide-winged LAAT carriers.

This time Mace and Kit didn't wait for the gunship to touch down. Jumping from five meters up, they raced across the brightly illuminated landing platform and directly into the access tunnel. Steps into the tunnel, their worst fears were realized when they saw three troopers hauling away a MagnaGuard, holed by more blaster bolts than would have been needed to demolish a police skimmer.

The hijacked gunship had rescued Grievous after his fall from the mag-lev, Mace told himself. But had the fall been deliberate—part of an increasingly elaborate ruse—or had Grievous originally planned to abduct Palpatine from the train?

Either way, how had the cyborg general known how many of his forces to commit to such a daring plan?

Unless, of course, he had received prior intelligence on the number of Red Guards in Palpatine's detail, and the number of troopers and other combatants stationed in the bunker complex.

Every meter of the tunnel presented Mace and Kit with fresh evidence of the ferocious fight that had taken place, in the form of slaughtered commandos and others. Without limbs, beheaded, shocked to death by EMP weapons . . .

Mace stopped counting after he reached forty.

The heavy, hexagonal entrance that was the terminus of the bloodstained tunnel was open. If the fight leading to the door had been fierce, the one inside the ravished bunker had been savage. Stass Allie, her face and hands blistered and her robes singed, was kneeling by the bodies of the four Jedi Knights with whom Mace had spoken to briefly during the mag-lev evacuation. Only

Grievous could be held accountable for what had been done to them. The same was true for those Red Guards whose corpses had been burned open by lightsaber.

Grievous had taken the blades with which the Jedi had fought.

Here, too, were the shells of two more MagnaGuards.

But Palpatine was missing.

"Sir, the Supreme Chancellor was gone by the time we arrived," a commando explained. "His captors exited the complex by way of the south tunnels."

Mace and Kit glanced at the door that led to those tunnels, then turned to Shaak Ti, who was standing by the bunker's holoprojector table as if lost. When Mace hurried over to her, she practically collapsed in his arms.

"I fought Grievous on Hypori," she said weakly. "I knew what he was capable of. But this . . . And taking Palpatine . . . "

Mace supported her. "There will be no negotiations. The Supreme Chancellor won't allow it."

"The Senate may not see it that way, Mace." Shaak Ti composed herself and gazed around. "Grievous had help. Help from someone close to the top."

Kit nodded. "We'll find out who. But our first priority is to rescue the Supreme Chancellor."

Mace looked at the commando. "How did they leave the complex?"

"I can show you," Shaak Ti said. Turning, she activated a security recording that had captured Grievous and several of his humanoid guards dragging Palpatine to the south landing pad, butchering the handful of troopers posted there, scrambling into a waiting tri-winged shuttle, lifting off into sunset clouds . . .

"How were they allowed through the shield?" Mace asked the commando.

"Same way they entered the bunker, General."

Mace hadn't even thought to ask. Had assumed they had burned their way in—

"They had the entry codes to the bunker, sir, as well as codes issued earlier today that permitted them to clear the screen."

Mace and Kit glanced at each other in angry bewilderment.

"What is the shuttle's location now?" Kit asked.

The commando conjured a 3-D image from the holoprojector.

"Sector I-Thirty-Three, sir. Outbound autonavigation trunk P-seventeen. Gunships are in pursuit."

Mace's eyes widened in alert. "Do your gunners know that the Supreme Chancellor is aboard? Do they realize they can't fire on the shuttle?"

"They have orders to disable if possible, sir. The shuttle is shielded and well armored, in any case."

"Who else knows of the abduction?" Kit thought to ask. "Has this been released or leaked to the media?"

"Yes, sir. Moments ago."

"On whose orders?" Mace fumed.

"The Supreme Chancellor's top advisers."

Shaak Ti forced an exhale. "All of Coruscant will panic."

Mace squared his shoulders. "Commander, scramble every available starfighter. That ship cannot be allowed to reach the Separatist fleet."

52

Dooku hadn't fled alone. The only indications of Tythe's invasion were the hulking remains of Separatist and Republic warships, tumbling indolently in starlight.

"We were all beginning to wonder if you were going to return," a human crew chief said by way of welcoming Obi-Wan and Anakin back to the assault cruiser's ventral landing bay.

Obi-Wan descended the ladder affixed to the starfighter's cockpit. "When did the Separatists jump?"

"Less than an hour, local. Guess they had enough of the pounding we were giving them."

Leaping to the deck, Anakin laughed nastily. "Believe whatever you want."

The crew chief furrowed his brow in uncertainty.

"Do we know where they're headed?" Obi-Wan asked quickly.

The crew chief turned to him. "Most of the capital ships jumped Rimward. A few appear to be headed for the Nelvaan system—thirteen parsecs from here."

"What are our orders?"

"We're still waiting to find out. The fact is, we haven't received any communications from Coruscant since the start of the battle."

Anakin took a sudden interest in the crew chief's remarks.

"Could be local interference," Obi-Wan said.

The crew chief looked dubious. "Several other battle groups reported that they have been unable to communicate with Coruscant."

Anakin shot Obi-Wan an embittered look and began to storm away.

"Anakin," Obi-Wan said, following in his footsteps.

Anakin whirled on him. "We were wrong to come here, Master. *I* was wrong to come here. It was all a feint, and we fell for it. We're being kept away from Coruscant. I can feel it."

Obi-Wan folded his arms across his chest. "You wouldn't be saying that if we'd captured Dooku."

"But we didn't, Master. That's what counts. And now no communication with Coruscant? You don't even see it, do you?"

Obi-Wan regarded him carefully. "See what, Anakin?"

Anakin started to speak, then cut himself off and began again. "You should keep me fighting. You shouldn't give me time to think."

Obi-Wan rested his hands on Anakin's shoulders. "Calm yourself."

Anakin shrugged him off, a new fire in his eyes. "You're my best friend. Tell me what I should do. Forget for a moment that you're wearing the robes of a Jedi and tell me what I should do!"

Stung by the gravity in Anakin's voice, Obi-Wan fell silent for a moment, then said: "The Force is our ally, Anakin. When we're mindful of the Force, our actions are in accord with the will of the Force. Tythe wasn't a wrong choice. It's simply that we're ignorant of its import in the greater scheme."

Anakin lowered his head in sadness. "You're right, Master. My mind isn't as fast as my lightsaber." He stared at his artificial limb. "My heart isn't as impervious to pain as my right hand."

Obi-Wan felt as if someone had knotted his insides. He had failed his apprentice and closest friend. Anakin was suffering, and the only balm he offered were Jedi *platitudes*. His body heaved a stuttering breath. He had his mouth open to speak when the crew chief interrupted.

"General Skywalker, something has your astromech very flustered."

Obi-Wan and Anakin swung to Anakin's starfighter.

"Artoo?" Anakin said in a concerned tone.

The astromech tooted, shrilled, chittered.

"Does he understand droid?" the crew chief asked Obi-Wan as Anakin hurried past him.

"*That* droid," Obi-Wan said.

Anakin began to scale the cockpit ladder. "What is it, Artoo? What's wrong?"

The droid whistled and zithered.

Throwing himself into the open cockpit, Anakin toggled switches. Obi-Wan had just reached the base of the ladder when he heard Palpatine's voice issuing through the cockpit annunciators.

"*Anakin, if you are receiving this message, then I have urgent need of your help . . .* "

The crew chief's comlink toned.

Obi-Wan glanced from the crew chief to Anakin and back again.

"What is it?" he asked in a rush.

"Tight-beam comm from Coruscant," the crew said.

He listened for another moment, then added, in obvious disbelief: "Sir, the Separatists have invaded!"

Obi-Wan gaped at him.

Above him, Anakin lifted his face to the high ceiling and let out a sustained snarl. Glaring down at Obi-Wan, he said: "Why does fate target the people who are most important to me?"

"I—"

"Crew chief!" Anakin cut him off. "Refuel and rearm our starfighters at once!"

Grievous had a good lead on them.

Seated in the copilot's seat of a Republic cruiser, Mace accepted that the shuttle couldn't be intercepted before it left Coruscant's envelope. And perhaps not before it was in the protective embrace of the Separatist fleet.

Regardless, the hot scrambled starfighters were giving all they had to the chase.

Having access to high-clearance codes, Grievous could have plotted a proprietary launch vector for the shuttle. But by doing so he would have put the shuttle at risk of arrest by disabling fire or tractor beam. Instead, he had elected to avail himself of the protection afforded by starship traffic in one of the outbound autonavigation trunks.

Police, governmental, and emergency vessels were permitted to use free-travel lanes that paralleled the trunks, but even with that advantage, Mace and Kit's cruiser was still several kilometers behind the rising shuttle. Below, vast areas of darkness stained the usual circuit board perfection of night-side Coruscant.

That the vessels surrounding it were compelled by orbital tractor beam arrays to adhere to standard launch velocities benefited the shuttle. The tri-wing benefited even more from the fact that Grievous was almost as adept at handling a ship as he was a lightsaber. Each time flights of starfighters attempted to hem him in, Grievous would lead them on spiraling chases through the thick traffic, inserting the shuttle between ships, initiating collisions, resorting to firing the shuttle's meager weapons when necessary.

Recalled from the battle outside the well, Agen Kolar, Saesee Tiin, and Pablo-Jill had come closest to incapacitating the shuttle, but, twice now, Grievous had managed to evade them by bringing the shuttle's laser cannons to bear on cargo pods and strewing local space with debris. Even when the three Jedi had gotten near enough to launch disabling runs, the shuttle's shielding and armor had absorbed the bursts.

With the pursuit closing rapidly on the rim of the gravity well, the Jedi pilots were executing maneuvers they had been reluctant to employ deeper in the atmosphere. Weaving among the vessels, the starfighters fired on the shuttle at every opportunity, scorching its wings and tail, as the shield generator became overtaxed. Grievous was unable to match them maneuver for maneuver, but his response to the attacks was to target any innocent in his sights, ultimately forcing the Jedi to fall back once again.

Punching through Coruscant's sheath of gases, the autonavigation trunk branched like the crown of a shade tree. Thrusters flared as endangered ships slued and rolled onto vectors meant to distance them from the fray. With local space crosshatched with plasma trails and brilliant with explosions, escape was scarcely an option. Even so, many ships were attempting to follow the curve of the gravity well toward Coruscant's bright side, while others veered for the safety of Coruscant's moons, and still others sped for the nearest jump points.

Except for the shuttle, which accelerated straight for Grievous's flagship.

Calling full power from the cruiser, Kit Fisto joined the three Jedi starfighters in a flat-out race for the shuttle. By then, too, several Republic frigates and corvettes were diverting from the principal battle to assist in the interception.

Despite his earlier misgivings, Mace thought for a moment that they might succeed.

Then he watched in disquiet as five hundred droid fighters—gushing from the great curving arms of a Trade Federation battleship—swarmed forward to safeguard the shuttle in its flight to freedom.

Three among a crowd several hundred strong standing in the Nicandra Plaza, Padmé, Bail, and Mon Mothma watched the late-breaking news report on the Embassy Mall's HoloNet monitor. When word of Supreme Chancellor Palpatine's capture had first been rumored, then verified, all anyone in the crowd could ask was, *How, in three short years, had it come to this?*

The armies of chaos were parked in stationary orbit above Coruscant, and the beloved leader of the Galactic Republic seized. For so many, what had been an abstraction was stark reality, playing out overhead, for all of Coruscant and half the galaxy to watch.

Now that time had passed, however, Padmé had begun to notice a change in the crowd. Though a climactic battle was raging as near as the night sky's frightening fireworks, most Coruscanti preferred to keep their gaze fixed on the real-time images of battle. That way, it was almost like watching an exciting HoloNet drama.

Would the starfighters be able to overtake the shuttle in which Palpatine was being held captive by a cyborg monster? Might the shuttle or the flagship that was its destination explode? What would become of the Republic should the Supreme Chancellor be killed, or Coruscant occupied by tens of thousands of battle droids? Would the Jedi and their clone army fly to the rescue?

When Padmé could take no more of the 3-D images or the remarks of the audience, she wended her way to the perimeter of the crowd to take hold of a handrail at the plaza's edge, and to lift her eyes to the strobing sky.

Anakin, she said to herself, as if she could reach him with a thought.

Anakin.

Tears coursed down her cheeks, and she wiped them away with the back of her hand. Her sadness was personal now, not for Palpatine, though his abduction hollowed her. She wept for a future she and Anakin might have had. For the family they might have been. More than ever she wished that she hadn't been a featured player in the events that had shaped the war, but merely one of the crowd.

Come home to me before it's too late.

Her gaze lowered, she caught sight of C-3PO, parting company with a silver protocol droid that disappeared into the crowd.

"What was that about, Threepio?" she asked as he approached.

"A most curious encounter, Mistress," C-3PO said. "I think that shiny droid fancies himself something of a seer."

Padmé looked at him askance. "In what way, Threepio?"

"In essence, he told me to *flee* while it was still possible. He said that dark times are coming, and that the line that separates good and bad will become blurred. That what seems good now will prove evil; and that what seems evil, will prove good."

Sensing there was more, Padmé waited.

C-3PO's photoreceptors locked on Padmé. "He said further that I should accept a memory wipe if it is ever offered to me, because the only alternative will be to live in fear and confusion for the rest of my days."

Slapped by fire, the tri-winged shuttle fairly crawled toward the docking bay of the *Invisible Hand*. Grievous held to his treacherous course, even while contingency plans formed in his mind. Wings of Trade Federation droid fighters had burned a path for the shuttle through areas of intense combat, but the vulnerable little ship was not yet in the clear. Many of Grievous's impassioned pursuers were so busy defending themselves that they no longer represented a threat, but three starfighters had managed to stay with the shuttle, and were continuing to harry it with surgical fire.

The spiraling chase up the gravity well and the twisting transit to the cruiser had left the ship battered. The sublight engine was whining in protest, the ray shield dangerously diminished, the minimal weapons depleted. Uncertain as to where Grievous had stashed Palpatine, the pilots of the trio of starfighters were being careful with their bolts, but every hit was inflicting further damage to the stabilizers and shield generator. Plasma fire from the *Invisible Hand*'s point-defense weapons had only prompted them to close ranks with the shuttle, using it in the same way Grievous was using Palpatine—as a kind of screen.

The mechanical voice of a control droid aboard the cruiser issued from the shuttle's cockpit speakers. *"General, do you wish us to deploy tri-fighters against the starfighters?"*

"Negative," Grievous said. "Save them for when we actually need them. Continue cannon fire."

"General, our computations suggest that continued close-range fire could subject the shuttle to fratricide."

Grievous didn't doubt it. As it was, the hull was blistering with each salvo from the cruiser.

"Ready the forward tractor beam," he said after a moment. "Fire a disabling burst at all four of us. Then utilize the beam to ensnare what remains of the shuttle and draw it into the docking bay—even if that means dragging a starfighter in, as well. Have battle droids standing by."

"Yes, General."

Grievous swiveled his seat toward Palpatine, who was strapped into an acceleration couch between two MagnaGuards. The Supreme Chancellor had been unexpectedly compliant since leaving the bunker, at times brazen enough to take Grievous to task for his less-than-perfect piloting skills.

You fool, you'll get us both killed! Palpatine had barked at him repeatedly.

What did Palpatine think was going to become of him after they reached the *Invisible Hand*? Grievous had asked himself. Was he under the delusion that Lords Sidious and Tyranus would simply hold him for ransom? Did it somehow escape him that he wasn't likely to see Coruscant again?

Once more, Grievous questioned the needless complexity of the Sith Lords' plan. Why not kill Palpatine sooner rather than later? If he hadn't been under orders . . .

You take orders? Palpatine had mocked him.

Which of them was the lesser, indeed?

"Strap in, Chancellor," Grievous said now. "This could get rough."

Palpatine sneered. "With you at the controls, I'm certain it will."

No sooner did Grievous swing back to the viewport than gouts of fire spewed from the *Invisible Hand*'s forward cannons. Two of the starfighter pilots must have sensed something coming, because they all but glued themselves to the shuttle. Rocked by the burst, the shuttle lost portions of itself to space, and all systems shut down. One of the starfighters was blown away, but the other two had lost little more than their wings.

The shuttle reeled as the tractor beam took hold of it.

With it came the pair of starfighters.

Grievous considered ordering that the docking bay be purged of atmosphere. Somewhere aboard the shuttle there would be extravehicular gear Palpatine could don. But with life support failing, Palpatine was already in enough trouble.

Grievous would just have to deal with the starfighter pilots when the ships were released from the beam.

The three were scarcely through the docking bay's containment field when explosive charges flung the canopies from the starfighters and two Jedi Knights leapt to the deck, lightsabers ablaze, deflecting blaster bolts from battle droids as they raced for the shuttle. Before the shuttle had even settled to the deck, one of the Jedi had plunged his glowing blue blade straight through the starboard hatch.

Hurrying aft through thickening smoke, Grievous caught sight of Palpatine's expression of derision.

"Surprise, surprise, General."

Grievous halted just long enough to say: "We'll see who's surprised."

He saw the lightsaber blade retract. By the time he had shouldered through the hatch onto the landing platform the Jedi had moved to either side. Even while continuing to parry blaster bolts, they surged at him, engaging the two lightsabers he drew from his cloak.

The duel raged through the hold. Battle droids lowered their weapons for fear of hitting Grievous. These Jedi were more proficient than the ones he had fought in the bunker, but not skilled enough to challenge him. The four blades seared through the recycled air, washing the burnished bulkheads with harsh light and outsized shadows.

Flanking him, the Jedi rushed in.

Grievous waited until the last instant to command his legs to raise him up several centimeters. Then he extended his lightsabers straight out from his sides, angled slightly downward. Slipping past the flashing strikes of his opponents, Grievous's blades pierced the chests of both. They fell away from him, faces contorted in surprise, of the sort only sudden death could bring.

Several battle droids hastened forward, almost prancing in eagerness.

"Jettison the bodies," Grievous instructed. "Choose a place where the Republic can have a good look at them."

Diminutive between two MagnaGuards, Palpatine was waiting at the foot of the shuttle boarding ramp.

"Take him," Grievous said.

Lifting Palpatine by his armpits, the combat droids followed Grievous through the cruiser, and at last through an oval of opalescent portal into a large cabin space containing a situation table surrounded by chairs. Grievous ordered the guards to set the Supreme Chancellor down in a swivel chair at the head of the table and to shackle his hands.

"Welcome to the general's quarters," he said while he did input at a console built into the table. Shortly the bulkhead behind the swivel chair became a hologrammic display, showing the battle of Coruscant. The flick of a final switch summoned a stalked, eyeball-shaped holocam from the tabletop.

"You're about to make an unscheduled appearance on the HoloNet, Chancellor," Grievous said. "I apologize for not providing a mirror, hairbrush, and cosmetics, so that you might at least camouflage some of your fear."

Palpatine's voice was sinister when he spoke. "You can display me, but I won't speak."

Grievous nodded at what seemed an obvious statement. "I'll display you, but you won't speak. Is that understood?"

"You will do all the talking."

"That's correct. I will do all the talking."

"Very good."

For no apparent reason, Grievous felt uncertain. "Lord Tyranus will soon be here to take charge of you."

Palpatine smiled without showing his teeth. "Then I am assured of being greatly entertained."

From aboard his cruiser, General Grievous addressed a captive audience of trillions of beings. His frightening visage dominating every frequency of the HoloNet, he delivered a message of gloom and doom, forecasting the end of Palpatine's reign, the long-delinquent downfall of the corrupt Republic, a bright new future for all the worlds and all the species that had been enslaved to it . . .

Crushed in among Nicandra Plaza's suddenly silent multitude, Bail touched Mon Mothma's arm in a gesture that promised his imminent return, and began to writhe his way to the edge of the crowd. Gazing around, he spied Padmé standing with C-3PO, arms cradled against her, elbows in the palms of her hands, her face raised to the light-splintered sky.

Hastening to her, he called her name, and she turned from the handrail into his comforting embrace, her tears wetting the front of his tunic.

"Padmé, listen to me," he said, stroking her hair. "The Separatists have nothing to gain by killing Palpatine. He'll be all right."

"What if you're wrong, Bail? What if they do kill him, and power falls into the hands of Mas Amedda and the rest of that gang? That doesn't worry you? What if Alderaan is next on Grievous's list of worlds to attack?"

"Of course it worries me. I fear for Alderaan. But I have faith that won't happen. This attack will put an end to the Outer Rim sieges. The Jedi will be back where they belong, here in the Core. And as for Mas Amedda, he won't last a week. There are thousands of Senators who think as we do, Padmé. We'll rally them into a force to be reckoned with. We'll put the Republic back on course, even if we have to fight tooth and nail to overcome anyone who opposes us." He put his hand under her chin to lift her face toward his. "We'll get through this, no matter what."

She sniffled; smiled lightly. "If I could keep my concerns focused only on the future of the Republic . . . "

Bail held her gaze, and nodded in understanding. "Padmé, if it's any comfort to you, please know that my wife and I would do anything to protect you and those close to you."

"Thank you, Bail," she said. "With all my heart, thank you."

On Utapau, an Outer Rim world of vast sinkholes and lizard mounts, Viceroy Nute Gunray watched a grainy HoloNet image of General Grievous lower the boom on Coruscant.

Had he been wrong to underestimate the cyborg? Might this war actually end with the Republic vanquished? It was almost too much to contemplate: unrestricted trade from Core to Outer Rim, undreamed of wealth, unlimited *possessions* . . .

Gunray glanced at Shu Mai, Passel Argente, San Hill, and the rest, a backslapping fellowship all of a sudden. Smiling broadly—for the first time in several years—he joined them in celebration.

In his quarters in the Temple, Yoda watched a HoloNet feed that showed the bodies of two Jedi drifting in space, close to the flagship of the Separatist fleet. The corners of his mouth pulled down in sadness, he turned to the comlink.

"See them, I do."

Mace's voice rumbled from the speaker. *"If we can ever break through this fighter screen, we'll storm the cruiser."*

"Kill the Supreme Chancellor, Grievous will."

"I don't think so. He's had plenty of chances already."

"Wait, then, to hear the Separatists' demands, we should."

"The Senate will give away Coruscant to effect Palpatine's release."

"Worse the situation will be if the Supreme Chancellor dies. Fall, the Republic will."

Mace fell silent for a moment. Yoda saw him in the cockpit of the cruiser he and Kit had piloted off Coruscant. *"What should we do?"*

"To the Force, look for guidance. Accept what fate has placed before us. For now, prevent Grievous's fleet from escaping to hyperspace, you must. Recalled, many Jedi and others have been. *Turn,* the battle will, when they arrive."

"Master Yoda, we were close to capturing Sidious. I could feel it."

"Knew this, Sidious did. Hiding, he is."

No longer on Coruscant, Yoda thought.

"We'll pin Grievous here, like the vermin he is."

Mace severed the transmission, and Yoda tottered to the windows. Western Coruscant was engulfed by darkness; the sky above, splintered by rabid light. Calling his lightsaber to his hand, he ignited the blade and waved it through the air.

Perilous the future will be. A cause for grave concern.

But the battle in local space wasn't the end.

Beginning, the final act was!

55

Dooku had ordered the droid pilot of the sloop to revert from hyperspace for a brief time at the planet Nelvaan. Should any ships among the Republic battle group at Tythe plot his escape course, it would appear that Nelvaan was his destination. The sloop's Geonosian technology would mask the fact that he had jumped almost immediately to Coruscant to join Grievous, and to play out the final act of the drama Sidious had composed.

The abduction of Palpatine had not only abbreviated the search for him, but also allowed Sidious to escape Coruscant undetected. But those events had been minor acts. Sidious would never have allowed the Jedi to expose him. And Palpatine was hardly the prize he appeared to be.

The greater prize, Sidious had told Dooku during their most recent communication, was Anakin Skywalker.

"Long have you watched him," Dooku had said, repeating words Sidious himself had spoken.

"Longer than you know, Lord Tyranus. Longer than you know. And the time has come to test him again."

"His skills, my lord?"

"*The depth of his anger. His willingness to go beyond the Force, as the Jedi know it, and to call on the power of the dark side. General Grievous will activate a special beacon that will call Skywalker and Kenobi back to Coruscant, and onto the stage we will set for them.*"

But not to capture them.

"*You will duel them,*" Sidious had said. "*Kill Kenobi. His only purpose is to die and, in so doing, ignite young Skywalker to tap the depths of his fear and rage. Should you defeat Skywalker easily, then we will know that he is not prepared to serve us. Perhaps he never will be prepared. Should he by some fluke best you, however, I will control the outcome to spare you any unnecessary embarrassment, and we will have gained a powerful ally. But above all you must make the contest appear real, Lord Tyranus.*"

"I will treat it as if it were my crowning achievement," Dooku had promised.

Hyperspace awaited.

"To Coruscant," he told FA-4 from his comfortable chair in the sloop's main hold.

And with that, the ship jumped.

56

The two starfighters sat side by side in the launching bay, only a few meters separating them, engines warming, droids in their sockets, cockpit canopies raised.

Neither pilot wore a helmet, so Anakin could hear Obi-Wan plainly when he shouted: "For all the jinks and jukes you've taken me through, there's no one else I'd rather fly with."

Anakin canted his head and smiled. "It's about time you admitted it. Can I take that to mean you'll follow my lead without question?"

"To the best of my ability," Obi-Wan said. "I may not always be able to remain at your wing, but I won't be far off, and I'll always have your back."

"When I call for help, you'll come speeding to the rescue."

"The day you call for help, I'll know that we're both in over our heads."

Anakin adopted a serious look. "Obi-Wan, you don't know how many times you've already rescued me."

Obi-Wan swallowed the lump that formed in his

throat. "Then whatever lies ahead for us shouldn't be a problem."

Anakin laughed lightly. "Who'll restore peace to the galaxy if we don't?"

Obi-Wan returned a tight-lipped nod. "At least you said *we*."

They lowered the starfighters' canopies and engaged the repulsors, lifting off, rotating 180 degrees, and easing through the launching bay's transparent containment field.

Flying abreast, all but sharing a wing, they enabled their thrusters and banked away from the massive ship. Accelerating on columns of brilliant blue energy, sluing slightly to port, slightly sinister, they coupled with their hyperdrive rings and disappeared into the long night.

[TO BE CONCLUDED]

Turn the page
for a sneak peak at
STAR WARS: DARK LORD:
THE RISE OF DARTH VADER,
James Luceno's exciting sequel
to
STAR WARS:
EPISODE III
REVENGE OF THE SITH

Dropping into swirling clouds conjured by Murkhana's weather stations, Roan Shryne was reminded of mediation sessions his former Master had guided him through. No matter how fixed Shryne had been on touching the Force, his mind's eye had offered little more than an eddying whiteness. Years later, when he had become more adept at silencing thought and immersing himself in the light, visual fragments would emerge from that colorless void—pieces to a puzzle that would gradually assemble itself and resolve. Not in any conscious way, though frequently assuring him that his actions in the world were in accord with the will of the Force.

Frequently but not always.

When he veered from the course on which the Force had set him, the familiar white would once again be stirred by powerful currents, sometimes shot through

with red, as if he were lifting his closed eyes to the glare
of a midday sun.

Red-mottled white was what he saw as he fell deeper
into Murkhana's atmosphere. Scored to reverberating
thunder; the rush of the wind; a welter of muffled
voices . . .

He was standing closest to the sliding door that normally sealed the troop bay of a Republic gunship,
launched moments earlier from the forward hold of the
Gallant—a *Victory*-class Star Destroyer, harried by Vulture and droid tri-fighters and awaiting High Command's word to commence its own descent through
Murkhana's artificial ceiling. Beside and behind Shryne
stood a platoon of clone troopers, helmets affixed to
their armored suits, blasters cradled in their arms, utility
belts slung with ammo magazines, talking among themselves the way seasoned warriors often did before battle.
Alleviating misgiving with inside jokes; references
Shryne couldn't begin to understand, beyond the fact
that they were grim.

The gunship's inertial compensators allowed them to
stand in the bay without being jolted by flaring antiaircraft explosions or jostled by the gunship pilots' evasive
maneuvering through corkscrewing missiles and storms
of white-hot shrapnel. Missiles, because the same Separatists that had manufactured the clouds had misted
Murkhana's air with anti-laser aerosols.

Acrid odors infiltrated the cramped space, along with
the roar of the aft engines, the starboard one stuttering
somewhat. The gunship was as battered as the troopers
and crew it carried into conflict.

Even at an altitude of only 400 meters above sea level,
the cloud cover remained dense. The fact that Shryne
could barely see his hand in front of his face didn't surprise him. This was still the war, after all, and these past

three years he had grown accustomed to not seeing where he was going.

Nat-Sem, his former Master, used to tell him that the goal of the meditative exercises was to see clear through the swirling whiteness to the other side, that what Shryne saw was only the shadowy expanse separating him from full contact with the Force. Shryne had to learn to ignore the clouds, as it were. When he had learned to do that, to look through them to the radiant expanse beyond, he would be a Master.

Pessimistic by nature, Shryne's reaction had been: *Not in this lifetime.*

Though he had never said as much to Nat-Sem, the Jedi Master had seen through him as easily as he saw through the clouds.

Shryne felt that the clone troopers had a better view of the war than he had, and that the view had little to do with their helmet imaging systems—filters that muted the sharp scent of the air, earphones that dampened the sounds of explosions. Grown for warfare, they probably thought the Jedi were mad to go into battle as they did, attired in tunics and hooded robes, a lightsaber their only weapon. Many of them were astute enough to see comparisons between the Force and their own white plastoid shells, but few of them could discern between armored and unarmored Jedi—those who were allied with the Force, and those who for one reason or another had slipped from its sustaining embrace.

Murkhana's lathered clouds finally began to thin until they merely veiled the planet's wrinkled landscape and frothing sea. A sudden burst of brilliant light drew Shryne's attention to the sky. What he took for an exploding gunship might have been a newborn star. For a moment the world tipped out of balance, then righted itself just as abruptly. A circle of clarity opened in the clouds, a perforation in the veil, and Shryne gazed on verdant forest so profoundly green he could almost taste its flavor. Valiant combatants scurried through the underbrush and sleek ships soared through the canopy. In the midst of it all, a lone figure stretched out his hand, tearing aside a curtain black as night . . .

Shryne knew he had stepped out of time, into some truth beyond reckoning.

A vision of the end of the war, perhaps, or of time itself.

Whichever, the effect of it comforted him that he was indeed where he was supposed to be. That despite the depth to which the war had caused him to become fixed on death and destruction, he was still tethered to the Force, and serving it in his own limited way.

Then, as if intent on foiling him, the thin clouds quickly conspired to conceal what had been revealed, closing the portal an errant current had opened. And Shryne was back where he had started, with gusts of superheated air tugging at the sleeves and cowl of his brown robe.

"The Koorivar have done a good job with their weather machines," a speaker-enhanced voice said into his left ear. "Whipped up one brute of a sky. We used the same tactic on Paarin Minor. Drew the Seps into fabricated clouds and blew them to the back of beyond."

Shryne laughed without merriment. "Good to see you can still appreciate the little things, Commander."

"What else is there, General."

Shryne couldn't make out the expression on the face behind the tinted T-visor, but he knew that shared face as well as anyone else who fought in the war. Commander of the 32nd Air Combat wing, the clone officer had somewhere along the line acquired the name Salvo, and the sobriquet fit him like a gauntlet.

The high-traction soles of his jump boots gave him just enough added height to stand shoulder to shoulder with Shryne, and where his armor wasn't dinged and scored it was emblazoned with rust-brown markings. On his hips he wore holstered hand blasters, and, for reasons Shryne couldn't fathom, a version of the cape-like command skirt that had become all the rage in the war's third year. The left side of his shrapnel-pitted helmet was laser-etched with the motto: *Live to Serve!*

Torso markings attested to Salvo's participation in campaigns on many worlds, and while he wasn't an ARC—an Advanced Reconnaissance Commando—he had the rough edges of an ARC, and of their clone template, Jango Fett, whose headless body Shryne had seen in a Geonosian arena shortly before Master Nat-Sem had fallen to enemy fire.

"Alliance weapons should have us in target lock by now," Salvo said as the gunship continued to descend.

Other assault ships were also punching through the cloud cover, only to be greeted by flocks of incoming missiles. Struck by direct hits, two, four, then five craft were blown apart, flaming fuselages and mangled troopers plummeting into the churning scarlet waves of Murkhana Bay. From the nose of one gunship flew a bang-out capsule that carried the pilot and copilot to within meters of the water before it was ripped open by a resolute heat-seeker.

In one of the fifty-odd gunships that were racing down the well, three other Jedi were going into battle, Master Saras Loorne among them. Stretching out with the Force, Shryne found them, faint echoes confirming that all three were still alive.

He clamped his right hand on one of the slide door's view slots as the pilots threw their unwieldy charge into a hard bank, narrowly evading a pair of hailfire missiles.

Gunners ensconced in the gunship's armature-mounted turrets opened up with blasters as flights of Mankvim Interceptors swarmed up to engage the Republic force. The anti-laser aerosols scattered the blaster beams, but dozens of the Separatist crafts succumbed to missiles spewed from the gunships' top-mounted mass-drive launchers.

"High Command should have granted our request to bombard from orbit," Salvo said in an amplified voice.

"The idea is to *take* the city, Commander, not vaporize it," Shryne said loudly. Murkhana had already been granted weeks to surrender, but the Republic ultimatum had expired. "Palpatine's policy for winning the hearts and minds of Separatist populations might not make good military sense, but it makes good political sense."

Salvo stared at him from behind his visor. "We're not interested in politics."

Shryne laughed shortly. "Neither were the Jedi."

"Why fight if you weren't bred for it?"

"To serve what remains of the Republic." Shryne's brief green vision of the war's end returned, and he adopted a rueful grin. "Dooku's dead. Grievous is being hunted down. If it means anything, I suspect it'll be over soon."

"The war, or our standing shoulder to shoulder?"

"The war, Commander."

"What becomes of the Jedi, then?"

"We'll do what we have always done: follow the Force."

"And the Grand Army?"

Shryne regarded him. "Help us preserve the peace."

—[CORUSCANT NIGHTS II]—

STREET OF SHADOWS

By *Michael Reaves*

THE BURNING REALM
THE SHATTERED WORLD
DARKWORLD DETECTIVE
STREET MAGIC
NIGHT HUNTER
VOODOO CHILD
DRAGONWORLD (*with Byron Preiss*)
SWORD OF THE SAMURAI (*with Steve Perry*)
HELLSTAR (*with Steve Perry*)
DOME (*with Steve Perry*)
THE OMEGA CAGE (*with Steve Perry*)
THONG THE BARBARIAN MEETS THE CYCLE SLUTS OF
    SATURN (*with Steve Perry*)
HELL ON EARTH
MR. TWILIGHT (*with Maya Kaathryn Bohnhoff*)
BATMAN: FEAR, ITSELF (*with Steven-Elliot Altman*)

STAR WARS: DARTH MAUL: SHADOW HUNTER
STAR WARS: MEDSTAR I: BATTLE SURGEONS
    (*with Steve Perry*)
STAR WARS: MEDSTAR II: JEDI HEALER (*with Steve Perry*)
STAR WARS: DEATH STAR (*with Steve Perry*)
STAR WARS: CORUSCANT NIGHTS I: JEDI TWILIGHT
STAR WARS: CORUSCANT NIGHTS II: STREET OF SHADOWS

Anthologies
SHADOWS OVER BAKER STREET (*co-edited with John Pelan*)